PRAISE FOR
# LIQUID LIES

*Berkley Sensation titles by Hanna Martine*

LIQUID LIES
A TASTE OF ICE

# A TASTE
# OF ICE

## HANNA MARTINE

BERKLEY SENSATION, NEW YORK

**THE BERKLEY PUBLISHING GROUP**
Published by the Penguin Group
Penguin Group (USA) Inc.
**375 Hudson Street, New York, New York 10014, USA**

Penguin Group (Canada), 90 Eglinton Avenue East, Suite 700, Toronto, Ontario M4P 2Y3, Canada
(a division of Pearson Penguin Canada Inc.) • Penguin Books Ltd., 80 Strand, London WC2R 0RL,
England • Penguin Ireland, 25 St. Stephen's Green, Dublin 2, Ireland (a division of Penguin
Books Ltd.) • Penguin Group (Australia), 707 Collins Street, Melbourne, Victoria 3008, Australia
(a division of Pearson Australia Group Pty. Ltd.) • Penguin Books India Pvt. Ltd., 11 Community
Centre, Panchsheel Park, New Delhi—110 017, India • Penguin Group (NZ), 67 Apollo Drive,
Rosedale, Auckland 0632, New Zealand (a division of Pearson New Zealand Ltd.) • Penguin Books
(South Africa), Rosebank Office Park, 181 Jan Smuts Avenue, Parktown North 2193,
South Africa • Penguin China, B7 Jiaming Center, 27 East Third Ring Road North,
Chaoyang District, Beijing 100020, China

Penguin Books Ltd., Registered Offices: 80 Strand, London WC2R 0RL, England

This is a work of fiction. Names, characters, places, and incidents either are the product of the author's
imagination or are used fictitiously, and any resemblance to actual persons, living or dead, business
establishments, events, or locales is entirely coincidental. The publisher does not have any control over
and does not assume any responsibility for author or third-party websites or their content.

A TASTE OF ICE

A Berkley Sensation Book / published by arrangement with the author

PUBLISHING HISTORY
Berkley Sensation mass-market edition / January 2013

Copyright © 2012 by Hanna Martine.
Excerpt by Hanna Martine copyright © 2012 by Hanna Martine.
Cover art by Tankist276/Shutterstock.
Cover design by Rita Frangie.
Interior text design by Tiffany Estreicher.

ISBN: 978-0-425-25725-8

BERKLEY SENSATION®
Berkley Sensation Books are published by The Berkley Publishing Group,
a division of Penguin Group (USA) Inc.,
375 Hudson Street, New York, New York 10014.
BERKLEY SENSATION® is a registered trademark of Penguin Group (USA) Inc.
The "B" design is a trademark of Penguin Group (USA) Inc.

PRINTED IN THE UNITED STATES OF AMERICA

10  9  8  7  6  5  4  3  2  1

ALWAYS LEARNING                                                                    PEARSON

*To my beautiful daughter.*
*Look what you can do when you have a dream*
*and do everything in your power to fulfill it.*
*You can be anything you want in this world.* Anything.

# ACKNOWLEDGMENTS

Everyone says that writing your second book is much harder than writing the first. *A Taste of Ice* is actually my fourth book, but Xavier didn't give me any less of a challenge. I am indebted to the following people for pulling me through and demanding the words were as good as Xavier and Cat deserved. My deepest thanks to:

Miles Lowry and Sharon Radzienta, for giving me time when I needed it the most.

Ellen Wehle and Erica O'Rourke, for very early comments about these characters and their goals.

Holly McDowell, for barroom word sprints, and for saying, "That's not enough."

Clara Kensie, for asking the most brilliant questions.

Eliza Evans, for personal motivation, and a killer critique.

Cindy Hwang, for helping to mold Xavier into a true hero.

Every reader of *Liquid Lies* who contacted me to say how much they hated Xavier at first, but then were so excited to hear he'd get his happy ending.

ACKNOWLEDGMENTS

# ONE

Xavier Jones lingered on the edge of chaos, and about a thousand people stood between him and his knives.

The first morning of the Turnkorner Film Festival and already he could throw a rock and hit a celebrity. For two weeks each winter, that's exactly what he wanted to do. He hadn't moved to White Clover Creek, Colorado, for the swarms of film lovers, the squealing fans, or the demanding Hollywood types. He'd come here for the other fifty weeks of the year, when the insular world of the historic mountain town wrapped its arms tightly around his life, and helped him forget what needed to be forgotten.

Today, however, the sidewalks teemed with strangers. Waterleaf Avenue, the main thoroughfare through town, had been barricaded on either end to disallow cars, and the central square had given birth overnight to several white tents. Music pumped from unseen speakers, the beats rising above the buzz of the shuffling crowd.

Shed, the restaurant where he'd been working for the last three years, was two blocks up, straight through a mass of people in sunglasses and down coats. More than half of them women. Xavier's fingers twitched, eager to wrap around the comforting handle of his favorite chef's knife. His mind burned, anxious for him to get to work, bend over his station, and tune out the world for the next fourteen hours.

He could do this. The first day of the festival was always the hardest. If he just got through this one, the next thirteen would be all downhill.

He left the relative safety of the residential neighborhood

and punched through the crowd. Head down, shoulders hunched, he soldiered forward, concentrating on the sting of arctic mountain air as he sucked it deep into his lungs. He loved the cold, the pain of freezing toes. Anything to remind him of what he'd missed his whole life.

Anything to remind him he was free.

The crowd thickened the deeper he went into town. Strangers jostled him from all sides. Salt and ice crunched under his boots. Noise, noise everywhere.

*It's okay,* he told himself on a loop. *You're okay. No one's looking at you.*

"Excuse me. Pardon me. Excuse me." The pleading, reedy voice cut through the white noise of the festival goers.

For once, Xavier was thankful for his height. Straightening, he found the crooked little man, his silver hair partially covered by a tweed cap, trying to pick his way against the crowd flow, toward the stairs of the Tea Shoppe. Mr. Elias Traeger, as much a local fixture in White Clover Creek as the bronze statue of the work-hardened miners in the middle of the town square. The old man had worked at the Tea Shoppe for twenty years and would probably totter from local job to local job until his life gave out. Crazy, but that's what Xavier dreamed of. So normal, so everyday.

Xavier was still getting used to the sight of people with wrinkles and brittle hair and bones. In the Plant, where he'd been conceived and raised, no one had ever lived that long.

A chorus of happy screams went up, meaning someone famous had just shown his or her face. The crowd shifted. A tourist with a cell phone plastered to his ear shoved hard into Mr. Traeger's shoulder and the elderly man tipped to one side. His eyes went wide, his thin arms scrambling for purchase on the smooth brick of the shop.

Five years ago, Xavier would've let Mr. Traeger go down. He would've walked on without a second thought. But Xavier wasn't that man anymore. Despite everything else, at least there was that.

Xavier lunged forward and caught Mr. Traeger under his arms before his knees could hit the ice. The old man found his feet, righted himself and blinked into the bright sunshine.

"Ah, Mr. Jones." Traeger's slight British accent trickled

through. "My thanks. Reaction times aren't quite what they used to be."

Xavier nodded, surprisingly pleased that Traeger remembered his name. "You should've taken the day off. The first day is always the worst."

A wave of the hand and a flash of false teeth. "Never sit idle, I always say."

Well, if that wasn't the truth.

Taking Mr. Traeger's elbow, Xavier helped him up the steps, which were blocked by two young women holding steaming paper cups of what smelled like Earl Grey.

Xavier cleared his throat. "Excuse us." Over the years, he'd perfected the art of speaking to people without looking at them. The women moved slightly to one side and Xavier gestured for Mr. Traeger to go up and enter. Through the glass door, Xavier watched the old man remove his cap and tip it in thanks.

The two women were staring at him. The blonde smiled, slow and obvious. "Hey," she said.

Three seconds. That's all the time he allowed himself to look. That's all that was safe. Three seconds to look at a woman. To note the shape of her mouth or the intelligence in her eyes. To make assumptions about her character. You could learn a lot about a woman in three seconds, not the least of which was whether or not she wanted to sleep with him.

The blonde did.

"Do you live here?" she asked as her friend laughed low.

He'd never get used to this, to the bold women of the outside world who lusted on their own terms and displayed that lust for all to see. Before, *inside*, he'd been the one with the desires. His captors, the water elementals called the Ofarians, had done a damn fine job of creating that monster, and he was still trying to exorcise it.

Xavier swiveled away, the three seconds over, his body aflame with need. He was so well trained, such a good pet, and it would take a hell of a lot more than the passage of years to break his conditioning. Five silly words from a girl and every muscle in his body, no matter how small, had tightened with expectation. Every blood cell raced faster. He *wanted*. He needed sex.

And yet he ran.

Man, he was messed up. He was still learning about the world outside the Plant, but that much was pretty clear. Normal Primary guys didn't sprint the opposite way when a hot woman showed interest. Normal Primary guys didn't spend more than half their days either cooking or thinking about cooking, and the remaining hours pounding the ever-loving shit out of a boxing bag, just to avoid getting naked with someone.

But then, he wasn't Primary. He wasn't entirely human.

And even though he wanted nothing more than to be "normal," he certainly wasn't that either.

He slipped back into the slow-moving crowd. Away from the women, who'd probably already sidled up to another guy, his body cooled.

Shed's entrance was tucked into the back of a cobblestone alley that ran alongside the nineteenth-century Gold Rush Theater, now used as the festival's main venue. The alley was barely forty yards away, but the crowd had completely stopped and Xavier was going nowhere. He bounced on the balls of his feet, willing himself not to duck his shoulder and barrel through the tourists. Willing himself not to have a panic attack in the close quarters. What was the holdup anyway?

Craning his neck above the sea of bobbing heads, made taller by colorful hats, he saw that two massive pockets of people—gaping at two different things—had converged, and no one could get through.

Some young, grizzled guy stood under the triangular theater marquee, a half-moon of five camera teams surrounding him and angling for a shot. A gaggle of fans shouting his name—a name Xavier didn't recognize—fought with the laughter and cheers coming from the crowd closest to Xavier. A giant circle had formed around a street performer.

A middle-aged man wearing a beige North Face jacket and a cheap, felt jester's hat danced along Waterleaf's yellow divider. Xavier's first instinct was to just lower his eyes and try to press on, but what Jester was doing froze Xavier in place.

Jester juggled a mass of colored balls, his hands blurring, a rainbow in the air. Some seemed to disappear then reappear. The audience gasped. Xavier did, too.

Was this guy like him—a Tedran, a Secondary human—capable of true magic, true illusion?

No. That would be impossible. Xavier was the last.

He peered closer, intently following the intricacies of Jester's hands. When Xavier caught the deft slip of Jester's fingers into the folds of his coat, he exhaled. He watched a charlatan, nothing more. He started to turn away, to head back into the thick of the crowd, then stopped. He wanted to be normal, right? If this was the sort of thing Primaries did, then maybe he should suck it up and try it, too.

He planted his feet. Closed his eyes. Shoved away the feel of strangers around him and pretended he was weightless and invisible. He drew in a deep breath through his nose and pushed it out. Opened his eyes.

Jester was storing the balls in a suitcase to the sound of applause. He pulled out a deck of cards from his coat pocket and shuffled them in an impressively high arc. He started to go around the circle, asking random people to pick a card, look at it, then put it back in the deck. His marks all happened to be women.

With a hand flourish, eyes deliberately averted, Jester offered the deck to Xavier, then finally looked up at him. "Whoa, sorry. Not you, big guy." Jester tried to play it off for laughs, but the nervous shock on his face was nothing Xavier hadn't seen before.

Since escaping the Plant, he'd put on a good thirty pounds of muscle on his already six-foot-five body. No one knew how horrible it was to be the person who stood out more than the person who actually stood out. But that's not usually what made people react when they saw him.

Pam, his boss at Shed, said it was because his eyes were the color of guns—shiny, silver, and full of *don't fuck with me*.

Xavier thought they were the color of death. And they were.

Jester offered the card deck to the person standing to Xavier's immediate left. "Well, hello, beautiful. Care to pick a card?"

Three seconds. Ready . . . go.

The woman watched Jester with genuine excitement. Laughter cast her in a spotlight. She clapped her mittened hands like a kid about to get a cookie. Her deep brown hair, streaked with gold and wavy like the ocean, streamed out from beneath a knitted red hat topped with a pompom. She was tanned, like so many Hollywood people traipsing around White Clover

Creek right now. A fine layer of freckles covered her whole face and neck. A price tag stuck to the sleeve of her green, fur-trimmed coat.

She radiated joy, so unlike those women on the Tea Shoppe steps who were clearly here to see and be seen. This one was . . . so unlike any woman he'd stood this close to before.

He forgot how long a second lasted.

Vaguely he sensed his skin start to tighten. Just barely did he notice a heat rising from deep inside. Then a hard, throbbing pulse kicked up that had nothing to do with his heart. It felt goddamn amazing. Like someone had chained him to a rock for centuries, and now he'd been given the go-ahead to jump from an airplane. Too fucking long to deny himself this rush—this want and need—day after day. What had he been thinking, going all these years without?

She must have felt the weight of his stare because a funny look passed across her face. She glanced over her shoulder at him. Did a double take. Their eyes met and hers widened. They were the color of the caramel he'd made at two in the morning last Tuesday.

She didn't look at him with apprehension, like Jester had, but with surprise. Like she'd been expecting to see him and, suddenly, there he was.

When she turned toward him, his body went haywire. That beating pulse took a dive for his dick and his mouth dried up.

"Hi," she said.

Nothing came from his lips, but inside he screamed. Told himself to walk away. To get away from her *now*.

Too late.

Here it came. That low, ragged voice breaking free from the dark place where Xavier had stashed it the day he'd arrived in Colorado. The gravelly, taunting voice of the Burned Man spiraled up from the past, and it hadn't lost any of its punch.

*Stay here*, ordered the Burned Man. *You're already hard for her. I brought her for you. Take her. She's yours.*

Three seconds. It had taken just three seconds to destroy three years free from the hallucinations.

They came back in a horrible rush, filling Xavier with terror and shame. One moment he was on the crowded festival street of White Clover Creek, the next he was back in the Plant's breeding block, known as the Circle. White walls, a well-used mattress. Him, naked and anticipating the Burned Man—the Ofarian guard who'd tormented Xavier most of his life—bringing him a woman he was supposed to impregnate.

Today it was the smiling freckled woman whose joy Xavier would quickly erase.

In his waking nightmare, she crossed the Breeding Circle's white floor without enthusiasm or emotion, like all the others had. In his mind, Xavier plucked the red hat from her head and tossed it to the floor, then he went for the zipper of her coat. Pulled it down, peeled the thick garment from her body. She was naked underneath, and the rest of her was as tan and freckled as her face, but he'd been trained to care only about the heaven between her legs.

He pulled her to the mattress, and even though he hadn't been made to lie on it in almost seven years, his nightmares recalled the stiffness of it, the bleachy smell of the sterile sheets changed before every breeding session. The freckled woman lay back, turned her face away, and he pushed himself inside her. He shouted at the feel of her—it had been so long—and took what he'd been made for. Years without release built and built and built inside him, propelling his thrusts.

Xavier—the man he had become since escaping this torture, the man who knew this was wrong—grabbed desperately for reality. It slipped out of his reach. In the hideous world of his past, his body still worked inside hers. Long-denied fulfillment—because it could never, ever be called pleasure—and self-loathing collided together at a violent crossroads.

He threw his head back, pleading for mercy. *She doesn't want this. And I don't want to want this.*

The square window he knew should belong to the Tea Shoppe morphed into the wire-crossed observation holes in the Circle. The Burned Man appeared on the other side of the glass, terrifying as ever. Unchanged over the last three years. The scarred cheek and chin, the missing hair, the melted ear, the webbed hand . . .

*Don't stop*, he growled in his fire-damaged voice, the puckered skin on his neck stretching. *If you stop, I'll just bring another.*

In the waking nightmares, as in life, Xavier always came.

It was what he'd been bred for: to create new generations of Tedrans. New slaves for the water-worshipping Ofarians.

*It's okay, what you're doing.* The Burned Man's tone rang syrupy false. Xavier had always suspected he'd enjoyed watching, and it had turned his stomach. *Her life will be better if she gets pregnant anyway.*

A red-mittened hand touched Xavier's arm, snapping him back to Colorado.

He gasped as though he'd been held under water—a paralyzing sensation he knew intimately—and gulped down the sweet, cold air. The loud drone of the festival slammed back into his ears. Sunlight bounced off the snow piled around the square, blinding him. He knuckled his eyes, hard enough to hurt. When he opened them, she was still there right in front of him, gorgeously and hideously innocent.

"Are you okay?"

Her voice was smoky, sexy, and it tugged him between reality and the evil place in his head. She wasn't naked beneath him, taking it because she had to. But the possibility of it terrified him.

"Fine." He ripped away from her touch. "I'm fine."

Right about then would have been the perfect time for the old asshole Xavier to return, to shove his way through the ever-increasing crowd and not care if he hurt anyone, like the guy who'd knocked down Mr. Traeger.

"I'm sorry, but"—her freckled nose crinkled and a curious smile lit her candy-colored eyes—"I know this'll sound weird, but do I know you? You seem . . . familiar."

He pictured a pristine cutting board, felt the phantom weight of a scary-sharp chef's knife in his palm, and imagined rows and rows of vegetables laid out before him, waiting. The vision brought him instant calm.

"No, you don't." He turned away, found the tiniest crack between bodies, and shoved himself into it. *Get away, get away.* He angled for freedom, pushing and mumbling apologies to strangers.

"Are you sure?" she called at his back.

The alley mouth leading to Shed was forty yards and forty thousand miles away. The crowd eased some, but the constant touch of unfamiliar bodies gave rise to panic. An elbow here, a hip there. The next one might be the one that made him crack. He had to get into the kitchen.

At last he broke the edge of the crowd and veered into the alley. At the far end flapped the yellow-and-white-striped awning over Shed's entrance. His long legs strode for it.

"Hey, wait." That smoky voice. Following him. "Can you hold up a sec?"

Didn't she realize that if she didn't leave him alone, the Burned Man would come for her again?

Giant pots holding yews decorated with bows in Shed's signature yellow and white dotted the wide alley, and Xavier wove among them. Stupid to think he could actually lose her, given that the alley came to a dead end, but he was grasping for any way out. When he ducked under the awning and still heard her footsteps crossing the cobblestones, he knew there was only one option left.

Xavier hadn't just given up sex the day he'd arrived in White Clover Creek. He'd abandoned magic, too. But standing there, in the cold shadow under Shed's awning, he reached deep inside himself and pulled out the rusty words of the Tedran language.

No reason to speak it anymore, since there were only two people on Earth who could understand him. Adine Jones, the half Tedran born without magic, had guided him through the basics of the Primary world and then disappeared. Gwen Carroway, the Ofarian Translator who had freed Xavier's people and stopped the slavery, had started a new life with her Primary lover in Chicago.

It had been ages since he'd spoken his native tongue, but with the first hesitant word, the rest sprang up like the quick gush of blood after a pinprick.

He chose his illusion, imagining the face and body he wanted, and whispered the Tedran words to bring it about. Glamour enveloped him in a light, airy caress. Head to foot, the new image fell around him in a shimmering cloak made of the thinnest material. Touch it and it would dissolve.

He couldn't deny that for some part of him, using his birthright after all this time was a well-deserved comfort.

He grabbed hold of the thick iron bar on the original granary shed wood door, and slid it wide on oiled rails. Rushing through the little foyer that blocked the winter wind, he pushed open the restaurant's main door and waddled inside, shouldering a huge purse that wasn't really there.

Pam, Shed's owner and executive chef, sat hunched over table eighteen studying receipts and supply orders in neat little piles. By the way her fingers toyed with her short, platinum hair, he knew that something wasn't adding up in the ledgers.

The only reason Xavier could work for Pam, a woman, and not fear the Burned Man, was because she sent out zero sexual vibes toward him. Probably had to do with the fact he had a penis.

Across the main dining floor, through the giant glass window of the open kitchen, Jose and Lars were setting up their *mise en place* for lunch service, their knives flying through prep. Ricardo was bending over the stock pots at the back burners. The familiar and welcome smells, sights, and sounds of the only place that had ever made Xavier happy.

He shuffled around the perimeter of the dining room, making a point to be noticed. Pam glanced up, distracted. "Hey, Carolina."

"*Hola*," he replied in the lilting voice of Shed's cleaning lady. Magic tingled on his skin.

Veiled in the disguise of a tiny Hispanic woman, he slipped into the back room where Pam stored her linens and cutlery. He shut the door behind him and sagged against the shelves.

Shed's front door opened.

Pam's shoes clicked across the dining room floor. "We're not open for lunch for another two hours."

"Oh. I'm sorry." *Her.*

Xavier groaned, her voice slicing through him like a newly sharpened blade. Desire flowed into the open wound, and despite his mind's direct orders to stay away from the back room door, his arm reached out and cracked it open.

She stood by the hostess podium, her eyes darting around the dim dining room. The cold touched her cheeks with a gentle pink. "I was looking for someone. Really tall, wavy blond hair to his shoulders? Navy blue down coat?"

Pam nodded and half smiled in the way that looked like she was laughing at some private joke. "You mean Xavier? Hasn't come in yet."

The woman tilted her head, the red pompom flopping to one side. What was it about that silly hat that forced Xavier to conjure images of tomatoes being diced to hell?

"I thought I just saw him come in here."

"Nope." Pam fiddled with the menus on the hostess stand, perfectly aligning their edges.

"But he works here?"

"Yeah. He's my saucier." When the freckled woman looked confused, Pam added, "One of my line cooks."

She shifted her weight and a snow chunk slid off her fuzzy boot. "Any chance you have a reservation open for tonight?"

Pam flipped open the mahogany leather reservation book and lazily dragged her finger down the page. "So. How do you know Xavier?"

The woman blushed almost as red as her hat. Xavier was horrible at guessing ages, considering his own was about as twisted as a screw, but she was younger than him. Mid-twenties, most likely. She kicked at the dislodged snow. "I . . . I don't."

Oh shit.

Pam looked like the fox who'd swallowed a chicken. Wrong person to learn a woman was looking for him. She'd been trying to get him to date ever since she discovered him working at an acquaintance's bistro in San Francisco. She'd even gotten her girlfriend to start badgering him. Between the two of them the barrage was endless. *Let's get the quiet cook laid.* They thought it funny, a game.

It was anything but.

Pam arched an eyebrow at the freckled woman, her wicked smile tipping toward flirtatious. "Oh, really?" She tapped the reservation book. "Look at this. Lucky for you. We have an opening at eight. For how many?"

Shed had been booked up for weeks, if not months.

"Um. Two. Put it under my name. Heddig."

"Got a first name? Just in case I need it?"

Pam would need it all right—to needle Xavier all shift. He considered calling in sick but knew he couldn't. Not during the festival when every table would be full from lunch through close. Not when the only other option was holing himself up in his house. With the Burned Man making such an abrupt appearance, Xavier didn't trust himself to be alone.

"My name's Cat," said the woman.

"Great, Cat." Pam clicked the pen closed and grinned. "See you tonight."

# TWO

**Here's what Cat knew about the guy she'd followed from the**
street performer's circle: His name was Xavier. He cooked at
Shed. And he was one of those incredibly good-looking men
who didn't know it and would never admit it, even with a gun
to his head.

Here's what she didn't know: how she knew him.

She hadn't thrown him a bad pick-up line out on the street.
She'd been standing there, laughing at the performer in the
jester hat, when all of a sudden she'd felt this tug on her subconscious. A burst of *awareness*—that's the best way she could
describe it. She'd looked up, and there stood Xavier.

She didn't recognize his face—she'd definitely remember
that—but there was something *about* him. She was far from a
granola hippie chick, so it felt silly to admit, but it seemed to
be something in his aura. It connected with her, hit some note
of recognition deep within her body, and she knew that even
in the throng of people she could pick him out with her eyes
closed.

But he was a local, and she'd never been to White Clover
Creek. Hell, she hadn't even left the Florida Keys in two years.

And, of course, he'd run from her like she was a leper. Nice,
Cat. Chasing down the guy who mowed over about twenty
people to get away from you.

She'd never done anything like that in her life. Never trailed
after a guy like a puppy. Certainly never stalked anyone by
making restaurant reservations just to get another look. No
wonder he'd told that woman Pam to cover for him as he hid

in the back. Cat would have done the same thing if a strange guy had followed her back to the hotel bar where she worked.

Except that for a long moment, when their eyes had first met, she could have sworn he was interested . . .

She shook her head to clear it, slapped her mittened hands together and straightened her coat. What was she doing standing there in an alley, propped up by a potted, leftover Christmas tree? Today was one of the most important days of her life and she was about to be late for it.

Back out on Waterleaf, she wove through the mob, keeping one eye on the salted sidewalk. She wasn't built for freezing temperatures, for snow. At least if she bit it, the tight crowd would keep her from falling on her butt. She was so cold she probably wouldn't feel it anyway.

Waterleaf cut away from the main square and climbed a steep, steady slope. Lovely old buildings with elaborate, nineteenth-century wood scrollwork lined both sides. Festival goers bundled in thick boots and puffy coats and expensive sunglasses spilled out of the shops and restaurants. A few she recognized from TV or the movies, and their way of sauntering about in the broad daylight was clearly meant to draw attention.

No one knew who she was, but, according to Michael, by the end of the festival that would change. Hell *yes*. The beginning of the rest of her life.

It had to be. She had no idea where to go or what to do if it wasn't.

The Drift Art Gallery capped the end of stair-stepped shops at the very top of Waterleaf, before the downtown blurred into residential neighborhoods. A century of Colorado winters had weathered the gallery's brick, but its wooden trim glowed in bright purple. Striped paper covered the windows, blocking the interior. On the neon green front door dangled a small chalkboard sign: CAT HEDDIG, PAINTER. FEBRUARY 6–MARCH 31. OPENING RECEPTION FEBRUARY 5, BY INVITATION ONLY.

Even though full-on hypothermia was about ten seconds away, she just stood there on the slanted sidewalk, staring at her name. So it was real. Her first show. Her big debut, to take place in front of scads of Michael Ebrecht's Hollywood folk.

Back when she'd first picked up a brush, almost six years

ago, she hadn't known this was where she wanted to be. All she knew was that there was something artistic and magical and frustrated swirling around inside her, dying to be released, and that she refused to be a bartender for the rest of her life. Now that she was here? It felt like she was standing on a stoop, lifting her hand to knock on the door of the place that was to become her home. And that's all she'd ever wanted, wasn't it? A true home.

Nerves skated around her belly—the good kind, the dreaded kind, all mixed together—but she wouldn't let them stop her. Not now. She opened the creaking wooden door. An old-fashioned bell tinkled overhead. Bass-heavy music played somewhere out of sight, mingling with the sounds of men's muffled voices. She stepped into a cloud of paint fumes. Ladders and folded drop cloths sat in the far corner of the long, narrow exhibit space.

She heard Michael before she saw him. "No, Helen. *No.* That's not what we agreed. *Pond #11* will go up front, hanging from the ceiling when you walk in. Bam! It hits you right away."

*Pond #11* was Michael's favorite painting of hers that he didn't already own.

He appeared from the back hall, trailing a statuesque woman in her late sixties with dyed black hair and glasses on a long, beaded chain. Helen Wolfe, presumably, Drift's owner and curator. Helen was shaking her head, talking to Michael over her shoulder as he snipped at her heels. Cat gasped. No one ever walked away from Michael. And if they did, he certainly never followed.

They didn't see her and she didn't call to them, painfully curious to hear what they had to say when clearly she was their topic of conversation. Helen whirled, jabbing her glasses at Michael. "That was before I actually saw it. It's too large. Cuts off the flow of the main gallery and the view from the street once the paper is taken off the windows. We'll do a ceiling mount of *Pond #11* in the back gallery, use it to draw the crowds into that room. Happy?"

Michael ran a hand around the back of his neck. "Then *Ocean #16* goes up front."

*Ocean #16* was Cat's favorite.

Helen considered him for longer moments than Cat figured

him patient for. Cat was dying to know how this woman was able to speak to Michael the way she did.

"Agreed," Helen said.

A young woman just barely out of college stepped from the side office. She, too, wore glasses, though they were likely just for show—she had that faux look about her. She made a beeline for Cat. "Sorry, but we're closed for installation. You'll have to come back February sixth." She emphasized *sixth* as though to underscore only certain people would be welcome for the opening on the fifth.

Michael and Helen looked over and finally saw Cat. She quirked a smile and saluted them with her mittened hand.

Michael charged toward the door, a Rottweiler in a stunning charcoal suit likely from some designer she couldn't pronounce. "No, no, Alissa. This is *Cat*. The *artist*."

Poor Alissa. Michael would never give her the time of day now. The assistant turned on a smile, fake as Miami boobs, and swiveled back into the office.

Michael pulled Cat in for a brief hug that had more space than contact, then stepped back, holding her arms. "You made it. How was the flight?"

He looked good, as usual, the wrinkles on his forehead and under his eyes making him look commanding, not old. The dusting of silver in his gelled-back hair perfectly complemented his clothes.

"Ugh." She stifled a yawn. "My first and last red-eye."

But he was barely listening, also as usual. He ran his hand down her arm, his fingers catching on something. He gave it a snap and lifted up the offending price tag with a raise of his eyebrows.

She snatched it from his fingers. "Er, just bought it yesterday. Do you know how hard it is to find a winter coat in the Keys?"

He was smiling at her in that way she never quite knew how to read. Like he wasn't sure whether he wanted to roll his eyes or kiss her. In the two years they'd known each other he'd never come on to her, but occasionally, like now, she wondered if he might be pondering it . . . or if he just saw her as some flighty bartender obsessed with painting water.

As for her, she'd never been attracted to him in that way.

The twenty-year age difference might have had something to do with it. Or the fact that he only visited his house in the Keys a few times a year. Or that sometimes he could be a serious jerk. Or that he was the one who'd plucked her from a life of showing her paintings to cruise tourists on a stopover. He'd believed in her, stuck his neck out for her, and she wasn't about to mix business with pleasure.

Helen inserted herself between them, hand outstretched. "Ms. Heddig. Lovely to finally meet you after speaking on the phone. Michael Ray has told me so much about you. Ever since he bought that first piece of yours at that art fair."

*Michael Ray?*

Cat blinked, realizing that she knew little to nothing about Helen herself—other than she was one of the most well-connected independent gallery owners in the U.S. Shaking Helen's hand, she said, "Michael speaks of your gallery very highly. I've seen some of the pieces in his private collection. You must have worked together a lot in the past."

Helen grinned while Michael shifted on his feet and stuffed his hands in his pockets. Who *was* this guy?

"I should say we have," Helen said slowly, with a hint of amusement and a sideways look at Michael. "You didn't tell her?"

He cleared his throat. "Helen's my first former stepmom. Out of four."

"Your favorite former stepmom," she added with affection.

Michael wiped at the corners of his mouth as his gaze bounced around the eggshell-glazed room. So he'd not only aligned his well-known name with a bartender slash beach-bum artist like her, but he'd involved a clearly beloved member of his own family. Cat slapped on her most charming smile—the one she wore for her five-star hotel customers—but the pressure inside made her want to put her hands on her knees and swallow a few deep breaths.

To hide her nervousness, she reminded herself of why she'd wanted to do the show in the first place. Years of wandering. Years of solitude. Day after day filled with false smiles and forced conversation with resort guests. The only thing that made it worth it was the daylight hours she could dedicate to painting her obsession: The thing that poked at her mind at

night until she finally fell asleep. The first thing to stab itself
into her consciousness when she awoke. The thing whose call
tugged at her all day long.

Water.

Not many people had an outlet for their crazy, but Cat had
her brushes. And it was time she put herself out there—*really*
out there—because painting alone had reached its threshold
of usefulness. If she didn't find a new path to travel soon, if she
didn't figure out what this strange connection to water meant,
she feared what might become of her.

"What do you think of the space?" Michael swept out
an arm.

Here it came, the bartender smile. "As if I've ever had anything to compare it to? It's . . . incredible. So much bigger than
I expected."

"We bought the old building behind us," Helen added, "and
knocked out the joining walls. Perfect for big shows like this."

Big show. For her. The floor undulated like waves and she
grabbed Michael's arm for support. When he looked down at
her hand with an odd, uncomfortable expression, she removed it.

Helen slid warm fingers over Cat's shoulder. An intimate
gesture from someone she barely knew. Strangely, it felt welcome and right.

"You okay, honey?" Helen asked. "Your eyes look a little red."

She glanced at Michael, whose expression reminded her of
the "talk" he'd given her a few months ago in preparation for
these next two weeks. *Be professional, Cat. Always be professional.* What he was really saying? *Don't embarrass me.*

Cat waved Helen off. "Yeah. I mean, *yes*, I'm fine. Not used
to the cold. Made my eyes water."

Helen humored her. "We're excited to have you. All the
canvases arrived safely and I've been paging through them
every day. Your work is fresh. Explosive, yet serene at the same
time. The perfect thing to show in the dead of winter. I expect
to sell the hell out of them during the festival and all through
ski season."

Her paintings in strangers' houses. At least some part of her
would find a home.

Helen crossed her arms. She looked like a kindly grand-
mother and a shrewd businesswoman at the same time. Heaven

help anyone who told her no. "Let me tell you, I had my pick of up-and-coming artists, all wanting to get in front of the Hollywood crowd. Nothing truly jumped out at me. Then Michael Ray called. He may be an arrogant son of a bitch, but he has an amazing eye and a sharp business sense. I'm not doing him or you a favor by showing you. I have a reputation to uphold."

Cat swallowed and glanced at Michael, but he just nodded.

"Then I saw your work." Helen rolled her eyes. "Wow."

Michael beamed. Cat realized they were waiting for a response. "I can't tell you how overwhelmed I am to have this opportunity."

Helen tilted her head as if Cat were the painting. "Let's see how long that humility lasts when the who's who of L.A. and New York walk in here and start clawing for your stuff."

Michael nodded. "She's the real deal, isn't she? And just look at her. Made for the media. Made to be big."

Cat stiffened but Michael didn't notice. He probably wasn't even aware he'd said it out loud or that he wore a disconcerting, hungry sort of look. He'd certainly never said anything like that to her face before. As a film producer, she supposed, he was used to treating people like products because to him, they were.

With a quick, perceptive glance at her, Helen deftly turned the conversation. "It's stunning, Cat, how you capture the personalities of various bodies of water and still manage to twist them. Oceans are intimate. Ponds are expansive. And the rivers—ah!" She pressed a hand to her chest. "I know Michael loves the *Pond* series, but the *Rivers* are my personal favorite. You give them all such mystery. Such melancholy. Like you love it and hate it at the same time. So tell me: why water?"

Cat toed a folded drop cloth. That was the big question, wasn't it? If she could answer that, she wouldn't have started painting in the first place.

A phone buzzed. Michael reached into his pocket, mumbling, "Sorry, sorry."

He'd never apologized before for taking a phone call, but Cat didn't mind because it saved her from answering Helen. Michael listened for a second or two, his mouth drawing a grim line, then clicked off the phone. "I gotta run. First screening starts in fifteen then meetings all afternoon through dinner."

He turned to Cat. "Meet up tomorrow? There's an actor I want you to meet. Big art collector."

She just stared. It always took a few seconds to track the speed of his brain.

"What?" Michael tapped at his phone's calendar. "Did we make plans?"

"Well, no. But I have a reservation at Shed tonight."

She wasn't really keen on having dinner with Michael—given that she'd made the reservation in order to stare at Xavier some more and try to figure out how she knew him—but she realized, as she said it, that she didn't want to be alone her first night away from the ocean. Already the dryness and isolation of this place scraped at her skin and mind.

He hissed through his teeth. "Sorry, can't. Wait. Did you say Shed? How'd you get in there?"

"Um. I asked?"

Suddenly she feared he'd cancel his plans to go with her, because if Michael was about one thing, it was status.

"Why don't you go with Helen?" he offered. "You two could talk more about the show. Get to know each other."

Helen grinned, sliding on her glasses, the beaded chain catching the overhead lights. "Sounds good to me. As long as I can pick up the check. We can giggle and talk about Michael Ray behind his back."

Michael snorted. "You already know everything. I'm an open fucking book."

As he gave Cat's arm an impersonal pinch, she wasn't entirely convinced that that was the case.

# THREE

**Michael kissed Helen on the cheek, gave Cat a squeeze on the** arm that felt more awkward than it looked, and left the gallery. No one could rattle him like the gorgeous, modest, as-yet-unknown artist from Florida . . . despite the fact she was still a nobody. With his help, that would soon change. And *then* she'd be worthy.

Out on Waterleaf, he flipped up the collar of his cashmere coat and tugged on his stiff, leather gloves. His gaze skated over the papered windows and the chalkboard sign with Cat's name scrawled on it. He shivered, but it had nothing to do with the cold.

Cat's opening was going to fucking *kill*.

Suggesting to Helen to schedule the gallery event in the middle of the festival, at the peak of the Hollywood presence and the greatest saturation of money and power, was brilliant on his part. Aside from the fact that he'd contracted with Helen to take a finder's fee from sales, really what he was selling was Cat.

The L.A. elite spent their lives grasping for whatever was "the latest." They worshipped new faces. They obsessed over beauty. They loved whatever someone else told them to love, whatever someone better than them deemed important or rare or special. Michael was a prime example of this, and he knew it. *Thank you, Raymond Ebrecht, for passing on the torch.*

Michael was merely doing his duty by telling the rest of the elite to love Cat's art. He was nothing, if not a trendsetter.

He was nothing, if not a man obsessed with the one woman

who didn't give a shit about his money or his job. The one woman who wasn't *quite* good enough for him.

His phone rang. With a grunt he pulled off a glove with his teeth. No wonder the industry was based in L.A. If everyone had to jump through these goddamn hoops all the time to get to their phones, the number of tantrums would increase exponentially.

"Yeah."

"Tell me you're on your way." Grant, his office assistant.

"I'm on my way."

Grant's voice lowered. "I have Tom Bridger in my eyesight and he's talking to some random. Get over here and you'll catch him before the main title."

Bridger seeing Michael at the theater *before* the screening went a hell of a lot further than Michael approaching the director right after. That meant Michael was about to actually sit through the film and hadn't just popped in during the denouement. Bridger needed to know Michael's pursuit of him was deadly serious.

The project for which Michael wanted the young, up-and-coming director was going to be a game changer. But Michael had to slow play him. Bridger was one of those annoying types who were into film for the "art" and publicly decried anything to do with Big Hollywood. So far, Bridger had barely acknowledged the calls from Michael's production company. Michael's number-one business goal while in White Clover Creek? Change Bridger's mind. And he was exactly the kind of guy who'd love Cat, with her aw-shucks likability and raw talent. He'd introduce them as soon as possible and let Cat's good vibes rub off on Bridger. Everything was coming together so nicely. With Bridger in the director's chair, the thing would sweep the Oscars.

The world assumed that winning more Oscars than the record-setting Raymond Ebrecht was every Hollywood producer's dream. Not for Michael. His goal was much more personal.

"You there?" Grant's tinny voice came through the phone.

"Be there in five."

At the bottom of the Waterleaf hill, a respectable crowd gathered outside the Gold Rush for Bridger's opus on eighteenth-century French prostitutes, shot with one camera and a max on Bridger's credit cards. A light snow started to fall and Michael had to slow his steps so his loafers wouldn't send his ass rolling down the sidewalk to the red carpet below.

His phone buzzed. A text this time.

"Jesus, Grant," he mumbled, "I'm almost there."

But it wasn't from Grant. It was Sean, his *other* assistant.

Need you up at the house. Now.

Problem? Michael texted back.

A surprise from Lea. Get up here.

Oh, God. She'd brought him another one.

Michael snapped his phone shut, adrenaline hurtling through his body. Growing up he'd never had the joyful Christmases like you saw in his films, but in the past two years Lea had become his own goddamn Santa: unpredictable, generous, and *magical*.

He stopped in the middle of the sidewalk, right in front of a boutique that had rolled out racks of sale sweaters and jeans under its awning. A woman walking behind him skittered on the slanted concrete trying to get around him. He didn't apologize.

Ten minutes to curtain on Bridger's film. His rental house up in the mountains a fifteen-minute drive away. He needed to be two places at once.

No problem.

He stalked down to the end of the block and hung a tight right. Shit, the narrow, one-way street was full of people posing for pictures against the backdrop of the main square and its horrid statue. He kept going and came out on Groundcherry Street, which bordered the backs of all the buildings along Waterleaf. An overflowing parking lot sat across the street. No celebrities, no gapers.

He ducked behind the boutique, into a little alcove where new snow was trying to make the old sludge look pretty again. A tower of empty Christmas decoration boxes tilted against the old brick wall and he wedged himself behind it, shielding himself from view, should anyone come along. Good thing he'd inhaled a giant breakfast. He needed the energy.

Pressing his back against the brick, he drew a deep breath and held it. He closed his eyes and dove into the black of his mind. There, straight down the center of his subconscious, ran a thick, pulsing seam of glowing red. He pushed his awareness into that seam, filling it until the crack widened and widened. He slipped ghostly fingers into the seam, taking hold of each side, and ripped his own mind apart.

He *split*.

The second it happened, Michael went weightless. His body felt like it shot upward from the ground, bobbing like a balloon. The next second, someone yanked on that balloon's string and he was jerked back downward. His stomach sloshed and lead lined his veins. He inhaled. Exhaled. The world evened out. Then he opened his eyes.

Michael Ebrecht stood in front of him. The same coat, the same posture, the same face.

It was not a twin, with a similar face and separate thoughts. It was not a mirror image or doppelgänger. It was him, Michael. Divided.

The double raised a gloved hand and smoothed down his silvering hair. Always, at the first look after a *split*, Michael was painfully aware of how he'd aged. How narrow his face had gotten, how all his years spent in L.A. and Miami had weathered his skin. If only he'd figured out how to use the *splitting* to his advantage at a much earlier age. If only Raymond had actually explained it to him. Or talked to him even. Ah, youth. Wasted on the youth. And Michael's was most definitely a waste.

He and his double didn't need to speak. The other automatically knew what he needed to do and by when. He nodded to Michael, stepped out from behind the boxes and headed back toward Waterleaf. They didn't share a consciousness, but instead melded together their separate conversations and emotions and occurrences upon reabsorption. He never worried the other would rebel; they had the same goals, the same mind. Within three hours, because that's how long the energy could last, the two would rejoin, and Michael would learn how the "surprise" meeting with Bridger went.

Michael stayed huddled behind the boxes until his watch said the screening had started. Then he turned out onto Groundcherry and headed back uphill. He waved down the first cab he saw, only realizing he'd stolen it from someone else when the jilted, irate couple stood on the curb and windmilled their arms. The rusting white minivan with the faded taxi decals pulled away. He couldn't have called back the limo driver who had toted him into town earlier that day because technically Michael was supposed to be in the screening. The first trick to being two people was to never get caught. The second trick was to use it for every advantage.

Divide and conquer, he always said.

**The cabdriver whistled as he pulled his rattling source of** income into the driveway of the sprawling, two-story fieldstone house Michael had rented for the next two weeks. The driveway made a wide circle around a dry fountain still topped with a decorated Christmas tree.

"Never driven anyone up here before," said the cabbie, his mouth hanging open as he peered through the windshield. "It yours or you renting?"

"Wait for me," grunted Michael.

"Hey, I keep the meter running."

"Hey, I don't care."

Michael approached the house, trying to keep his steps light and unhurried. People running in and out of houses tended to leave an impression on those who watched, and the cabbie was definitely watching.

The front door opened. Sean had one hand braced on the doorjamb and a ghostly expression on his barely adult face.

Michael waved Sean back inside and glanced over his shoulder to see if the cabbie was eyeing them, but the cabbie had turned his gape-mouthed attention to the east wing of the house. The fewer people who saw Sean the better. He was still technically "missing."

Sean backed into the foyer and Michael shut the door behind himself. The faint, stale smell of smoke lingered; Sean must have burned toast again.

"Talk," Michael said. "I had to *split* to get up here."

He didn't have to explain the time limits to Sean. Sean knew. He knew very well.

Sean ran a hand through his sandy hair and kept it there, clenching the straight stuff at the back of his skull. "Lea got you a new one."

Michael slid his hands to hips, parting the cashmere coat. "Yeah, that's what you said. Weren't we expecting another? She had her heart set on one in particular."

Sean was shaking his head before Michael had even finished. "No. A *new* one. Like, one that neither of us knew was coming. And it was delivered here."

Michael's arms dropped. So did his voice. "Why here? The L.A. house is all set up for collection."

Sean shrugged. "Said you'd want to see it right away."

The high that came with another addition to his collection, another new discovery . . . there was nothing like it. "Where is it?"

Sean paled even more. "In the garage."

"The . . . Jesus. Okay." Mentally he paged through his commitments that week, trying to recall if he was supposed to entertain anyone here at the house. Grant would know; that was his sole purpose. But Michael couldn't exactly text him right now, considering his other half was likely sitting next to his assistant in a darkened movie theater.

Michael tugged off his gloves and stalked through the echoing marble foyer, passing the curving staircase on his left. In the great room at the back of the house, just off the kitchen, was access to the garage through a door next to the two-story fireplace.

Two of Cat's huge canvases, protectively wrapped, sat propped side by side against the anemically filled bookshelves. These paintings were in his private collection, and ones he'd insisted Helen put in her show. Nothing like a placard saying "Property of Michael Ebrecht" to spark buying interest.

A third canvas—the smallest she'd ever painted, one of her first—rested on the fireplace mantel. That painting was how he'd first met her, walking past her flapping tent in the Key West art fair. He'd bought it within fifteen minutes, after talking her down twenty-five bucks and imagining her naked in twenty-five ways. Imagining her elevated to his level. Two years later, *Ocean #2* came with him wherever he went.

A low rumble detonated behind the garage door. Beside him, Sean froze.

Michael swiveled to the kid. "What the fuck was that?"

Sean swallowed, backed up a step. "The new one. When it started doing that, I called you."

Michael bolted for the door, threw it open.

A giant box consumed one half of the two-car garage. It was made of a thick translucent material, but for some reason he couldn't fully see inside. Like the inner walls had been painted with a substance that constantly shifted between shades of sick, menacing dark gray. The garage door had been opened a few inches on the bottom and a big fan ran on high in the corner. The smoke smell burned strong.

"It's *caged*?" Michael buzzed with frantic excitement. He jumped down the two steps into the garage. "How the hell did she get it in here?"

"Big truck."

"Yeah, but how'd she get it in *here*?" He stabbed a finger at the garage floor.

Sean shrugged. "She's got Jase with her. He moved it."

Yeah, Jase could move just about anything. What a find, that guy. And apparently Lea had been planning for this capture without telling Michael, given that she'd already had the cage and truck and all.

Another rumble exploded inside. The box rocked, one corner lifting a few inches off the concrete. The box was fucking huge. The power it must have taken just to nudge a thing like that . . .

Michael couldn't breathe for the anticipation. "What is it?"

"Lea said it was a surprise. Said you'd love it." Sean hovered in the doorway to the house, refusing to step into the garage.

Love didn't even begin to describe what Michael was feeling. He was already imagining how he'd throw this one in Raymond's face. How the old man would react. Michael inched closer. Something *thump thump thump*ed inside the blackened box. Like a toddler first facing flame, he stretched out a hand. And, like a parent, Sean said, "Don't touch it. It's hot."

Michael scoffed.

"No, really. It is."

Michael raised one hand, touching his index finger to the corner of the cage. He jumped back, hissing at the searing pain.

"Told you," Sean muttered.

Michael just stood there, staring. Holy shit, that was *smoke* inside that box. Thick, black, kill-you-with-a-single-inhale smoke. Goddamn it. What the hell was in there?

"Where's Lea now?" he barked.

"She and Jase and Robert dropped this off and then took off again. Said she'd caught the trail of a water she wanted."

Michael absently waved a hand. "That can't be right. We already have a water. We have Robert."

"It's what she said."

Well, hell. Two were always better than one. His Lea, a fountain of twisted information. The best magic bloodhound in existence.

Michael stared into the box, shifting his position every few seconds, trying to see through the thick murk.

"Lea said she probably wouldn't be back until the day of the opening at Drift," Sean said. "Maybe later."

*Shit.* "She didn't say anything else about what's inside? Anything at all?"

"No."

There was no seeing inside. He was *this close* to grabbing the ladder hanging from the garage wall, climbing up to the box top, and unlocking the latch, when Sean said, "I saw it, you know. Before it did . . . that."

Michael held his breath. "Did what?"

"Made it go all black and smoky inside. It did that when it woke up. Got pissed off." Sean slowly backed farther inside.

"What is it?"

Sean said nothing. Just pointed.

Michael followed the line of Sean's finger.

The black smoke swirled in a slow, deliberate circle. Thin streams leaked out from the box's tight seams. The fan picked up the wispy tendrils and sent them flying under the garage door.

Something moved inside the box. No, *against* the box. An arm, rubbing away the char. He crept forward, nothing making a sound in the whole garage. In the whole world.

A face peered out of the small, smudged hole. A woman's face. A face as beautiful as heaven and twisted as all hell.

The smoke cloaked her, twined around her like it was a

sentient being. He didn't know where the smoke ended and the black of her hair began. She didn't cough, didn't wipe at her dark, slanted eyes that eerily didn't water.

He bent closer to the box, the tip of his nose feeling the heat blazing from inside.

She came closer, too. Absolutely no fear on her face. She opened her mouth to speak, and though he couldn't hear her, he knew exactly what she said by the shape of her mouth.

*"Fuck. You."*

And he smiled.

Her eyes had burned dark before, but now they plunged into full black. Black and hard as coal.

The woman slammed her hands against the box wall, her palms making pale prints in the coat of ash. The box jerked from the incredible force. She opened her mouth and screamed, the tendons in her throat jutting out.

Michael just stood there. Staring. Lea had been right. He'd never seen anything like this woman . . . and he *loved* it.

She stopped screaming. She stepped back, one side of her mouth twisting up, like she was queen of the world and knew all. Her clothes draped in burnt tatters across the muscular lines of her strong, firm body. She was beyond exotic, her skin deeply colored and smooth, her features a hodgepodge of Asian and Pacific Islander and European.

"Guess what," Michael whispered, "you're mine now."

She drew a deep breath—so deep it seemed unnatural—her spectacular chest expanding up and out like her ribs were rubber. Her red lips parted and her mouth opened wide. There, in the back of her throat, sparked a flame. No more than a match strike, tiny and yellow. Her lips narrowed, the flame rolling in the depths of her mouth, her cheeks glowing from the interior heat and light. She lifted a hand and blew the flame onto a finger where it danced without being snuffed out. She rubbed her fingertips together and the flame grew into the size of a golf ball. Bringing her other hand into it, she rolled the fireball between her palms in slow, sensuous movements. The longer she worked it, the bigger it got.

Jesus, he was getting hard watching this.

She dropped one arm, cradling a fiery mass larger than her

head in her palm. That same arm fell back then launched forward. The fireball smashed against the inside of the box, leaving a new layer of char. Blocking his view.

He couldn't wait until Raymond saw this.

As Michael turned back to the house, he was aware of Sean's look of horror, of perpetual worry. But Michael was smiling. Exhilarated.

Fucking *jacked*.

# FOUR

**She walked into Shed at 8:03 p.m. Not that Xavier was watching.**
Or waiting. He saw everything from behind the wide pane of
kitchen glass. It perfectly framed the way Cat wove sinuously
between the black tables draped in white cloth, the way the low
light seemed to catch and hold on to her. The hostess seated
Cat and her companion—an older woman he swore he'd seen
before—in the center of the dining room. No table near the
busboy station for this last-minute reservation during high season. Thanks, Pam.

The three seconds over, he returned his eyes to his station
and tuned his ears to the beloved clatter and hiss of the kitchen
at his back. Pam was making her station rounds. At the burners next to Xavier, she was talking to Jose about the sear on
his chicken. With an encouraging clap on Jose's shoulder, she
came over to Xavier.

"Did you do something to my Cabernet sauce, X?"

The nickname made him shiver. In the Plant he'd only been
known as 267X, but he couldn't tell Pam that.

His hand went instinctively—protectively?—to the wooden
spoon in the pot holding the lovely crimson-colored, peppery
sauce for the filet special. "Maybe. Why?"

"Tastes different."

"What's it taste like?" He cracked an egg for the béarnaise,
passing the insides between shell halves to separate out the
yolk.

She drummed her short nails on the cutting board. "Like I
want to roll around naked in it."

He hid his smile.

She sighed. "I should fire you, you know."

He glanced over his shoulder at her pursed lips and raised eyebrows. "So fire me."

"Ah, fuck. You know I won't."

"Good. 'Cause I don't want to go anywhere."

"Double good. I'll just keep taking advantage of you."

"As long as we understand each other."

She let out a short laugh as he continued to crack and separate eggs. As he reached for the whisk, she asked, all falsely casual, "So who were you looking at out there?"

Here it came. "No one."

Pam made a show of standing on her toes and craning her neck to peer through the glass. "Angelina Jolie? Kate Winslet?"

Who? With a testing spoon, he checked the seasoning in the sesame sauce that got drizzled over the salmon.

"Ah, I see her." Pam whistled. "She's really pretty. Those tall boots with that skirt. Damn."

Pam turned toward the pastry station before he could tell her to leave.

Boots and a skirt. He ordered himself not to look. Béarnaise was tricky and if you didn't keep whisking it over the heat it would break . . .

Cat didn't wear her red pompom hat to dinner. In fact, she didn't wear much of anything. She'd pushed her chair out a bit, her legs crossed diagonally toward the table. Her black skirt was short and tight, her boots high. The line of her thigh muscle made his skin as hot as the burners to his right, but he couldn't look away. A fuzzy sweater exposed her shoulders, drawing a delicious, horizontal line of skin. Could women wear bras under sweaters like that?

While Cat's companion examined a bottle of wine, the sommelier standing at her elbow, Cat turned her face toward the kitchen. She found him immediately, as if she knew exactly where he'd been all along. Their gazes slammed together. She tilted her head.

The little balloons of dining room conversations popped. The clanking sounds of the kitchen fell away. The desire tackled him and he went down without defense. His blood began to pound, racing toward the throbbing part of him that would give everything away.

The kitchen glass fogged over, the swirls of hallucinatory white forming the ugly, mocking face of the Burned Man.

*How perfect*, he said. *You're used to an audience.*

Fuck *no*. This was not happening again. Not twice in one day. Not *here*, where he was supposed to be safe.

Xavier stretched over to Jose's station, snatched a red onion from his pile. Choking up on his chef's knife, Xavier bent far over the onion and made precise, quick strokes into the pliant pink flesh. Opening his eyes wide, letting the fumes rise up and curl around his face, he inhaled. The sting stabbed at his eyes and sawed at his throat. He did it again. And again.

When he lifted his head the Burned Man no longer haunted the glass. And Cat no longer looked at him.

**"You never answered my question back at the gallery." Helen** leaned heavily on the table, elbows pulling at the white cloth. They'd nearly finished the best bottle of wine Cat had ever had. Although that wasn't saying much, considering ten dollars for a bottle at home was a splurge. This one had cost two hundred; Cat had snuck a look at the leather-bound wine list.

"Which question was that?"

Helen flicked her wrist in a grand gesture, a massive diamond ring twinkling on her finger. "Why do you paint water? What draws you to it?"

Cat frowned and twirled her wineglass, leaving fingerprints on the bowl. "If I could put it into words, I'd be a writer, not a painter."

Helen had gotten it right, though, in what she'd observed that morning: Cat both loved and hated the source of her inspiration. Most days she really did wish she could put it into words. Might have made her life a heck of a lot easier.

Helen made an "*ah*" sound and nodded, like Cat had just imparted to her the secrets of the universe. It was impossible not to like this woman. Cat was close to so few people. Her job—the real one, the one that actually brought in money—made her skeptical of most human beings. Not many women chatted her up while sitting at her bar, and the men who did didn't seem to realize that small talk and false enthusiasm were written in to her job description. There were co-workers who were friends, sure, but when her shift ended, she was in front of her canvases, trying to figure out her life.

Cat threw back the last of her wine. The music filling Shed carried a steady, sexy, electronic beat, and the sounds of boisterous, wine-soaked conversations made Cat raise her voice. "What do you know of inspiration?"

Helen had started to peruse the dessert menu and now looked at Cat over her bifocals. Her eyes were done only in champagne eye shadow and black eyeliner. Age had only slightly overshadowed the beauty of her youth. "What do you mean?"

"I mean, is inspiration something artists talk about a lot?"

Helen smiled and folded the little dessert menu. It likely wasn't on purpose, but that smile made Cat feel about six years old. "They get asked about inspiration a lot. Where it comes from."

Cat inched forward on her chair. *This* was what she wanted to hear. "And what do they say?"

Helen shrugged. "That it just comes to them. That it's indefinable."

Cat looked at the table, trying not to let the defeat show on her face.

"That upsets you?" The bifocals came off again.

"'Upsets'? Not exactly. Disappoints, maybe. It's . . . never mind."

"No, go on."

Cat uncrossed then crossed her legs, and a warm trickle of awareness skated over her, moving slowly from hip to ankle. It tingled stronger than the wine in her blood. She didn't have to glance at the kitchen to know Xavier was watching. Just the thought of it exhilarated her, but she wouldn't look over there, not with Helen's eyes on her, too.

She tapped the table. "I don't understand why I love water so much. Only that I'm drawn to it, that it's part of me, and the only way to express how large a portion of me it is, is to paint."

Helen pursed her lips and bobbed her head side to side. "Makes sense. That comes through in your work. There's mystery to it. Agitation. A sense of the unknown."

"Yes! I'm so glad you see that." The wine made her all loose and comfortable, so she kept going. "I guess I'm partly here to learn what that's all about. Maybe, if I put myself out there, I'll find something that might be able to explain why my inspiration is so strong. Maybe, if I get to be around other artistic types, I could see how they work. Get a clue about myself."

"And sell some paintings." Helen smiled beneath a raised eyebrow.

"Oh. Yes. Of course."

Helen sat back, considering. "Are you prepared for criticism?"

"As prepared as I'll ever be, I suppose." Which wasn't at all, but she wouldn't tell Helen that.

"Are you ready for the spotlight? Because anyone standing next to Michael gets it."

Cat tried not to wince. "I had no idea who he was when I met him. I mean about the films and such. I didn't know until the third or fourth time he came to my bar."

"No?"

"I'd been showing my paintings at one of the island's art fairs to try to bring in some cash. My car needed work and . . . anyway, I needed money. Michael walked by one day. I remember it so clearly. He stopped and looked at my stuff, did a lap around the market and then came back. We got to talking and, I don't know, I just got a *feeling* about him. Like, even though I could tell he was vain and used to getting his way, underneath I felt a connection. Like, maybe he got me and I got him? He bought a painting. The rest is history."

The curator was watching her in that astute way again. "I'm glad you see that about him. But since he's not here I'm going to be completely honest with you. Michael Ray is selfish. The first person he thinks about is himself. Always. He didn't pluck you out of obscurity and involve me because of charity. Yes, he wants to see you succeed, but that's because there's something in it for *him*, whether it's money or recognition or both."

Cat pressed her lips together. She'd suspected as much. The fact that it came from Helen didn't soften it.

"On the other hand," Helen went on, "he's going to bring a serious level of clientele to your show. You will sell, and you will be able to fix your car ten times over."

Cat laughed. "Tell me more about him. About the two of you."

Helen folded her crumpled white napkin next to her fork. She took her time, made sure all the edges lined up. "I was married to Michael Ray's father, Raymond, when the boy was eight. I was told his mother just upped and left, and never looked back. My marriage to Raymond lasted less than a year; he was a demanding ass of a man who didn't understand I could be a demanding ass of a woman. It's how I got to where I was; I don't know why he never saw that. Anyway, almost as soon as the honeymoon was over, so were we.

"Except that I adored Michael Ray. First abandoned by his mom and then completely ignored by his dad. I insisted on keeping in touch with him even after I'd gone. I wasn't going to be the third adult to walk out on him. We used to have ice cream every Sunday, even after wife number three came around, and then wives four and then five. Even growing up in L.A., where kids' views of the real world are so twisted, and even with that ass of a dad, he was a good kid. And then something happened." She shifted on her chair, then turned and waved to the waiter for the check. "At first I thought it was just puberty but I'm pretty sure something else went on with him, too. We were close enough I'd hoped that if something was wrong he could tell me, but he never did."

"You still don't know?"

"No." Helen's gaze turned inward. "But it changed him. Made him hard and angry at first, then really, really arrogant. More so than he is now, if you can believe it. Things with his dad just got worse. It was like they were enemies; it was very strange. But I made sure to stand by him and treat him like a human should be treated. It was my hope he wouldn't turn out like his father." She laughed to herself. "Although at times that can be debated."

"I admit I don't know him that well. Our conversations have remained fairly on the surface."

Helen stretched across the table and patted her hand. "Well, I do. And deep down he really does have a good heart. I've seen it. He believes in you. And I do, too. We're partners now, Cat."

A knot of tension started to uncoil from deep inside her.

She let herself sink into her chair, relaxing in the aura of Helen's faith.

As Helen looked over the check and took out her wallet, Cat let her gaze drift toward the kitchen. Xavier stood tall behind the counter, front and center, owning it. His long hair was tied back in a band, a black handkerchief with SHED stenciled over his brow. Deep lines of concentration creased his mouth. He whisked something now, one arm churning madly in a stainless steel bowl. He paused to wipe his forehead on the sleeve of his black double-breasted coat . . . then froze. As though he knew she was staring again.

As if he could feel her, too.

For the second time that evening, his eyes met hers. The sight of his—so gray as to be silver—pulled a little gasp from her throat. Maybe they glowed, or maybe it was just the reflection of the bright kitchen lights. There was power in his stare. Yearning. And denial.

Their moment couldn't have lasted more than a second or two, but when his head bent to return to his work, she exhaled like she'd held her breath for an hour.

Helen dropped the pen into the check folder. "Do you know him?"

"Who?" Damn wineglass was empty. Cat had nothing to do with her hands.

Helen threw a pointed look at Xavier.

"No." Cat fidgeted with a spoon. "No, I don't know him."

"Huh," Helen said. Her eyes shifted between Xavier and Cat. "I recognize him, you know. I've seen him around town. And here, of course, when I bring in clients and artists. He's very handsome."

Handsome wouldn't have been the word Cat used. Stunning, maybe. Intriguing.

"You sure you don't know him? He looks at you like you've met." Helen leaned forward to whisper like a teenager. "Like you share a secret."

# FIVE

Xavier ducked into the Fresh Powder Pub at midnight, well and painfully aware he'd purposely thrown himself directly into the world of the Primaries. The pub smelled of damp wool and tangy beer, and he instantly wanted to turn back around and lose himself in the swirl of snow.

But where would he go? Home? For once his little kitchen offered no comfort. Tonight, Cat's image had been sewn into the chop and slide of the knife, the swipe of the spoon, the jiggle of the pan. He prayed that time would rectify that, unravel what had been inadvertently bound together. Cooking was all he had. If it became tainted by his past, he'd own nothing but his name, and not even that was his.

If he went home now carrying thoughts of Cat, the Burned Man would find his way through the front door, too. Xavier couldn't afford that. He supposed he could take the Burned Man into the basement, apply his face to the tattered bag hanging from the chain, and beat the crap out of it, but the Ofarian ghost would come back. He always came back. In the Plant and outside.

So Xavier would force himself to stay here, try to have a quiet beer, and unwind before he ventured back up the hill to his dark house. He'd stay, because he was fucking sick of himself already, and he wasn't going to get any better if he continued to hide.

"Hey, man." The bartender raised a hand attached to a thick, muscular arm. "I know you."

Xavier's eyes darted around the pub. There were very few

open seats, but those who were drinking didn't look Hollywood. "You do?"

"Yeah. Few years back. You took my class." The bartender nodded at the door, east, toward the small boxing gym at the bottom of Groundcherry Street.

"Oh, yeah." This guy had shown him how to throw a punch. How to make sure he gave as good as he got. "Ryan, right?"

"Yep. Never seen you here before."

"Never been in here before."

Ryan grinned, turned his baseball cap backward. "There's a seat free down at the end."

Perfect. The last bar stool, tucked against the back wall and near the short hallway that led to the bathrooms. He tugged the rubber band out of his hair, feeling a few strands rip, and let it fall around his face, an extra layer of protection. Ryan slid a pint of a reddish ale in front of him and said, "Try this. Local brew."

Xavier nodded in thanks, wrapped his fingers around the cold glass, and started to feel easier about his decision to come. This was all so ordinary, and no one seemed to care whether he sat there or not.

"So the insanity starts again," Ryan said, leaning against the mini-fridge and propping his foot on a shelf below the bar. "Read that Turnkorner'll break attendance records this year."

Xavier grunted and sipped his beer, and let Ryan's well-meaning but inane chatter keep his mind from tripping into darker thoughts. The beer eased into his belly and slipped into his bloodstream. He'd never been a big drinker, though he'd had a few rough nights here and there. Women had been his drug of choice. But now the Primary world—this tiny planet centered around the comfortable vinyl chair and filled with the soft drone of local voices—tucked itself around him and he was satisfied.

"Oh, *hel*lo." Ryan pushed to his feet.

And the world dropped out from under Xavier's.

He knew before he saw. The hair stood up on his forearms. Dread and excitement danced in his gut. A gust of something colder than winter whooshed across his body. Though he didn't want to turn, his traitorous body swiveled on the chair, following the line made by Ryan's gape.

Cat stood in the Fresh Powder doorway, snow billowing behind her. The red hat was back, that silly pompom flecked with white. She swept it off, shook the snow to the floor, then shrugged out of her coat. The wall pegs were already crammed with winter gear and she draped hers precariously on top. She'd replaced the short skirt from dinner with jeans but she still wore the sexy sweater that showed her shoulders.

She was alone. And she was here. In a bar he'd walked by a million times but had never entered.

Had she followed him again?

She innocently craned her neck, looking for an empty seat. Looking unsure about being there. Through the shifting bodies, she found Xavier and froze. No, the whole bar froze. Her mouth dropped open in surprise. The hard beat of Xavier's heart hurt. He knew he should face the bar again, hunch his shoulders. He knew he should give her a pretty strong hint to go away.

He didn't.

A shy smile tugged at her lips and the bar blurred back into motion. So did she, coming tentatively toward him. He should have gotten the hell out of there, but the pub was long and narrow, with a small path between the bar lining one side and the occupied highboy tables on the other. Even if he shoved to his feet and went for the door, he'd run into her. So he held his ground and watched her approach. The conqueror bearing down on the defeated.

Behind the bar, Ryan switched on a voice with a clear invitation. "Hi there. What can I get you?"

Cat must not have heard him, because she reached Xavier and stood as close to him as she had on the street. Closer even. The pub boiled hot. He hadn't showered after work and a new layer of sweat broke out over the old.

Melting snowflakes made the ends of her hair glitter and he stared like a baby watching shiny things.

Three seconds. Three seconds. Three seconds. Shit, how long had it been?

Her smile started to shake. "I asked the concierge at the Margaret to recommend a local pub. I had no idea you'd be here."

Ryan wagged a finger between them. "You two know each other?"

"No," Xavier and Cat said at the same time.

"But I can change that," she said, and her smile turned into a brilliant jewel. "I'm Cat."

Her throaty, wind-wracked voice made him rock on his seat. The movement told his mind what his body already knew: he'd grown hard and was only getting harder. This goddamn body. If he could abandon it in a cold, lonely hole, he would.

*Ah, good*, whispered the Burned Man close to his ear, and Xavier closed his eyes against the repulsive sound. *She came back to you. She wants it.*

He could sense the awkwardness surrounding him, and when he opened his eyes he saw it straight up. Cat gazed back at him with an odd look, and he knew she was considering whether or not he was crazy. Ryan's eyebrow crooked in a clear *What the fuck is wrong with you, dude?*

This is what the Burned Man had done to him, and Xavier hated it most of all: how his hang-ups made him appear to the Primaries he was trying to imitate.

*Look at her.* The Burned Man's smugness invaded Xavier's brain with barbed spikes. *You can just tell how good she'll feel around your dick.*

Shut up. Just shut the fuck up.

*I'm part of you. You can't ignore me.*

Maybe Xavier couldn't ignore the Ofarian ghost . . . but he could talk right over him. Drown him out.

Xavier looked her right in her toffee-colored eyes. "Short for Catherine?"

Her smile nudged its way back. Her bare shoulders dropped, relaxing. She shook her head, one long wave of hair falling over her shoulder. It swayed over her chest and he refused to give in to its temptation.

*Never knew you for a tit man. Just two roadblocks on the way to the real goal.*

"Caterina, actually. And you're Xavier."

He played along. "How'd you know that?"

"The, uh, blond woman at Shed. It's a great name. Xavier. Any story behind it?"

"Not an interesting one." Just a pathetic one.

*All this talking, 267X. It's not like you. You're just delaying the inevitable.*

Instinctively Xavier's body started to tense, but he fought it. Ground his teeth against it, determined not to give the Burned Man any satisfaction or acknowledgement. Determined not to give Cat or anyone else any more clues that he was seriously Fucked Up.

He took a giant swig of his beer.

Ryan tapped the bar in front of Cat. "What're you drinking?"

She swiped at her hair, now damp on the bottom half from the melted snow, and let out a short laugh. "Maybe I shouldn't have any more. Had too much wine at dinner. Look how brave it made me. Maybe a glass of water? With ice?"

"You got it."

Ryan left. Xavier's fingers started to twitch, his thumb and forefinger pinching together over and over, longing for a chef's knife. It wasn't too late to get up. It wasn't too late to . . .

Cat pressed a hand to her forehead. Though she wore all sorts of shimmery makeup that made her face glow, her fingernails were short and unpainted, the skin around them ragged.

"Jeez, I feel like a stalker. Really, I'm not. I swear. I came in on the red-eye this morning from Florida and I'm beyond tired. Figured I'd try to stay awake for a bit to adjust to the time change—" She cut herself off, pressing her lips together.

He realized, with a sort of virgin fascination, that she was nervous. To be around *him*.

"Well, Xavier, it was nice of you to allow me to embarrass myself in front of you. Again. I'll leave you to your drink." She gave this endearing salute with two fingers and started to turn away.

*You won't let her leave. You want inside her.*

"You're from Florida?" Xavier asked.

*Atta boy*, chuckled the Burned Man.

She peered at him. "You thought I'm from L.A, didn't you?" He nodded. "Shame on you."

Ryan slid a tall, narrow glass of water in front of Cat. Though he moved away, he still watched her.

*Don't worry about him. I brought her for you.*

"You're not part of the whole Hollywood thing?" Xavier's

voice sounded loud to his own ears, but the Burned Man's mumblings faded a bit into the background and he felt encouraged. A little pumped up, even.

"Noooo." She waved her hands as if warding off evil. "I'm a bartender. And a painter. I'm here to open my first show at the Drift Gallery. You know it?"

"Yeah. Sure." He traced a water ring on the bar with his finger. "That woman you had dinner with, she works there, right?"

By the way Cat smiled, he realized he'd revealed just how much he'd stared at her during dinner. "Helen Wolfe. She owns it. Do you know her?"

He shook his head. The Drift was for the wealthy tourists, not people like him.

Xavier still faced the bar, and with the lack of seats, Cat had sort of wedged herself between him and the guy on the next stool. Her arm, clad in that fuzzy red sweater, stretched long beside Xavier, boxing him in, sending his opposite shoulder into the wall. She held her water glass and absently began to stroke her thumb and forefinger up and down it, drawing seeping lines through its sweat.

The Burned Man lifted his gravelly voice. *Check that out. That could be you.*

But Xavier had already latched on to the movement. He tore his eyes away and swept them toward the ceiling. His whole body thrummed, tuned to every one of her breaths, every little flinch.

"On the street this morning, I really thought I recognized you."

He coughed and clenched his pint glass. "You don't. Believe me."

"No, I know that now. Still, there's something *about* you. Can't put my finger on it."

The low, dreamy tone in her voice drew his eyes back to her. Every time he did that—looked away and then looked back—the sight of her struck him. A full-body blow. Except now it wasn't just her face and mouth and legs and shoulders that left him bruised and wanting more. The humor in her words, the ease with which she'd approached him—several times now—awed him. She walked around with this casual, comfortable air, and he wished he owned that, too.

Her palm circled in front of his face, as though she were trying to divine a memory from the atmosphere. "Ah, well. It's probably something dumb, like you remind me of someone from high school or someone I met on the road."

Xavier knew she'd given him an opening, an opportunity to make real conversation—something he'd never done with any woman except Pam since moving here—but he couldn't get his mouth to work. And the Burned Man's suggestions were getting even more vulgar and nasty, morphing into bugs that wiggled through his ears, ate at his brain, and tried to put words in his mouth. If he talked, he feared what might come out.

*That's right. Years ago you would have just told her you wanted to fuck her and she would have let you. Weak women love that, when you take control. Do it now, 267X.*

Caterina was no weak woman. And that realization nearly pushed him off his chair.

Suddenly she frowned and reached into the pocket of her jeans. She pulled out a buzzing phone. "What does he want at this hour?" she mumbled, reading whatever it said on the screen. Then she turned it off with a "Sorry about that," and lifted her eyes back to his. "My sponsor, I guess you could call him. Double checking on a dinner we have tomorrow. Apparently he doesn't sleep."

First Ryan, then this "him" on her phone . . . and she was paying attention to Xavier. *Talking* to him.

Maybe talking to a woman was good. Maybe, instead of fleeing from the threat of sex and constantly trying to hide, he should stop. Plant his feet. Face it head on.

"So . . ." His throat dried up, closed. He swallowed, tried again. "So are you going to see any of the festival movies?"

Her eyes darted side to side in thought. "I don't think so. That seems kind of pathetic to admit, doesn't it?"

*Oh, holy stars in hell*, said the Burned Man. *You're boring the shit out of me. You're only making yourself miserable. It's been years. She's begging for you. You deserve her. You deserve a good, old-fashioned, guilt-free orgasm. Like the kind you used to have.*

What Xavier deserved was freedom. True freedom that had nothing to do with escaping a physical cage. Running hadn't done anything for him. His past always caught up. He'd run

from the Burned Man for three years, ever since Xavier had
left him behind in San Francisco, but time hadn't destroyed the
ghost. Xavier's completely whacked-out, funhouse-mirror view
of relationships had just skewed even further away from
normal.

He was really fucking sick of it, and it was going to end.
Starting tonight.

"Would you like to go?" he heard himself say, and didn't
quite recognize the voice. "To a film? With me?"

The second the question came out, panic swept in, tilting
the pub, making him grip the edge of the bar for stability. The
strangest thing set him right: her clear, sunny smile. And it had
absolutely nothing to do with sex.

"Which one?"

He shrugged. He didn't even know how to get tickets. Maybe
Pam could help. "Hey, Ryan. Do you have a festival schedule?"

The bartender reached behind the cash register and handed
him a folded brochure. There was a screening tomorrow
at 9:00 a.m.

Cat pulled out her phone again. "I'm free tomorrow morning.
Well"—she gave him a wry grin—"later this morning, that
is. Are you?"

He glanced at the clock. Nearly 1:00 a.m. He didn't have to
be at Shed until eleven. "Yes."

He slid from the stool. In the tight space his body suddenly
pressed against hers, and holy shit, he could feel her heat, smell
her scent, made all the more sweet by the melted snow. She
slowly tilted her face up to him, her shiny lips forming a lazy
O, as if she, too, had felt that zing of energy. That ripple of
desire.

She was a foot shorter than he, but in those tall heels her
mouth drifted closer. He could already tell she'd be soft.
Wet. He could tell she wanted him to grab her. He could tell
that everything the Burned Man had said about her was true,
that she'd open for him if only he'd ask.

His whole body went rigid. Goddamn, he was such a fool.
How had he managed to trick himself into thinking he was
better than he was an hour ago? What sucker actually believed
in miracles?

The Burned Man took advantage of Xavier's weakness and

broke through the barricades, screaming: *Do what you were fucking born to do!*

A great shudder wracked Xavier's body and he stumbled back, sending the bar stool into the wall. He hadn't touched his magic in years, and now this one woman had him stretching for it twice in one day. Maybe if he made himself invisible . . .

Cat reached for him.

He danced away from her touch. "I'm okay."

Ryan was looking at him. So were a few other customers.

Stop running. Turn and fight.

"Nine o'clock?" he mumbled to her, snatching his coat from where it had fallen to the floor. "Outside the Gold Rush?"

Cat nodded and said, "All right," but he could see the doubt playing across her face.

He didn't give her a chance to say anything more. He swung around her, shoving his arms into his coat sleeves as he headed for the door. He didn't zip the coat though, and when he burst outside the slam of zero-degree air froze his skin. He needed that.

As he stomped down Groundcherry, his raging hard-on told him the bag in his basement was about to get ripped from its chain.

If she didn't show up tomorrow, nothing gained, nothing lost. He'd go back to being who he'd always been.

# SIX

**Michael's double was taking a meeting with one of the directors** of a Croatian documentary. Rumor had it a bidding war over distribution was about to start, and he wanted in, if only to say that his studio won.

His main body stood in the garage of the rented house, staring into the ever-present ash and murk inside the fire elemental's cage. She'd finally fallen asleep and lay cloaked in smoke on her side, black hair swirling over her outstretched arm. Her body was insane. All hard muscle and not a fold of fat.

Sean had drilled holes along the top edge of the box to let out more of the smoke and, in the event she decided to speak, they'd actually hear her.

Michael's phone rang and he whipped it from his pocket. "Why haven't you called until now? And why aren't you here?"

"Didn't Sean give you the message?" came Lea's pleasant voice. "I'm out hunting."

"For another water elemental."

"That's right."

He heard the faint clicks of snaps, the rustle of fabric, as she dressed.

"Jesus." He shook his head, but couldn't keep the smile from creeping on to his face. "I can't believe you found another one."

"Well, I did. I'll bring her to you in a few days. There are some things I still need to hammer out."

"It's a woman?" His mind spun. "Do you know what this could mean? That I have more than one water elemental? A man *and* a woman? I could create more." Lea said nothing, and he started to pace. "Make sure the new one's not violent. Nice and trained, like Jase and Robert."

She made a sound like she was insulted. "Don't worry. It'll be taken care of."

"Yeah, well, the present you left on my doorstep is quite the handful."

The woman in the cage shifted, rolling half onto her back. She had great tits.

"You like her?" Lea's voice lightened. "I thought you might."

"If you call her 'fiery' I'll hang up on you."

She laughed. He'd always liked her laugh—innocent but with an edge. The few times they'd fucked she'd laughed a lot. No seriousness or overblown emotion to the act, just lots and lots of hot fun. Even though Lea wasn't the prettiest woman, she was definitely worthy, by his standards. So far, she'd lured, captured, and blackmailed into his service four humans with secret powers.

For many years Michael had thought that finding Sean would have been enough to show up Raymond. Then he'd met Lea, who'd revealed there was more magic out there that she could help him harness.

Which he'd realized he could then throw in Raymond's face.

"The fire elemental's the only one I couldn't blackmail, Michael. I got the tip where she was, saw the opportunity, and took it."

"How'd you get her? I can't even get near the cage. Sean feeds her through the trap door on top, just drops food down. She pees in a bucket, but we can't empty it because she won't let us near."

"What fights fire, Michael?" Lea asked dryly.

"Water." Michael scratched his chin. "Ah, so that's why you brought Robert. You're so good to me, Lea, getting me a pair."

"Who said they're for you?"

"What?" He didn't like that. This wasn't Lea's show. And yet, he absolutely depended on her uncanny ability to sniff out the magic. If she wasn't kept happy, she'd leave, and he couldn't afford that.

"Trust me. You'll keep getting what you want. And now, so will I."

"Which is?"

"Just trust me, baby. Have you informed good ol' Daddy about your latest acquisition?"

"Not yet." Timing hadn't been right. Michael should have been filming the garage that first day he'd awakened his prize. Now he just needed to piss her off again, make her call fire. Get it recorded. "Hurry up and get here." Suddenly he needed one of those fucks. He'd been fantasizing about Cat too much. And the fire woman.

"Just a few more days. Can't rush these things or they'll be on to me."

"Tell me you're not worried about the cops."

She clucked her tongue. "Give me a little more credit, would you? The cops don't know anything. This is our world. We don't let in outsiders. Ever."

It wasn't the first time she'd said that.

"You're welcome, by the way."

That made Michael smile. "I tell you thank you all the time. Now get over here and let me show you."

Deep down he knew Lea wasn't doing any of this for him. She didn't hunt down humans with weird powers for shits and giggles, or even to please him. She had her own agenda. He wasn't stupid. As long as he kept her in his sights, he wasn't worried.

But ever since a living match had been stuffed into his garage, he wondered if maybe he should be.

### She showed up.

Nine o'clock in the morning, and there Cat stood, leaning against the wall just beyond the Gold Rush Theater marquee. Waiting for *him*.

Xavier didn't know what surprised him more: that she'd willingly come after his disastrous exit from Fresh Powder, or that he had.

The action on Waterleaf reminded him of a turbulent ocean—bodies and motion everywhere, never-ending, making him a little queasy—and him clinging to a life raft as the waves pounded around him. But he was going to go through with this, however the hell it went. The Burned Man could scream in his ear for three hours and he'd see it through. At least he could say he tried.

He'd reached a pretty hefty decision around 3:00 a.m. After beating the boxing bag into submission and sprinting a few miles on the treadmill, and then slapping together three different kinds of herbed butter, he concluded that he would think of Cat as an experiment. Nothing more. He would meet her for the movie, think not one sexual thought about her, and learn how to *talk*. How to communicate.

*Yeah, right,* chuckled the Burned Man at his side. *You're weak. All your kind are.*

Xavier stood there in the middle of the surging crowd, watching Cat without her seeing him. The red hat was back in place, long waves of her hair spilling out from underneath. She blew on her mittened hands. The urge to turn around, head back to his kitchen, and dice every vegetable in his refrigerator into atoms thrummed strong, but he held fast. Today he wouldn't be weak.

He walked toward her, crossing the red carpet, now brown and squishy with slush, that had been spread under the marquee. She saw him and pushed away from the wall, surprise evident on her face.

"Hey." He stopped a few feet from her, hands shoved into his pockets.

"Hi." One corner of her mouth twitched and he had to focus on a neutral spot over her shoulder. Her mouth conjured too many ideas, made him think of too many weaknesses. "I wasn't sure you'd come."

"I'm sorry." The words just bubbled out. He didn't know if he'd ever said them before. If he had, he didn't remember.

She blinked. "For what?"

He tossed his head back, hair swinging away from his face. "Last night. Yesterday. My reactions . . ."

Then she did the strangest thing. She laughed. Not *at* him, not maliciously. But a low, soft chuckle that made his spine buckle. "No worries. I get it."

His turn to blink. "Get what?"

In the cold her nose had reddened. In the daylight every single one of her fine-sprayed freckles stood out like stars. She held up a hand. "Let me guess. Some tourist chick made you fall hard, screwed you over, then took off with barely a glance behind her. Now you're a little gun-shy."

Not at all where he expected this conversation to go, but he let her hold on to her theory if it steered them away from the truth. "How'd you guess?"

This time when she laughed there was zero humor behind it. "Because I'm a townie, too. Just in a different town. It's happened to me. I get it. Look, you don't need to worry about any heavy stuff from me. I'm only here for two weeks. I have a few hours before my meetings. Let's just see a movie and have some fun."

A great weight suddenly—surprisingly—rolled off his chest. He even touched it, to make sure he was actually still there, standing on the freezing sidewalk in front of this woman who knocked him sideways with every word.

"You have a funny look on your face," she said. "Could you not get tickets or something?"

He rummaged in his jeans pocket for the two slips of paper he'd begged Pam for an hour ago. She'd already been in Shed, taking deliveries. If you wanted to get into Shed during Turn-korner you had to have some kind of "in," so she was able to make a call and scrounge up a pair on short notice. She'd raised an eyebrow at him, however, so there would definitely be an inquisition later.

"I've got them." He looked at the title. "I don't even know what it's about."

Cat smiled and he had to look away again for fear of being blinded. "No one does. Let's get inside."

If he'd thought the scene outside was chaos, the theater lobby was chaos in hell. Shoulder-to-shoulder people, camera flashes every few feet, heat and noise. He let Cat lead the way. This was her domain, this crowded world of Primaries. Half-way up a set of short steps climbing toward the double doors of the main theater, she said something to him over her shoulder.

"What?" He bent closer, and unwittingly inhaled her scent. Like a drug, it hit his bloodstream and sent his mind hurtling toward the hard, spiked wall of desire. He dug in his heels. Dug them in hard.

*Ah, that's more like it.*

The lobby couldn't hold another body, yet there the Burned Man stood, leaning against the glass case with Skittles and

Junior Mints. He was smiling, but on the melted half of his face it just looked like twisted skin.

"I said that this must be old hat to you," Cat repeated.

"No." He jerked away, out of the sweet, simple cloud of her perfume or shampoo or whatever it was. "I've never been before."

She reached the top of the steps and turned around. "To a festival film? And you live here? Really?"

He'd never been to any movie, actually, but even he knew that was weird to admit, so he just shook his head.

"You have really amazing eyes," she said. "Who'd you get them from? Your mom or your dad?"

No Tedran born and raised in the Plant had any other color. It was the color of their magic.

The house lights dimmed and came back up. The crowd clenched around them, pushing in waves toward the double doors.

He didn't answer. "Let's get inside."

She gave a stiff nod, and he knew he'd been gruff and awkward. In the silence, they found a row with two vacant seats and they nudged their way down, apologizing with every knee clip. They plopped into the seats, and Xavier realized much too late how tiny the old auditorium seats were. The iron arm rests dug into his elbows. The seat pads had lost their softness decades ago. His knees touched the seat back in front of him. Cat's thigh rubbed against his. He pulled his away.

Three years of not touching a woman. Three years of not even touching himself.

His right hand pinched an invisible knife and started sawing through imaginary food. He ran through recipes in his mind—all the ones from Shed he knew by heart and ten more he made up on the spot.

Cat peeled off her coat and unwound her scarf. "Here. Can you hold this a sec?" Her hat dropped into his lap. He stared at the red pompom, knowing that he'd never be able to see that color for the rest of his life and not think of her. She pawed at her long, wild hair. "Now I need to ask what conditioner you use to get yours to stay down in this dry weather."

He looked up from the hat and realized that the Burned Man hadn't followed him in. He was still there on the fringes, waiting, but this sort of casual conversation thing bored him. Kept him at bay.

He turned to her. "What the hell's conditioner?"

Her face broke into a wide grin and it triggered something inside him. Something that had nothing to do with sex.

"Holy cow," she said. "You can smile."

So that's what it felt like. His cheeks tingled, but it was the levity in his heart and the swoosh of warm adrenaline through his blood that he didn't at all expect.

She threw up her hands. "Oh, whoops. Scared it off."

Not at all. The thrill of it lingered.

As the theater went dark, he took off his coat and stuffed it behind his calves. A grainy film title flickered on the screen.

"I hope it's a good movie," he mumbled.

Cat guffawed then slapped a hand over her mouth. The people in front of them turned around to glare. She leaned closer to Xavier. The euphoria from his smile disappeared and he concentrated hard on not glancing down to where her thighs, in tight jeans, spread over her seat. Instead he stared up at the little balconies lining both sides of the auditorium.

"Now I know you weren't kidding when you said you've never seen a festival film before," she murmured.

The auditorium had gone deathly silent and he was forced to bend closer to her. "Why do you say that?"

Her cheek brushed his hair and he held his breath. Did she think his hair was too long? He'd never given it a second thought, cutting it only when it got past his shoulders. And even then all he did was hack at it with scissors.

She was smiling again; he could hear it in her voice. "Maybe three movies out of the whole festival will actually be 'good.' Half are awful. The rest are *god*-awful." She rubbed her hands together. "Good is boring. I hope it's the worst movie I've ever seen."

# SEVEN

**It was the worst movie Cat had ever seen. A pretentious script,** melodramatic acting, and handheld camera work crashed together in a horrible accident she couldn't look away from.

The house lights came up and polite applause filled the auditorium. Xavier said out of the corner of his mouth, "I don't know about you, but I thought it was a masterpiece."

When she looked up at him, he was watching the stage where the director and lead actors pulled up chairs and snapped on lavaliere microphones for the question-and-answer session.

"Don't you dare," she whispered. "Don't you dare make me laugh now." But as soon as she said it, the laughter came up. She choked on it, her eyes watering and her stomach muscles burning.

Xavier tapped his lips with a finger. She doubled over and bit her own knee to keep quiet. Her face was probably as red as the velvet seat cushion. When she finally composed herself, she sat up and put her elbow on the armrest, shielding her face with her hand.

She couldn't see him, but it didn't make her any less aware of his long, lean thigh just inches from hers.

All that talk out on the street about avoiding the heavy stuff and just wanting to have fun was BS. She was insanely attracted to him. No one had ever intrigued her more. At first it'd had something to do with that weird sense of familiarity that clung to him, but that had been pushed away the moment they'd spoken in the bar.

And the killer? His modesty, his shyness. His cluelessness that people on the street strained to watch him go by, trying to figure out in which movie or TV show they'd seen that beautiful, tall man.

The director-and-actor gabfest ended. Xavier cleared his throat and unfolded his body from the cramped seats. When she looked up at him, he was staring at her with an odd look. Like he was surprised to be having a good time.

Her phone buzzed and she pulled it out of her coat pocket. It had gone off several times during the screening. All texts from Michael, confirming their meeting time later that day, reminding her who they were having a late lunch with tomorrow, what to wear . . . it was like every time a thought popped into his head, no matter what time of day, he reached for his phone.

"Do you have to go?"

She couldn't read the meaning behind Xavier's question. Was he looking for an excuse to leave, or did he want to spend more time with her?

"Not yet. You?"

He checked his watch, a battered thing barely clinging to his wrist with strands of worn leather. "No." He dragged a hand through the long, messy hair that she found surfer hot. He was like a granule of beach sand in this cold, waterless part of the world. "Shift starts soon, but there's a private party tonight so I'll be in the kitchen until after midnight." He swung on his coat.

"Thanks for the ticket," she said. "It was . . . an experience."

"Now I know why I don't see movies."

"At all?"

"No."

"But you watch TV, right?"

He shook his head. "I don't own one."

He was trying to say something else to her. He opened his mouth several times, closed it. All she could do was smile encouragingly. He didn't look at her. "You wouldn't want to . . . go for a cup of coffee. Would you?"

A shiver coursed through her that had nothing to do with the fresh, cool air sweeping in from the lobby. "I absolutely would."

He didn't exhale in relief or even smile. If anything, he looked even more tense. She pulled on the heavy coat she both loathed to wear and desperately wanted on at all times. As she yanked the red hat—the silly thing she'd grabbed from a clearance bin at the Denver airport—down over her ears, the tightness around his mouth and eyes softened. He watched her for a moment, almost dazed.

They silently walked out of the auditorium.

Outside under the marquee, now devoid of actors or reporters, he zipped up his down coat and tucked his chin under the collar. A line of people stamping in the cold snaked down the entire block, waiting for the next screening.

Xavier nodded across the square. "You mind walking a bit? The coffee shop I'm thinking of is back in the neighborhood, up in the hills."

"Not at all. Those are always the best places."

"Your teeth are chattering."

"Yeah, well, I live in Florida. Haven't seen winter in, oh, seven years."

They cut across the main square, circling around the white tents. She kept an eye out for celebrities, mentally ticking how many she'd seen. She hadn't even been there two days and she was on her third hand. Xavier just plowed through the nonsense, weaving her on an invisible path to a quieter side street behind the three-story Margaret Hotel where she was staying.

White Clover Creek was wedged into a tiny valley, mountains rising all around. Houses and churches cut into the mountainsides, a thousand eyes gazing down into the charming town like an amphitheater. Roads switchbacked up to the neighborhoods, but the sidewalks were a series of stairs that stretched straight up.

When Xavier first started up one of those staircases, Cat thought a little exercise might warm her up. Forty steps high, and she was sucking wind. "How much farther, Papa Smurf?"

He turned, perplexed, and gestured to the next street. "Just up here and to the left a half block. You okay?"

"Air's a little thin for me. You live here, remember?"

"Oh. Sorry." That sheepish look of his was killing her . . . in a good way.

She used the metal railing to pull herself up the final steps.

She exaggerated her weariness, rolling her eyes and sticking out her tongue, and it brought out Xavier's hesitant smile again. She liked that. A lot.

They stopped climbing at a narrow, empty road, NO PARKING DURING FESTIVAL signs stapled to the telephone poles. A stitch had lodged itself under her ribs.

"Over there." He pointed to an adorable brick ranch house with smoke curling out of the chimney. A small, rectangular bronze sign was nestled between the evergreen bushes lining the front fence: WHITE CLOVER COFFEE.

Tourist towns were the same the world over, so Cat was prepared for the second looks some of the customers gave her as she followed Xavier to the counter. *A stranger in our midst . . .*

"*X!*" A striking woman with a sleek, dark bob smiled from behind the counter, the tiny diamond stud in her nose glinting. "Fancy seeing you here."

"Hey, Jill." Xavier shuffled his feet. "Large coffee. Black." He turned to Cat. "What do you want?"

The way Jill's eyes widened—followed by her slow, sly smile—told Cat that this woman not only knew Xavier fairly well, but that she knew he was gun-shy around women. Particularly tourist women.

As Jill fixed Cat's cappuccino, the spurt of the milk foamer filling the warm, wood-floored coffee shop, she and Xavier wandered over to the last open table set against the picture window overlooking the town. The table was circular and tiny, and when Xavier leaned on it, it wobbled. Once they'd settled themselves on the purposely mismatched chairs, he stretched out his long legs underneath the table, one on either side of her chair. She was surrounded by him, and it warmed her more than the sun.

"How do you know Jill?" she asked.

"She's Pam's girlfriend. Pam, my boss?"

She nodded. Pam, who, upon hindsight, had finagled Cat's reservation so she could see Xavier. Pam, who had grinned knowingly at her while standing next to him in the kitchen.

Jill brought over their drinks, grinning at Cat the whole time. Then Jill sauntered behind the counter and into a back room.

"Why do I get the feeling she's going back there to call Pam right now?"

Xavier frowned at the swinging door. "Because she probably is."

And yet, he'd brought Cat here on purpose. She hid a smile in the foam of her cappuccino.

Xavier clutched his white coffee mug with both hands and shifted on his seat. His inner thighs brushed the outside of her knees. He froze, then jerked away, widening his legs to break the contact. The table rocked again. If awkwardness had a sound, that would be it.

As he turned his face to gaze out over the white-blanketed town, the sun shrank his pupils. His eyes were silver, not gray. Honest to gosh silver.

"You said you hadn't seen winter in seven years. Where did you live before Florida?"

He had such a measured way of speaking, like he had to think about every single word and perfectly organize his sentences before letting them out of his mouth.

"I grew up in Indiana. Bloomington. Left the day after my eighteenth birthday and I was no longer a ward of the state."

His mug stopped halfway to his lips. "Why'd you leave home?"

The cappuccino mug seared her fingers but she didn't let go. "Indiana was never home. Some of my foster families were all right. They tried their best but I never felt a connection, you know? Some other place was calling me, and the second I was old enough, I left to find it."

He was watching her intently now. After avoiding looking at her directly for so long, he probably wasn't even aware he was doing it.

"Did you? Find a home, that is."

She considered that. The day she'd arrived in the Keys on that bus she'd thought so. But something was still missing. "I don't think so. Not yet."

Her turn to break the mutual gaze. White Clover Creek was quaint and beautiful, but she'd been away from the ocean for going on thirty-six hours now, and she could feel its absence in her soul. Aware of how strange that might sound to him, this man she just met, she kept it quiet.

She toyed with her mug handle. "I keep thinking it might

have something to do with my birth parents. Who they were and all. Like maybe if I knew more about them I'd be able to settle this sense of wandering. But I'll never know."

"Why not? Aren't there ways to find out about that kind of stuff?"

She shrugged. "I was dumped at a police station when I was only a few hours old. You probably know more about them than I do."

"If you wanted to find out about them, shouldn't you have stayed in Indiana?"

"No. They weren't there anymore. I can't explain it, but I could feel it. They had me then disappeared." She tapped her finger on the tabletop. "You know, a lot of abandoned and orphaned kids I talked with described the feeling of not knowing their parents like a chunk of flesh had been torn from their leg and they couldn't walk without it."

"Do you feel that way?"

"Sort of. The others made it sound like their existence wasn't complete without parents, and if they could just find them, bam, their lives would be instantly fulfilled." She'd never said this next part to anyone before, and the words came haltingly. "I feel like I've been treading water my whole life. Just sort of lost . . . out there. To me? Finding out about my parents would be sort of like a raft floating along. I could grab on, rest a bit, get to safety. But I always thought that knowing them would be a new beginning, not an end. Not the culmination."

Xavier set down his mug and started to roll up the sleeves of his blue plaid flannel shirt. His forearms were strong, striated with muscle and tendons. A funny thing to find so sexy. Her gaze traveled up the length of his arms, where his biceps and shoulders pressed against the shirt seams.

"Okay, I spilled." She purposely leaned on the table to make it jiggle. Those forearms worked to steady it. "Where were you born?"

An easy question, not too personal. But his whole body went rigid. In the silence she could sense him retreating.

"I was born in Nevada," he finally said, each word deliberate. "I never knew my parents either."

What were the chances of that? No wonder he'd looked so spooked when she'd asked about his eyes in the theater lobby.

Distress tightened his features. Clearly it had taken courage for him to tell her that. And clearly he didn't want to say any more. She hadn't meant to resurrect old ghosts. And she sure as heck didn't want him to run off like he had on the street yesterday morning and in the bar last night.

"Bah." She flicked her wrist in a dismissive gesture. "Abandoned kids are the coolest. Parents are overrated."

The stiffness in him broke, muscle by tiny muscle. He sank lower in his seat. The death grip on his mug slackened. Pain still haunted his gunmetal eyes, but it was melting by the second. Something else started to invade, take over . . . it was that *want* for her. The hot desire he continually tried to push away.

It struck her, too, fast and intoxicating. It scalded her veins, made the underside of her skin pulse with sensation. Suddenly she was acutely aware of where the hard ridge of her jeans' zipper pressed against the apex of her legs. And when his thighs closed—barely an inch—to urge her legs together, she felt it even more powerfully.

"I think it's safe to say"—he swallowed, and his Adam's apple danced—"that I've never met anyone like you before."

His hungry eyes fastened on her mouth. The softness of his tone touched her in places she couldn't name.

"Xavier . . ."

Her voice shot through the spell, a cannonball destroying the intimate moment. It triggered his fight-or-flight response and, like on the street and in the bar, he flew.

His legs opened, releasing her. He shoved his chair back, the loud screech drawing Jill's curious gaze from behind the counter.

"I have to get to Shed." He didn't look at his watch.

*Play it cool, casual.* "Really? I thought we had more time."

"I just realized I need to . . ." As his voice petered out, his big right hand started to fidget, his empty fingers opening and closing, his wrist bending in a strange rhythm. He closed his eyes and said, slower and more carefully, "Come on. I'll walk you back to your hotel."

She nodded and stood.

That tourist had really messed him up good.

**Each step back down to town hammered the silence between** them. Cat's head pounded with it. For the first time since arriving in Colorado, she didn't feel the cold; she burned hot with frustration and curiosity.

Xavier walked several steps below her. He'd almost reached the very bottom, where the sidewalk that led to the square curved around the Margaret, when she stopped. The brick wall of a Mexican restaurant, painted with a giant green margarita, rose to her right. A cinder block wall for the Margaret's parking garage on her left. They were closed in, a canyon in shadow. She couldn't help but feel that if she let him walk away from her now, she'd never see him again.

"Xavier."

He stopped, his back to her, the hang of his head heavy.

"Am I imagining this?" she asked.

He looked over his shoulder, giving her his hard, beautiful profile framed by the surfer hair that absorbed the sunlight. "Imagining what?"

"You and I."

He briefly squeezed his eyes shut. "You're not imagining it."

"So is it the fact that I'm only here for a short time?"

"No." The word came out strangled and bare.

"Do I remind you of another girl? Of her?"

He hissed. Closed his eyes. Slowly shook his head. "No. Not at all."

She came down another step. No place to go but forward. She had nothing to lose, and the not knowing gnawed at her.

"Then why are you scared of me?"

He sighed. "I'm not scared of *you*." Slowly he shuffled around to face her, and with her a step above, they stood eye to eye. "What you do to me . . ." He put a hand to his chest, curled it into a fist.

Such honesty. It was the first time he hadn't weighed every one of his words before releasing them. The admission came from his heart. The hard lines that divided his golden eyebrows revealed the depth of his desire: it was severe, all-encompassing, and it stoked her own.

"What do I do to you?" In the cold, away from the madness of the festival streets, her whisper carried.

He inhaled slowly, as though sucking her words deep inside him. His silver stare shot shivering arrows through her body. "You excite me."

He was melting her in the middle of winter. "Isn't . . . isn't that a good thing?"

"No. Yes. Ah!" He stumbled back, fingers stabbing into his hair, eyes angled to the salted concrete.

Any other woman might have seen him as damaged goods, high maintenance. But Cat was not most women, and walking away would never satisfy.

"Xavier, I know that I don't know you—"

"No," he laughed shortly. "You don't."

"But I want to. And I think you want to know me, too. You and me, we're alike. I can feel it, though I can't explain it. I think we can help each other."

"A pity fuck?" he snarled. "Is that what you want?"

"No!" She gasped, but the way he said *fuck*, all gritty and forceful . . . it ratcheted up her lust. Made her thong rub achingly against the damp part of her that screamed for him.

But where had that come from? A *pity fuck*? Who did he think she was? Dear God, what had happened to him to make him think that's what she wanted?

"I don't pity you," she said. "I don't want you to pity me. That's not why I told you about my parents. I like you. I . . . I'm very attracted to you."

He stood with his hands clenched tightly, his big body coiled up and ready to spring. Imagining the power behind his restrained passion made her body hum. From him she didn't want a gentle kiss or a slow caress. She wanted the wildness that blazed behind those metallic eyes. And he was refusing to let it go.

They squared off, at a stalemate. "Xavier," she whispered. "Kiss me."

His chin lowered and his stare burned into her from behind the blond waves of his hair.

"You want me to kiss you?" His voice rumbled. The start of an avalanche, dangerous and uncontainable.

"God, yes. Do you want me to beg? Get on my knees?"

He lunged for her. Shouted. *"You want me to kiss you?"*

Here it came. She braced herself for his hands and his mouth, liquid desire surging in to replace every drop of her blood. But he pulled up at the last second and instead loomed over her, his chest pumping so hard she could see it through his coat.

All she said was, "Please."

He fisted the front of her coat and pushed her back against the brick wall, enough to knock out her breath. She didn't need oxygen, just him. He brought his mouth down on hers, hard as brick, hot as fire.

Their tongues swept across each other, mixing coffee and lust. Their lips formed an impenetrable seal, but inside it was all soft and burning. A silky, slow, undulating movement that made her shake. A high, trilling moan vibrated her throat. Her arms snaked around his waist, pulling him tight against her. Layers of coats and clothes between them, and she almost cried from the divide.

He released his death grip on her zipper and slid one hand around her neck. He hadn't put his gloves back on and his hands were cold and dry and desperate, pressing hard into her nape, pulling her so close their teeth scraped.

He kissed as though her mouth meant life or death, and she understood. She understood.

His other hand came up and swept the hat off her head. He drew back, breath stuttering between reddened lips, and did the strangest thing. He gazed at the hat—the cheap, silly thing—like it was a fancy bra and underwear and it was driving him over the edge.

His head was slightly turned, and the skin along his jawline beckoned. She came forward, flicked her tongue across the place that was still smooth from his morning shave. No cologne, just Xavier. He tasted like snow and hundreds of flavors of the kitchen. Like he was made of things he loved.

With a low groan he whipped his head around, taking her mouth. As he shoved her back against the wall again, his long thigh slid between hers. The pulse between her legs beat a bass drum.

She started to move. Slow circles of her hips that brought out stars behind her eyelids. She'd made him hard and she loved it. Loved that she could rub perfectly against that hardness. If she kept it up, she'd come. Right there on the staircase, fully clothed, thousands of festival goers only a block away.

*Keep going. Keep going.*

He kicked her legs apart and pushed his hard-on right to her clit. His turn to move. He skipped over the slow part and went right for the focused grind. She cried out, urging him on. The hottest sex she'd ever had that wasn't actually sex.

Suddenly he jerked back. At first she thought he'd come, then she saw he was shaking and there was no pleasure on his face. Anguished silver eyes danced in their sockets. When they met hers they were brimming with heartbreaking apology.

"Oh, God, Cat. I can't."

"What's the matter?" Her voice cracked like weak ice. She reached for him but he skittered away, her hat dropping from his fingers to the snow.

"You deserve better."

"Xavier, no. It's okay."

"It's not okay." He wasn't even looking at her. He glared hard at something over her shoulder, but when she glanced around there was nothing there.

Then he turned on his heel and stalked away, hair flapping around his ears, boots heavy on the road.

# EIGHT

**Michael lowered himself into the rolling chair behind the desk,** and switched on the webcam with hands that quivered with pure exhilaration. The lunch with Cat and Tom Bridger could not have gone more perfectly.

She'd been gracious and lovely. Engaging. Bridger had taken to her immediately, just as Michael had wanted. The two of them had blabbed on and on about art and film, and even though Michael had been bored to tears, he let them talk. Association was a wonderful, mysterious thing. Bridger had connected with Cat, whom Michael had discovered, sponsored, and befriended, creating good feelings inside Bridger for this Big Hollywood Producer he'd so sorely misjudged.

After Cat had unknowingly primed Bridger, Michael gave his pitch: the big budget historical meant to make audiences weep and Oscar voters cream their pants. After Michael had paid the check and they stood up, Bridger had been the first to extend his hand.

"I told myself I wouldn't let you convince me," the indie director had said, "but you have. I'm in."

"Excellent news." Michael gripped Bridger's hand and gave him a hearty slap on the opposite shoulder.

"I hope you forgive me for saying this," Bridger had begun, and Michael knew instantly what he was about to say, "but since it's a well-known fact that you and your father were at odds, I'd like to admit that I misjudged you."

Michael had nodded gravely.

Bridger had laughed uncomfortably. "You're not at all like I heard your father was. I was afraid you'd be an asshole, frankly. It's good to see you didn't inherit his personality along with his studio."

He'd glanced at Cat then, who'd been regarding him with a questioning expression. He'd forgotten that she knew little to nothing about him personally, and even though Raymond Ebrecht's death five years ago had been big news within the industry, for an artist/bartender in the Florida Keys, that didn't mean anything.

"Tell me the truth." Bridger had leaned in. "All those celebrity tributes at the funeral, they were all bullshit, right?"

Michael had smiled. A genuine smile. "Completely and totally."

Now, back at the rental house, his whole body filled to bursting with triumph, he sat down before the laptop. A tiny window in the corner showed his own face how it looked through the webcam. Satisfied. Confident. Fucking powerful.

He thought of Cat. She was starting to fit nicely into his world. A little puzzle piece wedging itself into place, becoming part of his greater whole. He'd chosen so well that day in the art fair. He was already starting to think of her as his possession—perhaps the finest piece in his collection—because he'd been the one to find her, build her up. Create her.

It felt good to think that. It felt right.

Raymond had mentioned once that finding the perfect woman could turn everything in your favor. Hadn't worked out so well for him, though. Five wives. Five divorces. That wouldn't happen to Michael. Cat would be forever. He'd show Raymond, once again, how it was done.

Michael took his phone out and made the call. It rang three times. The bitch always let it ring too long. Fiona liked to make him fear she'd left his service, but he wasn't the slightest bit worried. That would never happen. She was one of Ireland's most wanted and Lea had their government on speed dial.

"Michael." Fiona's lilt had long ago stopped being polite or even pleasant to hear.

"Put him on."

There was a long, heavy pause, and then he heard Fiona's shoes on the tile floor of his L.A. house's hallway. He listened to the familiar sound of the guest bedroom door opening, Fiona entering the room. She put the phone down, there was a brief rustling, and then the big black window in the center of his laptop screen lit up.

A gaunt, wrinkled face filled the window, pale lamp light illuminating only one side. The slow, steady, forced sounds of the man's breathing, and the persistent beep of the life-support machines trickled out from the laptop's little speakers.

Michael hung up the phone and stared into the comatose face of his father. "Hello, Raymond."

Raymond's chest pumped mechanically up and down, the hiss of the equipment providing the soundtrack. It gave Michael chills but also filled him with victory. Raymond's thin lips were dry where they clamped around the big plastic tube snaking down his throat. His eyelids remained permanently closed.

"I have amazing news," Michael said. "Just landed Tom Bridger for the big historical I told you about last week. That name won't mean shit to you because he wasn't around when you were head of the studio, but he's the next big thing. The next Cameron. The next Spielberg." He leaned his elbows on the desk edge and got real close to the camera so his face filled the lens. "And he's fucking mine. We're sweeping the Oscars in a few years. More than what you ever got in one year, let me tell you, and that's going to feel so fucking good."

He leaned back in the chair and started to click the mouse around, opening a movie file he'd taken just that morning. He connected it to the webcam feed and pressed *play*.

"Watch this."

He'd gone out to the garage that morning. Poked the caged tiger with a stick, so to speak. His little fire prize had performed beautifully. She'd raged. She'd spewed flames from between those perfect lips and thrown great fireballs against the cage. He'd clicked off the camera only when the smoke filled the box again and she disappeared into the billowy black.

The movie ended and Michael toggled his face back into the screen. "Isn't that incredible? You never found anything like that, did you? All your searching and you never found anyone else like us. You never even found your other son. But I did. You thought you were special just being able to *split*. That's nothing compared to what else is out there. What else I own." Michael pounded a fist into his chest for emphasis, echoing the thunder of his blood as his heartbeat kicked up. He rolled the chair back a bit, took a few deep breaths to try to calm down.

"I'm getting another water elemental, did you know that? Lea texted me on the way up here to tell me she got her. Now I have a man and a woman. Can you imagine what I can do with that? I can't wait for the day when I hold up a baby and tell you, 'Just look at what I created.' "

Raymond said nothing, as usual. No flicker of the eyelids as acknowledgement. No life whatsoever. But he heard, Michael knew. He heard. He just didn't want to wake up because he couldn't face the fact that the son he'd first ignored and then felt threatened by had become a far, far greater man than he ever was.

"So. Dad." Michael sniffed, despising the choke in his voice. Repelled by the man his father had created. He stared right into the camera, right into the flaccid face of Raymond Ebrecht. "Am I good enough for you yet? Do you love me now?"

# NINE

**Xavier needed fresh rosemary, but the singular plant in the little** greenhouse he'd attached to his garage had decided not to live through the autumn and he kept forgetting to get a new one. Not even 7:00 a.m., the overnight low temperature laughing at the peek of sun over the eastern mountains, and he was bundled up and trudging to Kensington's Market. The tents in the square stood quiet and slightly crooked, as though recovering from hangovers. His boots squeaked on the snow.

Inside the warm neighborhood grocery store, he shook off the cold and started to wander. A meandering detour through the aisles, drawing imaginary lines between ingredients, usually cleared his head of trouble and replaced it with culinary possibility. But what had lodged itself in his mind two days ago wasn't giving up the prime real estate so handily.

Years ago he'd used kissing as a means to an end. Women loved it; he never really understood why. Now he knew.

Sleep had never come easily to him, but these past two nights, since that kiss on the cold stairwell, it had become an impossibility. Every time he closed his eyes he relived the raw desire on Cat's face. Heard her high, yielding sighs. Felt the firmness of her thighs under his fingers and the heat where she'd ground against his cock.

All that control, gone.

The second he'd taken her mouth, he'd flown high. The sensation of their lips together, the hot glide of their tongues—the instruments they'd used to talk and laugh—leveled him. He'd never known desire that powerful. At first he'd thought it was only because he'd finally given in after three years of abstinence. But then, as Cat had clung to him and *begged*, he knew it was because of her.

Her passion ignited him. Her confidence floored him. Her responsiveness terrified him.

His mind knew this and welcomed it. But his body . . . the moment it had thought release was within its grasp, he'd retreated into that slave space. Automatic. Single-minded and selfish. Horrible.

The Burned Man had laughed in one ear and made awful suggestions in the other.

So Xavier had run, because he realized that Cat was worth so much more.

He'd wandered down every aisle in the market and couldn't remember a single dish he'd come up with along the way. Rosemary, that's what he'd come for. He should get some yellow pepper, too. He turned out of the condiment aisle, rounded the small display of winter grapefruit, and froze.

There she stood, pondering the plastic display case of pastries and doughnuts. The red pompom stuck out from where she'd stuffed the hat into her coat pocket. She pulled the loose waves of her hair over one shoulder and stretched for a chocolate éclair.

She hadn't seen him. He could walk out of the store right now and she'd never know he was there . . . except that in the short time they'd spent together, she'd shown him glimpses of the kind of person he could be, and he wanted to know that man better.

"They don't actually make those here." His mouth was dry as flour.

She stiffened. Straightened. Turned toward him. "Xavier."

He had no idea how to read her face, but hoped what he saw there wasn't pity. He was embarrassed as all hell, but he wanted to make it right. He didn't want her to think it had been her fault he'd freaked out. And he needed to prove to himself that it wasn't just physical with her, that sex wasn't all he needed. He remembered those moments of peace when they'd just talked, and he used them as a dangling carrot.

"What do you mean?" she asked.

"The breads and things," he stuttered. "They try to make it look like they're baked on site, but they're not."

Idiot. He was talking about *bread*?

"Oh." She looked longingly at that chocolate éclair. "I don't really care. I'm starving."

"You're up early."

"Can't kick the jet lag." She avoided his eyes, and really, could he blame her? "And I haven't been sleeping well."

Something skittered through his gut, and it wasn't hunger.

"I have biscuits in the oven at home," he said. "And I'm making omelets." He held up the little plastic bag of rosemary and the pepper.

She blinked up at him and didn't say anything.

"Never mind," he mumbled, and started to turn away.

"No, wait. Sorry. I'm just thinking about my schedule, if I have time."

He toyed with the rosemary in the bag, counting the leaves on a single stalk. Then he blurted out, "I'm sorry about the other day."

"Xavier, don't."

"For walking away. For shoving you into the wall like that."

She rolled her eyes and made a sound of frustration. Aimed at him. "Don't apologize to me. Please, just don't. I should be apologizing to you." She rubbed fingers across her forehead. "I knew about that tourist, how she broke your heart. I knew how resistant you were to going out with me, and I still went after you. I wanted more. You didn't. And you realized that while you were kissing me. Bottom line is, I suck."

He blinked. Twice. She had no idea what he wanted. But he knew that he wanted to smile again, and he wanted it to be because of her.

"You don't suck."

She let out a short laugh. "Thanks."

"I don't invite people who suck back to my house for biscuits and omelets."

It felt good, to say that. Even better when she pulled her hat down over her ears and gave up eyeing that sad éclair.

"Lead the way."

**"Okay, if you'd told me you lived on the top of Pike's Peak, I** might not have accepted the invitation."

She huffed hard as they reached the top of the staircase that ended at his street. He snuck a sideways glance at her, noting the flush in her cheeks and the faint smile. "Sorry. You okay?"

"I will be."

"This is it." He gestured to the blue-shingled two bedroom wedged between Massive New Construction to the north and Million-dollar Re-do to the south. As he led the way up the concrete front steps, suddenly he was painfully aware that they weren't level, and that the corner gutter was broken and that there was a large gash in the screen door.

He saw the unspoken question cross her face: how does a cook afford to own a home in this neighborhood, when even plots for tear-downs cost a fortune? The answer? He needed to live near town since he didn't know how to drive, and this was the cheapest house Gwen Carroway's money could buy him.

After Gwen had stopped the slavery and put an end to the business of selling the Tedrans' glamour, she'd given all her money to him to help him start a new life. Every day he was reminded of what he could afford, and why. He hated money.

He slid his key into the lock, ignoring the jitters in his hand. Hopefully Cat was, too.

Inside, the smell of the cheese biscuits greeted them. He toed off his boots and unwound his scarf. In the three years he'd lived here, he'd never given a second thought to the mustard-yellow tile in the tiny foyer or the dim, brown globe light that set the tone for the whole nineteen-sixties feel of the house. Not retro, just . . . old.

He walked into the living room with the big window looking down the slope toward town, and tossed his coat over the beige recliner. When he turned around, he almost choked at the sight of Cat. In his house. Not only was she the first woman he'd ever invited inside, she was the first *person*.

She'd draped her coat over the half wall dividing the foyer from the living room, and was now bending over to pull off her fuzzy boots. Her hair made a long, swinging curtain. The sight of her, here, in the place where he cooked and exercised and tried to sleep, messed with his head. Made him doubt his bravery back in the store. Made him think he'd made a terrible mistake.

*No, you didn't*, murmured the Burned Man. *This is only the beginning.*

She stepped onto the worn, shedding carpet in her socked feet.

Before she got to the coffee table he said, "You were wrong, before. I do owe you an apology." She stopped, and waited with those huge caramel eyes fixed right on him. He focused on the lime green table lamp he'd bought from Goodwill for five bucks. He took a couple of hard swallows. "I don't know what I want. I was aware of that when I met you, and when I went to the movie and then for coffee. I'm sorry for dragging you into my shit, for giving you mixed messages."

She crept closer but still kept her distance. If he stretched out an arm he couldn't touch her. "I think I understand," she said.

She couldn't possibly, but he nodded anyway. The gentleness in her voice made him ache. It made him want to collapse to his knees before her.

"Do you really want me to be here?"

She was giving him an exit, and man, it would have been really easy to have taken it. But he was tired of easy. It just left him jogging in place.

"Yes. Stay. Please. I just can't . . ." His eyes dropped to her lips, and he forced himself to ignore the way his mouth watered.

She smiled. No pity, no frustration. Just Cat. "Terms accepted."

And like that, with kissing and sex taken out of the equation, the Burned Man, who'd been growling in Xavier's ear, fell silent.

She crossed the line where the living room carpet gave way to the foot-worn brown linoleum of the kitchen. Onto sacred ground.

"Are you going to show me how a pro works?"

He went to the stove, turned on the burner beneath the pan, set the small plastic grocery bag on the counter and took out the rosemary. With a clamp of his fingers around the stem and a quick sweep downward, he removed the leaves. Swiping his favorite chef's knife from the butcher block, he took a deep breath and exhaled. Then he let his mind go and his hands flew through the tough, waxy leaves. The familiar *tap tap tap* of the knife on the cutting board instantly relaxed him. Even with Cat standing a few feet to his right, arms crossed, hip leaning against the counter.

"I suppose you're used to people watching you," she said. He nodded. "I don't know if I could paint with an audience."

He shrugged. "Different processes."

He had to stretch in front of her for the white onion and yellow pepper. Within her proximity, he could swear the hair on his arm stood on end. Magnetic, this woman.

He passed a damp rag over the cutting board, loving the sight of the clean streaks over the wood, and started on the onion. Some of the dice wasn't exactly a quarter inch, which made him twitch, but he'd do better next time. The yellow pepper followed.

"Wow," she murmured. "Very methodical."

"You have to be." He walked around her to get to the eggs in the refrigerator.

"I never would've thought to put rosemary in eggs. Velveeta maybe, but not rosemary."

He threw her a wry look over his shoulder. "Please tell me you didn't say Velveeta."

"Oooo, did I disgust you? How about . . . Lean Cuisine? Tombstone? Hamburger Helper?"

Holy shit, there it was again. The tightness in his cheeks. The euphoria slipping through his bloodstream. Like desire, only innocent. When he caught his reflection in the microwave window, he didn't recognize himself.

"I've eaten my share of Tombstones." He bent over a glass bowl, cracking eggs. "Not bad for a hangover."

She laughed quietly, nodding.

"Where'd you go to school?"

He whisked the eggs with a flourish. This was what he'd signed up for: conversation. Which meant he'd be asked questions about himself. He could answer; he'd just have to be careful about it. "Um, San Francisco?"

"Did you always want to cook?"

"No."

He dumped the beaten eggs into the hot pan, rolled the pan around to get a nice thin layer on the bottom. "I was sort of . . . wandering around in life and I took a job as a dishwasher in one of those brunch cafes. Was totally green, just needed the paycheck." Not really, but he needed a story more. He'd had money, lots of it; he'd just needed to do something other than troll for women to feed his Plant-made addiction. By that time he'd recognized what he'd been bred to need, and he hated it. He and the Burned Man's ghost had gotten real close.

"At first the atmosphere in the kitchen scared me. Non-stop, small space, people always moving and always right where you needed to be. I wasn't used to that at all. But then, on my first day off, I realized I missed it." The eggs bubbled and he pulled back the edges to prepare to fold them over. "Couldn't wait to punch back in. It was chaos, but ordered chaos, you know?"

He couldn't see her face. She'd gone quiet.

"And then there were the flavors." His tongue tingled reactively, the memory of those first few months coming back to him. "I didn't have . . . I wasn't used to eating food with a lot of flavor or variety growing up. You'd think that would ruin me, but it was the opposite. I think it made me better, more in tune with everything I put in my mouth. I ate pretty much everything I could, and when I'd talk about it with the other people in the kitchen, someone told me I had a great palate. That you have to have one to be a chef." He shook his head at the pan as he folded the first half of the eggs over and sprinkled the onions, herbs and peppers into the fold. "Didn't know what that meant at the time, where that would lead me. But I fell in love pretty hard."

"When was that?"

"Five years ago?"

"That seems really fast. How long have you been at Shed?"

"Three years."

"So, two years to go from dishwasher to school to a cook in the best restaurant in White Clover Creek. How is that possible?"

His kitchen—the place he felt most safe—suddenly felt very, very small. He glanced out the window, to the patch of sloped backyard that was nothing more than fallow dirt outlined by a chain-link fence. "I moved from the brunch place to a pretty popular bistro where I worked for free while I went to school. Pam knew the owner and visited one day. We met. She liked my technique and work ethic, what I cooked. Offered me a job here." Seemed like forever ago. And just yesterday. "Besides, I don't do much else." *It's all I have.*

He reached up to the cabinet to the left of the stove and took down two plates, feeling odd. He'd never taken down two plates at once before. The second one, the one that came with the double place setting, had no scratches on its surface, the red stripes around the edges still pristine and vibrant in their color. He tipped the omelet onto that one, letting it fold onto itself, then neatly divided it in half and gave Cat the better plate.

He turned around and did not expect at all to see what he did on her face. Wide eyes, clear expression, something that could be a smile but just as easily a laugh. That smoky voice turned breathy with wonder. "Nothing you do for fun?"

With a frown, he slid the plates onto his tiny faux maple table. He thought of the concrete-floored basement, the battered punching bag, the weary treadmill and the chipped set of weights. He wouldn't call that fun. Just necessary.

"No. I cook. When I'm not working, I cook more. In the summer I have a garden out back. Don't really like working in it, but I love the results."

"Sounds more like an obsession." It was a smile now. Definitely a smile. His heart gave a lurch.

"No. Just life. My life."

He opened the silverware drawer to scrounge for a second fork.

"Didn't you say something about biscuits earlier?" she asked. "Or was that false advertising?"

"No, you're getting biscuits." Using a potholder, he slid the baking sheet onto the stove top and scrutinized the puffs of golden brown. "Maybe less cheese next time," he muttered.

Cat came to his side. "Blasphemy. When in doubt, the answer is always 'more cheese.' Quick, get one on my plate." As he obeyed, she added, "I don't see any boxed mix."

He grunted. "Thought I'd play around a bit this morning."

She raised an eyebrow at the barely risen sun whose rays pierced the small window in the house's side door. As she slid out a chair she said, "Yeah, you don't seem like the type to fritter away a morning with coffee and the crossword puzzle."

"No." He pulled out the opposite chair and stared at the meager food he was suddenly embarrassed of. It should have been prettier or more creative. "I need to cook."

Her hand froze halfway to her fork. "Need to?"

He broke a biscuit, releasing the scent of herbs and cheese. "Yeah." His throat felt like he'd taken too large a bite and couldn't get it down. "Need to."

Then he ate. Out of habit, he couldn't chew anything without breaking down the flavors in his mouth and analyzing them.

Cat ate, too, a gentle, repetitive scrape of the fork on her plate. The silence of his house settled around them. It took another person to tell him how quiet his life was.

After a time, Cat slouched in her chair and slowly turned her plastic orange juice cup in a circle. She wore a faraway look. He barely recognized her.

"Are you okay?" The question rode funny on his tongue.

"You know"—her voice was soft as morning light—"I need to paint."

He remembered what she'd told him on the stairs, before she said she'd get on her knees: how they were alike in some way. He hadn't wanted to believe her then; he didn't think he could believe her now. He wasn't like anyone. "What do you mean?"

"It's the only way to get it out."

He held his breath. "Get what out?"

"What's inside me." She broke off a piece of biscuit.

Xavier just stared, like an idiot. "So . . . what did that feel like, the first time you painted?"

She wiggled her fork between her fingers, the tines tapping on the table. "Like I'd found something? Only I didn't know I was looking for it."

The last bite of eggs went into his mouth, but they tasted like dust.

"Like . . . somebody opened a door in my mind. It answered a lot of questions about myself, but created a whole mess of others." She laughed. "Like a kid cooped up all winter and then running free outside the first warm day. That sound weird?"

He remembered the first day he'd been given a knife and told to dice a whole box of jalapenos, then to de-leaf another box of flat parsley. While the other cooks had snickered at him having to do the crap jobs, when he'd finished, he'd looked around for more.

"Not at all," he said. "I bet when you put down your brush that door closed and that kid was locked back inside." She sat up straighter. "So you started to paint like crazy, just to keep that first feeling alive. To keep that door open. Is that right?"

"Yes."

He shoved his plate away and asked, "Did it work?" even though he already knew her answer.

"No. It created a monster. I was barely eating, barely sleeping. Just painting. Trying to get it all out. Trying to *figure* it all out." She stared deeply into his eyes. "It's what I do. Still."

"Working your life around it. Forever thinking about it."

"Yeah. Oh, my God. You know."

He knew. He knew it all too well.

"So this was different from the home thing? You said you left Indiana to find a home. Painting wasn't part of that?"

She contemplated her orange juice again. "I don't know. Maybe. All I know is that I took a bus east from Indiana, not caring where it went. It hit the coast. I'd never seen the ocean before. And the second I did, something came alive in me. So blue. Endless possibilities. And . . . something else. A kinship, maybe? I know that sounds silly. Anyway, I just kept traveling south, following the water. I knew I couldn't ever leave it. I just kept going and going, until I couldn't go any farther." She let out an embarrassed laugh, but there was a gleam in her eye. "God, growing up in Indiana, never knowing there was a place like the islands . . ."

He watched the glow course through her, while a faint dread started to build within him. "When did you start to paint?"

"When I got to the Keys. I spent every day on or in or near the water, and still it wasn't enough. Boating didn't do it. Snorkeling or swimming didn't do it. One day I was walking past an art supply shop and it just sort of hit me. I bought some paints and brushes and just . . . tried to get out what was in my heart."

Xavier shoved his chair away from the table, the sound loud and abrupt in the hushed kitchen. The first woman he'd ever been interested in outside of orgasm, and she loved water. Enough to build her life around it.

"You have a funny look on your face," she said. The second time she'd told him that.

It was stupid and reactionary to draw lines between Cat

and the Ofarians. First, any connection was impossible; the Ofarians knew where every single one of their kind was at all times. And second, Cat didn't deserve to bear the brunt of his baggage. He sure as hell had to stop thinking that he stood on one side and the rest of the world on the other. The Ofarians who had orchestrated and created his life, and then tossed it into the shitter, were locked away. Gone for good.

He met her eyes over the table. She made the whole kitchen warmer. She couldn't be further from an Ofarian. Millions of people—women—loved water. Hell, Pam and Jill took yearly trips to Hawaii.

"You must have a lot of paintings," he said, to cover up his awkward response and to fill the silence, "if you've been going at it as long as you have. If you need it as strongly as I need to cook."

Her shoulders dropped in visible relief, and he knew she'd prepared herself for him running away again. "Hundreds. I rent a storage space for them all. But Michael says I won't need that much longer if I start to sell."

"Michael?"

She popped the last bite of her biscuit into her mouth. "Ebrecht? Film producer? Oh, you said you don't watch movies. He bought one of my paintings a couple years ago, saw my other stuff, liked it, made some calls, and *voila*, here I am."

He snatched his dish and dumped it into the sink with more force than usual. He slapped on the hot water, squirted the soap in a swirl.

Cat appeared at his side, holding out her dish. "He's just a business acquaintance. I wouldn't even call us friends."

He'd never known the definition of *jealousy* in the Plant, where every man shared and you had no choice who you were with. He'd always thought it a silly emotion, a waste of energy, one that he never truly understood. Strange that the meaning finally came to him over a woman who wasn't even his, talking about a man he didn't even know.

The phone rang, a harsh jangling sound he didn't immediately recognize. Utility companies had this number. And Pam, for emergencies. And one other person . . . but he hadn't talked to Gwen Carroway since leaving San Francisco.

He looked at the phone, a hunk of red plastic slapped crookedly on the wall. It kept ringing. He'd never had need for voice mail.

Cat jutted a thumb at the kitchen corner. "Are you going to get that?"

He frowned at the phone. Didn't move. It kept ringing and ringing. Maybe it was Pam. Maybe, for the first time in three years, there actually was an emergency. Or maybe it was the electric company. At seven forty-five in the morning.

"You okay?" Cat's voice barely broke through the terrible sound.

The phone clanged like an alarm. The world was testing him. To make a woman like Cat remind him of the Ofarians and then possibly have one of the most powerful Ofarians call him?

The ringing stopped.

The silence forced him to suck oxygen into his lungs. When he faced Cat, she wore a quizzical look, but also a compassionate one. Like she knew he was odd but didn't care. She didn't back away. She didn't make a poor excuse and dive for her coat.

Gently, he added her plate to the scalding water and growing pile of bubbles in the sink. When he was done washing, she took the plates from his hands and dried them. The moment passed quietly, but in his head, the phone still reverberated.

The world was testing him, and he was going to pass.

He turned to face her, and she'd never looked more lovely. "Are you free tomorrow morning? I'd like to take you someplace."

# TEN

**Michael *split* in order to spend the afternoon with two different** women.

He'd arranged a meeting between Cat and an L.A.-based publicist. She'd been spacey the past few days. Pulling away from him. She'd arrived at the publicist meeting wearing a secretive little smile, and when Michael had asked her about where she'd been that morning, she actually seemed offended he'd asked. As if he wasn't in charge of her entire image and held her whole career in his hands.

He hadn't liked that at all.

His main body went back up to the house. He'd thought he could last a whole day away, but the lure of his fire woman was too great. It had become a daily occurrence, him sitting in the garage and staring at her. He'd even rented a car specifically for these back-and-forth trips, and had slipped a valet at the Margaret three hundred dollars to let him park there whenever he wanted.

Michael tossed his coat over the banister of the curving staircase. The dim sound of television applause drew his attention. The TV in the game room was on, which wouldn't have made him stop if it weren't for the fact that he could see Sean's short hair peeking over one of the leather recliners. Sean never watched TV.

Michael headed toward the game room. Picture windows lined the back wall. On the other side of the glass, beyond the frozen creek, rose a maze of white ski trails cutting through the snow-topped evergreens. The big-screen TV sat diagonally in a corner, with a semicircle of recliners facing it. The channel was tuned to a talk show, but Sean wasn't watching. He sat sprawled in a chair, his legs splayed out at angles, his arms dangling over the sides. His eyes gazed past the ski runs and seemingly into the heart of the mountain, and it was that troubled stare that drew Michael over.

He stood right in front of Sean. "Hey." No response. Michael lightly kicked Sean's sneakered toe. "I said, hey."

Sean startled, straightening. "Oh. Hey." He wouldn't look Michael in the eye.

Michael tried to get right in Sean's line of sight but the younger man's eyes darted around. "You *splitting*?"

"What? No, Mike."

"Good." Michael exhaled. Sean couldn't afford to be wandering around. You never knew who'd be watching. "So what's up?"

"Nothing."

Typical teenager response, except that Sean was twenty-two. He'd lost a lot of years to the hospital, and sometimes that lack of maturity came out in spades.

Michael ran a hand through his hair and watched a single skier round the last turn before the run ended at the lift. "How's my girl?"

One of Sean's hands clenched the armrest. "The same."

"Are you telling me the truth?"

Sean's hard blue eyes snapped to Michael's. "I hate babysitting a chick who keeps trying to kill me, all right?"

"Did she hurt you?"

"No, but Jesus fucking Christ, Mike. You've got her *in a cage*." Sean surged to his feet and Michael was forced to take a step back. Not good. "What the hell is this?" Sean demanded.

Michael calmly slid his hands into his pockets and recovered the ground lost. "You know what it is. It's my collection."

"Am *I* part of your collection?"

"No. You're my brother."

Sean ran an agitated hand around the back of his neck and let out a harsh laugh. "But you collected me, too, just like all the others. I didn't ask to join you. The others didn't come along until Lea found them, but I know they didn't ask for it either."

"Where is this coming from all of a sudden?" Truthfully, Michael had feared the day Sean started to question.

Sean ignored him. "For the longest time I thought they willingly came to us. But that's bullshit, isn't it? You think I haven't noticed those little yellow pills you make Robert take every day? How he glares at you behind your back? I'm pretty sure he'd kill Lea if he had the chance."

"So explain Jase then." Michael shrugged, hands still in his pockets. "The guy's as loyal as they come."

Sean ignored him again. Michael was starting to lose his patience, and no one in the world was granted a wider window of patience than his half brother.

"What do you have on them? How is Lea getting them to work for you? For free?"

"She has her ways."

"But she doesn't have anything on the fire chick or else she wouldn't be here against her will." Sean thrust a finger toward the front door. "Now Lea's gone off to bring back another water elemental? Are you crazy?"

Michael gave a stiff shake of the head. "The second one is her idea."

"So was the fire elemental. Who will kill us all. Who you are keeping in a cage."

Michael picked up the remote from where it rested on the recliner arm, and switched off the TV. "If it makes you feel any better, I don't like the cage either." He wanted her as free as Jase and Robert and Fiona. He wanted her as his. But what he really wanted was to waltz her in front of Raymond. "You're yelling at the wrong person. That was Lea's call."

"If you don't like it, why is she here then? She's a prisoner. You go in there every day and gape at her like she's made of diamonds."

Because she was. A rare, precious, beautiful thing that only he owned.

"What is this," Sean barked, "the Middle Ages? That shit just doesn't happen anymore."

Michael got right in Sean's face. "Don't you dare let her out."

Sean flinched back. "*Fuck* no, I'm not letting her out. Are you kidding me? I'm not dying that way."

Michael recognized the disgust that twisted Sean's mouth all too well. It's how Michael had looked at their father pretty much every day since the morning his mom had walked out.

Sean was everything to Michael. After Michael had broken Sean out of that hospital, he vowed he'd be better to Sean than Raymond Ebrecht had ever been to him.

Michael placed his hands on the younger man's shoulders. "Why don't you tell me what's really bothering you?"

Sean went to the window and stared out again. Suddenly he looked so much older. Just yesterday, it seemed, the hired mercenary had retrieved the boy from that hospital, and Michael had brought the scared fifteen-year-old into his house and his life. Now here was this person with broad shoulders and a deep voice, wearing the same face as that kid.

"When are you bringing me in, Mike?"

"You are in."

Sean released a shout of frustration that bounced over the pool table and around the room. Michael had never heard his brother make a sound like that before.

"No, I'm not." Sean rounded on him. "I'm your goddamn errand boy. I hide out, waiting for you to tell me what to do. I'm bored, I'm useless, I'm kept in the dark, treated like a kid . . . and I want to know how you plan on using me like you're using them."

He didn't admit it, but Michael had already used Sean. He'd shoved it in Raymond's face that he was embracing the son Raymond had refused to acknowledge.

"Look." Michael placed a hand on the window and leaned closer to his brother. "I'm not going to use you now or in the future. And I want you to be a part of the studio. I really do. But if you just reappear, the doctors—the government—will find you again. So much would be lost."

Sean crossed his arms. He was shorter than Michael but twice as strong. "What if I walk?"

Michael's hand dropped from the window, his fingers drawing sweat lines down the glass. "You wouldn't. I'm your only family."

"No, you're not. I have parents. Who want to know where I am."

"Who left you in a fucking hospital!"

Sean drew back as though Michael had slapped him. Good.

"If you left me now," Michael said, "and went back to them, they'd call the hospital. It was a government hospital,

Sean. You're not a minor, they couldn't commit you against your will again, but your reappearance could ruin everything."

"Ruin you, you mean."

Michael briefly closed his eyes. "Ruin *us*. We're both Splitters. And Lea is adamant about keeping all magic secret. She knows more than us, I'll admit to that. She knows giving the government access would mean death."

Sean shoved past him. Holy shit, he was leaving. He was actually going to leave.

"Sean. *Sean*."

There was nothing Michael could use to make him stay. *Splitting* wouldn't do it; two Seans would trounce two Michaels any day. None of the other elementals were here to get his back. Words were the only weapons he had.

"Stay," Michael said to his brother's back, "and I'll tell you how I found you. How I got you out."

Sean had almost reached the hall leading to the kitchen. He stopped walking. The muscles in his shoulders bunched. He turned around. There were tears in his eyes.

"Is that what it would've taken? After all these years? All I had to do was threaten to walk out?"

"It's time you knew. You're right. You're not a kid. You're not an errand boy. You're my brother and I need you. I got you out of there because you're family, and Raymond had denied you."

Sean ran a hand through his sandy hair. "How did you find out about me?"

Michael breathed stiffly through his nose. "It's no secret I hated Raymond. He fucked me up good. I was trying to find ways to get back at him and I was spying in his office. Found e-mails from your mom, telling him about you. And from him, refusing to acknowledge you."

*"Jesus."* There was so much hurt in Sean's eyes it pained Michael to see, because it was exactly how he'd felt growing up.

"So I dug around to find you. You were thirteen then, and your mom and the guy you'd thought was your father had committed you. I paid someone really well to tell me that they'd turned you in because they walked in on you after you'd *split*. You were playing checkers with yourself. They thought you were crazy, and after they'd committed you, you were starting to believe it. I wanted to help you, Sean. I've only ever wanted to help you."

What was this weird shudder in his chest? This odd tingle in his nose? Michael looked away and focused on a pair of skiers starting the run. "When Raymond found out I could *split* like he could, I thought it would be the beginning of a real relationship with my father. It wasn't. Just the opposite. He resented me even more because my existence made him less special. I knew I had to get you out, give you the support I never had."

"How *did* you get me out?"

"I found out who your doctor was. Followed him around. Learned his routine."

"Doctor Miguel?" The expression on Sean's face was odd. Almost wistful. Almost like he missed the guy.

"Miguel Rosa, yes. When I learned the hospital you were in was a federal psych research facility the public didn't know about, I knew I needed outside help. I took a code name, Tracker, and hired someone. Well, two someones. The first mercenary didn't work out. He bailed on the contract and disappeared, along with a shitload of my money. I tried to go after him, but he vanished and you became far more important. The second mercenary was the guy who broke you out." Michael opened his hands. "The end."

"But it's not the end," Sean murmured, slowly shaking his head at the carpet. "It can't be."

"It's been better with me, hasn't it? Better than with your parents?"

Sean lifted his head, but his eyes stared far away. "Yeah. It's been better than home."

"I'm on your side." Michael reached out and pulled his little brother into a tight embrace. "And don't ever forget that you are on mine."

# ELEVEN

**The first things Cat saw were Xavier's legs. Impossibly long,** they stuck out from where he sat in one of the hotel lobby's plush chairs. She'd taken the stairs from her second-floor room, and he was watching the elevator, so she gave herself a moment to stare when he didn't know.

The fingers on his right hand danced on his knee, and she recognized the nervous tic. She'd watched his arm and hand move his knife over the cutting board exactly the same way. He'd been so graceful and quick, so confident and beautifully calm. So very different from the agitated man who'd sat next to her in the theater, or the powerfully sexy man who'd pushed her against that wall and stolen her breath.

He held back so much, and she was beginning to see that maybe it didn't entirely have to do with the tourist. She'd thought, when he'd invited her back to his house and had made it clear that there couldn't be anything sexual between them, that she could handle that. Except that she craved him. She dreamed of that hard, unbridled passion on the stairs. Last night, upstairs in her hotel room, she'd pictured him lost to lust and felt the phantom weight of his hips as they circled against her. She'd touched herself, but it hadn't satisfied. She only wanted him more.

When he'd proposed this little outing, she'd hid her enthusiasm. Played it off like she could squeeze him in between appointments, when really she soared with happiness. He had no idea what he did to her, and since her time here was so short and he was obviously fighting any attraction to her, she wouldn't let him know.

"Hi."

His head whipped around. He jumped to his feet, and his height never failed to make her gasp.

"Cat." Denied desire colored the sound of her name. She smiled.

"So where are we going? I'm dying to know."

A small lift of his shoulders. "Still a surprise."

"Am I dressed all right? It's the warmest stuff I have." She raised her arms, bulky in a sweater and her thick coat.

He ignored her clothing and looked right into her eyes. "You look great."

"I need to be back by eleven. Is that okay?"

"Shouldn't be a problem."

"Where's your car?"

His lips flattened and he broke eye contact. "Don't have one. But the bus will get us where we need to go."

"I'm so intrigued."

"I hope you like it." The guarded panic on his face told her he was scared to death that she wouldn't.

The bus filled up with people in town, but as it snaked through the side streets and puttered to the outlying areas where the chain grocery store and big box home repair monstrosity loomed, it emptied out. Eventually only Cat and Xavier remained. The great bus engine whirred beneath them, and they said nothing to each other. Though he sat right next to her in the orange bucket seat, he'd nudged himself all the way to the opposite edge.

When they'd reached the very edge of civilization, when all that stood between the bus and the white wilderness was a lone gas station at the intersection of a couple of two-lane roads, he reached across her and pulled the stop chain. They exited the bus on the side of the road, where salt and tires had ground the snow into a disgusting black mess.

"Oh, Xavier." She pulled on the red hat. "What a lovely gas station. You shouldn't have."

Was that amusement on his face? Why didn't he just let it show?

He nudged his chin toward a small, empty parking lot flanked by the telltale bulky brown signs of the park service.

A thick layer of new powder draped over the words and she couldn't make them out.

He tugged on gloves but didn't bother with a hat. She'd never seen him wear one. Not that she was complaining; she loved the way he flipped his hair off his face. She remembered how the coarse waves felt between her fingers.

A rough set of stone steps rose up from the parking lot and he headed for them.

"More stairs? You're determined to kill me, aren't you?"

"Sorry. These are the only ones. Then it levels off. I promise."

He smiled. That rusty grin he didn't quite know what to do with. It made her catch her breath. Made her want to keep him in perpetual delight so those two lines of fear and self-doubt would never again appear between his eyebrows.

At the top of the steps, a gently used path meandered through a thick forest. It had snowed right after daybreak and a fresh layer of flakes settled into old cross-country ski and snowshoe tracks.

"This way," he said, secrets and cloaked joy pulling at the corners of his mouth.

It was like he'd shrugged off a coat of iron in the past twenty-four hours. Something had spurred this quiet assurance in him, and she loved it. She'd follow him just about anywhere right now.

They kicked through the pristine snow, barely entering the forest before the shush of the boughs swallowed the intermittent sounds of the road. Like on the bus, they didn't speak, but then, she didn't really feel the need to. Why did she feel so comfortable around him? Like she already knew him, already trusted him?

"How are you doing?" He peeked at her sidelong. "Feet warm enough?"

She waved a mitten. "I'm convinced I'll never be warm again, but it's fine. This is so beautiful."

"And you haven't even seen the best part."

He veered off the path and into the heart of the trees. The only tracks here were those from small animals, and she had to wade through nearly foot-deep snow.

Maybe that was it. Maybe the snow was making her feel this way. After all, it was water. Only it had been so long since she'd seen the frozen stuff she hadn't recognized its diluted call.

Xavier stopped and she almost ran into him, not realizing she'd been staring at the way the flakes rolled off her boots, like waves in the shallows. She lifted her eyes and saw where he pointed.

They stood on the lip of a smooth sheet of lake ice. The wind blew across it, gathering handfuls of snow and whipping them around in little tornadoes. On the other side, a tumble of gray rocks stair-stepped back up into the mountain, and there, frozen in bulbous, green-white ice, a waterfall hung in stasis.

She'd never seen anything like it.

Silent now, she imagined what would happen in the spring when the world released the pause button. The ice would crack and splinter, and water would return. Sound would flow through. First a steady drip, then a roar. She wished she could be there to witness it, to see the water come alive again.

"Do you like it?"

When she turned, Xavier wasn't looking at the ice-bound miracle. He watched her. Very intently.

"So, so much."

"In the summer this place is filled with hikers. I like it better now." He cleared his throat. "Want to walk out to it? There's probably a good foot or two of ice on the lake."

She'd gone ice skating once, when she was eight or nine and the pond on her foster parents' farm outside Bloomington had frozen over. She'd stuffed socks into the toes of the woman's childhood skates and hobbled out onto the ice. She fell a lot, and didn't remember it being much fun, but that was before her body had changed and she'd begun to feel water reaching out to her.

Now, as she nudged her toes onto the ice, she could almost sense the water chugging below her. She dragged her feet slowly, watching how the gray ice appeared once the snow wiped away. Water everywhere, in so many forms, and she still had no idea why it had such a great presence in her head.

When they reached the bottom of the thirty-foot falls, Cat gazed up at it in awe, but also with a lump in her throat. *Like you love it and hate it*, Helen had said.

"I've never painted ice," she murmured, then ran a mittened hand over the milky, lumpy surface. There it lingered, deep, deep below: that gentle pulse. A kind of heartbeat belonging to a living thing she feared she'd never understand.

But that was such a silly thought, to consider water alive. To believe that it wanted to talk to her, to know her.

*Ice #1* begged for her attention. She wondered if she'd be able to paint it when she went back, or if this sensation would die. She'd never had to wait so long to hold a brush, and her hand began to feel like Xavier's had looked, moving with the ghost of a knife.

When she faced him again, she made sure to smile. His head tilted to one side. He seemed to be searching for something.

"Thank you," she said. "I needed this after yesterday."

He frowned. "You mean breakfast?"

"No, no. After that. And maybe the day before. Nothing to do with you." No. Xavier, with his girl issues and his killer kiss, was the least weird aspect of her week.

"What happened?"

She stepped back to get a full view of the waterfall again. "I'm nervous about the show."

He did that thing where he pulled his hair away from his eyes with thumb and forefinger, and she bit her bottom lip because she liked it so much.

"Can you back out?" he asked.

"Oh, gosh, I can't do that. I want this. I *need* this."

"I don't understand."

She drew a deep breath. "I need someone else to tell me I'm good at something. To tell me what's inside my head is worth sharing. Or even worth knowing."

Where on earth had that come from? She'd never said that out loud. She didn't even know if she'd thought it before. His expression softened, and he was so beautiful she literally could not look at him too long in the bright sunlight.

"But at the same time I'm freaking out because what's going to go on those walls, what people may or may not buy, is *exactly* what's in my head. And if people hate it, I'll think they hate me. And then what will I have?"

"You'll have what you've always had. Is that so terrible?"

"No." But was it enough? When she compared her earliest

work from six years ago to the canvases completed only a few months back, it was plain to her that her confusion and discontentment were getting worse, not better.

"Ugh. Listen to me." She tried to grin but knew how awkward it must have looked. "Do you get nervous cooking?"

He pursed his lips and shook his head. "Is that all that's bothering you?"

She started to shuffle through the snow, tiny steps, feet together, to make a large figure eight. "I don't think I like being paraded around. Michael, he . . . he's selling *me*, not my art. And sometimes he's using me to help himself out, too. That's becoming more and more apparent. Like two days ago? He brought me to this lunch with a guy I was made to believe would buy my art, but it turned out I was, like, the fluffer for Michael's big movie pitch."

"Have you said anything to him?"

"And bite the hand that is, quite literally, feeding me?"

"I see."

Did he? He turned and walked carefully toward a jumble of boulders at the ice edge. He scooped up snow, packed it into a ball, then set it down and started again, until he had a nice pile.

"You throw those at me and we will have a serious disagreement."

The mischievous grin he tossed over his shoulder made her catch her breath. He faced her, grabbed one snowball, tossed it in a high arc, then grabbed another and another, until he had so many going in the air she lost count. The snowballs flew around in impossible ovals, seemingly multiplying then disappearing, defying gravity.

At last, one by one, the snowballs fell to the ice in unceremonious plops. She applauded.

"I remember you liked the juggler," he said. "Did you forget about your show for a few minutes?"

She gasped. "Yes. I did."

"Good."

He stood as still as the waterfall, his eyes like granite, searching her face. The intensity in them turned her to stone, too. Not even if the ice cracked and opened up beneath her did she think she could wrench herself away from his stare.

He said, "I want to try again."

Somehow, she found her voice. "I think you've got the juggling thing down quite well."

"Not juggling." He inhaled, shivering. "This."

He crossed the open space between them, his strides long and full of purpose. Like the ice didn't exist. Before she had time to process what was happening, he drew her into his arms and kissed her. Instantly she saw stars. Instantly her arms swept around his waist.

Though he held her tightly, as though that crack in the ice had indeed opened up and she was about to slip through, his mouth was achingly gentle. This was not the kiss against the Mexican restaurant wall—hard and hot, with pain spicing his tongue. This kiss moved slowly, softly. A deliberate opening and closing of his lips over hers. She tasted no pain this time, just a warm, moist mouth that erased all the chill from her body.

He was holding back, testing his own waters. She would hold back, too. She'd let him give whatever felt right to him, because she'd take whatever he offered. So when his lips parted and his tongue slid against her own, she almost cried with joy. A little moan came up from her throat. He stiffened for a second and then sank into a deeper kiss, nudging their mouths wider, coaxing their tongues into a slow drag.

Suddenly she knew this was greater than lust. For both of them. She felt it in the way he held her—the way he aligned his body with hers but didn't crush her. Didn't grind against her like the world was about to end and they were each other's final screw. But neither did she. They stood there on the ice, clutching each other, mouths fused, the heat between them threatening to make spring come early.

With a harsh groan he wrenched away, turned his face. But not before she saw the terrible grimace twisting his lips. Where did this frustration come from? This agony? He didn't want to stop kissing her but it was like her mouth had turned to poison.

He came back to her, pressed his forehead to hers. "It doesn't mean I don't want you," he whispered. "You make me hard. You make me want things. Make me imagine more of what I can do to you . . ."

*Oh, God. Yes.* This man who didn't always speak so easily

suddenly knew exactly what she wanted to hear. She'd sensed that power, that blatant honesty in him. He wanted her, but on his terms, and she was dying to know what those terms were. She wanted to destroy the shell he wore and kick the butt of whoever had done this to him. She wanted to hear more.

Kissing seemed to be a truth serum. She'd kiss him for days, just to keep him talking. She'd lick out his words, make him tell her all his desires.

He let out a strangled sound and stepped away, though it was clear he didn't want to. Icy wind rushed between them. She didn't want to give him another chance to run.

"Come to my opening," she blurted out.

He shook his head. "I don't usually get off work until eleven."

"It shouldn't matter. They've arranged the 'big unveiling' for midnight since there are late-night screenings and Michael wanted as many people to be there as possible." He looked completely dumbfounded. "Please. It would mean a lot to me. When I'm around you, I'm not nervous. When I'm with you, I feel like myself. And I . . . I would really love to have you there."

Oh, man, the hair flip. He stared at the ice for a long time. When he raised his head, his eyes burned silver. "For you, then."

Then he offered her his arm and she couldn't help but feel like some monumental battle had just been won.

# TWELVE

**The Burned Man growled and shouted and cursed at Xavier's**
back, but he held tight to Cat's arm as they crossed the ice. He
let the tirade go on and on, let the insults and demands fade
into a great, evil blur. The words didn't mean much to him now,
because his desire was cooling and he had Cat's strong warmth
beside him. And because this time *he* had made *her* smile.

He hadn't intended to reach for his illusions, but to see her
cheeks widen, her eyes fighting for brilliance with the snow . . .
it had been worth it. If he had thought his own laughter the
pinnacle of life, he'd been wrong. To give it to someone else—
to give that to *her*—was far better.

He'd been right to bring her to the lake. He'd started to doubt
it in the wake of the mysterious phone call that may or may not
have been from Gwen. If Cat had been Ofarian, he would have
seen the magic in her eyes when she first saw the waterfall. If
she'd been Ofarian, she would have touched the ice with her
bare hand, for those people touched the element with terrible
confidence and thought themselves better for it. Cat may not
have known her parents, but the water didn't know her either.

That brought a whole new smile to Xavier's lips.

He didn't let her go once they reached the snowy path. He
didn't release her hand as they crossed the parking lot and
waited. When she climbed the steps into the empty bus he
wrapped his fingers around her waist, and when they sat next
to each other with their backs to the side window, this time he
allowed their thighs to touch.

The Burned Man materialized on the bench opposite. Just
watching, hovering. Waiting for Xavier to weaken.

He took off his gloves and unzipped his coat. So did she. Though his hand rested on his own knee, his pinkie finger brushed her jeans. He could feel the flex of her firm muscle underneath, hear the shallow way she breathed. He shut his eyes and avoided the Burned Man's smirk.

The memory of her mouth ran too strong. He could still sense the hot puff of her breath the moment right before he'd kissed her, could still feel the way she'd tightly clasped herself to him. Too much blood began to flow too quickly. The Burned Man snickered.

Without warning, Cat stretched an arm across his body and touched his face. The chill of her fingers was strangely welcome. With a gentle insistence, she turned his face toward her. Her mouth touched his before he could protest or give himself a chance to fight the desire. She smelled of everything forbidden and lovely and delicious. The patient, sexual kiss ignited a flame inside him, which caught quickly and spread before he could contain it.

It raged through him. It hardened him.

*That's it. That's it*, the Burned Man urged.

Xavier pulled away. Cat sighed deeply and dug her fingers into the hair behind his ear. She buried her cool face into the warm crook of his neck.

"Xavier." His own name vibrated against his skin. "I think about you. About us. Together."

*Don't say that*, he silently told her. *Keep going.*

He dipped his head and rubbed his cheek against hers.

"I want this," she whispered. "I want us."

She opened her thighs. Just a few inches, but the invitation pounded into his brain and fought with the Burned Man's demands. Through the cacophony a single idea fought its way to the forefront and shouted in a clear, hopeful voice: What if Xavier gave her what she wanted but didn't take anything for himself?

His shoulder blocked her from the bus driver. When he slid his hand over to rest on her leg, she jumped. When his fingers tentatively curled around the underside of her knee, she exhaled. Her lips opened against his neck and started to travel upward, seeking his mouth, but he wouldn't give it to her, fearing how it might skid him off course.

He gripped her like he owned her. Pulled her legs open just a tad more. She made a high noise in the back of her throat and softened beneath him. Resistance completely fled her body.

*She's yours*, the Burned Man snarled.

*No*, Xavier thought. *Right now, I'm hers.*

He slid his hand higher up the inside of her thigh, inch by inch, the incremental rise in heat licking his fingers. When her hand came across and clamped on his upper thigh, he froze. Hissed through his teeth. With great pain and regret, he reached down and plucked her hand from his leg. Touching her was one thing; having her touch him was quite another. The former was a slow-burning ember, the latter a lit stick of dynamite.

"No," he said.

"Sorry." Even her whimper of frustration was sexy.

He paused, mind churning. She vibrated with need under his hand and he was quickly becoming obsessed with how he affected her.

"I want to touch you," he murmured against her mouth. His hand slid all the way up her thigh and found the hottest place on her body, hidden behind the hard crease of her jeans. "Here."

She shuddered. *"Yes."*

His thumb grazed the button on her jeans. Flicked it open.

The bus lurched, jolting him back into reality. Though the driver couldn't see beyond Xavier's body, at any time someone else could get on. Private versus public meant little to him, but it probably meant a lot to her. He moved to pull away, but her hand grabbed his forearm and held on. Kept him in place.

"Keep going," she whispered. Or was it just in his head? He had to make sure.

"Say that again."

She clung to his arm. "Don't . . . stop."

The zipper was cool and hard. He felt every tooth of it release, the tiny clicks reverberating all the way up his arm. Each one sounded like her name. *Cat Cat Cat Cat.* When the zipper was all the way down they both went motionless. Then, at the same time, she lifted her hips from the seat and his hand dove into her jeans and swept beneath her underwear. He'd never touched anything so wet or hot or soft. Had never known it was even possible for a woman to feel like that. His fingers slid right into her, palm cradling her like a fragile thing.

*Now what?* Instinctually he'd known he'd wanted to be here, to touch her like this. She'd begged for it . . . but he'd never done this to a woman before. Had never even cared to. What exactly did Cat want him to do? Whatever it was, he'd do it.

When she started to move, tiny circles against his fingers and palm, he caught on. Slowly, softly, he began to rub and stroke. A brand new sound left her mouth and curled into his ear. He'd never paid attention to what women sounded like before.

Suddenly he wanted to tell Cat everything. How he loved how smooth and slick and yielding she felt beneath him.

"Oh, God, Xavier." She was trembling, her thighs quaking around his hand.

One of her hands flailed around, looking for something to grab onto. It fell on his knee again and he let it, because all she was doing was holding on, digging in. The other scrabbled around on the hard, smooth plastic seat by her hip, her short nails tapping. Finally she grabbed hold of his hand down her pants, held on tightly, and moved him harder and faster. Harder and faster than he ever thought could possibly feel good to a woman. He had so much to learn.

"No," he said against her ear. "I want to do it."

He did. He wanted to make her come, right here on the bus. He wasn't getting off the damn vehicle until he did.

He reached around her shoulders and tapped her upper arm, silently telling her to give him the hand that covered his. She complied, and he laced their fingers together. Now she was all his. Open and waiting.

He took up the pace and pressure she taught him. Hesitantly at first, then enthusiastically when she responded with a lovely whimper. When he thought it might be too much, that he was hurting her, she surprised him again by rocking even harder against his hand.

Her head dropped back and he kissed her, pulling back only to murmur, in absolute honesty, "I love this. Doing this to you. Watching you."

It was easy to tell her these things. He'd been used to taking what he'd wanted. Even when the daily, nightmarish urges assaulted him, he would've said anything to convince a woman to sleep with him. After the Plant he could never, ever take someone who wasn't willing, but he'd gotten used to speaking his mind. Only difference was, Cat was the first woman he enjoyed saying these things to. For her and her alone, he meant every word.

Those candy eyes squeezed tightly shut. She went terribly still, as still as the frozen waterfall, then her whole body shuddered as if the thaw arrived suddenly, breaking through the ice. She was coming. For *him*. For a moment he just gazed at her in awe, then when she let out a little moan, he bent down and took her sounds into his own mouth. Swallowed them, tasted them. He kept going and going, feeding off the movement of her hips against his hand. More wetness, more heat filled his palm. The little muscles inside her clenched around his fingers. Though he felt the matching ghostly pressure around his dick, he pushed it away. Forced himself to be soft and unaffected. This was not about him.

She came down slowly and he took the cue to ease off. He kissed her softly. The clench of her fingers on his knee released. With a short tug he pulled up her jeans zipper and then she finished with the snap.

Cat's head, with its gorgeous spill of brown waves, lolled against his shoulder. She laced her fingers with his again and they stayed that way, side by side, silent, watching the white mountains pass outside the windows, all the way back into town.

It wasn't until they pulled into the White Clover Creek bus stop on Groundcherry that he realized that, through it all, the Burned Man had stayed completely silent.

A world of possibility bloomed inside him.

**Xavier was a book of a million pages, written in teeny tiny type.** One that Cat could read from now until the end of time, and she'd still never fully understand him. The amazing news was, he'd finally allowed her to crack open the cover. Now she was pretty sure it hadn't been just a broken heart that had messed with his head.

When they disembarked in White Clover Creek, the bus driver gave no indication he knew what had happened in the back. And really, at that point, Cat couldn't have cared less. She was flying high and the world moved below her in a slow gelatin haze.

Xavier took side streets, coming up on the Margaret Hotel from the side. As they stood at a corner waiting for a legion of golf carts trucking camera equipment to pass, she said, "I'll get the opening invitation to you. You'll need it to get in—"

The sudden way he turned to her, the fierceness with which he pulled her into his body, made her hold her breath, waiting for the heat of his mouth. He didn't kiss her though. He wanted to—he stared hungrily at her lips—but he instead just pressed his forehead to hers. He touched her face, his eyes closed, his fingers searing lines over her cheeks and jaw and neck.

"This," he murmured, "is more than sex for me."

His voice moved over and around her, as hot as a current of ocean air. A cryptic statement, but she suspected what he meant. Secrets decorated his soul like tattoos.

"It is for me, too," she said. He seemed to be her truth serum as well.

"No." He shook his head. "You don't understand."

"I think I might. At least part of it."

"But not all."

She pulled back a bit and forced him to look at her. "You can tell me."

He barked out a laugh. "Not likely."

At that, she fully stepped out of his embrace.

Regret darkened his eyes. "You're going to leave. I'm just protecting myself."

Sadly, that made sense. And if she had any sense of her own, she wouldn't allow herself to want this man in the way she did.

With a sigh her gaze drifted across the square, with its mass of tents and noisy mob that would disappear the same day she would. Today they lived in a temporary world, and to him, she was a part of that.

He said, "You're worth more than a quick fuck."

Her focus snapped back to him. It was crudely put, yes, but she appreciated his frankness. "Thank you for saying that. I wish more men would be that honest."

"Yeah, well, I'm not most men." He looked everywhere but at her.

"No. You most certainly aren't."

The train of golf carts passed and they crossed the street to the hotel. Over the din of the mingling crowd and the slam of taxi doors, she heard her name.

Michael pushed away from where he'd been leaning against a giant gold urn stacked with evergreen boughs and decorative plastic film spools. As he came over to her, he dropped the phone from his ear.

"There you are." His keen blue eyes settled on Xavier, who'd stiffened.

"Is it eleven already?" she asked Michael.

"Just about." He was notoriously on time. She should have guessed.

"Oh, Michael, this is Xavier."

Michael held out his hand and said, all smooth silk, "Xavier, how are you?"

A weird moment or two passed before Xavier took the hand, his face completely blank. "Michael Ebrecht?"

"Heard of me?"

She wondered if Michael practiced that particular smile in the mirror—the one secretly designed to patronize.

"Only from Cat."

Michael's smile started to strain. "You here for the festival then?"

"No."

When Xavier didn't offer any more, Cat piped in, "He lives here."

"Ah," Michael said, as though that answered a lot. Maybe in his mind, it did.

Cat was quickly starting to hate this situation. She hadn't realized she'd created a whole separate world around Xavier, but now that he'd met Michael, the melding of her universes did not feel right.

"Lunch with that actor of yours today?" she asked Michael, drawing his eyes back to her and away from Xavier.

"Not my actor yet, but yes." Michael rubbed his gloved hands together. "He's an up-and-comer. Starring in that Olympics film coming out in July. Just moved to L.A. Big empty house that needs artwork."

She nodded. Dual purposes to her presence, always. Sell her art. Use her to sell what he needed.

"Can you give us a second?" she asked him.

"Absolutely." Michael whipped out his phone and ambled back to the urn.

Xavier's eyes darkened to the color of iron, his pale eyebrows drawing down and in. "He wants you."

Cat blinked. Whipped around to watch Michael. He clutched the phone and gestured tersely with one hand. He didn't so much as glance in her direction. "No. I don't think so."

"Don't be naive."

She drew back, a little offended, and lowered her voice. "I'm not being naive. We've known each other for a couple of years now and he's never made a move. Never even suggested anything. He's been perfectly professional."

"He wants you, Cat. He's dying for you." There was an ugly twist to his words. Even he looked thrown by it, like he didn't know what to make of the emotions inside him.

Cat scrutinized Michael, who still hadn't looked back at her. "How do you know?"

"Believe me. I know."

*"How?"*

Xavier shifted on his feet. "Aside from the fact I'm a guy? He stared at your mouth. At where I kissed you. He saw that, didn't like it."

"He acts like he doesn't care."

"That's all part of it. He wants you to think that." The balls of his fists bulged in his coat pockets. The clench in his jaw sharply tuned the angles of his face. "Are you used to guys just coming right out and hitting on you?"

Pretty much every day at work. Nothing like men away from home drinking alcohol on an expense budget to bring out the flirting. She looked Xavier in the eye. "This conversation is making me uncomfortable."

"I'm sorry, but I think there's all sorts of shit going on with him below the surface."

"I said, it's making me uncomfortable." She leaned closer. "Considering what we did today, I think you're just being hypersensitive."

He exhaled and studied the sidewalk, looking regretful. "You might be right. Man, I hope you're right."

This time, when he yanked her to him, he did kiss her.

One arm around her waist, the other gripping the back of her neck, the kiss was condensed passion. Possessive. All the tension in his body came through in the force of his lips, and she nibbled at it, trying to take it from him. The taste and heat of him erased the world around her, which had been his intent, hadn't it?

He shoved back with a fierce grin. Wicked desire burned behind his eyes—the kind she'd witnessed on the staircase. The one tinged with pain. He rubbed his temple, eyes shooting across the snow like he saw someone he recognized—someone he hated.

He dragged one of his knife-nicked fingers down her cheek, then skirted around her, and crossed the square toward Shed. Stunned, set aflame and left to burn alone, she watched him go.

When she turned toward Michael, he was already staring at her. And it was then she saw exactly what Xavier was talking about.

# THIRTEEN

**Ten in the morning and Xavier hunched over Shed's burners,** three pots for sauces already going, his lunch *mise en place* taken care of. Another small pot of a doctored soup simmered silently and secretly in the back. When he was done tinkering with it, he'd hand Pam a tasting spoon. Something about it still wasn't right, and in the three days since he'd spoken to Cat, he had yet to figure it out. How fitting.

Jose was working back in the meat cooler and Lars hadn't punched in yet, so when footsteps crossed the tiled floor toward him, it could only be Pam.

"This came for you," she said.

Xavier looked up. She held a delicate silver envelope between her fore and middle fingers. The embossed Drift Art Gallery logo stared back at him from the flap.

She raised an eyebrow. "You don't want it?"

He eyed it for a few long moments before indicating the corner of the workspace with his chin. "Just put it over there."

"You're not actually thinking about not going, are you?"

How the hell did she know what was in that thing?

"Small town, Xavier. A million and two outsiders visiting, but still the same people behind the scenes. Wasn't hard to figure out who Cat was, once I walked past the gallery and saw her name. And the fact that she had dinner here with Helen Wolfe."

He gave the steak sauce a slow turn with a wooden spoon. "I was wondering why you or Jill haven't mentioned her yet."

Pam carefully set the invitation where he'd said and leaned

into the counter, overlooking his work with a frown. "You haven't figured it out?"

"Figured out what?"

"Why we tease? Why we try to set you up all the time?"

His turn to frown. "Because you're a control freak?"

Her head bobbed side to side. "Well, that, too." She edged closer, arms crossed over her chest. "You have no idea how women react when you walk past. How they watch you."

*Oh man.* He turned away, giving her his back as he took the long way around to the dish washing station.

"We tease," she called across the center island, "because we see it and you don't. But now that you're with someone—"

"I'm not *with* Cat."

"—there's no fun in teasing. And because you actually look semi-happy for the first time since you came here."

He swiveled back around.

She snorted. "Come on. You didn't think you'd actually done a good job hiding all that shit that eats at you, did you?"

"Pam." He moved around the island, the hanging copper pots hiding half his boss's face. "Is this about my work? Because if it is—"

"No. It's about you. We all have ghosts, Xavier."

His knees wobbled at the mention of ghosts but he drew himself up higher to compensate.

"Someone screwed with your head a long time ago. I get it."

Try hundreds of someones. And one really nasty one in particular.

She slapped the counter. "You need to unscrew it. Like, before you die."

He snapped the towel from his shoulder and wiped down an already-clean station. "Easier said than done."

"No. It's not. You just do it."

He tossed the towel back over his shoulder and challenged her with a stare, hands on his hips.

"Goddamn it, Xavier. You're a fucking genius. This whole thing would be a hell of a lot easier to say if I were trying to get you out of my kitchen."

Something tiny and sharp started to gnaw at his gut. "What whole thing?"

She threw her arms out in a wide vee, palms raised to the sky, a mirror of the frustrated gesture she threw at her cooks on overbooked nights when she so rarely lost her cool. "Why are you still here? Why? Why on earth don't you have your own kitchen?"

He picked up a spoon, poked at the stock. "Don't want one."

"How can you be such a fucking amazing cook and not want your own kitchen? What's the point of creating your own dishes if you don't want to be chef?"

"I'm happy here."

She stomped to the little cooler where the cooks stashed their bottled water. "No, you're not. You've been a moping mess since the day you started. A fucking brilliant moping mess, but a moping mess." She cracked open a water bottle and downed it.

Most cooks didn't want to work the line forever. You didn't learn how to blend flavors and obsess over presentation if you were only going to cook other chefs' food.

He shook his head, the rough tail of his tied-back hair swishing his shoulders. Pressing both palms hard and flat on the counter edge, he gave them all his weight. Pam hadn't moved. Just stood there, waiting for his answer.

"I found cooking," he told the stainless steel, "in a really ugly, dire time in my life. I love the repetition of the line. I need it. I'm scared that if I let it go, this thing I've come to know so well, I'll lose everything I've won."

Raising his head, he looked through the glass partition at the front door. He could still picture Cat entering through it that first morning after following him from the street. Pam came to his side, keeping the distance she'd learned he needed.

"You've changed over the past few days," she said, softer, "since you met Cat. For the better. Your work is even more inspired. Shit, I'm actually scared to taste that soup you're trying to hide from me because I'm sure I'll have to make room for it on my menu. I see what's happened to you since Turn-korner started—"

"She doesn't live here, Pam. She's leaving."

"And that's stopping you why?"

Because he told himself that morning of the movie date that Cat would only be a means to an end. That she would help him figure out a way to be normal. She was a moment in time. That's all she could be, when it came down to it, and he had to remember that.

"Because you're right," he said. "I do have some shit to work out, and I don't want her involved."

"Too late, Romeo. She's healed you some already. You're just too focused on that station in front of you to see it."

No, he saw it. He felt it on every inch of his skin, in every pulse of his blood, when he remembered how he'd made her come and the Burned Man hadn't said a damn thing.

He inhaled deep and long through his nose. "I can't rely on just a few days. I've been living . . . a certain way for so long that to change my thinking is . . . hard."

"I get it. I totally get it." She nodded so vehemently he wondered what events in her life had made her so understanding. "But the thing is, you *are* changing. And you can either accept that and move forward or retreat back into my kitchen where I will be glad to chain you to your station and keep you working for me until I retire."

This was the longest the two of them had ever spoken. It was cathartic and exhilarating and the most frightening conversation he'd ever had.

"Do you want Cat?" Pam nudged the envelope so the silver corner stuck out over the counter edge.

He removed the towel from his shoulder again, twisted it between his hands. "There's this other guy sniffing around. They've known each other longer—"

"Doesn't matter."

"And the last time we saw each other, I think I acted pretty badly. I might have been jealous, I don't know. I didn't really listen to her." *I didn't even say good-bye.* The Burned Man's appearance had refused to let him.

Since the day he'd walked away from her and Michael in front of the Margaret, Xavier had actually picked up the phone in his kitchen and tried to reach her at her hotel room. When she wasn't there, leaving a message felt too weird. He regretted that now.

Xavier now eyed the envelope where his full name had been written out on the front. *Xavier Jones.* That stupid last name Nora had picked generations earlier and then bestowed upon him like a newborn, the day after she'd rescued him from the Plant.

"Did Cat drop that off herself?" he asked.

"Don't know. It was in the main mailbox. Do you want her?"

After he recovered from Pam's abrupt change of subject, he turned around, leaned his ass against the counter, and took in the sight of Shed's kitchen, the place that was more home to him than where he put his head at night. He knew the location of every single pot and pan, the number of steps from the burners to the *garde-manger* station.

He met Pam's understanding eyes and replied, "Almost as much as I want to cook."

**Two other people were handing their invitations to the Drift** Gallery door guard when Xavier jogged up at twenty 'til midnight, his breath shooting sharp, white clouds into the frigid air. One of the coldest nights of the year—below zero, for sure—and Xavier was already sweating through his shower. Off shift at eleven, up the frozen streets to shower and change at his house, and back down to town, in a half hour.

The paper had been removed from the gallery's front windows. Bright light spilled out onto the sidewalk, making the ice glitter. Even out on the street, the buzz of the crowd beat at his brain. The people inside, standing shoulder to shoulder and drink to drink, wore clothes he didn't even know where to buy.

An ocean of Primaries, and he was about to purposely throw himself into it.

*Why* had he come exactly? Did he do this for himself—to prove he could, to take that next step into the Primary world, to knock the Burned Man down another notch or two—or was he here for Cat? To be here on her big night, to help ease her nerves?

With red, numb fingers, he slipped the invitation out of the silver envelope and tilted it sideways, reading what she had scrawled along the side: *I really want to see you.*

He lifted his head, blinking into the frightening brightness inside. An elaborate set of drapes covered the walls, linked together by a pulley system near the ceiling and dotted with purple tassels. No art yet, but everyone inside was here to see it. To see Cat. And she had asked for him.

Fuck it. None of this was about him. His selfish kiss on the sidewalk in front of Michael, his "moping," as Pam would call it . . . his problem was that he constantly internalized everything, circling everything back around to him. *That's* when he got into trouble. When the ghosts came back, when he retreated into himself, when he acted like an ass.

Tonight was about Cat.

"Sir?" The doorman, shifting on his feet, wore a parka built for an Alaskan dogsled race. A scarf wrapped around his face, showing only his chocolate eyes. "Are you going in?"

Yes. Like a soldier, he was going in. He nodded.

"Name?"

"Xavier. Jones."

The doorman looked to his clipboard and flipped through the pages that crackled like cellophane.

Xavier's fingers found the small patch of duct tape on the elbow of his coat. It was the first winter coat he'd ever bought, and it had seen better days. Scratching that little imperfection usually gave him an odd sense of peace. But right then and there, it felt like a label: Misfit. Hanger-on.

Secondary.

"You're good to go in," the doorman said.

Almost midnight. Xavier opened the door to a blast of laughter and conversation. The steady beat of bass surged somewhere underneath the voices, but otherwise the music was completely drowned out. He stamped up the three narrow steps into the gallery space and wedged himself into the solid wall of bodies. The scene was dizzyingly homogenous: pretty people balancing drinks and napkins with hors d'oeuvres. Same tone of conversation. Same muted colors.

He inched along the perimeter of the room, his back brushing the drapes and making them flutter. A tuxedoed server asked for his coat, but he declined, embarrassed of anyone else handling the sad thing. Besides, he didn't intend to stay long. Just enough to see Cat, to let her know he'd come for her. That he would continue to do so, whenever she asked.

Draping his coat over his arm, he craned his neck to scan the top of the crowd, looking for the familiar brown, wavy hair. Instead he found Michael, and Michael found him.

The other man talked with a couple, but focused steel eyes

on Xavier. Michael held a crystal glass filled with what Xavier guessed to be whiskey. If Michael took it with ice, it had already melted. Xavier told himself to nod, to be the better man. Michael just lifted his glass to his lips and shifted his gaze back to the couple, but not before Xavier saw the veiled surprise.

Cat hadn't told her benefactor Xavier was coming. That made him happier than it should have.

A brilliant burst of color fluttered in his peripheral vision and drew his attention toward the back hallway. All the breath punched from his chest as he watched Cat sweep into the main gallery.

In a room of people clothed in black, she wore a dress the color of tangerine: long sleeved, skin tight from shoulder to mid-thigh, and covered with sparkles that threw out tiny bolts of light. She'd somehow taken the wave out of her hair, and it hung straight and shiny over one shoulder. She was talking with Helen Wolfe, balancing a champagne flute in one hand and gesturing with the other. Helen pulled a woman over to introduce her to Cat, and Cat looked the new woman right in the eye, shook her hand, and listened to every word she said. Other guests passed by her, touching her arm or shoulder, saying words that made a luminous smile draw across Cat's beautiful face.

Xavier had chosen to stay on Earth, but Cat was clearly meant for the stars.

Her eyes widened. She looked up and immediately found Xavier, as though he'd called her name. Her smile magnified. It lit her entire body and fought with the radiance of that dress.

She began to move toward him, a slow process made all the more agonizing by his anticipation. She stopped just outside the reach of his arms. He had no idea what to do now, what was appropriate or what she wanted. Vaguely he felt several pairs of eyes on them—one of them assuredly Michael's—but couldn't bring himself to care. He could see every freckle on her face.

"You came," she said on an exhale.

"I did."

"I've missed you," she said. "I would have called, but I don't know your number and I know how you hate the phone. And we've both been so busy . . ."

And he missed *her*. The feeling shot through his gut, hard and swift as a bullet, then circled back and hit him again, this time a straight shot to his heart.

"Come here."

She teetered forward the same moment he opened his arms. He still held his damn coat and could only grasp her with one arm, but just that was almost more than he could handle.

Her dress was backless.

The shock of warm, smooth skin underneath his palm sent bolts of lust straight to his dick. He groaned, then bit it back. Suddenly he was acutely aware of the condition of his hands: the dryness and scratchiness from washing them so much during the day, the way he didn't trim his nails so much as rip off the rough edges with his teeth. The knife-cut scabs that just seemed to rotate locations every week.

Before he let her go—and before the Burned Man's hissing laughter escalated into something he couldn't ignore—he let his cheek brush the silk of her hair.

As he stepped back, he realized he hadn't had to fold himself in half to hold her. "Did you grow over the past three days?"

Holy shit, he'd done it again. Made her laugh. She pointed at her feet and the shoes that exactly matched the shade of her tanned legs. "Ridiculous heels." Her grin faded. "I was afraid you wouldn't come."

"So was I." She nodded in understanding, and he pushed back his hair. "I was watching you before, talking to people. You're amazing, Cat. You don't need me."

That's when he saw her break. Her cheeks cracked; worry and nervousness seeped into the lines at the corners of her eyes and made her husky voice quiver. "This is much scarier than I ever thought. I definitely need you."

He would give anything to possess the ability to not wear every single emotion on a sign around his neck. She did it so beautifully, like art itself. And she'd shown it to him and him alone.

Maybe she saw him in a similar way to how he saw her. Maybe they were each other's keys, meant to open a door to something new, but then disappear after they'd each passed through and into someplace else. By the way she regarded him now, head tilted, long hair swishing across her chest and shoulder, it seemed she might be thinking the same thing.

Helen's voice boomed through the gallery. In the corner, standing on a riser, the curator spoke into a microphone perched on a long stem, welcoming everyone. Midnight. The "big reveal," Cat had called it. Helen was talking about Michael Ebrecht and how he'd discovered this new artist, and how if Cat moved to New York or L.A., her prices were sure to go up. Xavier barely listened. He studied Cat's face. How easily and smoothly she erased any doubt or nervousness from her smile. How she threw back her shoulders and seemed to meet the eyes of everyone in the room, simultaneously. She gave the crowd a little bow, palms pressed together as if in prayer.

Then Helen went to the wall edge, where she lifted the tasseled end of a purple rope and gave it a good yank. In a coordinated, almost wavelike movement, the white curtains lining the wall swished apart, gracefully sailing into the corners, revealing Cat's art.

The room burst into applause, underscored by several audible gasps.

Xavier knew she painted water. Had prepared himself for the moment when he saw how she viewed the element that had caused him so much pain. He just hadn't expected to love the paintings so much.

The crowd ambled closer to the walls, leaving Xavier and Cat in a widening space in the center of the room. He turned in a slow circle, taking in each body of water. Her paintings were grand in scale, most taller than her. Three on one wall, two on another, and a great, wide one—of an ambling river under moonlight that reminded him of a stripe of glittering stars—taking up the whole wall just to the right of the entrance.

It might have been the only time Xavier would ever agree with Michael. Cat's passion was evident, and even though Xavier knew nothing about art, it was clear she was a star.

"What do you think?" Now that they were essentially alone, her voice came out so small, so unsure.

He ripped his eyes from the one whose pale turquoise waves

brought him instant, conflicting feelings of serenity and agitation. How on earth had she done that?

"Cat, they're . . . magical."

He didn't know where that word came from, and even though it hurt him a little bit to use it, it made her beam.

The paintings were wonderful and enigmatic and emotional, but they just reinforced the fact that the two of them were destined to be separate. Because in his heart, he didn't know how he could manage to stay with someone who continually reminded him of all that he'd escaped. In a way, it almost made their time together feel less frightening. She would leave, and her inexplicable relationship with water would make it a hell of a lot easier to let her go.

Except that he didn't want to.

"You are," he told Cat, and paused incredibly long because there were simply too many ways to end that thought, "very talented."

He couldn't say anything more, because his throat had closed and a terrible pressure settled in his chest.

"Thank you."

Some guests shook their heads at the art, and Cat took it like a champ, choosing to look elsewhere. But many others came over to talk to her, and Xavier stood to the side, listening and watching. She may not have had real magic, but she had *something*.

Then Michael stepped in. His whiskey glass barely held two drops. "Helen wants you to meet a buyer. I'm sorry. Did I interrupt something?"

"No." Cat shook her head, but took a long time to look away from Xavier. "A buyer already?"

Michael grinned, and it owned an inordinate amount of personal pleasure. "They've been primed well. All they needed was the store to open."

One hand rose to her chest. She looked a little pale. "Which one?"

*"Ocean #16."* He nodded toward the prominent painting near the window. "An agent and his wife. I guess they just won some sort of bidding war."

"Great." Cat smiled like a jewel but Xavier noted the wistfulness as she gazed at the painting in question.

"They're leaving soon." Michael pinned Xavier with a direct stare. Xavier wouldn't rise to it. Not again. This was no competition for Cat. Clearly that's exactly what Michael wanted, and if Xavier made it out to be one, it's what the Burned Man wanted to see, too. He wouldn't do it. This was Cat's night.

"That's my cue," Xavier said to her.

"No. Don't go." She touched his chest. "Not yet."

"Go do what you have to do. I'm glad I got here in time to see the curtains come down."

*"Cat."* Michael reached out and grabbed her elbow, but she yanked it away.

Xavier bent down and said, just for her, "I'm not running away again."

It didn't matter what her response might be. It felt fucking amazing to say.

She drew in a breath and blew it out through the O of her shiny lips. He wondered how different they'd taste with that stuff on them.

She said good-bye, then Michael steered her away.

Xavier got his first look at her back, the way the sparkling orange dress pressed against her skin, displayed the expanse of her shoulders and the brown line of her spine. Those shoes showed off the high, tight muscles of her calves.

They'd parted without further promise. He walked home with icy wind and trepidation and virginal fear rattling his bones, and still felt better for it.

# FOURTEEN

**The last two guests left the gallery at 1:46 a.m. Suddenly the** overhead lights burned too brightly. The adrenaline had begun its crash, the consistent need to smile and nod dropping away. Cat longed for dark, for quiet.

For Xavier.

Helen was in the back gallery with Alissa the assistant, giving instructions to the catering company employees who looked as beat-up as Cat felt. She remained exactly where she and Xavier had stood as the drapes had fallen.

"Nine." Michael locked the gallery door and turned to her wearing a Cheshire grin wet with whiskey. "Nine paintings. Look how far you've risen. A good night's work, wouldn't you say?"

He crossed the floor toward her. He looked at her differently, like she'd suddenly become a new person, changed before his eyes.

"For you?" she asked. "Or me?"

He stopped. "What does that mean?"

She hadn't meant to start this tonight. But she was tired, wrung out, and the ups and downs of this past week had erased her filters. "Michael." She kept her voice even. Very few people managed to hold his attention, but she seemed to be one of them, and she used it to her advantage. "It's become very clear to me what you've been doing this week."

Long pause. "And what's that?"

"Parading me around."

"I made introductions." He enunciated every syllable. "You think you would've sold tonight if I hadn't done that?"

Her mouth dropped open. Is that what he actually thought?

He pinched the bridge of his nose. "That came out wrong."

"Wow, Michael. Do you even *like* my work? You've bought enough of it."

His hand dropped. He hit her with a steel stare, one she felt in every vertebra. "I love it, Cat. It's special. *You* are special." She'd never heard his voice dip so low. It unnerved her in more ways than one.

"What is this about?" He came even closer. "I helped you make more money tonight than three months bartending. And it's only the first day."

"You did, yes." He'd always been very good at this, twisting conversations to hit points he wanted to hit. "And I'm grateful to you. Really, I am. I hope you realize that my art means more to me than money."

"So what's really going on?" Clever deflection away from the money angle. He threw out his arms, assuming a stance of impatience, one that was trying to make her feel wrong before she actually made her argument. It wasn't going to work.

She crossed her arms. "Tom Bridger, for one. Who isn't here. Who'd never intended to come."

He twisted his watch around his wrist. Once, twice. Looked down at it. Looked back up at her. "He's an artistic person. So are you. I thought you two would get along. You're very charming."

Goose bumps popped out along her bare legs and back. She rubbed her arms and shook her head. "Don't you ever, ever do that again, Michael."

"Do what?"

"Going in to that lunch you made me believe Tom was a buyer. He's a wonderful person, yes, but now I know you brought me there to help you accomplish something on your own personal agenda. I don't appreciate being used like that."

"Everything okay up there?" came Helen's singsong voice from the back, followed by a wineglass shattering on the wood floor.

Cat stared at Michael.

"Tell her yes," he said, leaning closer. "This is our conversation."

He was right about that. Helen didn't belong anywhere near this. The woman had been nothing but good to Cat, and she clearly loved Michael.

"Yeah, fine," Cat called back to Helen. "Alissa, could you get me a cab?"

"I've never used you on purpose." Michael actually looked aghast, but then, he was around actors every day and she had no idea if the reaction was genuine.

"If you wanted something from me, you should've asked. No tricks. I would've helped you, you know. I owe you a lot, but now I don't know if I can trust you."

His eyes flicked to the large front window, a sheet of black glass with crescents of snow tucked in the bottom corners. "I don't apologize much, Cat."

Much? Or ever?

His eyes swung back to her. "But I'm sorry for that."

"Good."

Was he actually sorry, or was he just saying that to end this conversation? He stared at her so hard she didn't know what to make of it. Was he trying to intimidate, or to make her believe him?

She wanted to believe him. She sure as heck wasn't going to let him intimidate her.

"And don't pull me away from Xavier again." Oh, she was opening a filthy, writhing can of worms with that one, but it had to be done. "It's rude to him and disrespectful to me."

Michael squinted. Was he actually trying to look confused, as though he couldn't remember Xavier?

She rolled her eyes. "Don't pretend."

Michael smiled, but it carried a vicious taint. "I'm not pretending. I'm just trying to figure out what makes him special. Why you'd go for him."

Having to work to peel back Xavier's layers was *exactly* what made him special, but Michael would never comprehend that. Michael needed everything always within his reach, always perfectly understandable. If it wasn't, he needed the people around him to be malleable, or he'd walk on. Which was why he'd thrown up a shield against her current attack. She was surprising him, and not in a good way.

His smile died fast. "He's not for you."

Now she was pissed off. "You have absolutely no say in that. You don't know him at all. You barely know me."

He shoved his hands in his pockets, shoulders taut, chin raised. "Oh, I know you."

The heat of his stare rubbed uncomfortably on all the bared parts of her skin. It was the thing that Xavier had warned her about, and now Michael no longer hid it.

"No," she said. "You *think* you know me."

But he was shaking his head. "I always know what I want. And then I get it." He tapped his temple with two fingers. "I think about things. I analyze. I'm not impulsive. It takes time for me to find a goal, plan a course of action—"

"Oh, God. Don't say it."

"I saw you in that silly art fair. I saw you and I thought 'what about her?,' then I walked on, thinking about it some more. I circled around the fair, came back to you. Talked to you. I saw your resistance, how careful you were about talking to me. To men, in general, which appealed to me. I do love a good challenge. I get so few of them. And I saw your potential, how you were this pearl waiting for me to take you and show you to the world. I know what I want—"

"Stop right there. Please."

"And I want you."

Utter silence plummeted between them. She bristled under its weight.

*"Why?"* she finally managed to say. "We're all wrong for each other."

He pursed his lips. "I can make you right. I've already started."

*What?* She shivered uncomfortably. "You have all those women, the ones who worship you, the ones who cling to you. I've seen you with them in the Keys. And you talk about that one all the time. What's her name, Lea?"

Something shifted on his face. She couldn't tell if it was anger or annoyance or something else entirely.

"Those women are what I have," he said. "They're not what I want. What I need."

"You don't need me."

"That's not for you to decide."

He was creeping her out. A horrifying thought came to her. "So all this," she swept out an arm, "was to get in my pants?"

"Don't reduce this to sex."

She hated that Xavier had told her almost the exact same thing.

"You only want me because you can't have me," she said, then turned to go get her coat from Helen's office. She said good-bye to Helen and told her they'd touch base tomorrow.

On her way out, Cat's eyes shot to the wall near the front door, covered by *River #2*. It was where she'd first seen Xavier that evening—him clearly feeling out of his element but trying his best not to show his discomfort. She could still see the look on his face when she walked toward him. Half-pained, half-drowning in desire. And the gentle, worshipful hand on her bare back when they'd finally embraced. Even though he'd made her orgasm and had stolen her mind with pleasure, it was that single hand on her skin that now sent her blood racing and her heart soaring.

An indefinable distance still yawned between them. He still held back, even though he no longer wanted to. And she was being careful because she didn't want to scare him away. So what came next?

A horn sounded outside. Her cab was here.

Michael still stood in the center of the gallery, watching her askance. She walked right past him, heading for the door. The brand-new nude pumps had destroyed her feet during the evening. The bite of blisters tore into her heels and the stiff patent leather sides had rubbed her skin raw.

"Wait." The ugly command in Michael's voice made her turn. He'd never talked to her like that. Never with such aggravation. He bit his lower lip then added, calmer, "Don't leave like this. Please."

"It's late. I'm done here." She swung her coat over her dress, fully aware of how silly the green parka looked over such fabulous sparkling material. She pulled the red hat over the hair that had taken almost forty-five minutes to straighten. "Michael, you and I are professional partners, nothing more. It will never be anything more."

He drew a breath he was obviously trying to keep steady. "At least let me walk you back to the hotel."

She turned back to him, looked him right in the eye. "Not that it's any of your business, but I'm not going to the hotel."

**Michael should not have been behind the wheel. It was bad** enough he was legally drunk, swerving on the mountain roads. Even worse that he had his cell phone slammed against his ear. He knew this. Didn't care. At least the snowplows had been out.

"Where the fuck are you, Lea?" Goddamn voice mail. Didn't matter that it was closer to sunrise than sunset. She should answer the phone when he called. Who did she think supported her? "Are you in White Clover Creek? That better be the reason you're not answering. When I get up to the house, I sure as hell hope you're there."

She wasn't.

Sean was asleep in the great room. Michael kicked his feet off the armrest of the couch and told him to go up to bed. Michael, on the other hand, snatched a lowball glass from the kitchen cabinet and dumped a healthy splash of whiskey into it.

He burst through the door to the garage. Flipped on the fluorescent light and blinked into its harshness. The box swirled with black, which meant his girl had recently been awake. Or pissed off. Or both.

Join the club.

The fan spun furiously and a harsh line of cold air streamed under the cracked-open garage door. Michael stalked around the box, swigging away at the whiskey, not really caring if he got it all in his mouth. He burned with such anger, such frustration, that maybe only his little fire prize could possibly understand.

*We're all wrong for each other.*

*You only want me because you can't have me.*

*I'm not going back to the hotel.*

Motherfucker.

Michael whirled, pitching the glass into the garage door like the count was three and two and he was going for the strike. The crystal exploded, but he barely heard it over the rage of blood zooming through his brain and making a racket in his ears.

He closed his eyes and reached for the seam inside his mind.

He should have done this back at the gallery. He should have *split* and followed Cat to that townie's house. It wasn't too late. If he *split* now, the two of him could head back into town. Yeah, the double could case some bars to ask if anyone knew where the tall local guy with the bad hair lived. Michael had already bribed the Margaret valet once. Maybe another hundred could get him the townie's address.

This was so much more than base lust. Cat was *his* creation. The anonymous girl he'd chosen and plucked from a life of nothingness. He'd brought her here for himself, just like all the others in his collection. No one was going to steal what was his.

The seam between his halves shimmered red and tempting. He pulled at it, widened it, feeling the beginning of the separation and thinking of Cat. How he was going to steer her back to where she belonged—with him. How he was going to make her realize he was the reason she was here. How he was going to bust down the door to that guy's house and . . .

What? See another guy's hands all over her?

Jesus, he didn't want to see that. He didn't want to *know* that. Nothing else existed outside of the world he'd created with his collection. *Nothing.* This wasn't the best outlet for his energy right now. He needed to sober up. To think.

Resigned, he zipped up the seam in his mind and bent forward, hands on his knees. Whole again.

Kicking aside a shard of crystal, he stalked toward the house door. He'd almost made it back inside when a dark, dark female voice rose up, curling out from inside the box.

"You don't know what the fuck you are, do you?"

He spun around.

His fire woman had smudged away a peephole in the soot. He hadn't seen her do it. Didn't know how much she'd seen of him when he'd almost *split*. Didn't care, actually, because there was her incredible face, her mix of striking, foreign features, staring back at him. And she'd spoken.

He rushed for the box, forgetting to hide his excitement. "What's your name? How can you breathe fire and not burn yourself? Where are you from?"

She hooked her black hair with a thumb and drew it all over one shoulder, like Cat had worn hers this evening. This woman stood before him without shame or fear, wearing only a sneer.

"Are you hungry? Are you cold?" he asked.

One eyebrow twitched up. "Are you a moron?"

What was he saying? Of course she wasn't cold.

She wiped more soot away then came forward, close enough her nipples brushed the ash. She slowly shook her head. "You don't know what you are. It's just become painfully obvious."

The fascination started to ebb. Annoyance settled in. "What are you talking about?"

She narrowed her eyes until they were little more than slits of glittering black. "It's why you took me, isn't it? Why you have the others with you—to massage your ego. You have no idea what you are or where you came from, so you surround yourself with other freaks. Clearly you're compensating for something." She gave a short, harsh laugh. "You must have the smallest dick in the world."

He got as close to the box as possible and chanced a touch. Warm, but not lava hot like it had been the first day she'd arrived. He pressed his palm to the fireproof material to show her he wasn't scared. She glared at his hand.

"Do *you* know what I am?" No use trying to hide what she must have seen him do over there in the corner.

She smiled, and it was gorgeous and evil. "You're a Secondary."

"Secondary?" A kick of excitement shot through his gut. Raymond had only ever used the term Splitter, and that was only that one day when he'd found out Michael had inherited the family secret. "What does that mean?"

She rolled her eyes. "How on earth did *you* ever get *me*?" Then she blew on the inside surface of the box until his palm almost ignited. He peeled it off with a hiss.

"Secondary human, asshole. As in, second to arrive on Earth. You're descended from aliens. God, I love the look on your face right now."

And he hated how his face felt. Drained of blood, of reaction. "Bullshit," he said.

"Where do you think your powers come from? Or mine? Or that hot guy who used air and a thought to pick up this entire box? You think Primary humans just *had* that kind of power? No, our ancestors have been coming here from all over the universe since the Earth was new."

He couldn't find his breath. "How do you know this?"

"*Every* Secondary knows where we came from. Everyone, apparently, except you." She tilted her head. "Are you all alone in the world, poor baby?"

Without thinking, Michael glanced at the door to the house.

"No shit," she breathed. "The kid is one, too?"

His head whipped back around. "Can you read minds?"

"Don't have to. You're just giving it all away tonight. Wish you would've gotten wasted days ago."

"This is all new to me." He ground fingers into his forehead. "You're saying there are more of these Secondaries out there?"

"Ever hear of the Senatus?" When he just blinked, she added, "Didn't think so."

"So there are more? Just tell me. Lea will find them anyway."

The fire woman's glare hardened. "Lea's a water elemental. She can sense other Secondaries. She can sniff out magic like your mom's apple pie."

"Now I know you're yanking my chain."

She made a condescending sad face. "What? Mommy never made you pie?"

"Shut the fuck up." No one was allowed to talk about his mother.

"Oh, you don't want me to shut up."

He removed his suit jacket and hooked it over the leaf blower hanging from a hook on the wall. "Lea's not a water."

The fire woman laughed. "Of course she is. How else do you think she found me? Found you, for that matter? All Ofarians can do that. That chemical they use to erase water powers doesn't do anything to that magic divining rod."

He heard little of that except for the name: Ofarian. The sound of it sent a little zing through his brain. A whole world—a whole universe, if this woman was to be believed—left for him to discover.

For him to parade before Raymond.

"Ofarian," he whispered.

Her mouth dropped open. "You didn't even know that much, did you? That her kind had a name? Why is it the clueless ones are always the cockiest?"

Never, ever had he thought of himself as clueless, and no

one had ever had the balls to call him that to his face. He always made sure to know the most out of anyone in the room, but this woman had his number. He needed to know everything inside her brain.

"Lea said her kind were rare."

"As rare as water, my friend. She lied to you." She ran her tongue along her lips and flame followed in its wake. "That's what her kind does. They lie, they twist things, just to keep the power. They're selfish. They're arrogant. They think they rule everything."

He realized he should be careful about what he believed. This woman was his prisoner. She'd say anything to get free, anything to cause friction between him and Lea. And that part about being descended from aliens sounded like hokey bullshit.

"So how many . . . Ofarians are there?"

"Not entirely sure."

He shifted a few steps to the right, just to make her follow. Just to remind her who really had the power here.

"And you? What are you called?"

Her smile was dragon-like, slow and full of teeth. "I'm a Chimeran. Look up what it means."

He didn't have to. His company had done a movie about ancient Greece five years ago. The chimera was a mythological monster that breathed fire.

"Clever," he said. "And how many Chimerans are there?"

That smile morphed into a snarl. "Does it matter? I'm not like you and Boy Wonder in there. I'm not alone. I can guarantee you that I'm missed."

"Twenty?" he guessed.

"Ha!"

"A hundred?"

A dry smirk.

*Holy fuck.* "A thousand?"

"How does it feel, to know you're not all that special anymore?"

It made him sick to his stomach, actually, because he'd thrown those exact words in Raymond's face the night he'd flaunted Jase, his first captive.

"Do you actually think you're the biggest, most powerful Secondary out there?" She nudged her chin toward the garage door. "That just because you can cage me and force a few other Secondaries into service, you're king of the magic world or something?"

She was seriously pissing him off, her attitude layering on top of Cat's resistance. "So where are all the others?"

She threw out her arms, displaying her powerfully lean body, dusted in ash and soot. "Everywhere, Michael. Absolutely everywhere."

He smirked right back at her. "So if I'm not king of the magic world, as you said, and you're this tough bitch, how *did* I manage to get you?"

"Did *you* get me? Or did Lea?"

"Lea works for me."

The fire woman laughed. And laughed and laughed. The mocking sound of it made him want to brave the fire just to strangle her. "God, she's done a number on you. You fucking her? Yeah, I bet you are. Thinking you're all powerful when you do it, too. Like it gives you some control over her." She pounded her fist on the box and the whole thing shook. "Let me tell you something about Ofarians, Michael. Ofarians don't work for anyone but their own. They think they're the top dogs in the Secondary world. Hell, they think they *are* the Secondary world. Lea's not working for you. She's working for herself."

Michael edged away from the box, remembering what Lea had told him about hunting a second water elemental for her own purposes. A water elemental. One of her own people. His fingers grazed his cell phone in his pants pocket. He needed to talk to Lea. Now.

"There's a lot more I want to know," he said. "Can we work something out? Maybe, like, if I let you out?"

She raised that eyebrow again as if to say, "I'm listening."

"I'll give you whatever you want," he said, "your freedom, a partnership, information about me and Sean. Just tell me *everything* about your world. You mentioned a . . . Senatus?"

She was shaking her head, *tsk*ing like a schoolteacher. *Shit*.

"Okay, then." He scrubbed his face, the alcohol beginning to wear off. He thought about why he'd gotten drunk in the first place. He thought about Cat. "If I let you go, will you take care of someone for me? Burn him to a crisp? Inside his house or something? Make it look like some sort of accident?"

"Sure," she said with a shrug, and he almost pumped the air with his fist, "right after I do the same to you."

*"What?"*

"You heard me."

"Don't fuck with me, woman. You're the one in that box."

She spit flame at him, the residual ash and smoke filling in the peephole.

"You took the wrong Chimeran," she screamed from inside the dark. "I'm their goddamn general, and my army will come for me! You're about to get a really rude introduction to our world."

That made no sense. She was grasping at straws and it was showing. There was no such thing as a Chimeran army. Shit like that couldn't be hidden from the rest of the world. Yeah, half of what this woman said had to be crap. She'd been trying to scare him and, for a moment or two, she'd succeeded.

He needed Lea. She'd clear all this up. Lea wouldn't lie to him. Would she?

# FIFTEEN

**The cab deposited Cat on the curb and rolled away through the** slush. The wind stung her bare legs, but she just stood there, staring up at Xavier's tiny house. The shade was drawn over the big front window, but a pale glow came from behind it. Light made a basement-level glass-block window shine. She'd gambled he'd still be awake; looked like she won.

She climbed to the front porch, her steps echoing up and down the hushed street. She swallowed a big gulp of cold air and opened the screen door to knock on the wood one, just below the off-kilter triangular window.

Movement inside the house. Inside her chest.

The door flew open and there Xavier stood, staring down at her in shock. She'd been hoping for one of his rare smiles. An eager embrace. Instead all he said was her name.

"Hi." Her teeth clacked together. "I didn't want to go back to my hotel."

He just stood there, one hand holding open the door, the other braced against the jamb. His hair was wet at the ends and even standing a few feet away, she smelled his fresh soap. A blue long-sleeved T-shirt stretched nicely across his chest and clung to the muscles in his arms. She loved the battered look to his jeans, how his bare feet stuck out from the ratty hems.

"Can I come in?"

He snapped out of his trance. Without a word, he stepped aside.

"You took a shower," she said like an idiot, after the door had closed behind her and they both stood in the foyer.

He coughed. "Yeah. I was downstairs."

Just opposite, the basement door stood ajar. At the bottom of steep, rubber-covered steps she got a peek of a weight bench and a set of giant dumbbells. One of his long arms stretched out and gently pressed the basement door shut.

"You were working out?"

He nodded.

"At two o'clock in the morning?"

Another nod. She took off her red hat and stuffed it in her coat pocket.

"And do I smell fresh bread?"

He glanced at the kitchen, where the only light came from a single bulb hanging over the sink. A pan with a golden crisp bread crust rising bulbous over the top sat on the counter, cooling. "Made the dough earlier. It was ready," he mumbled.

The foyer was tiny; only two feet separated them. Now that the basement door had been shut, they stood in deep shadow. He kept his face averted, but she could swear there was a pale sheen to his eyes. She wanted to touch him so badly. She wanted him to take her mouth like he had on the stairs—all need, no finesse. She wanted him to just give up and grab her.

"Come in." He shuffled backward into the dim living room, the kitchen light just barely touching his collection of old, worn furniture that reminded her so much of her own place. He put the coffee table with the chipped corners between them. She stepped onto the carpet, her legs shaking like a tarp in a hurricane.

"How did the rest of the opening go?" His quiet voice was loud in the still of his house.

He was so different from the man who'd stood by her side not two hours ago, and she knew it was because she had come to his home. He felt unguarded here. Was it wrong that that was exactly what she wanted? Should she feel guilty? Because she didn't.

"I loved having you there," she told him. "It helped so much."

"You've helped me, too," he said, almost too quiet for her to hear.

"How?"

He didn't reply.

She pressed her lips together. "You were right. About Michael. What he thinks about me."

The only part of Xavier's body that moved was his right hand. It didn't pretend to hold a knife this time. It tightened into a fist. "What did he say?"

"Exactly what you said he would." She laughed humorlessly. Xavier's face darkened. "I'm . . . I'm not sure he and I should be working together anymore."

Xavier went incredibly still. "You're strong enough without him. The way you and Helen have worked together . . . you don't need him anymore."

For a man of so few words, somehow he always knew the right thing to say. "Thank you."

"Is that what you came here to tell me?"

She advanced a few more steps into the living room, her fingers finding the zipper of her coat. Carefully, slowly, she lowered it. "What do you think?"

The way Xavier caught his breath—the way his stare devoured the stripe of glittering orange fabric showing between her coat flaps—erased any residual chill from her body.

They stood on opposite sides of the living room, drapes drawn against the sparkle of the town, the pale glow from the kitchen dusting light over half their bodies. His chin dipped low, hair hanging over one metallic eye.

"Do you want me to go?" she asked, at the exact same time he threw out a panicked hand and demanded, "Stay."

*Yes.* That's what she wanted. A Xavier who told her how he wanted her in ways she couldn't doubt or misconstrue. A Xavier who didn't doubt himself.

But then his hand that had curled into a fist threaded through his hair, and he looked like he didn't believe his own plea.

She shrugged out of her coat and let it fall in a heap at her ankles. From behind his hair, he stared at her dress as though it were made of chocolate, his jaw working.

"Do you want me?" she whispered.

"You know I do," he growled. "But it can't be about me."

Those cryptic words again. There was no room for them here. Not tonight. "I don't understand."

"You don't have to."

"Well, I want you, Xavier."

A strange sort of peace fluttered across his face. He cocked an ear, as though listening for something, or someone. "Say that again," he murmured.

Another two steps closer. "I. Want. You."

"I told you," he closed his eyes, "you're worth more than a quick fuck."

"So let's not make it quick."

His eyelids flew open, his stare striking her like two hot, iron spears. "I don't think I know how to do that."

"I'll show you. The first thing you should do is get me naked."

He winced as though she'd hurt him, but she knew that wasn't the case. Even across the room she could feel him vibrating, could see the mouth-watering erection rising underneath his jeans.

The thrill of her words—so brave, so unlike anything she'd ever said to any guy before—chugged through her blood and centered on her clit, turning her on in a way that made it nearly impossible for her to stand much longer.

She gestured to the coffee table he'd deliberately placed between them. "Still protecting yourself?"

"From you? Not anymore."

He kicked aside the flimsy coffee table. It flipped over and struck the couch. In three long strides he erased the space between them. He grabbed her without pretense or care, wrapping both arms around her back, forearms clenching over the bare patch of skin, lifting her off the carpet. Like wings, her arms flew around his neck, clutching him as close as humanly possible.

The moment their mouths met, in a wet, open, passionate kiss, pleasure exploded in her brain. She forgot her own name, why she'd ever even come to Colorado. The only thing she knew was the taste of his tongue and all the places she needed to feel it on her body.

One of his large hands slid up her back, shooting gooseflesh and desire throughout her entire system. That hand buried in her hair, yanked her head back. His mouth left hers to feast on her throat. The sounds that came from her mouth were unrecognizable. She'd never been one to give in or give up, but that must have been what surrender sounded like. Like heaven.

Her toes touched the ground again. She gripped fistfuls of his hair—thick and knotted and damp, and sexy as all hell—and pulled his face back to hers. She could kiss him forever, but tonight was made for new things. Knocking down walls. Facing fears. Daring one another.

With a groan she pulled her lips from his and broke the seal between their bodies. He looked drugged, lost. She understood. His fingers dug hard into her waist. They both breathed hard.

With great effort, she released him and dropped her arms languidly to her sides. "Will you take off my dress?" She barely recognized her own voice, all throaty and saying these bold things.

"Caterina," he said, meeting her eyes. "Tonight I'll do anything you want."

# SIXTEEN

**Closing his eyes, Xavier silently psyched himself up. He could** do this. This was what his beautiful Cat wanted, what she told him to do. Like on the bus. Just do whatever she wanted and the Burned Man couldn't say a thing.

Xavier loosened his grip on her waist, slid his hands around her back and sucked in a breath when his fingers touched her bare skin. So smooth, so taut. He found the dip of her dress, sitting there against her lower back, and traced the fabric edge all the way up to her shoulders. She shivered under his touch, and he told himself that everything he did was for her pleasure. He got absolutely nothing out of the way his fingers skated over her softness, or the encouraging sounds she made at the back of her throat, or the way she swayed on those shoes and had to reach out to steady herself on his biceps. The taste of her, the eager way she clutched at him . . .

Nope. No pleasure there whatsoever.

Yeah right.

The Burned Man sat behind him at the kitchen table, just waiting for him to fuck up. Or just waiting for him to fuck, period.

Xavier put his cheek against hers. His fingers curled under the fabric of her dress, his knuckles brushing her collarbone. Only her shoulders held up the sparkling dress. Instinct told him to rip the garment from her body, but a burning desire to do right by her overtook him.

*Do it*, her eyes pleaded. And then, so did her mouth.

So he obeyed, because it was all for her. Everything, for her.

He slid the fabric down over the curves of her shoulders.

Down the long, freckled lines of her arms. Slower than he ever
thought himself capable of. He didn't know if he could watch
himself unwrap Cat like a present, so he let his eyelids flutter
closed and listened to the excitement in her breathing.

The dress caught on the slope of her breasts. When he
cracked open his eyes, he saw how the bright orange fabric
hung on the peaks of her hard nipples. Oh God, he was going
to get to see them. She wanted him to, he reminded himself.
She wanted him to.

Need pounded behind the zipper of his jeans. He shoved it
away.

The dress was heavy, the thousands of little sequins giving
it a coarse, cool texture against the hotness of her skin. He
pulled it away from her breasts, felt her body give it up. He let
it drop. Gravity sucked it to the carpet. It jingled as it landed,
puddling around her feet. And there she stood.

He stepped back. Couldn't breathe for the sight of her.

The only thing she wore were the sky-high heels the same
color as her skin and a tiny triangle of pink lace underwear,
whose strings made heavenly indentations around her hips.

Her lungs pumped, her gorgeous, round breasts heaving,
her nipples pink and hard. For *him*. A piece of her newly
straightened hair fell over her shoulder. With a thumb he
pushed it back so he could see all of her. Because it was what
she wanted.

"You look scared," she whispered. "And excited."

"Yes," he said. Let her pick which word he'd agreed to.

"Touch me." Her voice shook with plaintiveness.

"You are so fucking beautiful." It came out much more
forcefully than he'd intended, but Cat just swayed on her feet,
her lips parting.

He reached out and palmed her breasts, her nipples in the
place where he normally cradled his knives. She thrust her
chest toward him. It drove his eyes shut, made his dick throb
with need. Blind with desire, he lowered his head and somehow
found her mouth. It was a quick kiss, this one, because to have
her naked in his hands and his mouth on hers detonated his
senses. And behind him, the Burned Man was stirring.

Xavier withdrew, his hands falling to her hips. The tiny
strings of her underwear teased him.

"Don't move away," she whimpered. "Don't leave me cold."

"I'm not." He slid a hand around her scalp, digging his fingers into that sleek hair. "I just need to slow down."

"Okay." Her voice shuddered. "Okay."

He wanted to touch every inch of her, especially that place inside her where she went all wet for him, but he started with her hand.

Lacing his fingers with hers, he gave a small tug and pulled her from the circle of the puddled orange dress. The way she looked at him, he knew that she'd do anything he wanted her to, but it couldn't be that way. He'd already told her; she didn't deserve that.

He glanced around the tacky plainness of his dated living room, made even worse by the yellow light coming from the kitchen. Cat was too perfect for this room. He wanted to make her come like on the bus. But not in here.

"Will you come with me?" he asked softly.

"Anywhere."

He couldn't help it. He glanced over his shoulder at the Burned Man, who was grinning maliciously.

Xavier shook his head of the image and started walking backward down the short hall to his bedroom, gently pulling Cat with him. He watched her walk, nearly naked in those heels, the muscles in her thighs working just below the barely there underwear.

His bedroom was pitch black. He edged inside, Cat still standing in the hall. Her silhouette, curvy and backlit, was the most erotic thing he'd ever seen. Until the Burned Man materialized just beyond her.

"If we're going to do this," he told her, "I need you to tell me what you want."

She came forward, crossing the threshold into his room, and pressed herself to him. Holy shit, she was warm everywhere, perhaps the warmest in her mouth, as her lips touched his.

"Can you turn on a light?"

He flipped on the nightstand lamp and angled it toward the wall so a soft light filled one corner.

"I want to see you." She was having difficulty getting the words out, he could tell. "I want . . . to see your body."

He froze. "You do?"

*"Yes."* The word sounded strangled.

He thought back to their first kiss, how he'd brutally shoved himself at her without any consideration, ground into her like a crazed animal. And that had been when they'd both been buried in heavy winter gear. Could he trust himself naked? Maybe, but only if he kept to his rules, if he let her steer the ship.

She touched his waist and his stomach muscles jumped, automatically sucking in. "I want to take your shirt off," she whispered.

In the dim light he could see the longing on her face. Slowly he raised his arms and let her lift the hem of his shirt. Let her peel it away. Tried to ignore the murmur of her approval. She raised her palms to his chest, leaning in like she might kiss him there. He shrank back.

"Say, 'I want.'"

Did he imagine it? Or did she like being told what to do? The Burned Man had said that only weak women liked to be ordered around, but Cat was nowhere near weak. She knew what she wanted, and that was the best kind of strength.

"I want to touch your chest," she said, her voice coming stronger now, "and kiss your neck."

Before he got a chance to nod, she was there, warm hands on his chest. Hot, wet tongue moving up and down his neck. His muscles started to lose their rigidity. She pressed against his erection and he stifled a groan. She loves this, he reminded himself. She loves . . .

He hadn't felt her hands slide down his chest and abs until her fingers curled around the waistband of his jeans. Her nipples brushed his ribcage and he shuddered, because what she wanted was driving him out of his mind. He'd do anything for her, anything to please her.

*Anything to fuck her*, offered the Burned Man out in the hall.

"I want to take your pants off," she whispered, tongue in his ear.

She didn't wait for his assent. As she pulled open the snap on his jeans and worked on the zipper, his hands found their way around her neck, under that silky hair. He rubbed his cheek over the top of her head as she opened his jeans and let them fall. Only when he felt cool air over his cock did he realize

she'd also dropped his underwear. For a split second he panicked, thinking this had gone too far, that she'd tripped an ugly
wire in him and any second now he'd blink and find himself
in a waking nightmare. That he couldn't do this.

Then she lifted her face to his, her eyes glistening, and said,
"I want you in my mouth."

His cock screamed *yes*. His mouth said, "Are . . . are you
sure?"

"God, Xavier. Yes."

"Will you kiss me first? On the mouth?"

*That's not what you want*, came another's garbled voice,
because Xavier had had the audacity to ask for something for
himself.

She arched high up on her toes to press her lips sweetly to
his mouth, before sinking gracefully to her knees before him.
His legs started to shake. He breathed heavily through his
mouth. When she pressed soft hands to his thighs, dragging
her fingernails up to his hip bones, he stilled. They stared into
each other's eyes, his hard cock jutting between them. She
licked her lips and he repeated over and over in his mind, *She
wants this. She wants this. She wants this.*

He stood tense, every muscle primed to the point of pain.

As her beautiful lips slid over the head of his cock, two
thoughts came to mind: One, what a fucking idiot he'd been,
to turn this down so many times before. And two, he was so,
so glad he'd saved this moment for Cat.

She started so slowly, licking around him, sucking him
inside her mouth a bit at a time. He couldn't breathe, couldn't
think, couldn't even hear whatever vile things the Burned Man
spouted from out in the hall. She wrapped a hand around him.
Squeezed. She sucked farther down. Her cheeks hollowed
around him, the pressure and the slide building and building.
His knees buckled. He could barely stand.

He must have had a million orgasms in his lifetime, but
never one quite like this. Never one given to him as a gift
because the other person wanted it even more. Never one he
hadn't had to work for himself. It was humbling and powerful
and the sexiest fucking thing he'd ever seen a woman do.

Three years without, and the mind-bending power of
impending orgasm knocked him sideways and back again.

*Don't come like this*, said the Burned Man. *Don't you dare waste that. Remember what happened last time.*

He did. Oh, shit, he remembered. The first and last time the Burned Man had caught him jacking off. The Ofarian had tortured him in a vat of water—dunking him in, holding him down. Xavier had yet to ever take a bath.

He panicked, tried to pull out of Cat's mouth. Placed a hand on her head, attempted to push her away, but she dug in her fingernails and gave him a long, slow pull.

"Cat . . ." he began, but the sound of her name triggered the orgasm and he was helpless to stop it. Three years of caged sensation burst through him, jostling his body, wiping his mind blank then overfilling it with pure pleasure. His head dropped back, and he could have sworn that the ceiling above him disappeared and he could see all the way into the stars, all the way to Tedra. A sound filled the bedroom—a low pant, a moan—and he realized it came from his throat. Xavier, who had never uttered a sound before during sex.

She took him until he was done. When his chin dropped back down, she kissed him right on the tip, released him, and sat back on those high heels. She looked up at him under her lashes, rubbing her smiling lips with the back of her hand. He stared down at her in utter wonder.

The Burned Man was blessedly silent. It emboldened Xavier, made him feel invincible.

He stroked Cat's cheek. "My God," he said. It wasn't his god, but it didn't matter. The expression was appropriately reverent, when it came to her.

She rose gracefully, then slid backward onto the bed. His bed. He had to blink twice to realize the image was real. She took his hands and hooked his fingers under the strings of her underwear. He followed her wordless command, pulled them down her legs and snapped them off her foot. Then he realized, just like on the bus, he had no idea what the hell he was supposed to do next.

She gave him a hint, slowly opening her legs. Turned out, it was all he needed.

Sliding his hands under her hard, tanned thighs, he pushed her legs up and stared down at the only place on a woman he'd ever gotten off on before tonight. Only those women weren't one tenth as lovely as Cat. She was smooth down there, and wet, which meant only one thing.

"You liked going down on me?" He hadn't meant for it to sound so shocked.

"Yeah."

Her hips writhed on the wrinkled bedspread. The movement mesmerized him and his mouth salivated for the taste of her. But was he doing this for her or for him? He couldn't chance it. Not tonight.

"Say it."

As he brought his hands around to grip her inner thighs and open her more, she shivered. "I want your mouth on me." Her voice was broken and tempting, and she was barely finished speaking before he leaned down and dragged his tongue through one of the most lovely things he'd ever put in his mouth.

She sighed loudly. He swathed her with his tongue again. Instinct took over, and he opened his ears to her sounds. The sounds she didn't—couldn't—make on the bus. He learned by moans and gasps where she liked his tongue and lips, and at what speeds. He was educated by the little tremors of her thighs and how they clamped around his ears.

*For her. For her. All for her.*

But he couldn't ignore how his body was starting to harden all over again. How making things good for her so easily created a direct line of pleasure for him.

When she came, he absorbed her energy, fed off it. She was wild, her body loose, one of her hands in his hair, the other clamping around his wrist. Like the bus, he kept going until she calmed, her ass lowering from where it had bucked off the bedspread.

She said his name, her lower lip fitting between her teeth, her eyes so wide and dark in the dim light from the lamp.

His jeans still looped around his ankles and he kicked out of them. He started a slow assault up her body, leading with his mouth. First her flat belly, then the indent of her navel, then across the hard ridges of her ribs. *Is this what you want?* he asked silently, and the undulations of her body answered affirmatively. When he took her sweet nipple between his lips, she quivered.

Using his body, he pushed her farther up the bed so they

could both lay upon it. He settled on top of her, so much skin beneath him. Her legs wound around him. Then her arms. Then her soul.

They kissed and kissed. Hard, hot grinds and slow, tender pecks, all mixed together. He let her lead, and he loved where she took him. It was so easy to make her happy, to give her this.

At last he released her, rolled to one side, and ran a hand down her thigh, his skin so pale against her Florida tan. When he came to her foot he slipped off her shoe and she moaned. He quirked an eyebrow up at her.

"You like that?"

She laughed languidly. "No. It just feels amazing to finally take those ridiculous things off."

Glancing down, he saw the angry, red marks from the shoes. He bent her knee and slipped the other shoe off and gently palmed her feet.

He sat up and set the shoes neatly at the foot of the bed, and when he turned around, torso half bent over her, she was staring at him.

"You were wrong," she said on an exhale. "You're the one who's beautiful."

No, not beautiful. Never him.

She ran a hand down his arm. "When you're ready, I want you inside me."

He looked down, where he was nearly hard again. "I don't know."

"Please." Her fingers tightened on his biceps. "For me, Xavier. For me, if that's what you need to hear."

He turned fully toward her then, coming to his knees over her. She saw his erection, then looked up at him with gleefully shocked eyes. "Wow. So soon?"

*That's my boy.*

He went still, cringing at the shredded voice coming from the hall as much as at her surprise. Was getting hard again that soon unusual? It was all he knew, how he'd been conditioned. Get it up, get it inside a woman, do it all over again. Squeezing his eyes shut, he slid his body up hers and kissed her fiercely.

"You make me hard."

She smiled against his lips. "Good."

God, she was so happy. She made *him* happy, and not just

because he was cradled between her thighs, the tip of his cock brushing her wetness.

Taking his face in her hands, she said what he needed to hear. "I want you inside me."

Anything for her. He started to push inside.

"Wait. Stop." She pushed lightly against his shoulders. "I can't believe we didn't cover this already, but do you have condoms?"

Dread turned his blood to sludge. How could he have forgotten? That could have been a disaster of the biggest kind, given what his body could do.

Did he have any condoms? He remembered a shoe box, reluctantly brought from San Francisco, that contained a long string of square foils. He'd considered throwing the box out, but like an alcoholic hiding his bottles, he'd shoved the box into the farthest reaches of his closet, thinking that maybe if he fell off the wagon, at least he'd be ready.

He lunged for the closet and rummaged around, the mess he was making niggling in the back of his mind. He'd clean it later. Tomorrow.

There. On the top shelf, the tattered shoe box. When he brought it down his hands were shaking. The box fell to the floor but in his hand dangled a rope of silver-wrapped condoms. He ripped one off and opened it with his teeth.

Out in the hall, the Burned Man said, *Nice to see you back. Get this one done, then move on to the next.*

On the bed, Cat lifted herself to an elbow with a wry grin. "Excited or something?"

"Tell me again," he said softly.

Her grin faded and she gazed at him in all seriousness, with so much desire it made his heart ache. "I want you. I want you inside me."

That want filled his ears and his body, nudged into the places where he'd cracked over time. For the first time in years—maybe ever—he felt whole. He swiveled, marched to the bedroom door and stared out into the hall. The Burned Man stood there, sneering.

*Go the fuck away,* Xavier told him. And slammed the door.

Cat jolted off the bed. "What was that about?"

Xavier went to her, unfettered. Gathered her in his arms

and kissed her. She softened, reaching between them to stroke him. With a groan he pulled back, rolled on the condom. She lay back on the bed, her hair streaming over the pillow he slept on every night. He covered her with his body. Instantly she went soft and open.

*Now. Yes*, his body screamed. And he obeyed, nudging himself inside her. The heat and tightness of her drove his eyes shut. This was more than good. This was the best he'd ever had, ever felt, and it had everything to do with the sounds she made, the little words of encouragement, the greedy clutch of her hands on his back. With the fact that it was his Caterina beneath him.

He rocked into her, inch by glorious inch. Then suddenly it wasn't enough. It was too slow and too gentle and if he didn't fuck her as hard as he could—as hard as the desire demanded—it wouldn't satisfy. He only knew how to do this one way. He hadn't lied before; she deserved better. She deserved worship, and he didn't trust himself to give that to her.

His eyes flew open. Sweat broke out all over his body. He stopped moving altogether. She swung her drug-lidded eyes to his.

"What is it? What's wrong?"

He didn't want to stop. His hands and mouth were one thing—they were virginal and they could be trained—but his hips and cock had minds of their own, and he was scared to death of unleashing them on her.

He rolled to his side, wrapped an arm around her slim waist and swung her up on top of him. "I need you to do it."

She looked at him only for a moment, then bent to kiss him on the mouth, her tongue touching his in understanding. She rose high and lovely above him, slid a hot hand around his dick and fitted him inside her. Deep, all the way, until he couldn't be inside her any deeper . . .

*"Oh God,"* he cried out, that prayer again.

She began to move. Slowly. Up and back, up and back, creating a rhythm she loved.

"Take what you want," he croaked. "I'm yours, Cat."

She threw back her head and moved faster. It was the most perfect sexual experience he'd ever had. Tonight was a night of firsts, and this, by far, was the best. To be at her mercy, to let her ride him, pulled out the most primal of sensations inside him. He watched her until he simply couldn't anymore; it was like staring into the sun. Even when he closed his eyes and just *felt*, he could still see her body undulating on top of him.

When he came, he almost bucked her off the bed. He couldn't control the pump of his hips, the stroke of him upward inside her. His eyes flew open. There she was again, a goddess with her hair swinging in front of her face. Her body collapsed under the power of her orgasm and he caught her as she tilted to one side.

He laid her alongside him, got rid of the condom, and the world went right on its axis again.

He wrapped her in his arms, as though shielding her from the ghost outside, when really it had been the other way around. She'd protected him. He smiled into her hair, so she couldn't see how grateful he was.

What surprised him most was the strength in Cat's return embrace. No woman had ever held him so tightly. He stroked the length of her hair, smoothing it down her back as she curled one hand around his neck, her thumb running along his jaw. Her cheek rested against his chest. Another first.

He watched the green digital clock in the corner click past three, then three thirty.

Her breathing slowed. Her muscles relaxed. Seconds away from sleep, she murmured, "What happened to you?"

And to chalk up another first, he actually had the urge to tell her.

He listened to her breathe in sleep for a long time. Only as he finally drifted off himself did he realize that Cat's pleasure truly had been his as well, and the whole time he'd been inside her, the Burned Man hadn't forced his way into the bedroom . . . or his head.

# SEVENTEEN

**Foggy gray sunlight fell over Cat as she woke up in Xavier's** bed. *In Xavier's bed.*

She rolled over to find him lying on his side, one arm propping up his head, already watching her. The blanket covered him to his waist, and she let her eyes wander down the lean, chiseled body she'd run her hands all over last night. The urge to touch him again overtook her, but the pensive look in his eyes stilled her hands.

"I've never slept with a woman before," he said.

She smiled. "Could've fooled me."

"I meant I've never woken up with one."

So he'd been one of *those* guys. Suddenly a lot of his behavior made sense. A "mimbo" trying to reform or redeem himself, trying to stay away from women. Maybe he'd played the field for so long that when he finally met someone he really liked—that tourist girl, perhaps—and she hadn't returned the infatuation, he'd just given up altogether.

"I'm glad I was your first."

He ran a hand through his hair. "So what's the protocol here? I'm flying blind."

"Wellll"—she stretched a hand across the cool expanse of sheet that separated them—"it feels like something died in my mouth, so kissing's out of the question, but if you pull me to you and wrap yourself around me, you won't hear any protests."

He reached out those strong arms and did exactly as she said, all that naked skin sliding against hers and making her sigh. She buried her face in his warm neck and wrapped one leg around his hips. There was confusion and satisfaction in his touch. One moment he clenched her tightly, the next he loosened as though he was about to let go.

"Make you breakfast?" he murmured into her hair.

"Absolutely." She kissed his neck. "That's really why I came over last night, you know. To trick you into cooking for me again. All this sex? Just a ruse."

When he pulled back and gazed into her eyes, his close-lipped smile made her fall just a little bit harder for him. Because that's definitely what had started to happen last night.

He rolled out of bed, his long legs striding for the dresser that had seen better days. He stepped gracefully into boxer briefs and then gray sweatpants. Though last night he hadn't believed that she wanted to see his body, in reality he wasn't at all shy about moving around without clothes.

"Can I borrow a T-shirt?" she asked.

He popped open the top dresser drawer an inch. What a strange thing to bring out his secret smile, but it did. "Help yourself. Take your time."

Before he left the bedroom, he stood for a few seconds with his hand on the doorknob, staring at the wood. As though preparing himself for something that might be waiting on the other side. She recalled that odd moment last night when he'd slammed it. Now he opened it fast. His torso contracted as he exhaled heavily, then he walked down the hall and disappeared into the kitchen.

With a reluctant glance at the digital clock, she realized she didn't have much time at all. She was supposed to have a lunch meeting with Helen to debrief last night's event. No Michael, thank God. It was ten thirty now. Only an hour left with Xavier.

By the time she washed her face clean of last night's makeup and padded out to the kitchen wearing one of his plain black T-shirts, Xavier had set the table and was at the range, hair tied back in a bandanna like he did at Shed, flipping pancakes that smelled like apples and cinnamon.

He looked at her over his shoulder, pancake balanced on a spatula. His eyes drew a hot line from her face to her bare legs, and back again. "Hope you don't have a lunch meeting."

"Nope," she lied, because she wasn't about to miss this.

Breakfast was, as with everything he cooked, careful and wonderful and all the more delicious because he'd made it for her. She ate until she was full, and then she kept eating because he'd rocked back in his chair and was studying her, and she loved the way it felt. She made him talk more about Shed, about the daily grind and a bit about Pam. He told her how Pam wanted him to be her competition, to have a kitchen of his own, but that he was comfortable where he was.

"Too much responsibility?" she asked.

"Yeah. I guess."

"Wouldn't the money be better, though?"

He swept a gaze around his house and frowned, then started to pick at the edge of the kitchen table where the veneer was peeling away. "Maybe. But I don't really need any more than I already have."

She liked that. He was never going to use her to make more money, or to get what he wanted, like Michael.

She pushed aside the plate and took a long drink of water. Setting the glass down, she stroked its sides. Xavier looked at the motion of her hand, and the way his expression heated, the way his chair slowly came back down to rest on all four legs, told her he, too, was remembering how she'd stroked him like that last night.

"I loved being with you," she murmured.

One of her fingers dipped into the water, started to swirl it around, the clinking ice cubes the only sound in the kitchen.

"I, uh, loved it, too."

He'd trusted her with something last night. That much was wonderfully clear. He'd let go of something menacing—even if only for a little while.

She'd never done this before: this prolonged, mutual stare, lips twitching in dazed smiles, completely lost in the other person.

The water churning around her finger in a good, swift hurricane added something else to the experience. An undercurrent of heightened sensation, a feeling of exposure. It buzzed through her blood, making it pulse harder, warming her. This was nothing new; it was what she felt every time she nudged a toe into the surf or trailed her fingers over the side of a boat.

Except that she'd never felt it while with Xavier, and the experience very nearly unhinged her.

The water had always filled her soul, but with Xavier now consuming her vision and most of her heart, the water was getting some stiff competition. His lips parted, as though he'd just come to the same conclusion. As though he, too, felt that swelling in his chest, the need racing across his skin. He stretched a hand across the table to touch her and she automatically leaned into him. She removed her finger from the water glass to take his hand.

He glanced down. Gasped.

"What?" she asked, confused.

Xavier jumped up like she'd drawn a gun on him. His chair tipped backward, clattering to the tile. He stared at her water. The little hurricane she'd created inside the glass had turned itself inside out. A tiny funnel of water spiraled above the lip of the glass, stretching for her finger that now hovered just above.

"Holy shit." He stumbled away, stopping only when his back struck the wall next to the phone.

She didn't know which shocked her more: the way the water spun toward her, or Xavier's dramatic reaction. "Wow," she breathed, and the water collapsed back into the glass with a *gloop*. It looked like any old glass of water now, leaving her to wonder if she'd imagined it all. Except that Xavier's pale skin, unblinking eyes, and horrified expression left no doubt that it most certainly *had* happened.

"What did you do?" His voice was hoarse. "How did you . . ."

"I don't—"

The phone rang, a scream cutting through the tense room. He startled, his shoulder jostling the phone from its receiver. It crashed to the linoleum, dangling from an honest to gosh cord.

"Xavier?" A woman's desperate voice crackled in the receiver. "Xavier? Are you there?"

Cat might have asked him the same thing. He looked beyond spooked; he didn't even look present. What the hell was going on?

"Hey." She rose from the chair, started to circle around the table to him.

"It's . . . you're . . ." he stammered. He threw out a hand to ward her off.

"Xavier, oh thank the stars you're there," came the disembodied woman's voice from the phone on the floor. "I can hear you. Can you hear me?"

He crouched, snatched up the phone, and slammed it back into the cradle. His hand remained clenched around it, his stare fierce on the hunk of red plastic.

"That sounded important," Cat said. "She sounded scared."

Emotions warred on his face. One second he looked ready to punch the wall, upper lip curling. The next second he looked lost. The next on the verge of tears.

This was the hardened, hurting man who'd shoved her away on the steps after their first kiss. He was alive and well, thank you very much. And now she knew for sure that girls were the least of his problems. Everything they'd gone through together last night disappeared. Vanished into thin air like a stupid rabbit pulled out of a hat.

Her frustration started to morph into anger. "I'm trying to understand. You don't just snap like this and not tell me why. Or if I can fix it. It's unfair. And immature." Still nothing. "Xavier, what on earth—"

His scared eyes found her. "Just. Go."

*Screw you*, she thought as she backed out of the kitchen. You didn't sleep with a woman and treat her like this the next morning. Not after what they'd shared.

But she didn't say any of that, because instinctively she knew that Xavier's reaction had nothing to do with them as a couple. Something had triggered a terrified—and terrifying—response in him, and whether it was that weird water thing or the phone call from the scared woman, she couldn't be sure. She just knew she had to get away, to give him space right now. Or maybe forever.

That last thought made her ill. Was this enough for her to walk away for good? Could she handle this manic behavior, if it kept going on? And really, their "forever" was only a week more. Until she went back to Florida.

Except that she'd already seen the beauty inside him and she couldn't, in all faith, abandon him. Still, if he wanted her to leave, she would.

She turned, giving the kitchen, and Xavier, her back. There, still crumpled on the living room floor, lay her fabulous orange dress. Sitting there, mocking her. She snatched it up and went into his bedroom.

The mess of the sheets, his jeans still lying in a puddle, her shoes perfectly aligned at the foot of the bed, made her heart twist and her gut ache. What the heck was going on? He didn't get to wrap himself around her, kiss her senseless, ignite something intense inside her, then shove her away. What gave him the right? Who taught him it was okay to treat people like that?

What kind of pain made him *do* something like that?

She ripped off his T-shirt, meaning to throw it in the corner, but instead folded it neatly and placed it on the dresser, because that's what she knew he'd like. She couldn't find her underwear and stepped into the orange dress anyway. The sequins felt cold on her skin and she broke out in goose bumps. Hissing with pain, she slid her swollen feet back into the ridiculous shoes, trying not to remember how they'd looked at the ends of her legs, wrapped around Xavier's head as he buried his tongue in her.

No, she couldn't give up on him. There was something there—in the air between them, in the way they connected and touched. The way they made each other smile, the way they could talk. Forget the fact she didn't live in Colorado, that she was supposed to leave in a week. She wasn't a coward. She didn't run away. She ran toward problems, and she sure as hell tried to fix them before they grew into something out of control.

It was very clear that he'd taken a chance on getting involved with her. She couldn't call him a jerk and just walk out. One, that was what he expected, to be left alone again. And two, she wasn't built that way. That was what a teenager would do. Not someone who cared for the other person.

She went to the front hall closet where he'd hung her coat. There were only two other coats inside, and when she pulled hers down, the metal hangers rattled, awful and lonely.

Standing in the middle of the living room, where he'd undressed her so carefully and, yes, so lovingly, she pulled on her coat over her dress. He hadn't moved an inch. His hand still clutched the phone, his arm straight out from his body.

"When you're ready to talk," she told him gently, "I'm here for you. Anytime."

His forehead dropped to his biceps. His eyes squeezed tightly shut.

She left.

# EIGHTEEN

**Going on midnight, lonely as fuck. Xavier didn't remember** trudging home after work. Hell, he didn't even remember working. If it weren't for the preps and dishes he'd done a thousand times, he probably wouldn't have survived.

Now he slouched in the beige recliner in his living room. House completely dark. The streetlight on the corner outside cast pallid light through the picture window and draped him in weird shadows. He thought about Cat because he couldn't *not* think about her. Not when she'd become the center of his world after mere days.

Ofarian. If what he'd seen that morning was true, Cat was a fucking *Ofarian*.

The easiest way to deal with this would be to go about his life until she left town. Then he'd never have to see her again. Except . . . he'd never see her again. And wasn't it screwed up that that prospect sickened him more than the source of her blood?

Three years ago he'd fled San Francisco, the hotbed of Ofarian culture, and he managed to run right back into their arms. He'd never get away.

Elbows perched on the worn armrests, he buried his face in his hands. They smelled faintly of garlic, though he'd scrubbed them until they stung.

For the first time ever, he hated the silence of this house he'd bought with Gwen Carroway's money. The money she'd earned from the lives of his kinsmen and lovers and children. The money she'd given Xavier to clear her conscience. He didn't like spending it, which is why his place was decked out like a time warp, but he'd always loved the refuge it provided.

Now it felt like his cell in the Plant. Cold, dark, the loneliest place in the universe.

When he took his hands away from his face, the Burned Man was perched on the arm of Xavier's brown velour sofa, one boot propped up on the cushions. He wore the old blue Plant guard uniform, and the shadows from the streetlamp settled into the twisted webbing of his melted skin. The acrid odor of cigarettes filled the small room. Xavier had always found that disturbing, that the man covered in fire damage always smelled like smoke.

*Interesting turn of events.*

"Fuck you," Xavier said aloud.

*No, thanks. Though I never knew you liked to fuck my kind.* The Burned Man peered down the hall to the bedroom.

"She's not Ofarian. She can't be."

*Yes, she is. She's messed with your head so much you don't believe your own eyes.*

For once the Burned Man was right. Xavier had lost perspective.

He shoved from the chair and stalked into the kitchen, flipping on the weak bulb over the stove, because it was all the light he could stand at the moment. He yanked out the junk drawer, found the tiny scrap of paper taped to the very back. He stared at the ten numbers for a long while, then picked up the phone and dialed.

*Love it,* the Burned Man scoffed at his back. *After all this time, all this effort trying to escape, and you just come running back to us. Say hi to Ms. Carroway for me.*

Xavier whipped around, but the Burned Man had vanished from the couch.

The phone rang on the other end of the line. The waiting made him nauseous.

Gwen answered, out of breath. "Hello?"

Years since they'd talked. Even longer since she'd stood with him on the Lake Tahoe dock as he chose to stay behind on Earth. He'd been the one to use his glamour to help send every other Tedran safely and secretly back to the stars.

"Uh, yeah." He ground the heel of one palm into his eyelid. "I just realized it's after one in Chicago."

"I don't care, Xavier. It doesn't matter. I'm just glad you're there."

The relief in her voice was palpable and it terrified him. He sidled back to the stove, clicked off the light. Darkness drew around him again.

"That Xavier?" came Reed's groggy voice close to Gwen's phone.

"Yeah," Gwen told her lover—husband? Had they ever gotten married? Then she asked Xavier, "Are you all right?"

"You didn't call just to check up on me. What's going on." He was fully aware of the flatness of his voice, and that Gwen's concern was very real. She didn't have a false bone in her body.

"I've been trying to get a hold of you for days." Her voice shook. "Two Ofarians have gone missing."

He rubbed absently at his temple. "Sorry to hear that." Not really. "What does that have to do with me?"

"Because the first one vanished last month from Denver. The second one seven days ago. From Vail. That's not far from you, is it?"

"Less than an hour away." Suddenly his mouth went sticky-dry. "Why are there Ofarians in Colorado? I thought you were the only one to leave California." *Please, please say that's true.*

"When the Board was in control, they deliberately contained us there. Griffin stopped that. We can live anywhere we want now. We even work in the Primary world. You're not going to believe this, but we hired Adine to help us transition in smoothly. Identities and paperwork, and the like."

But all Xavier heard was the part about them living anywhere. "Why did you call to tell me about this?"

Gwen sighed. "I know you want to forget it, but you're Secondary. I've been worried about you."

"Me? Why? Isn't this an Ofarian problem?"

He heard the rustling of bedcovers.

"Others are gone, too," she said.

"Others?" He steadied himself on the counter edge.

"Other Secondaries. Besides Ofarians. Besides . . . you."

The motor in the refrigerator kicked on, filling the small

kitchen with an easy hum. "What are you saying? That there are other races here on Earth?"

"Yes."

That changed so much. Too much. His head started to spin and ache. "I had no idea."

Gwen made a faint, exasperated sound. "Of course you didn't. You made it perfectly clear you didn't want to be a part of our world any longer. And I've respected that. But I hope you can forgive I had to break that wish to warn you that something bad is going on."

He wandered back into the dark living room, the phone cord stretching to the max, and stood before the picture window, one hand on his hip. "How do you know it's something bad?"

"Because the disappearances seem to be systematic. We haven't been given access to all the information, but Reed's analyzed the patterns. There are no . . . bodies. It's like they've just disappeared. Or been taken."

"Yeah, well, he should know."

"He does know. It's definitely foul play. And with Vail so close, I wanted to warn you, to tell you to keep an eye out for anything unusual."

"Turnkorner's going on right now. There's all sorts of unusual happenings."

"Xavier." Her patience snapped. "I've been freaking out over here. Why didn't you answer your phone the other day? Why don't you have voice mail or a cell phone like everyone else? Why'd you hang up on me this morning?"

He inhaled, and Cat's phantom scent came to him. It buckled his knees and he fell back into the recliner. "I've been busy."

"I've been this close to getting on a plane to Colorado."

"Don't do that."

She sighed again.

"Tell me about these other Secondaries," he said. "What are they?"

"Hold on a sec."

"Where are you going?" Reed mumbled in the background.

"Go back to sleep," Gwen told him, and Xavier heard her give him a kiss. "Going to talk to Xavier in the living room." There was the sound of bare feet on tile, then nothing, then Gwen's voice again. "Okay, I'm here."

"The other Secondaries," he prompted.

"The Board, before we took them down, had apparently known about them. Not much information, just vague sightings and hearsay and chance encounters, that sort of thing. The Board was starting to research them, go after them, right around the time I was . . . well, you know. That project fell away once Griffin took over and we had to restructure, but soon it became his number-one priority: find others like us."

"And he did, I take it."

"Xavier, it's incredible. It's not like there are five or six random people scratching out a life in the backwoods. There are whole societies of other races who originated in the stars, who immigrated here over time. Huge enclaves all over the world. Thousands of each kind. And they all knew about each other—that's what's so crazy to us. They'd already banded together and they knew about *us* but they never came forward."

Xavier didn't find that all too crazy. The Ofarians had once been pretty unapproachable. Probably still were.

"There's even a whole system of government between them," Gwen went on. "It's called the Senatus and it meets yearly. About three years ago Griffin appealed to the Senatus for the Ofarians' inclusion, but there was this big, awful misunderstanding."

"Let me guess. They didn't let you guys in."

Awkward silence. "It's worse than that. Things are pretty strained right now between us and them. Hair-trigger, I might even say. But we were still able to get some basic information about their missing people—Adine's amazing. That's how we know something bad is happening on a big scale. What Griffin and I want is to find their missing people and bring them home. Maybe that will get the Senatus to see we're not as selfish as they think."

Wow, so much had happened in the years since he'd hid in the kitchen. The Secondary world had expanded while his had contracted.

"Who are they?" he asked. "What kind of Secondaries?"

"Elementals, mostly. They can control air and earth and fire . . . it's pretty amazing. We want to know them better. We want them to know us." She sounded wistful and frustrated.

He nudged his toe into the beam of fuzzy light striping his carpet. "Can I ask you something?"

"Anything, Xavier. You know that." Her goodness—her honesty and selflessness—had almost destroyed him once. Then it had saved him, and for that he owed Gwen more than he could ever repay.

"You guys still keep pretty close tabs on all your people? You know where they are, who they mate with, that sort of thing?"

"Yes. Even though we can live and work anywhere now, Griffin has insisted we stay closely knit, for safety's sake. But he's made everything transparent. Things are so different now."

He couldn't believe he was about to ask this, but he had to know for sure. "What about records from twenty-five or so years ago?"

She made a doubtful noise. "We've been trying to piece together everything that happened while the Board was in control, but data is splotchy. They hid a lot, destroyed more, encrypted others." Her voice dipped low. "Why? What's happened?"

"Would it have been possible for an Ofarian to have been born outside of California? Is it still possible for one to not know who or what she is?"

The silence on the other end dug deep into his brain.

"There's this girl," he rushed on, "and I think she might be Ofarian. She was abandoned as a baby, doesn't know anything about Secondaries, but she's obsessed with water. And today I thought I saw—"

"What?" Gwen went breathless. "What did you see?"

He looked over his shoulder at the kitchen table. "She was, ah, spinning the water in her glass with a finger. And when she pulled it out, the water stayed connected to her hand. The water came out of the glass, Gwen. Rose straight up and stayed there, defying gravity. I'd swear it on anything."

"Did she say anything? Words that sounded Ofarian?"

"No. Nothing. It just happened."

"If she was raised by Primaries," Gwen said slowly, "the water's been trying to communicate with her. She's probably like a magnet to it. It wants to be part of her, so when she pulls away without *touching* it, it follows."

Xavier swore under his breath.

"How well do you know her?" Gwen padded the question in a casual tone, but there was a layer of sympathy underneath, as if she knew exactly what was going on between Xavier and Cat.

"Well enough," Xavier said, closing his eyes.

"Is she there with you?"

The emptiness sat hard on his chest. "No. Not anymore. I don't know . . . Gwen, I don't know if I can face her again."

"Have you heard nothing of what I just told you? If she's Ofarian and two others have gone missing nearby, she could be in danger. You know that, right?"

He waved a hand at no one. "You're making assumptions."

"About the disappearances, yes. But it's better to be cautious, don't you think?"

He pressed his lips together, bowed his head.

"There's another danger, Xavier. If she doesn't learn to communicate with water in the way her body is meant to, her mind could revolt. In fact I'm a little surprised it hasn't already. It wants her to do one thing and her body simply can't. There's a risk of mental instability."

He recalled how Cat had spoken of her confusing inspiration, how painting was the only way to express how water made her feel. He could still see each of her paintings—the agitation and mystery and devotion behind each one. Perhaps that instability had already manifested.

"I don't want to be the one to tell her," he said.

Gwen made a frustrated sound. "You were always good at convincing yourself of things that would make your own existence easier. But this is someone else's life. Someone you clearly care about. Ofarians have *disappeared* near you. There's no more time. Are you willing to gamble her safety?"

His gums hurt as he ground his teeth together.

"I'm not," she said. "If she's one of ours, she needs to be protected. She needs to be told."

He pushed up from the recliner, started to pace across the matted carpet. "You want me to do it."

"I'm in Chicago. You're there. Tell her. Keep an eye on her."

"Fuck." He stopped and braced one arm on the wall. *"Fuck."*

"Tell me you get it." He recognized her tone of voice. The one that said she'd set her mind to something and if she didn't get the help she was looking for, she'd come in and do it herself, and to hell with anyone who got in her way. "Tell me you understand why she has to be told and what I'm asking you to do."

"You're not ordering me?"

"I would never do that."

He exhaled. "I know you wouldn't."

That made it all the more difficult, because Gwen was so reasonable and so *right*. She would never, ever bring up all she'd done for Xavier and his people, but she didn't have to. He'd never forget all that he owed her.

But he wouldn't do this solely for Gwen. He realized that he wanted to protect Cat. "I freaked out, Gwen. I shut down. I shut her out. When she left, things were bad."

"What was the last thing she said to you?"

He drew a breath and it rattled in his chest. When he spoke the sound was thin. "That she'd be there to talk, if I wanted."

"See, that's woman code for: I'm not giving up on you."

"She's *Ofarian*."

Gwen paused. "It's hard, Xavier, to fall for someone against your better judgment. You don't think I know that?" Five years ago Gwen and Reed, a Primary, had valiantly fought their attraction, but love had always come back to them, no matter how hard they flung it away. "And this is more than your relationship with her. This could mean her safety. Her life. Please. Go to her. Tell her."

"What if she doesn't believe me?"

"Tell her to put her finger back in that water and say this." She gave him an Ofarian phrase, made him repeat it until he got the inflection just right. It was the first time he'd ever said anything in that language and it made his skin crawl.

"Good," said Gwen. "Now give me everything you know about her and I'll get on research."

He related all Cat had told him about growing up in Indiana, and what he'd guessed to be her birth year based on that story. He could hear Gwen's fingers typing as he talked.

"Will you give her my phone number? Tell her to call me?"

The prospect of telling Cat actually started to appeal to his baser male instincts. Stand guard over a woman. He'd never been able to do that before; they'd always been snatched from him in the Plant. And Cat was so very worth saving.

But to put Cat in touch with Gwen? To give Cat full access to the world that still haunted him? He'd found Cat when he needed someone most, but she wasn't just any old female who'd wandered in and filled an open slot—she meant something to him. What that was exactly, he couldn't articulate. But he wasn't ready to hand her over to the people who'd created his hell of a life.

"Please." Gwen was still typing, but the plea wasn't any less sincere.

He was scum for even considering not to. "All right. I'll tell her. She'll call you."

*And I'll give her to you, because if she belongs with anyone, it's you, not me.*

# NINETEEN

**Xavier found Cat's cell phone number where she'd scribbled it** on a corner of the Cantonese House takeout menu. His foot wouldn't stop tapping, making his shin ache.

She answered on the fourth ring. A loud party went on in the background. Lots of laughter and what sounded like a live jazz band.

"It's me," he said.

"Xavier. Here, let me go . . . what time is it? Can you hold on?" She sounded a little drunk. He didn't blame her. A door clicked shut and the sounds of the party were muffled. "There. I should be mad at you, but I've been wanting to hear your voice."

"I need to see you."

"What, now?"

"Yes. Now. Where are you?"

"At a party. At Helen's."

He rubbed his sweating hand on his jeans, then switched the phone to the dry hand and rubbed the other. "Can I come get you?"

"Um." There was a burst of party noise, like she'd opened the door to look outside and then shut it again quickly. "Why don't I just meet you somewhere? I've been wanting to leave anyway."

Michael must have been there.

"Just stay there," he said. "Go back to the party. Stay next to Helen if you can, where there's lots of people."

Pause. "You're kind of scaring me."

"Which house is Helen's?"

"The big white one on Windflower Lane. There's a gazebo in the side lot and some sort of freaky sculpture next to the garage."

"I know it. Just stay there. Be there as soon as I can."

"I'm so glad you called. I don't care what time it is." She sounded soft and dreamy, like those moments after she'd come against his mouth and hand and around his cock.

He had to remind himself why he'd called in the first place, why he was about to race across a wintry town in the middle of the night. That stole away the desire good and fast.

**He didn't bother knocking. The jazz band inside Helen's house** could be heard a block away and no one would ever notice the doorbell. The great oak door, stained a deep brown, swung inward to reveal a formal living room to the right, its windows overlooking town, and a dining room to the left. A wide hallway stretched toward the back of the house. Primaries mingled everywhere. Just yesterday Xavier would've thought himself alone among them.

Not anymore.

He scanned the crowd and saw Cat walking up from the back, her coat draped over one arm. She was wearing ridiculous heels again, this time with slim black pants that made her legs look a mile long, and a shiny gold top that gathered at the waist and made her chest look incredible. His mouth started to water and he ran his tongue along the inside of his bottom teeth.

Michael trailed after her, his expression ominous. "Come on, Cat. Don't go."

"Isn't Lea supposed to arrive tomorrow? What would she think, if she saw you clinging to me like this?"

"I'm not clinging," Michael snarled, then looked up and caught sight of Xavier by the door. "Oh. I get it now."

"No," she cast over her shoulder. "I can't imagine you do."

She approached Xavier with a guarded expression. It made sense, given how he'd treated her—confused her—earlier that day. "Hi," she said, her voice cautious.

Michael stood just behind her, torso tilted forward as though his cocktail glass weighed forty pounds, chin jutting out in a challenge. "Don't fuck him again," he slurred.

Xavier's whole body snapped to attention. Rage started to build inside.

Cat, to her beautiful credit, just turned and told Michael, "You don't get a say in who I do or don't sleep with." But when she faced Xavier again, he saw how unsettled Michael's words had made her. "Can we go now?" She slid one arm into her coat.

"I built you, Cat!" Michael lunged, grabbed her shoulder and spun her back around.

Crimson, the angry red of flame, shot across Xavier's eyes. Three years of punching a bag in his basement and he was finally going to be able to substitute in the real thing. And what better target than this cocky asshole.

Xavier barreled forward and rammed his elbow into Michael's breastplate. The two men shot across the hall and thudded into the far wall, jostling a delicate table and sending the lone picture frame on it to the dark wood floor with a crack of glass.

Michael was drunker than he had been at the gallery opening, and it took him a second to figure out what had actually happened. That Xavier was hunched over him, ready to pound him to dust. Michael swept around the arm that held his cocktail glass, meaning to smash it over Xavier's head, but Xavier easily blocked him. The glass hit the floor and shattered.

"I'll fuck you up," Xavier gritted into Michael's face, "if you touch her again without her consent. Don't think I won't."

"You're insane. Who the hell are you anyway? Don't you know—"

"I don't give a shit who you are. You're nothing to me. You treat her like you own her, like she owes you, I come after you. Plain and simple."

Michael's eyes drifted to where Cat now stood by the umbrella stand. Helen had rushed over—along with the rest of the party. The music had stopped.

"Cat," Michael said. "I'm just trying to get us back on track. The things we can do—"

"She's not yours," Xavier said, low. "She never was."

Michael sagged in Xavier's grip, throwing up his hands. "Look, she can do what she wants. Sorry for the misunderstanding." But the look he threw at Cat was pure possession.

Even though it killed him, Xavier let Michael go. Xavier crossed to Helen, glass grinding under his boots. "I'm sorry about your floors. And the picture. I'll pay for them. I'm good for it." Helen watched him warily, her fingers tightening on Cat's arm. Xavier cleared his throat. "Cat, will you come with me?"

"You don't have to," Helen said, loud enough for everyone to hear.

"I'm not the bad guy here," he told Helen.

When Cat looked at Xavier, a lovely clarity crossed her face. Kind of like the moment on the ice when he'd kissed her.

"I don't have to," Cat told Helen, "but I want to." With a gentle pat, she removed Helen's hand from her arm. "I want to keep working with you, Helen, but as of now, I'm severing my professional relationship with Michael. This has no effect on my work. I want to sell. I want a career. And I want you to be part of it."

"Cat. No." But Michael protested to deaf ears.

She opened the front door and stepped out into the night. Xavier followed. Out on the porch, they faced each other and listened to the party rumble slowly back to life.

"Who's Lea?"

"His girlfriend, I guess. Or the closest thing he has to a girlfriend. I've never met her, but she follows him to different cities. He probably has a bunch of women like that. Why he wants me, I'll never know."

He just stared. "Are you kidding?"

She looked into his face, dark eyes wide as new moons. Then she slowly shook her head and zipped up her coat. "You confuse me," she whispered.

All he could see was her. All he could think about was how her body had felt under him. Over him. Around him. The body of his enemy.

The beautiful Ofarian body that had kept the Burned Man at bay.

This was it. Why he'd come. Except that he really wanted to talk about this morning first. He owed her some form of an explanation, some context for all the other shit he was about to dump in her lap.

He swallowed a huge gulp of icy air and drew strength from

it. "I haven't slept with anyone in over three years," he blurted out.

Her head swiveled around from where she'd been contemplating the snowy birdbath. Her mouth dropped open.

"By choice," he added. "And you're the first woman I've ever touched twice. You're the only woman I've ever *wanted* to."

"Seriously?"

"I need you to know"—he felt his throat start to close up—"that my issues, how I acted this morning, are not because of you. It could never be you."

"I'm confused. Is that why you came here tonight? To tell me this?"

He stared hard into her eyes. "No. There's much more. Stuff I don't want to say here, in the cold." He started down the steps.

"Where are we going? Back to your house?"

Grimly he remembered the awful image of the Burned Man, sitting on the couch like he owned the place. Maybe he did. "No. Not there."

He took her to Shed.

The heat in the restaurant had been turned down to sixty-two, but it was still a hell of a lot warmer than outside. Emergency exit lighting glowed red over the main door and the delivery door in the back. A single can light streamed down over the center table—the one Cat had eaten at with Helen that first night.

The booths along the outer edge of the floor sat in blackness. He moved over to one, feeling comforted by the shadows, shedding his coat as he went. When he didn't hear her following, he tossed his coat onto a bench and turned around. She was standing near the hostess stand.

"Why am I here?" During peak hours she would have had to shout to have been heard. Now, in the wee hours of the morning, her murmur carried excellently.

He ran a finger around the rim of a water glass. Though it was empty he could picture it full. Could picture Cat's graceful finger moving the liquid around.

"You're here," he said, "because I know what you are."

It took a long time, but she began to cross the restaurant toward him. "You know *what* I am?"

He laughed, though there was nothing funny going down

at all. "It actually crossed my mind, the first time you ever talked about your paintings. About water. How much you loved it."

"What are you talking about?" Her steps slowed. "What do my paintings have to do with this?"

He ignored her question. "I actually *thought* it, and I pushed it away. I told myself it was impossible, that I was imagining things. That it was my past finding new ways to haunt me, since I'd given up sex. And then you did that thing this morning. With the water."

She gasped. "But I don't know *what* I did, what that was."

"When you did it, when you spun the water and it followed your finger, I knew for sure what you are. And it changes everything, Cat. It takes what I feel for you and spits on it."

His eyes closed. His hands made fists at his sides. He couldn't say it. He couldn't admit it out loud.

"What am I?"

His eyes flew open and she was standing right in front of him. Her big eyes were made brilliant by unshed tears, and there was terrible panic behind them.

"Oh, God, just tell me. What do you know about me?"

Goddamn selfish bastard. Of course he could tell her. She needed to know to fill the emptiness she'd spoken of. To find the home she'd always wanted and to learn why water tormented her. To protect her mind from turning on itself. To give her shelter among her own people.

He was nothing, in the grand scheme of things. He would tell her because, out of all the women in the world, she'd been the one to give him the dream of love. And if he couldn't have her, at least he could walk away with that.

So he drew a deep breath and just . . . said it. "You're a water elemental."

She stared. And stared.

"A water elemental." Her voice flattened. Her gaze switched to someplace far away.

He licked dry lips. "You have magic, Cat."

"Magic . . ."

"Real magic. Not jester street-performer magic. It's trying to get out. It wants you to communicate with water. And the water wants to be a part of you."

She was so still, so quiet.

"What you are . . . your kind is called an Ofarian." The name lodged like a nut in his windpipe, and if he didn't expel it, he'd die.

"Ofarian," she whispered, drawing out each syllable. "That's insane. You know this sounds insane, don't you?"

He just nodded. She staggered away, collapsing onto the bench of booth six. She looked at him for a long moment, and he saw the doubt cross her face.

"I don't understand," she said.

"You're a different kind of human. Changed. Different. What's called a Secondary."

He took a deep breath. So did she. He let her sit there and think, work it all out. He wasn't going anywhere.

# TWENTY

"Ofarian," Cat said to herself. And then, "Water elemental."
Maybe saying the names out loud might actually make them
true. Or believable.

She looked up at Xavier, who was watching her without
emotion. Could have been that he was seriously, medically
crazy. Except that she knew he wasn't. He was injured, deep
down, and wounds you couldn't bandage never truly healed.

She had *magic*? Connected to water?

Some part of her—a very large part of her—believed him.
The part that twitched and hummed and stretched whenever
she touched water. The part that wanted to be explained every
time she set a brush to canvas.

The part that knew she'd manipulated the water that very
morning.

"Tell me more." Her voice was scratchy.

He drew a shaky breath, looking like he had to psych himself up, then nodded. He walked past her, snatching a water
glass from a table. He went into the kitchen. She heard him
clanking around. He didn't turn on the light. An unseen faucet
blasted on then turned off. He reappeared, coasting across the
dining room floor holding a half-full glass of water straight out
from his body like it might burn him. And given his reaction
to what had happened that morning in his kitchen, maybe he
did actually believe that.

She felt suspended in time, hanging there, waiting for him
to speak. Anticipation spiked her heart rate and made her mind
swim. It hit her that her reasons for coming to White Clover
Creek had boiled down to this moment. Perhaps that was what

she'd felt on the street that first morning; she'd sensed Xavier's importance to her.

"Take your coat off." His lips barely moved. "We might be here a while."

She did as he said, laying the coat across the booth bench. When she straightened, his hot gaze was making a slow path over her body. She recognized the lust; she'd seen it plenty last night as he'd peeled her dress off. As he'd stared at her spread legs. As she rode him until they both shuddered.

Only now there was terrible pain behind it. Like he hated her and wanted to screw her at the same time.

Then he blinked it away. He set down the water glass on the table and gave it a nudge. "Put your finger in it, like you did this morning."

She couldn't deny it; excitement purred through her. Excitement and trepidation. She covered the top of the stemmed glass with her hand, then crooked her forefinger into the bowl so just the tip of it broke the surface.

There it was. That curl of emotion swirling up, greeting her. Inviting her in. She gasped; Xavier grimaced.

"Now repeat after me," he said.

He spouted a short phrase in a language that sounded like water burbling over rock. Even though he struggled with some of the sounds, she repeated them back with ease, word by glorious word.

The magic exploded inside her.

It rushed in to fill the holes the major questions of her life had gouged out. It flooded her senses and took control of her muscles. Her legs felt weak and powerful at the same time; her mind both wandering and more focused than ever. Her heart was too large for her body and not nearly big enough to contain everything she felt. The water held out its lovely arms and took her into its embrace.

She was home.

Her eyelids fluttered closed and she *listened*.

*Cat.*

Her name drifted all around, the sound melodious but also anguished.

"Caterina." It wasn't the water speaking. It was Xavier, and he was calling her back.

With great effort she opened her eyes.

"Look at what you did," he said.

She glanced down and gasped. There was no more water in the glass. In a thin, glistening stream, the liquid wrapped ribbonlike around her bare forearm, snaked with gorgeous precision over her elbow, and swirled around the cap sleeve of her gold party top.

She could not feel the water on her skin. It made no damp lines. Yet she *sensed* it, its power and voice seeping into her. When she moved, turning her arm to stare in wonder, the water moved with her. It waited for her to command it, the loving master and willing slave.

And then suddenly, horribly, it was too much. Too scary. Too strange. The awe crashed and burned, and she was just a lonely girl from conservative Indiana wearing an eerie bracelet of water. She shook her arm. It wouldn't come off. She shook it harder, panic setting in.

"Get it off me. Oh, God, get it off."

"Easy, easy." Xavier reached out but didn't touch her. "Say this to release it."

He had to give her the new words twice, because the freakout drew whines of fear from her throat and she couldn't hear over herself.

The water collapsed to the floor with a splash. Her lungs pumped like she'd just sprinted up one of White Clover Creek's neighborhood staircases. Xavier's gunmetal eyes had glazed over.

At great length she asked, "Are . . . are you one, too?"

"If I was, those words would've worked for me."

She backed away from the puddle. "So how do you know all about this? About this magic?"

He turned his face away. "I'm something else. Someone who knows you and your kind."

"Something else?" She almost laughed. "What does that mean? Who are you?"

"I'm Tedran." He still wouldn't look at her. "I have different magic. I have illusions. It's how I got away from you after bolting from the street performer. I made myself look like Shed's cleaning lady. Pam didn't know."

Then he whispered something that sounded as natural

coming out of his mouth as the Ofarian words had escaping hers. In a glimmer of light and shadow, he transformed from being Xavier to a squat Hispanic woman. Cat jumped, hand to her pounding heart.

"Touch me," the strange woman said in Xavier's voice. Cat just stood there. "Touch me."

She inched forward and pressed a single finger to the woman's arm. The image shimmered and disappeared. Xavier rose before her again.

"Oh, my God," she murmured. The enormity of what she'd just witnessed—on both their parts—made her start to hyperventilate. Not because she didn't believe, but because she did.

It was real. She'd found her answers.

"The snowballs," she said, "on the lake."

He licked his lips. "Yeah, that was an illusion."

She turned and went to the large corner booth.

"Remember what you said to me the morning we met?" he asked at her back, his voice hushed. "You thought you recognized me."

"Yes."

"Because you did. In a way. Your kind . . . Ofarians . . . can sense other Secondaries, other magic-users. I think they're called signatures, and each kind of Secondary's feels different. That day you felt my signature."

She recalled so vividly that first mental tap on the shoulder, when she'd become aware of Xavier standing next to her before she'd even seen him. "I can still feel it," she said, "though it's different now that we've spent so much time together. Muted. I think I've felt them before, the signatures." She flipped back through her memories, to all those strangers coming into her bar. "Like, a lot. I've been around others and I just never knew."

"It's possible. I'm told there are a lot of Secondaries."

Xavier leaned his forearms on the divide between two booths and pressed his forehead into his clasped hands. "So there you have it," he said. His tone made her want to cry.

"Have what?"

He turned his head to look at her. "A home. I just gave it to you in the form of your people." He pushed off the booth and cut through the air with a hand. "And I can't be a part of it."

"Because I'm . . . Ofarian?" Would that ever get easier to say?

He winced. "Yes."

"Why not? Why not, Xavier? As long as we're in the confessional, we might as well bring it all out." When he still said nothing, she added, "You have issues with . . . Ofarians."

He released a short, pained laugh. His face was so haunted, and the sight of it scared her more than the water wrapping around her arm.

"Please," she said. "Talk to me."

It took a few moments, but he straightened. Faced her. And told her the most awful story she'd ever heard in a flat, emotionless voice.

"I told you I came here three years ago. For two years before that I lived in San Francisco. But the time before that . . . I was a slave. I was born in what was called the Plant, a facility the Ofarians used to drain captive Tedrans of their glamour and sell it on the black market under the name *Mendacia*. They'd been doing it for generations. To keep it going they needed a steady supply of Tedrans. They had an elaborate breeding system set up. I was born inside a building with no windows. I lived there until seven years ago."

Cat covered her mouth with her hands. Xavier just plowed on.

"Nora and Adine, the only two Tedrans not enslaved, broke me out of the Plant. Their plan was to kidnap the daughter of the Ofarian leader, Gwen Carroway, and force her to take down her own people and return the Tedrans back to the stars. She did both, but on her terms. In the end, the old Ofarian leadership was destroyed, the Plant shut down, and the Tedrans returned home. But in order to get them all back safely, I had to stay behind on Earth. To mask their departure with illusion."

Xavier just stood there, hands in his jeans pockets, eyes so far away he seemed blind. It was so much to digest. That piddly little water bracelet had scared her? She was a simpering coward next to this man.

"I have no words," she said slowly, each word hurting as it came out. "Nothing I can say will make things better for you. I know what you must see when you look at me. I understand your reaction this morning, when you must have realized—"

"You want to hear about it?" A million ugly emotions were

balled up in that nasty question and flung at her with destruction. "You want to know what the Ofarians did to me in the Plant?"

The backs of her knees hit the bench. She hadn't realized she'd been edging away from him. "Only if you want to tell me." But did she want to hear it?

"That's not true. You want to know. I heard you ask me about it before you fell asleep last night. You want to know why I didn't want to kiss you on the stairs. Why I wouldn't let you touch me on the bus. Why I made you tell me what you wanted last night, and why I had you fuck me when I would've given anything—*anything*—to have just gone crazy on you."

His words sparked something inside her. Something she shouldn't have been feeling at that moment. "Yes. I want to know all that."

His face turned terrifyingly blank. "It started right after my body changed. The guard who'd been in charge of me for pretty much my whole life took me to the Circle, which was what the Ofarians called the block where they bred the Tedrans. He sat me on a chair in front of the window. Made me watch a man and woman going at it. Made me understand what I was supposed to do with that hard stick between my legs."

Cat wasn't one to swear, but *holy shit*.

"The first time he put me in a breeding cell, I didn't know what to feel. I wasn't scared. I'd seen the other couples doing it and no one looked scared. He brought in a woman older than me by ten years at least. She lay down, spread her legs and showed me where to put it." Xavier shook his head, his hair falling over his face in shame. "And I loved it. I thought the top of the world had been popped off and all the stars and sun shoved inside my body, even though at the time I had no idea what those things were. It was the greatest fucking thing." He swallowed hard. "Until I saw how she *didn't* love it. She didn't resist, didn't say no or push me away, but she went dead inside. And even though this was the only life I'd ever known, I sensed in my heart how lopsided the whole thing was. I was fourteen, did I mention that?"

An awful sound filled the dining room and Cat realized it was her, trying to hold back a sob. The threatening look he threw her made her bury any tears before they fell.

"I became their prize stud. I was a machine, hard all the time, ready whenever they needed me and even when they didn't. He wouldn't let me touch myself. At night he tied my hands behind my back and my blood would boil, dying for the next day. Dying for a woman."

*He. He.* That same guard, she guessed.

Xavier was pacing now, making short work of the path between the outer booths and the tables in the center of the dining room. His body moved tightly, all constrained power and sexuality. She imagined him pacing like that in his cell, waiting for release.

"And for some reason"—another ugly laugh—"I could get any Tedran woman pregnant. The ones who had problems, they brought to me. It always worked. Always. Never knew why, never questioned it. Just took whoever they gave me."

It was a long time before she could ask, "How many kids do you have?"

"Don't know."

Those weren't tears glimmering in Xavier's eyes. That was hatred, boiling up from inside and turning into something viscous and tangible.

"This 'he.' This guard . . ."

He tilted back his head and said to the ceiling. "Never knew his name. They didn't exactly wear name tags. But he was the most consistent presence in my life. How fucked up is that?" His fingers wiggled near his throat. "Half of him was burned, like he'd been caught in a fire. One of his arms was a big mess." He held out his shaking hands like they were filthy. "I can still feel that hand on my arms, Cat, pulling me through the corridors. He hated Tedrans more than anything. Amazing how people who don't even understand why they hate, hate the strongest. And he took out that hate on me."

He wiped his hands on his jeans, long, slow rubs up and down his thighs. "He wasn't there, when I went back with Gwen. I thought I was home free, that I'd never, ever have to see him again. Even though I was just as miserable on the outside as I was in the Plant, that was the one thing that I could be happy about."

He looked at her with horror, like *she* was one of *them*. How had that happened, when she'd started the day waking, blissful, in this man's bed?

She wrapped her arms around her middle, knowing that apologizing would only piss him off. What to say? Everything sounded dumb and patronizing and useless in her head. She went with: "He can't hurt you anymore." It was the truth, at least.

Two long strides and he was inside her space, looming over her. "Oh, you think so? I saw him almost every goddamn day after I left Lake Tahoe. Adine and I went to San Francisco and I was jumping out of my skin. The Burned Man appeared to me in hallucinations. He haunted me, pushing me toward women like he had in the Plant. Tempting me. I was helpless."

"You said you hadn't slept with anyone in three years."

He leaned closer, bending her backward over the table. She had to put her hands behind her to steady herself. "Because I slept with pretty much every woman in San Francisco before that. There wasn't anyone left." He reached up as if to touch her face, but then changed his mind. "I was careful, Cat. So careful. Adine shoved condoms at me like food, told me all about Primary diseases, dragged me to an Ofarian doctor Gwen told her about. But, above all, I didn't want to get anyone pregnant."

In its crazy way, it all made so much sense now. Every stricken, lust-filled look he'd given her. The way he talked to her, so frankly, like he'd said it all before. How he wore sex like a second skin and exhibitionism meant nothing to him. How he'd pushed her away.

"You stopped," she whispered.

"I had to. It was ruling me, and I was scared. I was scared for who I'd become and how far I had to fall."

He was staring at her mouth, his thighs pressed to hers, shoving her back into the table.

She took a chance and touched his arm. The muscles underneath his long T-shirt were bunched so tightly she thought they might snap. His breath hissed through his flared nostrils.

"And then you found cooking," she said.

"Oh, man." His head dropped, cheek brushing hers. His other hand snaked around her lower back, holding her gently. "You get it," he murmured. "It feels so good that you get it."

She rubbed her cheek against his. "How did you know when to stop? Sleeping around, I mean."

"When I realized I wanted to be normal, like a Primary. To blend in. I had to stop what had been bred into me."

She looked into his eyes. "You gave up sex."

He laughed shortly. "No, I abandoned it. Kicked it from a car going seventy and watched it roll around in the dirt. I didn't look back. Moved here. And I didn't have any problems with the Burned Man appearing except when—"

"You talked to a woman. Or when one talked to you."

"Yes." It was more an exhale than a word. "He was there the day I met you. When I looked at you and immediately wanted you."

"And when you kissed me on the steps."

"So many other times. The lake, the bus, the hallway of my own damn house . . . Every time I lost sight of you—the second it became about me, about fucking and coming and taking what I'd been trained to take—he was there."

A wave of guilt washed over her and she tried to shove him away. "I'm sorry. I'm so sorry. Last night . . . what sex must have done to you."

"No, that's the thing." His arm around her back tightened. His eyes found hers and clamped on. His voice lightened and he actually sounded excited. "He wasn't there last night. I kicked him out of my bedroom and he stayed out. Because it was all for you; I made sure it was all for you. I was tested and I passed."

The words touched her deeply but still made her sad. "It wasn't all for me. I saw how much you loved it. Sex shouldn't be one-sided. It's give and take. And you did both last night."

"No. It can't be about me."

"Yes, it can. When I went down on you, you loved that. When I was on top, you should have seen your face. You're healing yourself, Xavier."

His brow furrowed deeply and she drew fingers across the lines. She gave him a smile.

"Do you think that maybe you're a little scared to live wholly in the human world? Do you think that your subconscious is clinging to the Burned Man because of that fear?"

"Ah, fuck. Don't say that. I don't want that to be true."

"Sex isn't about him anymore. You're moving on."

He was denying it, shaking his head, but she knew it to be true. She just had to get him to see it.

His hands slid up to her face and he cradled it like he had on the ice. "When I met you," he said, his eyes closing, "I told myself that I was just going to use you to help me get better, to be a normal Primary. To learn how to talk to a woman, nothing more."

"And now?"

"Now?" He slid his lips across her temple and let them hover over her ear. "I want to learn how to love you."

# TWENTY-ONE

**Just when she thought she'd won, that she'd broken through to** him, that her heart couldn't balloon any larger, Xavier sucked in a breath and pushed away. Torment veiled his eyes and the chill in the restaurant sliced between them. His anger was slowly starting to become hers.

"But you won't let yourself," she said, more bitterly than she'd intended, "because of what I am."

His wide shoulders bunched up. "You think I want you to be one of them? It's *killing* me, Cat."

"Just—"

With a slash of his arm, he spun away. "How did this get so turned around? I didn't want any of this to come out. This isn't about me."

A fist closed around her stomach, squeezed it tight. "What is it about then?"

He scrubbed his face with his hands then stabbed his fingers into his hair.

"Just say it, Xavier."

"Okay." He blew out a breath. "Other Secondaries have gone missing. Apparently some Ofarians from very near here. I came to get you tonight to warn you, to make sure you're safe." He was back to saying every word very precisely and very slowly.

"Missing?"

"Yeah." He shrugged. "I don't know what the other Secondaries are—maybe an air elemental, or a fire; she wasn't specific—just that they're gone."

"She?"

He toed a chair to make it perfectly flush with the table. "Gwen."

"Gwen." She flipped back through the story he'd just told her. "The Ofarian you kidnapped. The one who brought down her own people."

"Yeah. We haven't talked since I left California but we spoke tonight. She's the one who called during breakfast the other day, and then again this morning." He cleared his throat. "I told her about you."

"You told *her* before you told *me*."

"She convinced me to tell you."

Cat gasped. "You weren't going to say anything otherwise. Were you?"

"At first, no." He focused on a little pile of crumbs on the floor the cleaning crew had missed. "I was going to let you leave. Go back to Florida, where I wouldn't have had to face it, or you, ever again."

"Jesus, Xavier." The curse tasted sour.

"But then I realized how much I've hated being a coward all these years. And how much I want to see you safe, for you to have the life you deserve." Chin down, he lifted just his eyes to hers. "You're my enemy, Cat, and I—"

"I'm not your enemy!" The shout pinged all around the empty restaurant. She took a hard swallow and stepped closer. "You know that, right? Deep down, you know I'm not your enemy."

He drew his lips in so tightly they disappeared. She could tell by the glassiness of his eyes that he was just going to run right over that one.

"Gwen says you need to learn how to use your powers before it starts to affect your mind. She wants to teach you."

That explained a lot. The constant distraction. The shift in her art over time, how at first it had been rapturous and free-flowing, and lately, in the past year or two, it had grown more agitated, more frustrated. Like her.

She could only imagine, at this rate, what her art would look like in another year. Or two.

Or what would happen to her brain.

"She wants you to call her." He dug into the back pocket of

his jeans and pulled out a piece of paper. When he handed it to her, his hand shook so badly the paper rattled. And when she took the paper, she saw that it had been wadded up and flattened and wadded up and flattened several times.

"Okay, I will." He'd just handed her everything she'd always wanted. Why wasn't she happier?

They stared hard at one another.

"I'd been thinking," he began, then gave a little shake of his head, breaking eye contact. "I'd been hoping that you and I could . . . be together. Somehow. You made me hope. You made me believe."

"You say that like it's a bad thing."

"I can't afford that belief."

"But why?"

"Because the idea of us is more powerful than the reality. Now that I know what you are, I can't help it; I've put up this wall. I tell myself that you're different, that you're not really one of them. But if you call Gwen and she brings you into the Ofarian world, I don't know if I could handle that."

"That's not remotely fair. You have no idea what will happen. You're shutting everything down before it can even get started. What happened to wanting to heal?" She went right up to him, stood toe-to-toe, and tilted her face up to his. "What do you see, when you look at me now? No, don't close your eyes." She placed her palms on his chest. "Tell me what you see."

"I see you." His voice was hoarse. "I see confidence and joy. I see warmth and strength. I . . ."

She saw the moment the desire kicked in, shame chasing it right on its heels.

"Go on. It's okay."

He lifted a hand and touched one of the waves of her hair, tracing its swirl across her shoulder. When his palm slipped from the glittery fabric of her shirt to the skin on her arm, he released the smallest sigh.

"Do you think about sex with me?"

Now he closed his eyes. "All the time."

"That's not a bad thing. Stop telling yourself it is."

"Ask me to stop breathing. That might be easier."

She pressed closer, close enough the fabric of their clothes brushed together. "And what do you see? In your mind. Us together."

Him, standing there with his eyes closed, pale surfer hair framing the planes of his ethereally beautiful face, brought to mind a few seriously wonderful scenarios of her own. All of them included him letting down his guard.

"Because I see us like we were last night," she whispered, and he groaned. "Naked. Lovely. Intense. Now what do *you* see? Open your eyes and tell me."

His eyelids cracked open and the glimmer of his irises made her heart stutter. "I see your skin," he said. "Every part of it. And it's so soft and tastes so good."

For a second he looked like he was about to give in to panic and shutter himself away, but she couldn't let him. "More. Tell me more." *Touch me.*

His palms skimmed lightly across her shoulders and slid around the back of her neck. Holding her, claiming her. "I see all this hair. I . . . I see it spread across your back. I'm inside you from behind. I wrap your hair around my hand and I pull your head back. I see myself making your back arch."

The faint pulse between her legs exploded into a pounding rhythm. He'd made her wet with just words. And he wasn't done yet.

"I see myself going animal. I've kept it chained up with you, Cat. I've tried to be gentle with you, but since you asked, I see myself letting it out now. I want my mind to go blank of everything but you and how I feel inside you. I see my body taking over, just obliterating all the shit I've been carrying around for so long, and I'm free."

*Yes.* That's what she wanted to hear.

"And when you come around me," he growled, "I'll know you're free, too. That you're with me. That you're my cure."

Something shifted in his eyes and he flinched back. She gripped his biceps, held him steady. "He won't come for you again. If you do all that, if you let yourself go with me, the Burned Man won't come."

"You don't know that. You can't say that. This is the kind of shit he loves. I'd be inside you and he'd sit right over there"—he stabbed a finger at the back of the booth—"and grin and say awful things about you, knowing he'd won."

"Will you listen to yourself? He isn't real." She grabbed his shirt in her fist, held on tight. "It doesn't matter that you know what I am."

Something sparked in his silver eyes and she dared to believe it was hope. He gave a tight shake of his head. "Oh, man, Cat, it does—"

"I am not the Burned Man. But I'll be whatever you want me to be, if it will help you."

A half-crazed look seeped into his gaze.

"Do you hear what I'm telling you, Xavier? I. Am. Yours. Everything you told me you want, I want, too. I will love it, I promise you. And the Burned Man will not come."

"If you're wrong . . ."

"I'm not wrong. All right, I'm putting my money where my mouth is. If you fuck me the way you want to fuck me"—a fire raged across his expression, and it was a hot and wonderful vow that made her all warm and achy—"yeah, I said 'fuck,' and apparently you like it. If you fuck me and the Burned Man comes back, I will walk right out of here, call Gwen and never speak to you again. Because that's what you're saying you want."

In an unexpected move, he lowered his face to hers, cheek to cheek, warm voice curling around her ear. "And if I let myself go and he doesn't appear?"

She turned her head slightly, just enough to brush her lips across his. Just enough so he would know she was smiling wickedly. "Then you come back to my hotel room and sleep next to me. Naked. You'll be there in the morning when I call Gwen, when we tell her about us. And everything will be just fine."

She saw it then, the tremble in his lips, the faint furrow of his brow. That's what lust looked like, yes, but in that moment she knew he might love her, too. Which was absolutely fine, because she thought she might love him back. Out of all the crazy things they'd talked about that night, that just might have been the craziest.

He crushed her to him. His mouth came down on hers, his tongue pushing inside. His lips slanted, took, devoured. She'd thought the kiss on the wintery stairs had been hot, but that day he'd still been hiding behind fear and ghosts. Now he ripped them both to shreds.

He held her so tightly she could barely breathe. Stupid lungs, she didn't need them. All she wanted was this. Him. Unleashed.

Nothing existed between them anymore. Nothing but clothing that was starting to burn like acid.

She let him push her backward, his hands strong and commanding. Her butt struck the booth table so hard the water glasses tipped over. Somewhere in the back of her mind she heard one or two roll off and shatter on the floor, but the sound couldn't compete with the hard beat of her blood and the roar of desire in her ears.

"Say it again." He clenched the back of her neck in his big hand and nipped at her mouth.

"I'm yours." She shuddered. "In every way. I want what you want."

He kissed her hard, and the sting of pain was very, very good. His tongue met hers in determined pushes and sensual pulls. Then he leaned back, using the grip on her neck to yank her head to one side. He dove for her throat like a vampire and feasted on the sensitive skin there. The suction and the swirl of his mouth made her shiver so hard the table vibrated.

Then he stepped back, his expression fierce. "Take off your clothes. I want to watch this time."

She'd never stripped for a man. She kicked off her black pumps. He watched them skitter away, then his eyes trailed to where her fingers slowly lowered the zipper of her pants. Pushing the black fabric down her hips, she watched with severe satisfaction as his mouth dropped open at the sight of her black lace boy-style underwear.

"Leave those on," he ordered.

Taking the glittering gold top, she lifted it over her head and tossed it into the booth. The heat from his eyes and the chill of the restaurant mixed deliciously on all her exposed skin.

She fingered the black lace strap of her bra. "Leave this on, too?"

"Absolutely not."

As she slid it from her body, he attacked.

Warm breath covered her nipples before he took each one of them between his lips. Pulling. Licking. She bent backward, offering him more. Offering him everything.

His hands fell to her waist and he forcefully flipped her around. Through his jeans, his hard-on jutted against the crack of her butt. His hands smoothed down her belly and slipped over the black lace covering her hip bones, jerking her even tighter against his erection.

The long fingers of one hand slipped under the lace and easily slid over her slick flesh. He groaned, head dropping to her shoulder. He pushed two fingers inside her, filling her shockingly fast, then used his other hand to press on her shoulder. With a lovely shake of anticipation, she complied with his unspoken order, stretching forward across the table. The cold surface pebbled her skin. With a moan of regret, he removed his fingers from inside her, cupped both her elbows and raised her arms above her head. Shoving aside forks and spoons and rolled napkins, he curled her fingers over the table edge.

"Don't let go," he murmured, then took his time tracing her body with his hands and mouth. Down her arms and shoulders, her back, her hips and curves. She could do nothing but lay there, dying slowly under his touch.

She heard the gentle rasp of his jeans as he crouched behind her, then felt the soft, tender caress of a single finger as he nudged the lace of her underwear to one side. The hot kiss of his breath fluttered over her before his tongue found the best, wettest place.

"You don't have to . . . oh, *God*." But his tongue kept circling and flicking. "This is about . . . you. What . . . you want."

He removed his mouth but dragged a finger across her clit. "This *is* what I want. I want to hear you scream my name."

She was naked, stretched forward over a table, while he, fully clothed, worshipped her with his mouth. It didn't take much to make her comply. Every nerve stood at attention, completely dependent on him. Her whole body hummed, that hum spiraling and spiraling, becoming more and more centered on the movement of his mouth and tongue.

"Let me hear you," he said against her.

She came, bucking against him, and the sensation was all the more intense because she could barely move. His name escaped her lips in a tremulous cry.

He didn't ease her down this time. He just stopped, leaving her achingly empty and panting for more.

"Condom. In my purse. Front pocket."

"Prepared," he muttered as he rummaged where she said. And even though she couldn't see him, she could tell he was wearing one of those crooked half smiles that drove her out of her mind.

"Hopeful," she whispered back.

He came back to her and spread his body over hers, pressing her into the table. Even through his clothes she could feel him shaking. He pressed an apologetic kiss to the back of her neck. "It's going to be hard. It's going to be fast."

He said it like it was a warning, but her ears heard only a wonderful promise. He slid away, his mouth the last to leave her.

She turned her head. "Sometimes hard and fast can be very, very good."

A big hand slapped her thigh, just below her butt, and clenched, as though she might try to get away or something equally as ridiculous. The other hand started to roll on the condom.

She said, "Don't forget to pull my hair."

With a single motion, he entered her. Another cry—this one of relief, of such intense pleasure—ripped from her throat and bounced around the empty restaurant. Her body offered no resistance whatsoever.

He was nothing if not honest, and he took her hard.

She sensed the freedom in his body, in his movements. And even though he plunged into her with ferocity, his hands moved softly across her back, arranging her hair, like he'd said he wanted to see. Like last night, he barely made any sounds, but she listened to the thick pattern of his breath, and she realized that she wanted to hear him scream, too.

He slid in and out of her, so thick, so consuming, that her whole existence spun down into the small, slick place where their bodies joined. He felt impossibly good, and every second was better than the second before.

He started to slow down as his thumb worked across her back, gathering her long hair into his fist.

"*Yes*," she hissed.

Without warning, he tugged her hair, bringing her cheek off the table. She arched her back, and with a low groan of approval, he picked up speed, driving her with an emotional intensity she didn't have to see to feel. He was losing himself, and she loved it. Loved how his freedom set them both on the edge of something greater than just sex.

She loved proving him wrong. Proving that they were together in this.

His body loosened, his strokes inside her losing the driving rhythm. He was getting close; she remembered how the movement of his hips had changed when she'd ridden him last night.

"Now I want to hear you," she managed to say. "Please."

There was only the slightest pause. In it he released her hair, planted his hands on either side of her hips with a slap to the table, and fucked her, exactly like he said he would.

When another orgasm snuck up on her, and started to throw her into bliss, she bit her own tongue to keep from making a sound. Because behind her, he was shouting his release, and it was as dramatic and glorious as a symphony.

When it was done, he pulled out and took her waist. Flipping her over, she finally got a good look at him. She gazed into his beautiful silver eyes and found them clearer. Less unsure. Less afraid.

He picked her up, cradling her gently against his chest, his warmth enveloping her. She wrapped her legs around his hips, her arms tight around his neck, and buried her face in his tangled hair.

A vision came to her: a new painting, of swirling, pale colors dominated by bolder strokes. Water held by something strong and yet fluid. Possessive and yet yielding.

He squeezed her tight, drawing tender hands down her hair in slow strokes. She knew what he was going to say before it came out, but it made her eyes fill with tears nonetheless.

"He's gone, Cat. The Burned Man . . . oh, God. Thank you. Thank you so much."

# TWENTY-TWO

**The bathroom filled with thick steam. Michael drew the razor** around his jawline, swiping away the last bit of shaving cream. Putting the razor into the filled sink, he swished it around, watching the dirty water and white foam mix with the short black and silver whiskers.

Where had it gone wrong with Cat? A woman who breathed fire was caged in his garage, threatening war, and all he could think about was the one woman he wanted to introduce to Raymond as his.

She'd rejected him. In public. She'd taken all that he'd given her and thrown it in his face, walking off with that townie. So she liked nobodies, huh? Made sense, since she still technically was one.

He slapped down the sink plunger and watched the water swirl down the drain. Towel wrapped around his waist, he slid open the bathroom door and stalked into the master suite.

"Lea."

The master suite was a long room with a king-sized bed on one end, and a sitting room with a couch and TV on the other. Wooden posts carved like trees divided the two halves, and Lea leaned against one. She was smiling at his half-naked state, but it wasn't meant to be seductive. There was a coldness to her that appealed to him on occasion, when he wasn't looking for someone more—or someone like Cat.

He advanced on her. "Where the fuck have you been?"

She uncrossed her arms. "Nice to see you, too."

"Is Jase with you?"

She smoothed her shoulder-length blond hair back into a

ponytail. "And the new girl. The whole happy family's together again."

His arm snapped out, his fingers digging into her neck. He pushed her back against the post.

"Hello, Ofarian."

Her brown eyes narrowed and her upper lip twitched. Then she erased it all and donned an air of nonchalance. "Finally did your research, huh?"

"No. Your little fire gift told me. She seems to know a lot."

A million unsaid things danced across Lea's expression, and he vowed to learn every last one of them. Secrets weren't going to erase all the ground he'd gained with Raymond. Lea wasn't going to make a fool of him.

"Why didn't you tell me what you are?"

Lea shrugged. She had such an innocent look about her. Plain, straight hair. Wide-set eyes, very little makeup. Unassuming clothing. She didn't look frightening at all. "Because for all intents and purposes, I'm not Ofarian anymore."

"You led me to believe that Secondaries are rare."

She lifted an eyebrow. "Wow. Big word."

"The Chimeran told me. Yeah, she and I are tight now."

Lea sighed. "I've never lied to you, Michael. I stumbled upon you and Sean in Miami, told you I could find more people with magic, and you just assumed we were all like you. Special. Few and far between. But that's typical. For you."

"So why'd you take another water—another Ofarian?"

"Relax." She slid a hand around his wrist that still held her to the post. He was getting hard, because power did that to him. And because Lea had already proved herself worthy to him—unique and formidable and elevated to his level. "I'm not trying to *take* anything from you, Michael. I help you, you help me, is all."

"I wasn't aware I was ever helping you."

"Again, not my fault."

He removed his hand from her throat and dug his fingers into her shoulder. She winced. "Ow. What the—"

"The Chimeran said her people would come for her. That they'd bring an army."

Lea's face was blank. Dangerously blank. She didn't deny it, and suddenly clues fell into place.

"Little Lea." He slowly shook his head, *tsk*ing his tongue. "Are you trying to start a war?"

"You go about your business," she replied darkly. "I go about mine."

He squeezed harder. "I'm afraid I can't let you do that."

"Do what? Stop that. That hurts."

"Want me to go back to the throat? You know what I'm talking about. Going behind my back. Using the Chimeran—and maybe this second Ofarian—for something you're not telling me about. Don't give her to me as a gift then plan to snatch her out from under me. What's mine is mine."

"I'm not planning on taking her from you, asshole. You and I have different goals, and they don't cross each other."

"She's not leaving me." His voice quivered with fury.

"Don't worry about that."

"What about this army? I don't want any exposure. This is between me and Raymond."

"I told you, the Secondaries move and work in secret. Under the radar. You think her people are going to attack someone as visible as you?"

His hand dropped. "I don't know what to think."

"Just trust me. Have I ever done anything to compromise you?"

She had him by the balls and she knew it. He couldn't find Secondaries without her. And he'd never finally earn Raymond's respect without the collection.

She pushed away from him and sauntered toward the bedroom door. He watched her ass jiggle and she peeked over her shoulder to check if he was looking. She never flaunted herself if she meant to tell him no.

"Where do you think you're going?" He snapped off the towel. "I'm not done with you."

**Gwen Carroway sounded as receptive and intelligent on the** phone as Xavier had made her out to be. That told Cat a lot, that Xavier spoke so highly of her—an Ofarian and a woman, to boot.

To his credit, he'd taken his loss like a man. The Burned Man hadn't shown his face when Cat and Xavier had had sex in Shed, or here in her hotel room. Now she sat on the edge of the bed, his legs bracing the outside of her hips and thighs, his arms around her waist. As she held the phone to one ear, he kissed the opposite side of her neck.

"We're looking for your parents," Gwen told her. "We have to sort through a lot of messed-up info, but we'll find them. In the meantime, I want you to stay out in public as much as possible, just to be safe. Stay with people you know, people you trust."

"I'm with Xavier right now."

Gwen paused. "You can trust him, Cat. Above everything, I know that."

Xavier squeezed Cat's waist, shifting his mouth on her skin.

Gwen said, "I think you should go to San Francisco after you're done in Colorado. It's Ofarian HQ. Griffin Aames, our leader, is there. You can learn all about us, all about you. Immersion, if you will. You've already missed the Ice Rites, but maybe you could stick around for the summer Water Rites . . ."

Immersion. Ofarian HQ. Rites . . . That dizzying, sinking feeling of being overwhelmed rolled over her. "I don't know, Gwen."

Gwen sucked in a breath. "Sorry. Too much?"

"Maybe a tad? Guess I'd rather wade in than be thrown in."

"That makes sense. I'm just excited to have found you. That Xavier has found you, I mean." Cat didn't think she meant that solely in context to the threat against Secondaries. "What if you came to Chicago instead? It's just me and Reed here. I can teach you a few things."

Cat exhaled. "That sounds better."

"Xavier says you're an artist. I love art. Seriously love it. Remind me to tell you how Reed and I met. Oh, man, I could take you to the Art Institute . . ."

They talked for a bit longer and Cat grew more comfortable. As they said good-bye, Gwen said something in the Ofarian language. "That means, 'may the stars' blessings be upon you.' It's very formal, but I think it's fitting."

Though Gwen was lovely, Cat couldn't help but feel like she was shaking her arm again, trying to throw off the water bracelet.

She turned in Xavier's arms and kissed him. "You won't go to San Francisco with me."

He met her eyes. "No. I can't go back. I'm sorry."

"How about Chicago?"

She watched him weigh it in his mind: face one Ofarian or face many. Gwen versus the whole lot. "Yes," he replied. "If you come somewhere with me."

"Where?"

"Shed. While I work today. At least until your lunch with Helen, just so I know where you are."

So Cat sat at Shed's bar all morning, watching him work. The other cooks and servers eyed her. Then teased Xavier. He just smiled furtively at his cutting board.

Once, at the same time, they both looked over at the corner booth. They'd cleaned up their mess and re-set the tables so Pam would never know, but Cat could still picture what they'd done there. How he'd bent her over. And then how he'd given himself over.

Two other singles sat at the bar. A thirtysomething guy pecked at a laptop with one hand and nursed a glass of draft beer with the other. A petite blond woman occupied the seat at the far end of the bar, and she alternated between reading snippets of what Cat guessed was a movie script and flirting with the receptive bartender.

At one o'clock, Cat slid off her bar stool. She tapped the kitchen glass. Xavier looked up, and she mouthed, "I'm going." He frowned, scanning the restaurant with worry. He'd wanted her to cancel, but she'd insisted that she'd be with Helen all afternoon, in the middle of White Clover Creek, and that she'd come right back to Shed the moment the meetings were over. He nodded reluctantly, and she kissed her fingers and pressed them to the glass.

Helen waited in the alley outside, leaning against one of the potted yews, tapping at her phone. She'd arranged for a meeting with Jim Porter, an art dealer in L.A.

"Jim's a few minutes behind," Helen said as Cat greeted her. "We're meeting him at the restaurant."

"Okay." She glanced warily back at Shed.

Helen assessed her. "Everything all right?"

Cat threw on a smile. "Why wouldn't it be?"

"Last night? The way you left the party? I'm worried."

"No need to be. I'm fine."

"Cat, I feel awful. I had no idea things between you and Michael Ray had soured."

And just like that, like Helen speaking his name had conjured him out of thin air, Michael appeared at the mouth of the alley. The silver in his hair glinted especially bright in the winter sun. Cat held her breath, hoping he'd pass by, but instead he turned and made a beeline right for her. His eyes were carefully blank, his mouth drawn into a hard line.

"I'm so sorry," Helen said, her voice low. "I meant to tell you before he showed up. Jim insisted he come. They're old friends."

Or Michael had called Jim and slyly inserted himself into the lunch meeting.

Cat really wanted to hit it off with Jim Porter. Having him represent her in L.A. could catapult her career. She couldn't cancel on a guy who'd come specifically to Colorado to meet her. She drew herself up with a deep breath. "It's all right. This is business. If I can remember that, so can he."

Helen smiled, but it was clear she was torn between Cat and the former stepson she cared about.

"Good morning," Michael said as he reached them.

"Morning," Cat managed.

His presence buzzed around her brain, poisoning her consciousness. It brought to mind the day they'd met in the local art fair, how she'd felt this instant affinity for him—a trust that was more feeling than proof. Similar to what she'd felt toward Xavier that morning on the sidewalk. Similar . . . but mostly different.

Could Michael have Secondary ancestors, too?

The way he stared at her unnerved her. She felt like prey. He seemed to enjoy her discomfort, and remained that way the entire lunch.

Jim Porter was terribly elitist but well connected, and had encouraging things to say about her paintings. Jim wasn't a geyser of compliments like Helen, but assessing and critical. Art was business and status to him, and he seemed interested in what Cat had to offer. The lunch ended with his business card in her hand.

"White Clover Creek is one thing," Michael murmured in her ear as he helped her with her coat. "L.A. and New York are another. See what I can do for you?"

She carefully stepped away, shivering.

Outside the restaurant, a black Lincoln Town Car idled at the curb. Michael turned to Helen and Cat. "Given the direction of events over the past few days, I think the three of us would benefit from a quiet talk. Away from the crowds." He nodded at the car. "Why don't we head up to my house?"

Cat's first instinct was to decline—she'd promised Xavier she'd return to Shed—then she thought about her future. And her past. How Helen and Michael had launched her career, and how it would help them all to clear the air. They did have a lot to discuss. Gwen had told her to stay in public with people she knew, so that's what she'd do.

"All right," she said, and Michael smiled. "But how about the bar up at the ski resort? I hear the views are lovely." Michael peered at her for a moment, then nodded. Helen agreed, too.

Michael threw his coat in the front with the driver and took a seat in the back. Cat wedged in next to him, giving Helen an easier in and out since she'd seen the older woman favoring a hip on occasion. She peered at the driver. A young guy, nice looking but nowhere near the beauty of Xavier. He seemed really familiar, too. Gave off almost the same vibe as Michael, and she shifted uncomfortably on her seat.

They'd just pulled away from the curb and into traffic when Helen's phone beeped. She turned it on and gasped.

Michael leaned over. "Everything okay?"

"No, no. An emergency at the gallery. Water leakage in the basement storeroom." When Cat gave a little cry, Helen amended, "None of yours are down there. The ones not on exhibition are kept off-site. But I have to go. Driver, can you pull around to the Drift? Take a left on Begonia Street and drop me off at the corner."

The driver did as she asked, and Cat couldn't help but feel sorry for how distraught Helen looked. Helen jumped out at the corner of Begonia and Waterleaf, apologizing, and was swallowed up by the crowd on her way into her gallery. Left alone with Michael in the backseat of the car, Cat prepared to make her own excuse and ask the driver to circle around to the back of Shed on Groundcherry.

Michael turned to her. The leather seats gave a slow creak, echoing the sudden sinking feeling in her stomach. That tingling sensation of familiarity clicked up several notches in intensity, turning into something else entirely, freezing her in place.

"Cat," he said, calm as ever, "I'd like to introduce you to some people who are very special to me."

*What?*

He gestured to the Town Car driver, whose narrow-set blue eyes watched her in the rearview mirror. "That's Sean, my brother."

Cat couldn't say anything, couldn't move. Dread slammed into her.

The door on Cat's right opened and a strange woman slid onto the seat. No, not a stranger. The blonde from Shed, who'd been sitting at the bar with the script. The blonde who was now making Cat's mind buzz and her skin prickle.

*"You thought you recognized me,"* Xavier had said.

*"Yes."*

*"Because you did. In a way. Your kind . . . Ofarians . . . can sense other Secondaries, other magic-users."*

The blonde yanked the door shut. The Town Car pulled away from the curb. The doors locked as one, sounding like a gunshot. Secondaries surrounded her. This woman. Sean. And Michael.

Oh no. *No no no no no.*

"And this is Lea," Michael said, all casual. "Lea, this is Cat Heddig, the artist I was telling you about."

Lea's smile was positively chilling.

# TWENTY-THREE

**The front door of the Drift chimed open. Xavier shot off the**
metal folding chair he'd been sitting on at the back of the gallery and barreled down on Helen.

"Where is she? Have you seen her?"

Helen jumped, her half-unwound scarf dangling in her hand.
"What?"

"Cat," he barked, eighteen hours of fear packed into his
voice. "Tell me you've talked to her."

"Sorry, Helen." The curator's assistant hurried out of the
side office and over to them. "He came by last night after you'd
gone, and now he's been sitting in here all morning. Waiting
for you."

Xavier rounded on her. "If you'd given me her damn phone
number I wouldn't've had to."

"Do you want me to call the police?" the assistant asked
Helen.

Helen removed her coat, draped it over her arm. So slowly
it was pissing him off. "No, Alissa. I'll talk to him. Come."
She beckoned to the office.

"Christ, just fucking tell me you've seen her."

Helen spun and eyed him with disgust. "There's no need for
that language. I said I'll speak with you, but we'll do so in my
office."

He followed her in and she closed the door behind him.

"She had a late lunch with you yesterday," he said. "She was
supposed to come right back to Shed when she was done. She's
not answering my calls. The Margaret says she checked out
last night. I'm going out of my mind."

Helen licked her lips and pressed them together, taking a moment to ponder something inane on her desk. He knew very well how he was coming across: the stalker townie boyfriend. The jealous type who'd rough up another man in the middle of someone else's party and then steal the girl away.

He couldn't care less. He hadn't slept at all last night; instead, he'd scoured White Clover Creek. This morning he'd asked in every single shop and restaurant and bar.

Helen looked up. "She didn't tell you?"

"Tell me what?" he shouted.

Helen held up a hand and glared. "I'm sorry to be the one to say it, but she's gone home."

*"What?"*

Helen jumped again. Good. She was starting to understand. He was livid. He was scared shitless. And he wasn't leaving until he got answers.

"Apparently she had an emergency back home and left yesterday evening."

"No. *No.*" He shoved fingers into his hair and pulled so hard his scalp stung. "I don't believe that."

She sighed and dug into her purse for her cell phone. She tapped a few keys then turned it to face him. "This is what she sent me last night at around six thirty."

Helen, I'm sorry, but my landlord called and said there was a fire at my place. I'm flying home tonight. We'll talk soon about the show and the new deals. Thanks for everything.

Yep, that was her cell phone number, but there was no way Cat had sent that message.

Home, she'd typed. Cat had told him she'd never called the Keys home. And Xavier knew how she cherished her opportunity with Helen. She wouldn't just take off after sending a text message.

"That's not from her," he growled. "I know it isn't. What happened after you had lunch with her yesterday?"

She was actually considering not telling him. She squinted and glanced at the phone. The Primary police were just a quick call away, and he couldn't afford that.

"I got pulled away. I left her with Michael Ray."

*Michael.* Xavier fell forward, arms braced on her desk, staring her down. "And then?"

She crossed her thin arms, meeting him stare for stare. "And then I don't know. They dropped me off here; I got that text several hours later."

"No. Don't you see? She's not . . . she didn't just up and leave Colorado. Not without telling me."

Helen's expression softened. "Look." He despised the condescension in her voice. "Maybe whatever you thought you two had, she didn't feel the same way."

He knew exactly how Cat felt, but what the fuck was he supposed to say to Helen? That he was descended from goddamn aliens, and so was Cat? That she had all sorts of freaky water magic and that her kind were being hunted? That Helen never should have left her side yesterday?

"Michael," Xavier sneered.

"I know you two have had your differences, but he knows Cat isn't his. They've moved past that. I talked to him last night; he helped Cat get a last-minute flight out."

Xavier laughed in Helen's face. "Of course he did. Where's he staying?"

"I'm not telling you that."

He pushed off the desk and pressed the back of a hand to his mouth.

"Do I have to be the one to say it?" All sympathy left her eyes; all kindness departed her voice. "To Cat, it's over between you two. And from what I've seen from you today, and the other night at my house, that's a good thing."

"No." Xavier drove his boot into a plastic wastebasket by the door, cracking it and sending papers and leaking Starbucks cups spinning out onto the hardwood floor. "It's *not* over."

He stormed out. Stomped into the big room filled with Cat's paintings. The great, beautiful canvases filled with her Ofarian heritage. They surrounded him. Reached out to him. Cried out to him for help, in Cat's voice.

**Xavier cut his way down the sloping sidewalk, weaving around** slow walkers who, it seemed, had been deliberately placed right in his path. He shoved off the sidewalk and loped into the blockaded street, hoping to find a better passage there. Nope. Just as packed.

He was supposed to punch in at Shed in thirty minutes. He'd

never been so much as late in three years and now he couldn't give a shit if he never showed up again. He wasn't going anywhere without finding Cat.

She was still here in Colorado, hopefully still in White Clover Creek. He could feel it. Not in the way she could sense Secondary signatures, but in his gut. In his heart.

The music was pumping again around the square. Camera teams and circles of fans wound around the miner statue. None of the faces belonged to who he needed to find. He was tall but still not tall enough. He stalked toward a bench, launched himself up, and lifted his head high above the mob. A million and a half people swarmed the streets, all wearing basically the same thing. The noise made voices indistinguishable. Then . . . *there*.

Not just any random person, but the devil himself.

Across Waterleaf, Michael Ebrecht was exiting the Gold Rush Theater with a man who wore glasses. Michael was talking, the other man listening, frowning. Then the man nodded, gave Michael a wave, and walked away. Michael started across the street toward the Margaret, head dipped as he became mesmerized by his phone.

Xavier launched himself off the bench and shoved through the crowd, this time not caring who he offended or toppled over. Not even guilt would stop him now. He planted himself right in Michael's path.

"Where is she?"

Michael halted, looked up. When he saw it was Xavier blocking his way, he grinned. "Dumped you, did she?"

Xavier leaned down, got right in his face. "Where is she?"

"Haven't seen her." Smug satisfaction smeared over Michael's expression. He glanced casually at his phone, made a show of scrolling through something.

Xavier's hands began to twitch at his sides. He wanted his knives, but this time for something other than cooking. "Bullshit."

Michael dropped the phone into the pocket of his long coat. "Look, asshole. The last time I saw her was at Helen's party. When she left me for you. Maybe I should be asking you the same thing."

"You're lying."

"What the fuck's wrong with your eyes?" Michael was trying to laugh, but Xavier heard the fear behind it. And the wonder. And something else.

He bent even closer to Michael, let him see the sickly silver irises that were probably pulsing with magic and anger. Let him be *all* that Michael saw. "You had lunch with her yesterday."

Michael may have been an accomplished liar, but not even he could cover that one up. "Oh yeah. Forgot about that."

"Where is she?"

"I. Don't. Know."

Xavier lifted a fist. Michael did exactly as scripted, flinching away. But he recovered quickly, glancing knowingly around to remind Xavier they weren't alone, that a public assault would be on his head. Any other day Xavier wouldn't have cared, except today Cat needed him, and getting busted would only pull him farther away from her.

"You thought she'd become yours after a week?" Michael scoffed. "Even I wasn't that deluded. I've been working on her for two years."

"We've already gone over this. She's not anyone's."

*That* brought out the strangest reaction, one that made Xavier shiver. Michael got in Xavier's face now, his neck blotchy with rage. "Fuck you."

Then Michael shoved past Xavier, knocking his shoulder hard.

Xavier gave him a good lead, watched him hurry up to the pudgy valet standing in front of the Margaret's revolving doors. The valet ran around the side of the hotel to the parking garage. Three minutes later a Lincoln Town Car pulled into the Margaret's horseshoe drive. Michael slid behind the wheel, his face twisted into something possessive and angry, and the car turned away from the square.

Xavier slipped around to the side street lined with waiting cabs. He ran for the first cab in line, tapping it on the roof as he fell into the backseat.

"Follow that Town Car. And don't make it obvious."

The cabbie enthusiastically threw his sedan into drive, grinning like he was stunt driving for one of the movies being shown here in town.

Xavier perched himself in the middle of the backseat and stared out through the windshield at the Town Car up ahead.

*I'm coming for you, sweetheart.*

**The two vehicles swerved higher into the foothills, only one of** them visible.

The moment Xavier's cab pulled out of downtown White Clover Creek and away from other cars, he'd cloaked the entire vehicle in illusion. The cabbie had no clue; he just puttered away, whistling, following Michael's car as it climbed farther and farther away from homes and civilization.

A huge house appeared around a bend, nestled perfectly in a little valley and overlooking a ski run. The home was beautiful and desolate, and just ostentatious enough for someone like Michael. It made Xavier's blood run cold.

Michael sped his car into the long driveway and stopped with a spray of snow by the front door.

"Don't go in the drive. Stop right there, just outside the gate, on the curb." Xavier threw money at his cabdriver as the white sedan rolled to a stop. "Now get out of here as fast as you can." Because he could only hold an invisibility illusion a certain distance away from his body, and if Michael witnessed a taxi appearing on the road out of thin air, well, Xavier could kiss his advantage good-bye.

The cabbie looked at him funny, then shrugged and peeled off, back down the road toward town. Xavier stood on the curb, watching the taillights disappear, feeling the strain of the illusion pull and pull, like a rubber band stretching too thin and too hard.

The rubber band snapped. Magic slammed back into Xavier and he stumbled where he stood. There was very little power left in him and his energy quickly drained; the two went hand in hand. He had to get inside that house before he had none left.

He sprinted up the driveway, trying simultaneously to cover up his footprints in the thin dusting of snow. His vision was starting to turn fuzzy, his stomach a little nauseous. It took extra effort to move his legs, but there was Michael, just up ahead, starting up the rounded front steps to the house. Seeing that man worked like a checkered flag waving Xavier around the final turn.

He dug deeper. Ran harder.

The front door to the house opened. A young man stood with his hand on the knob, watching Michael approach with a grave expression.

"I don't like this," said the younger man, his voice carrying easily in the quiet mountains.

"I don't give a fuck," said Michael. Only not the Michael climbing the steps. It was another Michael. A Michael who was pushing past the younger man to exit the house.

Xavier skidded to a stop. Holy stars in hell. There were two. Twins? was his first thought. They looked exactly alike. Even wore the same clothes, parting their silvering hair in the exact same way. Then . . . *no.*

The Michael from the car hopped up onto the top step. The Michael from the house rushed to meet him. For a brief moment it looked like they were going to embrace like long-lost brothers, the momentum was that strong. Instead, the Michael from the house slammed into Car Michael, chest to chest. Hard. There was a pause, a glimmer, a shifting of images, like someone had taken two pictures of the men and overlapped them, then slid them together until they matched perfectly.

And then they were one man. One Michael Ebrecht.

Holy *fucking* stars in hell.

The singular Michael stood motionless for a moment, head bent, gathering himself. Then he shook it off and lifted his eyes to the young man who didn't look remotely surprised to see any of this.

The two men turned to go into the house. The door started to close on silent hinges. Xavier shook off his shock and surged forward, sprinting with everything he had, not able to maintain the footprint illusion and his speed at the same time. He bounded up the steps. The door was just wide enough for his body, but it was closing, closing. He shot through the opening, past the younger man—careful not to touch him—and into a brightly lit foyer done in white marble and darkly stained trim.

The younger man, his hand still on the doorknob, stiffened, his eyes shifting around wildly. "What was that?"

"What was what?" Michael wrenched off his coat and stretched to hang it on a tall, freestanding iron rack.

The other man shut the door with a click and turned the

dead bolt. He looked spooked. Good. "I felt something. Like wind. But not."

Michael rolled his eyes. "You're in the goddamn mountains. We have another problem—"

A blond woman came rushing into the foyer from down the hall. There wasn't anything threatening about her appearance except for the vicious point of her finger at the front door, the wildness in her eyes . . . and the words that came out of her mouth.

"Someone else came in, Sean," she cried. "Another Secondary. A *new* Secondary."

Who were these people? And Michael had an *Ofarian* with him?

With a giant breath, Xavier released his illusion. Visibility shimmered over him. "Yeah," he said, fists tight and ready, "that would be me."

The blonde's eyes widened. Her skin paled. Xavier didn't give Michael time to react.

"You mother*fucker*," Xavier snarled, whirling. His knuckles connected with that cocky prick's face.

Michael went down hard, but not before Xavier saw the complete shock in his eyes over having been done over by Xavier, the poor townie. He lifted a boot, ignoring the weakness in his muscles, and pressed it into Michael's wheezing chest.

"Where. Is. She."

Even if Michael had answered, Xavier didn't hear. Because one second he was prepping to crush Michael's ribs under his foot, and the next the floor had swept up to crash against his head.

Xavier rolled over. A jet breaking the sound barrier exploded through his brain. His vision was winking out. Before it completely disappeared, however, he was pretty sure he saw Sean standing over him, that big metal coat rack clutched in both hands.

# TWENTY-FOUR

**Xavier came to. Searing pain pounded against the left side of** his skull. He'd been moved. The right side of his face pressed into a cold, rough slab of concrete. The daylight from the foyer was gone, replaced by the bluish tinge and incessant hum of a fluorescent light.

"Michael," a strange man's voice called, distant and throbbing. "He's waking up."

With a groan, Xavier rolled onto his back. Michael appeared in a stairwell. His fuzzy form crossed the floor toward Xavier then crouched five feet away. A giant purple shiner blossomed across his cheek and expanded the skin around his eye.

Xavier grinned. "You look good."

Michael bared his teeth. "Hell of a punch. Didn't think you had it in you."

"Oh, I have a lot more in me."

"Yeah," Michael murmured, assessing Xavier's prone body. "You do have more in you. Don't you."

Xavier seized the unexpected moment, those few precious seconds as Michael let down his guard. He shoved aside pain and harnessed his own fear and anger. In one motion he swept to his feet, intending to take Michael down to the concrete and finish him. Michael's body position was weak and Xavier owned the power advantage. Roaring, he surged forward, arms cocked back and ready to thrown Michael down.

He struck a wall instead.

An invisible wall. A wall that pushed back with a force ten times his own. A moving wall that abraded his face. He tumbled backward, striking the concrete hard, needles of pain shooting up his spine. Sprawled on his ass, he shook his head.

"What the—" Xavier snapped to his feet, his brain feeling like it was sloshing around in his skull, and attacked again.

The invisible wall thrashed him, a whiplike surge of energy that tossed him backward. Again. And again.

Through it all, Michael just stood there, arms folded. His smirk showed no fear. "You doing okay, Jase?" He looked lazily over Xavier's shoulder, to the far corner. Dazed, Xavier turned.

A strange man sat on the edge of a blue-and-white-striped lawn chair. Elbows on knees, hands clasped between his legs, the one called Jase leaned forward. His light eyes focused intently on Xavier.

"Yep. Good to go," Jase said. "Going to have to sleep sometime though." He slowly rose from the chair and ran a hand through the shaggy brown hair that curled around his face and neck. He looked, at best, bored. At worst, even cockier than Michael.

Michael waved an impatient hand as if to say *yeah, yeah*.

Xavier made a show of struggling to come up on one elbow, then pushed to his hands and knees. Seemed to him that Michael was expecting attacks on him, so Xavier took a deep breath, changed course, and lunged for Jase instead.

That wall shot out, a thousand needles scraping across his body. The hardest surge yet. Xavier landed badly on his elbow. He rolled to his side, trying to hide the wince, and stared at Jase, who saluted Xavier with a tip of an imaginary cowboy hat.

Holy shit, Jase was an air elemental. Just like Gwen had described.

"Lea's on it," Michael told Jase, with a vague wave toward Xavier. "We just need to keep him contained until she gets what she needs."

"Is Cat all right?" The pain in Xavier's elbow bloomed, but he didn't cradle it, didn't show weakness.

The door at the top of the stairs opened and down came the little blond Ofarian woman from the foyer. Lea, he presumed.

What the hell was Michael—who was some form of Secondary perhaps not even Gwen knew about—doing with an Ofarian and an air elemental? Or maybe the better question was: what were they doing with *him*?

Lea slowed when she saw Xavier sprawled on the ground. She went to Michael's side, her head tilted as she raked a haughty, hate-filled look over Xavier. He knew that look all too well.

An Ofarian looking down on a captive Tedran.

Years of thinking he wandered alone in the Primary world—and that the Ofarians, the only other known Secondaries, had been relegated to the west coast—and here Xavier was, trapped in some sort of wind cage in a basement room entirely filled by Secondaries.

"Cat," Xavier snarled. "Is she okay?"

No need to ask if they actually had her. Michael's smug look said as much.

Michael ignored him and turned to Lea. "Did you get what you need?"

"Not yet. What I really need is on its way, being sent by courier. Should be here tomorrow. I have these for now." She reached into her back pocket and pulled out a pair of ordinary handcuffs.

The sight of the plain metal rings made Xavier smile. Just let them try to get close. Michael's busted face was evidence of what his fists could do. He could easily take Lea. Jase looked like he might be a bit of a challenge, but if he was anything like other Secondaries, there was a limit to his magic, and it had to run out sometime.

Xavier heard someone moving around upstairs; his guess was Sean, the kid with the killer swing. When he peered up the steps, he saw that Lea had left the door open. Beyond, he could see the corner of an outside window, gone dark with night. If he could wrap himself in invisibility glamour and sprint out of this basement before they slapped those handcuffs on him, he could lose himself outside in the dark.

It was a big gamble. He'd used a lot of magic getting up to the house and he could feel that the glamour in his system was almost depleted. He'd need a good long rest and food to replenish it to full capacity, but what he had left could be enough. It *had* to be. This was his chance.

Closing his eyes, he opened every available portal to his magic. He commanded his source to yawn wide, to give him all it had. He dug into the pockets of illusion, scraping out the kernels of glamour that clung to the sides. He cobbled them together, a hasty and ugly batch of magic, but it was still usable. He whispered Tedran words, felt them doing their thing.

Michael and Lea started to laugh. To *laugh*.

Xavier forced his eyes open.

Jase's lips weren't moving. He wasn't laughing. Wasn't even smiling. But the basement room seemed dimmer now, as though someone had shaken out a dusty sheet in an old house and the air was now clogged with months of neglect. Xavier waved an invisible arm, the air swirling in its wake. Dust motes clung to the edges of his invisible arms, perfectly delineating the placement of his body.

"Nice try," Michael said.

Xavier collapsed. His glamour died, flickering and fading as the last of the wick burned out. He couldn't hold himself upright any longer, and his head felt so very heavy on his neck.

"Cat," he croaked out. "If you fucking touch her . . ."

"Knock him out," Michael told Jase. "I don't want to hit him again. Damaging the goods and all. I have a phone call to make when he gets his strength back. Raymond'll shit his pants over this one."

Jase turned to Xavier without hesitation. The wind kicked up. Suddenly the air in the room came up short. Xavier scrabbled for it, trying to take deep gulps of what wasn't there. He clawed at his throat but the other three people were unaffected. Black spots floated in front of his eyes, growing bigger, stealing his sight. Jase whipped away the last bit of oxygen and Xavier blacked out.

**The next time he woke, he was stretched on a stiff, splintered** slab of particleboard, wrists locked above his head in the handcuffs, ankles fastened with plastic strapping. All limbs attached to long, heavy chunks of metal in the board that weren't going anywhere. The pain from the earlier blow to his head had lessened some, but his magic was still gone. Not that it would've done him any good at that point. Because really, what good were illusions? Useless fucking bit of magic.

Not for the first time, he wished Tedrans had something like *nelicoda*, the chemical that erased Ofarian water magic. If he could, he'd permanently delete what made him different.

Give Michael no reason to want him. Get the hell out of there and take Cat with him.

He did have a bit of an advantage. If Xavier was right, Michael hadn't been hunting him or Cat. Michael had only recently learned about her powers—from Lea, surely—and Xavier had stupidly revealed himself. Michael was unprepared.

"You're awake." There, on the lawn chair again, reclined Jase, the faux cowboy, flipping through a magazine. He pulled a phone out of his pocket, typed something, then set it back down and picked up the magazine again.

"Who are you?" Xavier's throat ached. Jase didn't answer. "What does Michael want with Cat? With me? Who's Raymond?"

Cowboy's eyes flicked up to Xavier then back down to the page. He looked to be about Xavier's Earth age, late twenties/early thirties, and he'd mastered the art of nonchalance.

Xavier tried another angle. "Why are you working for him?"

That got a much longer look. Interesting.

The basement door opened. One set of footsteps descended. Xavier prepared himself to face Michael, but it was Lea who sauntered to the edge of the particleboard rack. He looked to Jase, who'd very nearly come to attention at the appearance of the little Ofarian. Jase, who hadn't called Michael after Xavier woke up, but Lea.

Interesting times two.

"Where's Cat?" Xavier asked Lea. A broken record, but he didn't care. He'd ask every minute until he got an answer.

Lea shrugged and ran a finger down the board. "Upstairs. In Michael's bedroom."

Xavier thrashed, the board rocking on the cinder blocks that lifted it off the floor. His whole body burned with a rage that made muscle and bone want to pop out from his body.

Then he caught the way Lea was looking at him, and an icy chill shivered across his skin. He had to close his eyes against it, to not see that Ofarian staring down at him, her eyes roving over his body like so many others' had before her. It made him feel dirty. Tainted. Used.

"So you're Tedran," she murmured, half to herself. She touched his knee and he flinched, despite his resolve to not react. "Which means you must be *that* Tedran. The one who escaped and freed your people. The one the Board was most upset to have lost."

Her hand left his leg. He opened his eyes. She leaned over him now, staring into his face. If he had any sort of moisture in his mouth, he'd spit at her.

More footsteps on the stairs, these Xavier recognized as Michael's. The guy who could split himself in two stalked over, hands in the pockets of his tailored black pants. He wore a pale gray button-down shirt still carefully buttoned at the wrists, his blue tie knotted neatly.

"What the hell do you *want*?" Xavier demanded.

Michael pursed his lips and rubbed his nose with his thumb.

"You can't just take people off the streets and expect them to not be missed. After this week, with all those people you introduced to Cat—Helen and everyone else who shook her hand and bought her damn paintings—you expect them to believe she just up and disappeared? You fucked up, Michael."

Michael knew it, too, with the way his jaw worked and the crazed look in his eyes. Taking Cat had been 100 percent emotional and impetuous.

"I told Helen I suspected foul play," Xavier said. "I told her I thought you were involved."

"I'm not worried about her." Michael went to the end of the board and looked down at Xavier's bound legs. "And now you've disappeared, too. Isn't that going to seem like quite the coincidence, considering how an entire party saw you attack me and rip her away?"

"You've taken others, haven't you? Other elementals, other Secondaries. Why?"

"I have my reasons." Michael slid a look at Lea, who wasn't affected at all. She continued to focus narrowed eyes at Xavier.

"Cat's part of my collection now," Michael added. "I found her. I made her. And now she's perfect and worthy because I know she has magic. Raymond will love her. He'll love *me*."

"You sick fuck. You don't need her." Xavier rattled the handcuffs. "Whatever petty revenge or twisted fantasies you want to play out with Cat, just don't, okay? Please. I'm the one who took her from you. Take it out on me."

"I plan to," Michael said.

"She *just* found out what she is. She knows nothing about

the Secondary world. She's completely innocent and you'll destroy her. She's lost in all this and you're stealing her entire life. That has to hit you on some level. You've got to understand that. Please don't do this to her." Xavier didn't care how the panic was making him sound. He wasn't too proud to beg, not when it came to Cat.

"How'd you know she was Ofarian?" Lea asked.

"Wasn't hard to figure out." That was all he was going to give them. He had to think fast. "Look, you say you have a collection." He nodded at Jase. "An air elemental, a couple of waters from what I understand. Maybe another Secondary or two. But what you don't have is me."

Michael laughed. He grabbed Xavier's cuffs, gave them a good shake. "Could've fooled me."

"Yeah, but I'll fight you. Any chance I get, I'll revolt." He licked his lips. "*If* you keep Cat, that is."

Michael squinted. "What do you mean?"

"You heard me. Let Cat go and I'll stay with you and whatever fucked-up circus you've got going on here. I won't make a sound. Won't say no to a thing. I'll be like Cowboy over there, all 'yes, sir' and 'no, sir.' I'll do whatever you say, stand in front of whoever you want me to, as long as Cat has her life and her freedom."

He hadn't thought of the bargain before it came to his lips. The words just fell out.

Five years ago he swore he'd never belong to anyone ever again. Now here he was, offering himself back in chains. His life was nothing. Cat's was just starting.

Lea made a sound of approval. Michael still didn't seem convinced.

"Ask her." Xavier nudged his chin toward Lea. "Ask her what I am. How many of my kind there are in the world."

"He's Tedran," Lea said, her voice breathy.

Hands on hips, Michael bent toward her. "Is that supposed to mean something?"

"It means"—her eyes never left Xavier's face—"that he's the last one left on Earth. He's one of a kind, Michael."

"How valuable is that?" Xavier pulled against the restraints. "Who's worth more to you? Me, who has something no one else has? Or Cat, who doesn't deserve any of this?"

Lea and Michael exchanged a look, then she took his arm and pulled him to the other end of the room, out of earshot. She talked at him for several minutes, her gestures minimal but her eye contact severe. Every now and then she glanced over at Xavier and it made him feel oily.

He didn't want to know what they were planning. In the Plant, it was better when he hadn't known what they were going to do to him. The anticipation only made it worse.

At last Michael's head snapped up, a frightening clarity smoothing his features. He moved Lea aside and stomped toward Xavier. "Who's going to miss you?" he demanded. "And don't fucking lie to me or Cat is mine."

*Yes.* This was going to work. Michael was a selfish enough bastard to want Xavier over Cat. He'd let her go. She wouldn't go to the Primary police because she'd be afraid to endanger Xavier and all the other Secondaries. Michael would be banking on that. But she knew how to get a hold of Gwen—and neither Michael nor Lea had any clue she and Gwen had already spoken. Gwen and Griffin would protect her.

Gwen and Griffin would then come for Michael and Lea.

"If I did this," Michael nearly shouted, "if I exchanged you for Cat, who would know you'd be missing? What would we have to do to clean up behind you?"

Xavier exhaled. He was doing this: willingly surrendering his freedom. And he'd do this and more if it meant Cat's safety.

"Just Pam. At the restaurant." He purposely left out Gwen, but the admission still left him empty. One person in the whole world who'd actually miss him? Pathetic.

Michael bent close to Xavier's face. "You'll call Pam. Tell her you went after Cat to Florida. Would she believe that?"

Xavier closed his eyes. "Yes. Yes, she'd believe that."

So would Helen. It was the perfect excuse for him leaving town. The obsessed new boyfriend with a history of reclusiveness. The one who'd threatened to beat up Cat's mentor. The one who staked out the gallery and then kicked the crap out of Helen's wastebasket. Abso-fucking-lutely perfect.

Michael planted his fists on the particleboard. "You stay confined until we pick up shop and move back to L.A. You do what I say, when I say it. You don't touch me or threaten me or say one word to me unless I talk to you first, or I send Lea after

Cat. She's really, really good at finding people. Even better at getting them to do what she wants. Got it?"

He looked to Lea, who nodded with a smirk. She'd taken at least two other Ofarians from their communities and done God knows what to deliver Jase into Michael's twisted employ. Menace burned under that innocent facade. It reminded him of someone else from a long time ago: Nora, the old Tedran woman who'd broken him out of the Plant and then twisted his naiveté into blind trust. She'd been the most cunning person he'd ever met. Until Lea.

Michael got even closer, his hot breath whispering over Xavier's face. Taunting him, telling him that he could get as close as he wanted and Xavier couldn't do a damn thing to hurt him. "Do we have a deal?"

Captive again. A great shudder coursed through Xavier's body. Let Michael see it. Let Lea see it. Let Jase see it. He rolled his head toward the stairs.

There, sitting on the third step from the bottom, was the Burned Man. He was grinning in his own horrible way, his scarred face contorting. He lifted his hands—one unmarred, one covered in melted, webbed skin—and he applauded.

"Yes," Xavier whispered. "We have a deal."

# TWENTY-FIVE

**When the younger guy named Sean removed Cat from the** bedroom she'd been locked in for the past two days, she knew things were about to get much, much worse.

Sean pulled her into a huge bedroom that was larger than Xavier's house. She fought him, kicking and screaming and biting, but he got the ropes around her wrists and tied her to one of the giant posts in the middle of the room carved to look like pine trees. The finely sculpted boughs dug into her skin, making new bruises.

The smell of old fire was less in this room, but still present. Sean wrapped a red handkerchief around her face, gagging her. As he tied it behind her head, she noticed him shaking. He even softly apologized when the knot tugged at her hair. Then he stalked out, leaving her alone in Michael's bedroom.

His cologne clung to the air. When she craned her neck to the left, she could get a peek of familiar suits and shirts hanging in the closet.

Michael was a Secondary. This was his room and his house and he had kidnapped her.

Oh, God.

The ropes made it all finally sink in. Sean had been bringing her food and water and clothing for two days, but she'd been able to move about freely in that cell of a bedroom down the hall. Michael had visited her once. He and that Ofarian woman, Lea, who'd apparently sniffed Cat out that morning at Shed.

Lea had said nothing during that brief visit, but Cat had seen the gears in her brain churning. Dangerous, that one.

No matter how much Cat had screamed at Michael, he

refused to say what he wanted with her, why he'd taken her. He'd just stood there, watching her like she was meat and he hadn't hunted in weeks.

"You're perfect now," he'd told her. "He's going to love you. And you'll always be safe with me. Always."

She couldn't cry anymore. Two days alone had dried her all out, and tears wouldn't get her anywhere anyway.

Closing her eyes, she ground her cheek into the tree post. She'd done exactly as Xavier and Gwen had suggested—only trusting people she knew, always staying in public—and she'd still been taken. Of all the people in the world, Michael Ebrecht and his bloodhound Lea were the ones who'd been kidnapping Secondaries. And the worst part? Cat had all this magic inside her and no idea how to use it. No clue how to get herself free.

Xavier . . . he must have been out of his mind by then. He would've called Gwen. They'd be searching for her. Yes. Cat had to believe that. And Helen . . . her current show artist couldn't just up and disappear without her noticing. Maybe she'd have called the police. Maybe the Primaries had gotten involved.

Then Cat remembered Lea had taken her purse and phone. Who knows what the other woman might have done with them, what sort of lies she'd spun?

The bedroom door opened behind her. Someone was walking across the carpet. Cat tried to nudge herself around the post to see, but the ropes wouldn't let her. Her Ofarian sense was pinging all over the place, but that was nothing new. This whole house was filled with Secondaries.

*Not Michael*, she prayed. *Please don't let it be Michael.*

The person stopped just behind Cat, out of her peripheral vision.

"I bet now you wish you didn't know what you are." Lea. She came around the post and crouched. She pulled the gag out of Cat's mouth.

"Did you sense my signature when I came in?" Lea smiled out of one corner of her mouth and there was absolutely no happiness behind it.

"Yes."

"But you couldn't tell it was me. Jeez, you really are a virgin."

"Teach me how to tell them apart." Cat strained against the ropes. "Get me out of here and teach me."

Lea laughed softly. "Can you sense the others?"

Sense wasn't a good enough word. More like her whole brain had gone topsy-turvy. When it had been one Secondary—like Michael that day she met him in the art fair, or Xavier that morning by the street performer—the signatures had come across as familiarity. A weird feeling of kinship that had steered her wrongly.

"Sort of," Cat said. "They're really faint. Five, maybe six others. One of them"—she cocked her head toward where she remembered the garage being—"is pretty scary."

Lea made a grunting sound of assent.

"Did Michael purposely send you after me?"

"No. He told me to watch you. Keep tabs on you. At the time, he didn't know what you are. Neither did I, until I walked right past you in that restaurant. Sometimes when a lot of Primaries are around the signatures get muddled. In a crowd, you have to be pretty close."

This was surreal, Lea talking to her so casually.

"Anyway," Lea said, "I texted Michael and told him what I'd found out about you. He was shocked, to say the least, but really, really happy. He immediately told me you'd be our newest acquisition. So I took a little detour to Drift, posed as Michael's assistant and got access to the vaults, tweaked some pipes, and left Helen's assistant to find the damage and call Helen back to the gallery."

"But *why*?" Cat pleaded. "What does he want with me?"

Lea cocked her head. "I think you can figure that out. Michael likes to own things he thinks are special." Then she rolled her eyes. "He's got other reasons, but even *I* don't quite understand them."

"He's crazy," Cat whispered. "He can't own people."

Lea chuckled. "Some people might argue that most driven, successful, narcissistic people are crazy. Even if he'd never found out about you, he would've pursued you in the Primary way. But once he found out you're one of us—"

Cat gasped. "He's Ofarian, too?"

"No. He's something else. If there's a proper name for his kind, it's been lost."

"And you're helping him?"

"Who's helping whom exactly? Little Cat, little Cat. He and I are helping each other."

She wondered if Michael knew that, because he wasn't the type of guy to let others rise above him. The fact that she gave no more explanation, and looked at Cat with that wide-eyed, faux-innocent face, made Cat shudder.

"You've taken other Ofarians," Cat said, turning her face toward the hall door, trying to pick out their signatures in the house.

Lea nodded with false pride. "Very good. So you're starting to be able to differentiate them."

Cat dug into her memory, trying to recall all that Xavier had told her in Shed when he'd revealed the world of the Secondaries. He'd mentioned others—other elementals, specifically. She closed her eyes, concentrated on the whisper of sensation across her body and the different kinds of twinges in her brain. "Is there an . . . air elemental? Maybe a fire?"

That condescending look of satisfaction melted off Lea's face. "Quick learner."

"Are they all working with you?"

Lea paused. "The fire is a little temperamental."

"Wants to burn you alive, huh? I know the feeling." Cat didn't look away from Lea's scorching look. Lea seemed to respond to being goaded, so Cat started to poke around. "So how in the world did *you* capture someone like that?"

"Not much can overpower water, you little bitch," Lea hissed. "If there's one thing you need to know about us, it's that."

Bingo.

"Ah. So that's why you took the other Ofarians first. To collar a fire elemental?"

Lea stood up, looking down her nose at Cat on the carpet. She examined Cat like she was a lamb going to slaughter, and Cat feared she'd just poked the wrong person.

"Among other reasons," Lea said, that smirk reappearing. She turned away, heading for the bed.

"You're kidnapping your own people."

Lea whirled back around, snatched Cat's chin in her hand and wrenched it up at a sharp angle. "They are *not* my people."

Her nails dug in. "Whatever delusions you have about beautiful Ofarian people joining hands and singing sappy songs worshipping water are so *wrong*. They are not good people. They don't care about any Ofarian unless they follow every one of their twisted rules exactly to the letter. It's fascism, Cat. They control everything about you, and when you want to follow your heart, they rip it out, stomp on it, then abandon you."

"What the—I don't understand."

Lea shoved Cat away, the back of her head striking a particularly sharp carved tree branch. Lea went to the dresser, where Michael had a neatly folded tie and a bottle of that awful cologne. Lea brushed her fingers over the tie. She took several deep breaths, each one more calm than the next, then turned back around. Leaning against the dresser, legs crossed at the ankles and arms folded at her waist, she said, "Let me tell you a story, Cat. It's an oldie but a goodie.

"Once upon a time there was an obedient little Ofarian girl who did everything her daddy told her to. She said what he wanted her to say, she went where he wanted her to go. And as she got older, she always believed she'd marry who he wanted her to marry. Because that's how the Ofarians worked, you know."

Wait . . . what? Arranged marriages?

"Only when the betrothal announcement came, this girl had already fallen in love with someone else. And he wasn't Ofarian. She gave in to the Allure—the itch to fool around with Primaries before you give yourself entirely to the Ofarian world. She thought it was going to be a one-night thing, as most Ofarians do, but there was something there. Something powerful and wonderful and stronger than anything she'd ever find with an Ofarian man. So when the time came for her to marry and her daddy marched in an Ofarian man she'd only met briefly once or twice before, she refused. She told her daddy she'd fallen in love with a Primary and that she was going to marry him instead."

Cat didn't move. The hardened, calculating Lea had suddenly become this desolate woman with tears shimmering in her eyes.

"You know what happened next?" Those glassy eyes focused on the carpet somewhere near Cat's feet. "Her daddy made her choose: the Ofarians, or the love of her life. She chose love. And her daddy had his big bad soldiers grab her, inject her with about five needles of this potion that completely erased her water magic and said, 'Bye, then. You made your choice. You're never welcome back.'

"So she left with her love. Married him. Never thought twice about the backstabbing dad and sister who claimed to love her then threw her away when she longed for their support. Until she got pregnant and had a beautiful baby girl, and there was no one in the world she wanted to share it with other than her older sister. But her sister was rising in the ranks of the Ofarian Board, being groomed for the next Chairman's seat, and the banished girl was forbidden from making contact. So she tried to forget about them and lived her life. Until everything was stolen from her. Again."

Cat couldn't remember the last time she'd blinked or breathed. *These* were the people she wanted to belong to? Suddenly Xavier's terror—his reaction to her heritage—made sense. If the Ofarians could do that to their own people—their own daughters—imagine what they could do to a race they held enslaved.

Lea swiped at her tears with the back of her hand and looked down at the wet streaks in disgust.

"My husband and child died in a dumb car accident. Not because of anything I did, not because magic went awry or some terrible alien force took them out. He was taking my baby to the grocery store and a distracted moving van driver slammed into them. I had no one to go to. No family to hold me. No one of blood left to comfort me. No one!"

Oh, God.

"When did this happen?"

"Six years ago."

So much conflicting information. Cat had no idea which way was up. And she couldn't let on that she knew anything about the Ofarians at all, how Xavier and Gwen had claimed the whole system had changed. "That's a long time, six years, to go without family. Couldn't you try again?"

Lea laughed through her tears and it was nasty and devious. "Nothing will change with them. Ever."

"How do you know that, if you've been gone so long? How

do you know your sister isn't sick with worry? Maybe she's tried to contact you."

"She hasn't. She couldn't even say his name when I told her about him. Neither could my dad. It was John, by the way. My John. But Gwen's all high and mighty now. She's *part* of what's leading them. She was the one who brought the old Board down and then built everything back up in the way she wanted. If she's my daddy's daughter, then nothing has changed, no matter what she says."

Whoa. Gwen was Lea's sister?

Something wasn't right. Either Lea had Gwen pegged wrong, or Xavier had been tricked into believing something about Gwen and the Ofarians that wasn't true. He'd told Cat that Gwen was one of the most honorable people he'd met, and that she'd changed her people for the better. The thing was, Xavier wasn't easily tricked into anything. He was cautious with a capital *C*. He hadn't *wanted* to trust Gwen, but some part of him did.

"Wouldn't matter anyway." Lea pushed away from the dresser, and the cologne bottle rocked and tipped over. "I made myself disappear. Changed my name. If she and my daddy couldn't be there for me when I needed them the most, I wasn't going to turn around with open arms whenever they decided it was okay to talk to me. It doesn't work that way. I've picked my side and, like them, I'm sticking to it."

Lea was dry-eyed now, that cunning, hard look settling like ice crystals over her features. She was doing this—helping Michael take Secondaries, particularly Ofarians—for revenge. And that scared Cat most of all.

"It makes me happy," Lea said, "to see Ofarians not in control. I like to see them scurry about, all confused. I want to see them used, in the way I was used all those years ago, when I was young and trusting, and was made an example of the consequences of disobedience and punishment for the entire Ofarian world."

Cat rubbed her cheek on her shoulder. All of this was so foreign, so out of her league. But there were general truths and emotions behind it all, reasons that defied Primary or Secondary definitions. "There's an easier way. Go to Gwen and talk to her. Chances are she's changed as much as you have. You're sisters. She talks, you talk. She listens, you listen."

"Says the newbie," Lea spit. "I can't wait until you're out of here and you can see what they're like for yourself."

Cat gasped. "You're letting me go?"

Lea rolled her eyes and sighed dramatically. "Technically, Michael doesn't need you. He already has two Ofarians in his collection. He wants you, but he doesn't need you. Plus"— she glanced at the hallway door—"he has something better now."

Cat's gut roiled. Her voice bottomed out. "What do you mean." Then, suddenly, she knew. "Oh, God. Xavier."

Lea sauntered back to stand over Cat again. "He came for you, you know."

Cat couldn't catch her breath. Xavier had come for her. Where was he? Was Gwen far behind?

"He made a trade." Lea examined her fingernails. "You for him. So Michael agreed to let you go and Xavier's now bound to him."

Oh no no no. If he'd done that, the action had been borne of passion, out of impulse. Chances were he'd gone hunting for Cat without contacting Gwen. He was alone.

Xavier was strong and would survive whatever it was Michael wanted him for, but kneeling at an Ofarian's feet again, cowering under Lea's whip . . . Cat feared it might destroy him, piece by piece.

And he'd done it for her. Stupid, brave, selfless man who'd already suffered enough for a generation.

Wait. Maybe this was exactly what Xavier wanted. Maybe he had a plan after all. If Michael was letting her go free, the solution was simple. All she had to do was contact Gwen and the Ofarians. Tell them everything. Lea had no idea Cat knew Gwen, or that they'd spoken. Lea and Michael would assume she wouldn't know where to go, and that she'd never alert the Primary police. But she'd bring the Ofarians back here—or to L.A. or Miami or wherever Michael would be. They'd save Xavier. Break apart Michael's sick "collection."

And Lea would be in her people's custody, at their mercy, again.

"Where is he?" Cat demanded, because she couldn't give away her cards. "In this house?"

"He's kind of sexy, your loverboy."

Cat took that as a yes. A yes that enflamed hatred.

"You know that's what he was made for, right? To fuck women? I know which Tedran he was, too, when he was in the Plant. How they prized him."

"Shut up, Lea. Just shut up."

Lea ignored her. "Michael's coming to terms with your freedom. He may still want you, but Xavier's far more valuable in the end. The last Tedran and all that." She started for the door. "Anyway, that's why I came here, to tell you the good news, so to speak. And to get a last look at you."

She left, and Cat tried not to feel like Lea had taken hope with her.

# TWENTY-SIX

**The daydream played on a loop.**

Xavier imagined Cat standing on a pristine, secluded beach of white sand, staring out at water so clear he could see the bottom. A storm rose behind her, turning the world ugly and violent, but ahead, over the water, only a few clouds danced across an otherwise sapphire blue sky.

A boat appeared in the shallows, rocking and drifting toward her, the waves slapping lightly against it. She pulled the boat to her, and with barely a glance at the great expanse of water, she stepped into the boat and picked up the oars. Her arms moved steadily, propelling the boat farther and farther out. The look on her face was determined but also excited.

After she broke through the waves she drifted across the open ocean, one tanned arm draped over the side, her fingers trailing through the water. Nothing around her in any direction—the land had since fallen away and so had the storm—and yet she was perfectly content.

Cat, out in an element that terrified him. An element that had managed to cage him once again.

In the distance, another boat appeared. In it sat Gwen and Griffin, who smiled at Cat and paddled over with long, smooth strokes. They pulled Cat's smaller boat to theirs and helped her over the side and into their craft. They rowed away.

The basement door opened, throwing a weak shaft of daylight down the stairs. Xavier raised his head from his crossed forearms. They'd taken him off the particleboard slab and had removed the cuffs, but hadn't let him out of the bleak basement cell in nearly twenty-four hours. When the kid, Sean, brought him food and a bucket to piss in, he'd either *split* himself in two like Michael, or he'd brought with him Jase, the wind cowboy.

Didn't matter. A deal was a deal. Xavier wasn't fighting, as long as Cat was safe.

"You came yourself," Xavier said, standing as Michael crossed the empty floor. "Thought that might've been beneath you."

Michael gave him a wry look then turned back to shout up the stairs. "He's good. You can come down, Lea."

"I'm only 'good' if Cat's hell and gone away from here."

"She is." Lea reached the bottom of the steps and came over, holding her hands behind her back. "Put her on a plane myself this morning."

Cat's boat was drifting out to sea . . . Gwen's was coming to meet her . . .

"We also put a man on her," Lea added. "Someone just as loyal to Michael as Jase and Sean. I'll know where she goes, who she talks to. And if you so much as flinch in my or Michael's direction, he has orders to take her out."

If she was trying to get Xavier to reveal something, it wouldn't work. He narrowed his eyes at Michael. "What now?"

With two fingers, Michael gestured Lea forward. The snide look on her face should have prepared Xavier for what she hid behind her back, but, in truth, he never expected to see a neutralizer cuff again.

In the Plant, the whole place—with exception of the rooms where the Ofarians had drained the Tedrans' magic—had been decked out in neutralizers, which prevented Tedrans from starting a glamour spell. When the Ofarians had tried to move the slaves, they'd slapped neutralizer cuffs around the Tedrans' wrists. Cold metal, a sickly green glowing light. No magic.

Then the Plant was shut down, all the Tedrans freed, and a new Ofarian government came to power. The neutralizers shouldn't have existed anymore, but Lea dangled one from her finger.

Hadn't he just wished for something like this? For what made him Secondary to be taken away? He stared at the little green light, already feeling it sucking the magic from him.

He truly had come full circle.

Blank faced, he addressed Lea. "How'd you get that?"

Michael looked shocked that Xavier knew what it was.

Lea shrugged, extended the neutralizer out farther. "I have my ways." Her eyes shifted slightly as she said it. Discomfort. Lies.

Unless she just happened to have that thing lying around, she'd had to have gotten it from the Ofarians. The technology wasn't used anymore—no need, if he was the only Tedran left—which meant Lea had to have secretly contacted someone inside the Ofarian world to get it for her. Otherwise it would have raised a big red flag that Xavier was in some kind of trouble. A benefit to being the last of his kind.

There was only one possibility: Lea had a spy somewhere inside the Ofarian ruling class.

Xavier wordlessly held out his arm. Lea slapped the cold metal around his wrist and the sallow green light peered back at him. He couldn't stare at it too long; the gentle pulsing of its power hypnotized him, sent him hurtling back in time to the place he'd almost—*almost*—managed to leave in the past. He rolled his long sleeve over the light. If he didn't have to look at it, he couldn't be reminded of what he'd lost. *Who* he'd lost.

Satisfied, Michael headed for the stairs. "Come with me."

Xavier followed, exiting on the main floor that was filled with bright morning light reflecting off the drifts of snow piled high outside. Jase slouched on a stool at the kitchen island.

"Where are the others?" Xavier asked. "Sean? The Ofarians?"

Michael ignored him. "I want you to cook."

"What?" Xavier shook his head. "That's not why you took me. What you really want from me."

Michael smirked. "No. That's not what I really want from you. But for now, it'll do. Remember, you're mine." He pushed a small pad of paper and a pencil over the island. "Dinner menu for seven. Anything you need, we'll get. Heard good things about you."

Then Michael and Lea left by the front door, leaving Xavier in a kitchen that was as big as Shed's. Jase idly drummed his fingers on the countertop, then reached into his back pocket, pulled out a tiny music player, and stabbed the earbuds into place. As Xavier edged toward the pencil and paper, he could feel currents of air surge around his body. Jase was testing him, feeling him out for any sudden moves. The cowboy, corralling him.

He wondered where Michael was keeping the other Ofarians. If they were locked up in some other part of the house, or if they were wandering free like Jase, their power knocked out by *nelicoda* and their loyalty won by some horrific bargain. He thought of this other person they claimed was watching Cat. Was he Secondary, too? Or just some hired muscle?

A deep, dangerous rumble came from behind the door next to the fireplace. More than a sound, more than a vibration, it was a *feeling*. Ominous and filled with rage, and very, very real. The scent of smoke seeped into the house. Jase threw a long look at the door, but otherwise seemed unworried. He faced the counter again, casual as ever, and Xavier knew that asking the air elemental about what was behind Door Number One would be futile.

He took the pad of paper and pencil, and switched his brain toward food. He'd hold up his end of the bargain long enough for Gwen to pull in Cat's boat. He'd cook, because that's what he always did to forget.

**Shortly after sunset, Xavier banged and clanged at the stove.** There were sauce splashes all over the burners, dirty bowls piled on the counter and crumbs tucked into every crevice. The mess went against everything he'd been taught. He didn't care.

Around the corner, in the office nook tucked into a hallway, Lea tapped away at a laptop. Behind him, Jase still sat at the island. The two Ofarians, Robert and the new "acquisition," Shelby, sat holding hands at the kitchen table. They'd both been dosed with enough *nelicoda* to numb their powers for the night, and Robert, who was pockmarked and a little greasy at the temples, was telling Shelby that if she just did as she was told, all would be well back home.

As Xavier ran water over the cooked noodles, he felt Shelby watching him. "He's Tedran," she said to Robert, as though Xavier couldn't hear her.

"Yeah," Robert said, and cleared his throat.

"So he has to be the one who helped take down the Board and stop *Mendacia*. He has to be—"

"The last one," Robert offered. "Yep."

Just then, Michael entered the kitchen. Xavier would know the sound of those leather dress shoes anywhere.

"It's ready." Xavier snapped the kitchen towel off his shoulder and threw it against the backsplash. "Come and fucking get it."

Jase actually cracked a smile. But Michael wasn't looking at the food or the fucked-up little family he'd created and forced to sit around the table. He was staring at Xavier with the most disturbing expression—eyes so wide and clear and crazed. The corners of his mouth twitched into an uneven grin. His shoulders dropped, his arms going lax at his sides. He looked to Shelby, then back to Xavier.

"What?" Xavier snarled.

"Jase," Michael said, his voice eerily distant. "Take Xavier downstairs."

Lea appeared in the kitchen doorway, arms crossed at her waist. She eyed Michael, and though she was trying to sound nonchalant, she was clearly wary. "What're you doing?"

Michael ignored her. Jase obediently slid off his stool, and Xavier lurched under the sudden pressure of air at his back, which steered him toward the basement cell.

**Hours later, Jase came back to get him. As he ushered Xavier** through the house and up the stairs, he heard voices in the game room—Sean and Lea and the Ofarians. Someone switched on the stereo and awful dance music with a driving beat thundered through the house.

Jase took Xavier to a small bedroom at the very back of the second floor, decorated in red plaid and knotty pine. Something was up, and it had to do with the terrible way Michael had examined Xavier earlier. As presumed, Michael entered the bedroom, looking incredibly pleased with himself. Jase stood guard in the open doorway.

Xavier's heart was pounding. "What's this about?"

A twisted glee lit Michael's eyes. "In a moment I'm sending Shelby up. You're going to give her a baby."

Xavier was sure he hadn't heard correctly. He blinked. Opened his mouth.

Michael said, "You heard me."

Xavier squeezed shut his eyes. This wasn't happening. Not again. "I won't do that. I can't."

"But that's what you're good for," Michael said with false innocence. "Lea told me you were some sort of breeding stud to the Ofarians. That you could get any woman pregnant, even those with problems." He lifted his hands in a praise-Jesus gesture. "Oh, ye of the magic sperm."

The Burned Man materialized on the bed. His scarred hand smoothed over the comforter, the melted side of his lips pulled back to bare his teeth in that horrible smile. The real world spun away from Xavier as he was pitched into hell. "Fuck you," he whispered. To Michael and the Burned Man.

"No." Michael's nasty grin died. "Fuck Shelby."

Xavier didn't have to do this. Cat should have been freed a day and a half ago. She would have made contact with Gwen by now. He had to believe that, had to trust that the Ofarians were on their way.

Xavier shoved his hair away from his face and glared at Michael. "I said no."

In the doorway, Jase shifted on his feet.

Michael narrowed his eyes. "Excuse me?"

"I'm not having sex with Shelby. You can try to go after Cat, but here's the thing. I don't think I believe you when you say you put someone on her. I think that you like to carry everything, and everyone, you own with you at all times. Like her painting sitting on the mantel down there. Part of you actually believes that's her. And I don't think you have any other Secondaries under your control down in Florida. I think that was all bullshit just to scare me into doing whatever you wanted. So guess what? I'm calling your bluff. And I'm telling you that not only did Cat make it back to Florida safe and alone, but that she knows exactly how to contact the Ofarians. She's already spoken to them and they already suspected she might be in danger. They protect their own, and I'm guessing that they're already mobilizing, already on their way here. So my answer is no. There's no fucking way I'm sleeping with Shelby or anyone else. Not while Cat's still out there."

Michael just stood there. *Just stood there.* And Xavier realized, with a sickness that almost doubled him over, that everything he'd guessed had been wrong.

Michael ambled toward the TV parked in the bedroom corner.

*Oh, please, no . . .*

Picked up a remote and switched the TV on.

*Please . . .*

Up popped the black-and-white image of Cat. Gagged and bound at the ankles and wrists, she was tied to a post in the middle of a bedroom. A bedroom decorated almost exactly like this one.

"You're right," Michael said. "I do like to keep everything I own with me."

Xavier roared and charged Michael, forgetting about Jase until the great gust of air swept around and threw him backward. Xavier didn't care. His fists flew, his arms striking nothing but gale force winds.

Michael just said, "I know how you feel. I don't want to give her up either. Look what she's become since I met her. Beloved, respected, successful. And now I know she's special in ways I never even imagined."

Xavier finally collapsed back, chest heaving, arms aching. Nora had made him kill once. He'd fed a homeless man *Mendacia*, made him look like Gwen, and then stabbed him in order to make her people believe she was dead. After that, he'd vowed never to kill again. But staring at Michael, he wasn't so sure he could honor that vow.

"You know what you have to do, Xavier." Michael slid his hands in his pockets. "And it should be easy. You were born for this. I won't even tell Cat."

"You think this will make me? You think keeping Cat tied up is going to make me do what you want? You're delusional."

Michael leaned forward. "I haven't touched her. Yet. If you do this with Shelby, I won't ever touch her."

Xavier scrubbed his face, feeling the itch of the skin he was dying to crawl out of. "You've already double-crossed me. I don't believe you."

"Are you really willing to take that chance?"

Fuck Shelby so Michael wouldn't fuck Cat.

*It's just once*, said the Burned Man. *Sex hasn't meant anything to you for years. You expect that to change in a week?*

Xavier stumbled to the TV, touched the image of Cat. Her

eyes were filled with anger. She hadn't given up. Not his Cat. She was aware and strong and smart.

"Why?" Xavier croaked. "Why Shelby? What's the point?"

Michael's fist flew to the side, struck a print of the mountains hanging on the wall. Glass shattered. "Because Raymond Ebrecht may have ignored me, he may have tried to hide my powers from me, and he may have been the most successful studio head in Hollywood history, but he didn't create new races. I can. And I will. I'm going after fucking *godhood*."

There was no reasoning with insanity.

The music coming from below wasn't stopping. The same beat over and over, driving into Xavier's brain. He knew for a fact that mating a Tedran and a Primary produced no magic—Adine was proof of that—but Tedran and Ofarian? Or Tedran and another Secondary? Even he couldn't predict what would happen.

The Ofarians had no idea where he or Cat were, not even that they were in danger. Because he'd been blind and desperate while he'd searched for Cat, and Gwen hadn't entered his mind. The Ofarians weren't coming. Xavier and Cat only had each other. They'd get out of this, away from Michael and Lea, but to do that, they had to remain alive. And Michael had to believe they were his.

"For you, sweetheart," Xavier whispered to the TV in Tedran. "Everything, for you."

"That's a 'yes,' I take it?"

Xavier just bowed his head.

"Bring Shelby up," Michael told Jase on his way out. "Make sure it happens."

Jase watched Michael leave, then with a final glance at Xavier, he shut the door and locked it from the outside.

Xavier rushed to the TV, gripping its sides in his hands. Cat was jiggling her ropes, trying to figure out the knots, trying to get free. Her mouth worked against the gag. Suddenly she went stiff as though she'd heard something. From the left side of the screen, Michael walked in. Xavier gripped the TV harder, his nose almost to the glass.

"Don't do it, asshole. Or I won't."

Michael walked slowly toward Cat, saying something to her that made her eyes bulge. His lecherous gaze slid down

Cat's immobile body and Xavier almost put his fist through the TV.

Michael loosened his tie. He looked right into the camera lens—right at Xavier—then turned, walked past Cat and sat on the edge of the bed. Waiting.

*Don't know why you're so worked up,* said the Burned Man from the bed. *This is you. You're home.*

"This is not my home!"

The lock clicked. The door swung open to reveal Shelby and Jase in the hallway. Xavier slapped off the TV. Whatever was about to happen, he didn't want Cat in the room with him, not even in two dimensions.

Shelby peered into the bedroom. "Who were you talking to?" She had short, curly brown hair and a round face, the skin under her eyes heavily smudged.

"I don't want to do this," he told her outright.

Though her own reluctance was painted plainly across her face, she still said, "We have to." She charged across the room, right for him. He panicked, backed up. His shoulders struck the wall near the bathroom and then she was touching him, her foreign hands grabbing for the snap on his jeans.

"Jesus! Stop!" He shoved her off and spun away, blood hammering in his veins. The trained desire sunk its talons in nice and deep, enough to hurt. He could feel the erection starting, growing, no matter how hard he mentally stamped it down. This woman had touched him, the Burned Man watched from the corner, and Xavier had no control over his own body.

*Cat, I'm so sorry.*

He thrust out his arms to Shelby, his eyes closed, quick breaths hissing from his nose. The need made him tremble.

When he opened his eyes, she'd moved closer to him. Gone was the reluctance, replaced by determination. "We *have* to," she told him again, stronger this time, "because if I don't, Lea will give the Campos family my brother. She and Michael took over my debt and saved the only person in my family I care about. I'm not about to have them take it all back. I already screwed up my life once. I'm not doing it again."

In the doorway, Jase hung his head.

Xavier scrubbed his face. Another innocent person at stake. Destroy a life . . . or make one.

"You'd have a baby?" he asked, incredulous. "For *him*?"

Shelby slowly shook her head. "Don't care. I have a lot to make up for."

Part of him understood. What one person would do to make up for past mistakes wasn't for him to decide. But her solution and his were very different, and satisfying Michael wasn't on his list.

*Think think.* He scanned the bedroom—the dresser, the corners, the TV. Was there a camera in here, too, so Michael could watch them? He couldn't find any; but then, would Michael really need cameras if he had Jase to enforce his orders?

Xavier threw a long look at the blank TV. Cat's image still lingered, maybe not in wires and light, but certainly in his mind. Even though his body was reacting in the way he'd been conditioned, she'd changed him. Ruined him, even. Because mentally he'd never be able to sleep with any woman ever again if that woman wasn't her.

That was it.

Shelby was inside his space again. Eyeing him with very little desire and a whole lot of desperation. She'd trapped him between the bed and the wall. The Burned Man's vulgar words layered with the bass of the music still coming from below.

"All right. I'll do it," he said. Shelby eased back, exhaling in what he could only take as gratitude. Xavier looked to Jase. "But I need help, man."

Jase pushed off the doorframe where he'd been leaning. "With what?"

Xavier looked to the TV again, and Jase's gaze followed. "I'll do it—no protests, no questions—if Shelby looks like Cat."

Jase swiveled his head back to Xavier. "And how do you propose that?" But by the clench of his jaw, he knew exactly how.

Xavier lifted his cuffed arm, the end of his sleeve tugging back to reveal the sickly green neutralizer light. Jase was already shaking his head. "No. No way."

"I don't care who I look like. Just do it," Shelby said, taking another step closer.

"See?" Xavier said. "Shelby is up for it; you won't get any fight from her. She's probably dosed with *nelicoda* anyway.

And you and I both know that if you're commanding air, I'm not going anywhere."

Jase just stared. Xavier had to touch Shelby's shoulder to get her to move aside. She offered no resistance, but he felt the stirrings of a wind cage swirl around his feet.

"Look," Xavier said to Jase, lowering his voice. "You're not playing lackey to Michael and Lea out of the goodness of your heart. Like Shelby, I bet you've been forced to do this because of someone you love. Well, guess what"—he thumped a fist to his chest—"so am I."

Jase swallowed. Pain and regret flickered behind his light blue eyes.

"It's just glamour," Xavier went on. "I'll weave it, give Michael what he wants. *Everyone* gets what they want. The people we're all protecting stay safe. Michael told you to make this happen. I'm telling you, if you take off the neutralizer and let me use the illusion, it'll happen."

For someone who could control wind and create powerful forces of movement, Jase stood very, very still. Xavier thought for sure Jase would refuse, but then the air elemental reached into his back pocket and pulled out the cuff key.

Xavier almost collapsed to the floor, he exhaled so hard.

"We both know," Jase murmured as he slipped the key into the neutralizer lock, "that if I'm commanding air, you're not going anywhere."

Xavier listened to his own words, thrown back at him. The cuff fell off. "Take that thing out in the hall," he told Jase, and the other guy tossed it far away.

"I want to see you do it," Jase said.

So Xavier turned Shelby into Cat. He didn't even have to think about it. Cat's wavy, sun-kissed hair, the tanned skin coated in delicious freckles, the glimmering smile . . . her image came to him instantly, and suddenly she was there in front of him. Only it wasn't her, because there would never be another man in the bedroom when he wanted her as much as he did just then.

"Let's get this over with," Cat said, and the illusion—in Xavier's mind—winked out. That was Shelby's voice, not his Cat's.

Xavier slowly pulled the tails of his shirt out of his jeans. He reached for the buttons. If he looked too anxious or nervous, Jase might see through him. "You going to watch?"

For a brief, terrifying moment, Xavier thought Jase would say yes. That he'd sit over there in the corner with the Burned Man and snicker. But Jase cleared his throat, ducked his head, and left.

# TWENTY-SEVEN

**Thirty minutes later, Shelby rapped lightly on the bedroom door.**

"Yeah?" said Jase out in the hall.

"We're done," she said.

The lock clicked. The door swung slowly open. Jase took a long look at the woman standing just inside the bedroom, her short, curly hair a bit messier. Clothes on but rumpled, her shoes dangling from her fingers.

Shelby wouldn't meet Jase's eyes. He peered over her head at the bed, where Xavier lay naked, half covered by a sheet. His mouth hung open in sleep, one long arm thrown up high on the pillow.

"You okay?" Jase asked her softly, making careful assessment of her face and body. His concern surprised her.

"I'm fine," she snapped, because she'd done what she had to do. "Can I go?"

He nodded. "Find Lea downstairs. I'd walk you down but I can't leave him." He jutted a thumb at sleeping Xavier.

She waved the hand that wasn't carrying the shoes. "Basement jail cell, here I come."

Shelby left Jase standing in the hall and walked down the corridor, being careful not to run. Careful not to panic.

Because Shelby wasn't really Shelby, and the Xavier asleep on the bed wasn't really Xavier.

Xavier wore Shelby's image like a coat. For this to go down the way he wanted, he was banking on Jase not touching who he thought was Xavier lying in that bed. If he did, the glamour would vanish.

Ryan, the Fresh Powder bartender and part-time fighting instructor, had taught Xavier how to apply just enough pressure to someone's throat to make them pass out, but Xavier had never actually done it for real. Shelby had been his practice and trial, all in one.

The moment Jase had left the bedroom, Shelby had lunged for him. The glamour dissolved. She realized Xavier's duplicity too late. His hands had gone around her neck and she'd clawed at him. He'd pushed her to the bed and hoped that the creaking sounds of the mattress and her struggling grunts sounded somewhat sexual. The whole time he'd whispered apologies and promises that he'd get her away from Michael, and tried not to let guilt stay his hand.

When she'd fallen unconscious, he'd woven another glamour spell over her, making her into him. He'd stood beside the bed for a moment, staring down at himself. It had been a really long time since he'd paid any attention to his appearance, and he prayed he'd gotten it right.

Then he'd wrapped himself in Shelby's body and voice, and knocked for Jase's attention.

Now Xavier rounded the corner, exiting the east wing of the house. The music downstairs drowned out his footsteps. Where were Lea and Sean? According to Jase, Robert was probably locked in the basement. And Cat was with Michael in one of these bedrooms on the upper floor.

He'd need a weapon. Glamour and fists weren't enough, not in this house of freaks. He slinked down the stairs, careful to keep his feet on the center, carpeted parts. The dining room was at the bottom of the stairs, the table still piled with dirty dishes from his half-assed dinner. Perfect. Xavier padded for the table, found what he was looking for, and climbed the stairs again, two at a time. The big steakhouse knife felt cool and comfortable in his palm.

Back in the upstairs hall, he jogged to the west wing.

There. A crack of pale light in an open doorway halfway down on the left side. The sound of muffled voices—one male, one female—shifted his adrenaline and rage into high gear. He wasn't even fully aware of his body's movements. The demanding pulse of his blood and the need for vengeance and freedom flogged him into action.

Xavier charged for the door. Of course Michael wouldn't have locked it. Of course he was confident that Xavier would remain contained. And of course Michael hadn't kept his end of the bargain. Again.

The asshole covered Cat's body from behind. He'd untied her ankles and brought her to stand. Her chest pressed against the post carved like a tree, and Michael had his arms around her, picking at the rope knots at her wrists. His face was buried in the crook of her neck, his lips making words Xavier couldn't hear over the furious thud in his ears.

Xavier shut the door behind him. At the sound, Michael looked up. Did a double take. He released Cat and stepped away, combing fingers through his hair. "Shelby? What are you doing here?"

Xavier charged across the huge bedroom, shedding the glamour along the way.

Michael's squinty, confused eyes bulged in surprise. Xavier launched himself through the air, knife drawn back, coming down down down toward Michael's shoulder. Michael's image blurred in a shudder of light, a shifting of atoms. Crazy how fast it happened, how quickly he split apart. Cat was calling out warnings, but it was too late.

The two Michaels stepped away from each other. Xavier, his momentum carrying him forward, sailed through the middle, past the bed, and crashed into the bedside table. He tumbled to his side, his head and shoulder striking the wall. His only thought was to keep the knife away from his body so he wouldn't fall on the blade, but that left the weapon exposed.

One Michael kicked the knife out of his hand, and it flew back toward the posts. The second Michael kicked Xavier, a hard-soled shoe to the ribs. Pain exploded in his torso; Cat's pleading voice filled his ears. Both Michaels fell on him, two full-fledged attacks—fists and knees and feet—with Xavier literally backed into a corner. He had to get out. He had to get *up*.

Michael was no fighter—smaller and older and weaker than Xavier—but there were two of him, they were relentless, and Xavier was on the floor. He finally managed a leg strike of his own. He lifted his knee, got a decent angle, and plowed his foot into One Michael's gut. One Michael stumbled back and Xavier got a half-second look at Cat. She was pulling at the loosened ropes with her teeth, almost free, her eyes wide with hysteria.

One Michael was picking himself up off the carpet, coming back for another attack. Xavier found his feet, pushed to standing, and threw successive punches into Two Michael's kidneys and then his ear. Digging deep into the power of his thighs, he propelled himself forward, tackling Two Michael. The force sent them both flying into the bed. Xavier locked his legs around Two Michael and rolled, tumbling them over the far side. As they hit the floor, Xavier glimpsed Cat peeling away from the post, the ropes falling away. Xavier flipped Two Michael on his back, braced his knees on either side of his hips, and just pummeled away.

"Xavier, he's coming!" shouted Cat.

Over his shoulder, Xavier saw One Michael had recovered from the kick and was rushing around the bed.

One Michael threw a brilliant punch to the side of Xavier's head, which sent a shock of sickening, swimming lights across his vision. Xavier sagged then immediately drew himself up. There was no way he was going down from a sucker punch from *Michael*.

Two Michael was weakening under Xavier's fists. Blood poured from his nose and several cuts around his face, and he had no leverage with his legs, since Xavier still had them clamped between his. Two Michael's arms had turned into useless spaghetti tools of defense, things that Xavier could easily get past.

One Michael jumped on Xavier's back and threw an arm around Xavier's windpipe. Tightening, crushing. Xavier reached back with one long arm, grabbed One Michael's hair and pulled hard. The other arm pressed Two Michael into the floor. Xavier threw back an elbow, landing in One Michael's gut with an *oof*, but his attacker held on. Xavier chucked his head back, knocking skull to nose. Still, Michael held on. Black spots swam at his periphery, but Xavier had to try one more thing. He rocked forward, intending to throw One Michael off balance, maybe to the side. Such little strength left in his muscles, though, and so few pockets of air left for him to grasp.

This *was* how he would go down. He knew that now. From a stranglehold. At least he'd beaten the shit out of Two Michael. At least one was down for the count. At least he'd tried to get Cat free.

Then One Michael gave a strangled, wet cry and went limp across Xavier's back. A gush of hot liquid spread over his shoulders. The arms around Xavier's neck slackened and he clawed for breath. Energy surged back into him and he heaved himself to his feet, throwing One Michael off him. There was no resistance. One Michael slid off Xavier's back, falling to the carpet in a tangle of limp limbs and blood.

Blood. Red was everywhere. One Michael clutched futilely at the hole in his neck, blood bubbling and gurgling between his fingers. A soggy puddle of crimson spread beneath his body. His legs twitched, his eyes wide, begging. Slowly, slowly, life leaked out of him.

*What the—*

Xavier looked up. Cat was backing away from One Michael. Tears streamed down her face and her whole body shook, but no part more than the hand that held the steak knife. A high wail escaped her lips, and the chattering of her teeth shredded the sound.

"Cat." Xavier stretched for her. Her legs gave out. She sank to the floor, the knife tumbling from her fingers to land point up in the carpet. He remembered, all too clearly, what it felt like to kill someone. To *stab* someone—because that's how Nora had made him do it. That dirty, guilty, awful feeling of a life disappearing in your hands. He'd thought he'd shed it years ago, but the feeling surged back as he reached for Cat.

Two Michael had somehow gotten up. He grabbed Xavier's legs from behind, pitching Xavier forward. Not expected, not expected at all. He'd made bad assumptions, underestimated his opponent.

Xavier used the momentum from the rear attack, tucking and rolling. He clasped his legs around Two Michael and threw him over his body like a doll. Two Michael landed hard next to his dying double. Xavier fell on top of Two Michael and flipped him over. Wrenching his arms behind his back, Xavier pressed one knee into the center of his spine. Two Michael's face was three inches away from his bleeding and dying look-alike, his lips smashed into the wet carpet.

*"Fucking cocksucker."* The insult came out in bubbles of blood.

"What's it like"—Xavier got so close to Two Michael's face the stench of the blood nearly overwhelmed him—"to watch yourself die?"

And just like that, life left One Michael. The twitching ceased, the horrible gargling in his throat stopped. His eyes remained open, however, staring right into his double's terror-stricken face.

"What does that mean?" Xavier leaned hard into Two Michael's back. "You don't get to do this again?"

Michael, the alive one, the one in Xavier's grip, started to convulse. At first Xavier thought it had something to do with the magic. But no. His captive was crying—great, heaving sobs that wracked his remaining living body.

Xavier didn't give a shit about Michael anymore. He lifted his head and found Cat. She sat on her butt, legs sprawled messily in front of her, shock making her body loose. Her vacant eyes stared at the bloody knife. Splatters of red covered her hands and forearms.

"I killed him," she whispered.

"Part of him, yes." Xavier longed to go to her, but he didn't dare release Michael, not knowing what he could still do. What could happen.

She brought her wet, red fingers in front of her face, gazing at them like they weren't attached to her body. "I just wanted him off you. I didn't want him to hurt you. I just wanted him off . . ."

"Cat, it's okay." He knew he should keep talking to her, keep her present. "We'll get out of here. I'll fix this. We'll figure something out . . ."

Pounding footsteps thundered down the hall, off tempo from the pulsing music. "Michael! Xavier's gone! It's Shelby in the bed."

*Oh shit.*

Jase careened into Michael's bedroom, immediately saw the bloody mess, and froze. "Christ Almighty."

Xavier had forgotten all about the glamour on Shelby. He must have lost control of it the moment he'd attacked Michael, and Jase must have peeked in on who he assumed was still Xavier in the bed. Or he'd tried to put the neutralizer back on Shelby's arm and the touch had dissolved the illusion.

Xavier lunged across Michael's sniveling, spasming body and snatched the knife from the carpet. He pressed the tip to the soft place just below Michael's ear. "Use your air," he snarled, "and Michael's gone. Both of them."

Jase looked to a shivering, bloodied Cat, then to the dead Michael, then back to Cat. "Christ Almighty," he murmured again. "You did that?"

Beneath Xavier's hands, Michael's substance shifted. Xavier didn't know of any other way to describe it. One moment Michael's body was corporeal, heavy and hot from exertion and pain and anguish, the next moment it turned to thick air. Pillow like, as though if Xavier pressed down, Michael might pop. Xavier scrambled back as Michael's image started to wink, flickering like a TV set on its last day before the landfill.

Michael stretched a fading hand toward the dead body that was also beginning to pale. Then, simultaneously, the two Michaels drew toward one another, the bodies sucking together. Their images shuddered and joined, becoming one again over the sticky, bloody mess.

The whole Michael flopped onto his back, the saturated red carpet making awful slurping sounds under his body. He sounded like he was choking, suffocating, mixing the death of his other half with the life he still clung to. Then his arms went flaccid. His eyes rolled around in their sockets. A long, agonizing moan leaked from his now singular throat.

He wasn't dead yet and Xavier wasn't taking any chances. Xavier grabbed Michael under the arms and pulled him toward the giant bed, careful to keep the knife in a threatening position. "The rope, Cat. The one that held you. Bring it to me."

Xavier got Michael to the bed with no resistance. Michael was dead weight—alive, but just barely. Xavier propped him up against one of the massive bed legs and held his arm out for the rope. The rough length slapped into his palm.

"Thanks." He looked up. Cat hadn't moved from where she was still sprawled on the floor ten feet away.

Jase stood over Xavier, holding on to one end of the rope.

"What are you doing?" Xavier breathed.

Jase glanced fearfully at the door and dropped his voice. "Michael's not who you have to worry about."

Xavier could only kneel there, watching in shock, as Jase crept to the bedroom door. He peered into the hall, then ducked back in and shut the door behind him. The music dulled.

Jase ran a hand through his curly hair. Gone was the cool, devoted henchman who'd so easily thrown Xavier on his ass several times. Jase pointed to Michael. "I'd still tie him up if I were you."

Xavier blinked out of his surprise and complied, wrapping Michael's wrists and then securing his torso to the thick leg of the bed. It didn't really matter, though. Michael Ebrecht, as he lived just minutes ago, was gone. His torso leaned awkwardly, the rope the only thing holding him up. His head, bruised and battered from Xavier's fists, lolled backward. His eyes jerked back and forth in their sockets, sometimes not even in the same direction.

Xavier leaned down, got right in vegetable Michael's face. "You're not even half a man, Michael. You never were."

A familiar hand touched Xavier's back. The pressure of Cat's fingers felt cold and wet, and he realized it was because the back of his white shirt was completely soaked with Michael's blood. So were the ends of his hair, and when Xavier moved his head he could smell the sharp, acrid tang of that prick's life all over him. Cat had shoved aside most of her fear, or at least she was giving it a valiant attempt, and for that, Xavier couldn't help but love her.

As Jase moved closer, Xavier pulled Cat behind him. Jase raised his palms as if in surrender. "It doesn't matter if Michael's dead or alive. This is all Lea. She was using Michael like he thought he was using her, only he never had a chance."

Xavier wanted desperately to believe Jase, but he'd been double-crossed twice already. "Why? What does she want?"

"Revenge on her people," Cat said at Xavier's elbow, "because they exiled her for loving a Primary. She's Gwen's sister."

Xavier sucked in a breath. Gwen had never told him about any sister, but then, he hadn't been that close to her.

"'Hell hath no fury,'" Jase said, wiping at the back of his neck. Sweat dotted his forehead under the shaggy curls.

"Why are you here?" Xavier snapped. "Why are you standing here talking to us like you want to help us?"

Jase licked his lips and threw another wary glance at the closed door. "Because you were right. What you said earlier, about having to do this for someone I love."

Cat came out from behind Xavier. So trusting. She always had been. "What do you mean?"

Jase shook his head. "This is my chance, dude. The first chance I've had to escape in years. Lea's in the game room with the music turned up so she wouldn't hear what you were doing, Xavier. Shelby's unconscious. Robert will be locked in the basement. Sean's probably in the garage with the fire elemental. Michael's out of the picture. You two are up here, and I want to be on your side."

Xavier ground fingers into his forehead. "Fire elemental?" That explained the rumbling and the smoke smell.

"In the garage. Scary as shit. Taking her was completely against Lea's MO. I have no idea why Lea wanted her. It definitely wasn't just so Michael could try to impress his dead dad. She's got a plan."

"What about Sean?" Xavier asked. "Who's side is he on?"

Jase kicked at Michael's foot. "Michael's. Forever and ever. We can't rely on him. And Lea's got connections everywhere. Her phone is always on. One text, one call, and so many of us are done. The people we love, done."

"Except for me," Xavier said. "She's got shit on me, I have nothing to lose, and I want this *over*."

A fierce determination sparked in Jase's pale blue eyes. He squared his shoulders, tipped that imaginary cowboy hat again. "So what's the plan? You had to have had one, genius, to have broken out."

"It didn't go past getting Michael away from Cat."

Cat looked down at her captor. "He lives in the Primary world. We need to do something about that."

Jase ran a thumb over his bottom lip. "So we need time. Make him seem like he's gone missing." He snapped his fingers. "The rental car. I'll return it to the local airport. I'll tell Lea I'm picking up Michael's double in town. Then you two go after Lea and Sean, and I'll meet you back here."

Xavier didn't like that at all. "You can't help us now?"

Jase's lips tightened, his voice hardened. "Do you understand what I'm risking? You think if I'd been able to take them down by now, I wouldn't have?"

"How do we know we can trust you?" Xavier asked.

An emotional pain curtained Jase's eyes. "You don't. No one's trusted me for decades. I haven't done a single thing on my own, for any sort of good, in God knows how long. And I want to now, more than anything."

Xavier looked down at Cat and wove his fingers into hers.

"But," Jase added, "if you two don't succeed, I have to make like you got the best of me. If Lea wins, I'm saving myself and what I left back home. There's too much at stake."

"I understand." And Xavier did. If Cat's life was put on the line again, there's no telling what lies he would say or what he would do. Who he'd betray.

Another tip of the invisible cowboy hat. "See you on the other side."

Then he was gone.

Cat and Xavier looked at each other. The other side of what?

## Michael was half-dead.

Raymond Ebrecht had never given him a "don't do drugs" talk, because the elder had been a bit of a cokehead and he hadn't even been able to dig up a "do as I say, not as I do" speech. Raymond hadn't taught Michael to drive, or tossed baseballs with him in the front yard, or lectured him about safe sex. He'd never smacked him upside the head for a grade below a C. Hell, he'd never even asked to see a report card.

Michael had never been anything more than a tumor to Raymond. A reminder of the first woman who'd left him— arguably the only woman he'd ever loved. A hated leftover from a failed relationship and a weight around his ankle.

And, when he'd discovered that Michael had inherited the family Splitter gene, his competition.

The day Raymond had found a pubescent Michael shivering and delirious after his first *split*, he'd hauled the frightened, trembling boy up by his shirt and shoved him against the wall, snarling.

*Guess you really are my son. So now you know that you're better than everyone else out there. But you're still not better than me. Got it?*

*Yes, sir.*

*Good.*

All these years, Michael had clung to those words like food or water.

He hadn't ever told anyone he could *split* until he found Sean, who could do the same. But then came Lea . . . and now that motherfucking townie knew. And Cat.

Who'd killed him.

Raymond had had a Primary-style heart attack. Michael had brought him back, kept him breathing, and the asshole still hadn't had the courtesy to open his eyes and admit that Michael really *was* better than him.

*Splitting* had given Michael a better life than his father's, and now the magic had taken that life away. Because even though Michael's heart still beat and he could still see and hear, he was no longer Michael Ebrecht. He was now no better than fucking Raymond. Dead but still alive. Breathing, but lifeless.

He'd watched himself die. When it had happened, he hadn't felt the double's pain or experienced the other's panic. Until the reabsorption.

Usually combining halves brought him a surge of information and ideas, a wave of conversations, emotions, and decisions. It had always been an additive experience. Not so when one half died.

It had been the longest second of Michael's life, sucking back in his dead half. All the agony and terror the double had gone through ripped through his skin and shredded his organs. Death had slashed his mind to shreds and left it dangling in tatters. He had a dead person inside him.

The dead part wanted to cross over into that foggy atmosphere that permanently lingered on the outskirts of his awareness. The alive part wanted to destroy Xavier . . . and to make Cat watch.

The bitch had killed him. After all he'd done for her.

He tried to scream, but the dead half wouldn't let him speak. Now he'd never get the chance to show Raymond the new race he'd created. Even in death, Dad won.

# TWENTY-EIGHT

**Cat had killed someone. She'd picked up a knife and deliberately** shoved it into Michael's body. The thick resistance, the tangible horror, all that blood . . . Maybe he wasn't completely dead, but she'd felt that one life leave. She'd never be able to wash that feeling away.

Cat clung to Xavier, not wanting to let him go. Ever. They were fused together, each grappling for a better, tighter embrace, never able to find it.

"Lea said you traded yourself for me," she whispered, realizing she was crying.

He took her arms and gently pried her off. One of his big hands swept over her forehead and around her hair. "I'd do it again," he said.

And that's when she fell in love.

Xavier glanced down at Michael. "I should've known. I should've known he wouldn't have let you go, but I had to take that chance." He wiped her tears and cursed, looking down at his own bloody hands. "Did he touch you?"

"No," she lied, because it didn't matter now how Michael had groped her over her clothes. How he'd cryptically told her how worthy she was now. How she'd turned out to be so much better than he'd ever imagined. Special, like him. How his father would love her and therefore love him because of the woman he'd brought home. Creepy, all of it.

Xavier kissed her. Hard and fleeting. But she tasted all of him in that moment and it fueled her. It momentarily steered her thoughts away from the dark, terrible memories of Michael's life and death. Xavier knew; he somehow knew her mind was tripping away from her and he wasn't going to allow it.

"You ready?" he asked, then opened the door. Music poured in. Xavier waved her behind him and they crept toward the stairs. They left bloody footprints on the carpet, but she couldn't worry about the evidence. This was a one-way street. No going back for either of them.

For such a big man, Xavier was remarkably silent. But then, he'd spent years avoiding attention. At the top of the stairs, he stopped. Jase appeared, hurrying from the opposite wing and cradling an unconscious woman in his arms.

"Who's that?" Cat asked, even though her senses had already named the woman's race.

"Shelby," Xavier replied. "She's Ofarian."

There was more to the story—Xavier's eyes said as much, and Jase had hinted at it earlier—but now was not the time. They were moving forward now, not backward.

"I'm going to put her in the basement with Robert," Jase murmured when he reached them. "That's where she was supposed to go anyway. Wait until I'm gone to make your move."

They waited. And waited. At last the music cut off.

"Oh, thank the stars they're done," came Lea's muffled voice. "Took him long enough."

"I'm heading out," Jase told Lea. "Picking up Michael's double in town."

Cat could feel Lea bristling from one floor up. "I didn't know he'd *split* tonight."

"Well, that's what he said."

From the top of the stairs, they watched Jase go out the front door. Listened to the gentle purr of a car starting in the drive. Then the car peeling out. The house was pitched into heavy silence. Xavier took Cat's hand and squeezed.

Where was Lea? She could be anywhere. Cat had a terrible vision of Michael's blood seeping through the floor and dripping into the kitchen, giving them away. Sean would *split*, she and Xavier would be surrounded, and they'd lose.

"I could get you out of here," Xavier whispered.

"How? Where?"

"Away from here. Safe."

The idea actually offended her. "Send me off into the cold

while you stay here and face God knows what? I'm part of this world now. You're here because of me. The others need to go free. Lea needs to be stopped."

He kissed her again, smothering her mouth with his. When he pulled away they were both breathless. He paused, bowed his head, and closed his eyes.

"Shit. No glamour left." Strain pulled down the edges of his mouth. He looked really tired. "Was hoping to make us look like Sean or Michael, but I don't have anything left."

Cat took his chin and looked right into his eyes. "So she sees us coming. She doesn't have any water magic. All it's going to take is force."

A heavy emotion crossed his face, something like pride. "Ready?"

The whole world had contracted to this house, to whatever it was they were about to do. Saying no wasn't an option.

Step by slow, soundless step, they edged downstairs. A clock ticked somewhere. Cat pointed down a hallway leading to the back of the house, from where the faint Secondary signatures wafted. When Lea caught wind of Cat and Xavier's signatures, an alarm would go up. They'd have to move fast.

Xavier tugged Cat into the kitchen and great room. The pull of several signatures burned strong in her senses. *Sean*, she mouthed, pointing to a door between two bookcases. *And the two Ofarians.*

*That's the basement*, he mouthed back, and frowned. Jase had told them Sean was likely in the garage, but apparently that wasn't the case.

The door next to the fireplace must have been the entrance to the garage, because from behind it came a loud *bang* and a low reverberation. Fire elemental. Cat memorized the feel of that new signature.

Something on the mantel caught her eye. *Ocean #2*. The one Michael had bought from her the day they met. The one he said he'd never sell, the object that had started this all. He'd brought it with him here, which told her so much about how he'd viewed her: his, to carry around and look at or take down whenever he pleased.

She turned her back on it. Another Secondary signature tugged at her, coming from the hallway branching off the kitchen. The hall was long and dim, and at the far end she could see where it opened up into a game room, the corner of a pool table and a blinking dartboard in view. From within that hall came the faint blue light of someone working on a computer. The tiny *tap tap taps* on the keyboard filtered into the kitchen.

"Xavier?" Lea called, warily. "Is Shelby with you?"

Xavier charged across the kitchen and dove into the dark hall, a predator zoned in on his prey, Cat on his heels. "It's me and Cat. Surprise."

The keyboard clacking stopped. "Oh, no . . ."

Lea scrambled up from the wheeled office chair. It shot backward and slammed into a set of cabinets. The quiet house exploded with noise.

Lea took off down the hall, her high-heeled shoes making harsh sounds on the hardwood floor. Xavier pounded after her, whirling the office chair out of his path. Cat chased them both.

When the hardwood met the game room carpet, Xavier tackled Lea from behind. Halfway to the ground, he spun. Arms around Lea's waist, he flipped so he landed on his back, Lea flopping on top of him. Then, lightning quick, he rolled again so Lea's face was crushed to the carpet. Xavier clamped her arms behind her back. She started to kick with her high heels and Xavier sat back on her legs, just like he'd done with Michael upstairs. Lea groaned and thrashed, not giving up.

Xavier looked around frantically. "That lamp," he told Cat, indicating a standing lamp in the corner. "Bring it over here."

Cat ran to the fluted wood lamp that stood as tall as she, and ripped the cord from the wall. She rolled the base over to Xavier and he snatched off the shade, laying the lamp post lengthwise over Lea's back. He started to wind the long cord around her wrists.

Lea wrenched her mouth away from the carpet and screamed. "Sean! Do it, Sean! Now!"

Xavier froze, his eyes lifting to Cat's. Sean was in the basement with the other Ofarians.

"Oh, God," Cat begged. "Go, Xavier. Please help them. I've got her."

She saw the deliberation in his eyes, the awful split-second decision. Try to save the lives of two Ofarians and go up against Sean, or keep control over the mastermind.

"*Please*, Xavier. You're not alone in this. I have Lea and you can get to them."

His mouth twisted as he shoved the end of the cord into her hands. Cat jumped on top of a struggling Lea as Xavier sprinted back down the corridor. He ran through the kitchen, threw open the door to the basement and bounded down the steps.

Lea was smaller than Cat, but she had some fight. She bucked, popping Cat off her. She almost managed to roll onto her back, but the square lamp base prevented her from making it all the way and she had no leverage with her tied hands.

A male roar Cat recognized as Xavier's rumbled up from the basement. Another man shouted in surprised response. And then another, sounding exactly alike.

Oh, no. Sean had *split*.

Lea yanked desperately at her cord restraints. Cat kicked out. Her bare feet struck Lea's stomach and the bound woman went motionless for a moment as the pain rolled in. Cat rose, standing over her.

The fighting escalated below. Loud, terrible crashes. Male grunts and curses. How much energy did Xavier have left? He'd had none to work an illusion upstairs, and he'd already fought two Michaels. She'd sent him into that—to save two people who belonged to a race he hadn't forgiven—and she couldn't live with herself if he didn't make it out.

The moment of wonder proved stupid. Lea's arms were still tied to the lamp, but her legs were free. With a screech, Lea threw out a leg. Cat caught a stiletto heel across the stomach, the sharp, stinging pain feeling like it scraped all the way back to her spine. Cat snapped backward, stumbling into one of the chairs surrounding a chessboard table. She righted herself, whipped around, and dove.

Lea was struggling hard against the lamp, her elbows flapping under the loosened wire. Cat pushed Lea back onto her stomach and sat on her. Hard. She found the trailing end of the cord and brought it down with a *smack* on the backs of Lea's legs. Lea cried out and tensed up, and it was that moment of stillness that gave Cat what she needed.

Cat wound the cord around Lea's wrists once, twice. Leaning back, she yanked one of Lea's ankles, bringing it all the way to her butt. Cat looped the cord around Lea's ankle and tied it off, pulling tighter than what was necessary. Lea writhed, finally immobile.

"Water bitch!"

Breathing hard, Cat crouched down near Lea's head, careful not to get too close. "Who, exactly, is the bitch here?"

It might have been comical, to see this seemingly innocent-looking woman strapped to a floor lamp, except that the awful sounds of a vicious fight in the basement were far from funny. Cat paced, every collision, every groan, making her wince. Should she get down there? Could she help? What were the Ofarians doing? Were they fighting Xavier, too?

She didn't dare leave Lea. The woman had no magic and yet she'd been capable of so much already.

Lea glared up at her, her makeup smeared all around her eyes, her blond hair in tangles. If hate had had physical power, Cat would have been the one tied to a lamp.

"Is Michael dead?" Lea ground out.

"Part of him. And I'm the one who did it."

Lea spit out carpet fuzz. "Good."

It took a moment to process that. "Why partner with Michael if you just wanted him dead?"

Lea snorted. "Do you know how much money he has? Our interests overlapped. I got him what he wanted, and then used his resources to get what *I* wanted."

"It's the end for you, too, you know. Whatever you wanted isn't going to happen now."

Lea just laughed.

The fighting downstairs was starting to lessen. Cat thought of Gwen's blessing that invoked the stars. Cat had been brought up worshipping the Christian God, but the stars seemed just as powerful a thing to pray to. So many of them, always visible, full of possibility. So she did that now, praying that the fighting wasn't dying because Xavier was weak.

She looked down at Lea. "How do I free the fire elemental?"

The laughter died. "You don't want to do that."

"Yes," Cat said. "I do."

"She'll burn you to ash. On second thought, keys to the cage's top hatch are in a bowl by your painting on the mantel. Have at it."

Cat bent closer and pulled back some of Lea's hair so she could look right into Lea's brown eyes, unobstructed. "I'm not the one who took her. I don't believe she'll come after me. But I'll be sure to let her know where I've wrapped up a nice bundle of firewood for her in the game room. I'm sure she'd love to face you again."

The look of satisfaction that passed over Lea's face made Cat shiver. Lea said nothing, but her nostrils flared as if she'd smelled smoke. Then her eyes shifted down the hall and toward the kitchen. Cat swiveled in that direction, wondering what she saw. There was nothing.

That was it: nothing. The fighting had stopped. A ponderous silence pressed down on her. Both she and Lea stared at the basement door in expectation, their breathing loud and very nearly synchronized.

Leaden footsteps started up the basement stairs. Only one man ascending, but two Secondary signatures. The footsteps moved so slowly, so unevenly. The basement door opened, hinging outward and hiding whoever it was that had claimed victory. If it wasn't Xavier, Cat didn't know what she'd do. Run? Try to fight Sean off?

A floating pair of feet poked out from behind the door. Then a pair of legs. Then Xavier, shouldering an unconscious Sean.

Cat let out a sound that was part sob, part laugh.

Xavier's long legs wobbled. He teetered toward the big couch making a U around the fireplace and dumped Sean onto it.

"Xavier!" Cat called, unable to keep the relief and joy from her voice. "Are you okay? What happened?"

He didn't answer, just went to a side table, ripped out another lamp cord from the wall, and secured Sean as he had Lea.

Xavier finally looked up, saw Cat, and started for the game room. His steps were uneven and dragging. When he hit the kitchen he stumbled and had to balance himself between the island and the stainless steel refrigerator.

She met him in the middle of the dim hallway, pulled one of his arms around her shoulders, and helped him into the game room. In the light, the sight of him made her gasp. He was already covered in Michael's blood, but now the buttons on his shirt were half gone. New bruises and cuts marred his beautiful face. His great shoulders slumped, his eyelids drooped at the corners.

"Goddamn Tedran," Lea snarled up at him, giving a new thrash that only tightened the wires around her wrists and ankles. "There's a reason we kept you locked up."

Xavier just stared down at her. Nothing moved except the twitching corner of his top lip.

"Don't listen to her," Cat told him.

He lunged for Lea. She squeaked and tried to shrink away. Xavier bent over and scooped her up into his arms. Where he found the strength, Cat didn't know. Barely able to stand by himself, his arms shaking from strain, he started back to the great room. He deposited Lea onto a section of couch opposite Sean.

Still not saying a word, he went back to the kitchen and started rummaging through drawers.

"Jase'll be back soon," Lea said.

"Good," Cat replied with a smile, and Lea glanced with fear at the front door.

"That's right. We got a little help from him. Weren't expecting that, were you? But what I want to know is, what exactly did you want from him? He's not Ofarian. He doesn't fit into your revenge scheme."

Xavier came back around the couch, holding a roll of silver duct tape. He pulled out a section, ripped it off with his teeth. Cat held up a hand to him. "Let her answer first."

Lea eyed her captors then sank further into the couch. "I didn't want him. Michael did. He was our first. The rest were mutually beneficial."

*"Why?"*

Lea just laughed again. "Fuck you. Fuck you, too, Xavier."

He made a sound of disgust and slapped the duct tape over Lea's mouth. He went over to Sean and knelt beside him. He covered Sean's mouth, too, but much gentler. Xavier tilted his head to look into Sean's unconscious face. "He was a decent fighter," he said, almost to himself. "He fought because I went after him. He *split* to protect himself, but I could tell he didn't want to. It took a lot out of him. Wore him down faster. In the end, I kicked one of them in the face, made him go down. He reabsorbed the second, but by then it was over." He exhaled and placed a hand on the cushion near Sean's head. "I don't think he wanted to be down there any more than the Ofarians."

Cat threw a fearful glance at the basement door. "Are they . . . alive?"

Xavier nodded shallowly. "They're restrained, unconscious. Jase must've tied up Shelby to keep up appearances. Their allegiances are twisted. I think we should keep them like that until we know more." Xavier sighed. "Sean was stalling, taking his time, I think. I saw vials of *nelicoda* nearby. Looks like he got some of the syringes into them, but I don't know how much . . . how much it takes to burn out the magic. There was other stuff down there. Poison, maybe. I don't think he got it in them."

"I think we should call Gwen," she blurted out.

His shoulders curved inward and he nodded. "I think so, too. I have no idea what to do with all this. If she doesn't know, Griffin will."

She didn't really want to ask, but did so anyway. "Why didn't you call them earlier?"

"Cat." He looked up at her, his heart in his eyes. "All I could think about was you."

There was a phone on the wall next to the mini wine fridge. A laminated piece of paper taped to the wall above explained how houseguests would be charged for long-distance phone calls. She easily remembered Gwen's number—heck, she'd studied it for hours before actually dialing it.

Her hands shook from the dying adrenaline. Gwen answered on the second ring, and the sound of her voice instantly made Cat cry. The enormity of the past few days plowed into her. She sank onto a stool at the kitchen island and let it all out.

She told Gwen everything. What had happened to her since they last talked. How Xavier had saved her. The caged fire elemental and the turncoat air elemental. The fates of the two missing Ofarians and . . . the role of her sister, Lea.

Gwen went so quiet Cat thought she hung up. "Hello? Gwen, are you still there?"

"It can't be Delia," Gwen whispered.

"Delia?" On the couch, Lea stiffened, her blazing eyes boring holes into Cat. "I think it is her. Short, maybe five foot three. Blond hair, brown eyes." Cat lowered her voice. "Married a Primary named John."

And then it was Gwen's turn to cry.

"Hold tight. Be strong," Gwen said after she'd steadied her voice, and Cat might have told her the exact same thing. "We're coming."

She hung up the phone and turned to Xavier, who was watching her with such pride . . . and such strain. She knelt next to him on the floor and took his face in her hands. When his eyes lifted to hers, the hardness and pain and torment in them melted.

There was no "he kissed her" or "she kissed him." They came together at the same moment, with the same high level of desperation and relief. The blood didn't matter. The physical pain faded away. The fear over what came next lifted up and escaped her body. It would come back, but for now—for now—they'd be together. Taste each other.

In the cold of the room, Xavier was heat. In the stress of this house, Xavier was calm. Facing a future of the unknown, Xavier was the present, and Cat absorbed him. She kept her lips to his, her tongue taking him in. She wrapped her arms around his neck and gasped when he crushed her to him.

When they separated, he was trembling. No, they both were.

Something crashed outside. It sounded like stone falling on stone, with that telltale hollow *clink*.

Xavier surged to his feet. "Stay here. I got it."

He grabbed a knife from the kitchen block and padded to the front door. There was a pause, then Xavier called back to her in surprise, "It's Jase."

The door opened and closed as Xavier went outside.

And then, from the garage, came a huge *groan* and a series of heavy thumps.

Cat rocked to her feet and looked to Lea, whose wide eyes watched her. Without second thought, Cat marched to the fireplace mantel, reached into the little pot sitting next to *Ocean #2*, and removed the key to the fire elemental's cage.

# TWENTY-NINE

**It really was a cage. A bizarre cage of some sort of thick,** translucent material. Scorch marks striped the inside walls and little scraps of burned cloth littered the corners. Smoke leaked out of small holes at the top of the box, and a fan tried to dissipate it, but the old fire stench stung Cat's nostrils.

A woman appeared from the billowing smoke, parting the plumes like an ancient goddess standing on top of a cloud. She was dramatic in every sense of the word, from her muscled naked body, to the shiny streams of black hair, to the exotic tint of her skin. The best features of at least three different races granted her a powerful type of beauty, made all the more intimidating by her piercing stare. Cat didn't think she'd ever felt so inadequate, and this woman was *caged*.

The fire elemental wiped away some of the soot with her forearm and peered out. "Who the hell are you?"

"I'm Cat. Michael took me, too."

"Did he now?" The fire woman crossed her arms over her full breasts. "Another one of his kidnapped minions? Come to feed me or try to keep me company or something? Get on in here and try, beautiful."

Cat blinked. This wasn't going at all like she'd imagined. "No, I'm, uh, here to get you out."

"Nice try. I'm not fucking working for him. Or that Ofarian."

"Michael's dead. Or at least, part of him is. This is his blood all over me." Cat ran a hand over her sticky, reddened hair. "I escaped. I'm trying to help you do the same."

The fire woman moved closer, her movements smooth, absolutely no fear on her face. "And that bitch Ofarian?"

"You mean Lea?"

"Yeah, that's the one."

"She's inside, right through that door. Tied up. So is Sean. The other Ofarians are drugged in the basement. Jase just returned, but he's on our side."

The fire woman pressed her palms to the wall. Her lips formed an *O*, and for a second the tough warrior demeanor dropped away and she was just a captured woman, overjoyed by the good guys' victory. The hardened look rolled back. "What are you waiting for then? Get me out of here."

A ladder leaned against the far wall of the garage and Cat glanced over at it. "Lea said you'd burn me to ash if I let you out."

The fire woman smiled, blinding white teeth against her dusky skin and the smoky backdrop. "Now, why would I do that? You didn't put me in here, did you?"

Cat relaxed. Somewhat. She had no idea where this woman's magic came from, how she wielded fire. Could she really burn someone to ash? "No, I didn't."

The two women stood there, watching each other. An unease prickled over Cat's skin, but she chalked it up to the fear Lea had tried to plant in her. This poor woman was as much a prisoner as she'd been, and Cat hadn't been the one to take her. "What's your name?"

"Kekona," she replied at length. A tiny smile. "The ladder?"

"Oh. Right." Cat walked over to it, saying, "I've called the leaders of the Ofarians. They're on the way."

"The Ofarians." Kekona's voice was strangely flat, but maybe Cat was hearing things, given the banging and clanging of the aluminum on the concrete floor.

"They'll know how to clean this up, straighten out this mess. I'm sure they'll take you wherever you need to go."

"I'm sure."

As Cat set the ladder against the cage with a loud clatter, she caught Kekona's intense, doubtful expression. "Lea's not one of them. Well, she used to be, but she's gone rogue."

Kekona raised an eyebrow. "Is that what she told you?"

Cat started to climb. "You don't need to fear them. We . . . I trust them."

Chances were Kekona's trust was lying in ash on the floor along with her clothing. Cat didn't blame her, but she felt the weight of Xavier's word and Gwen's vows in her bones, and she wanted to get that across. She would see Kekona free and prove Lea wrong.

As Cat awkwardly pulled up the ladder, Kekona eyed it hungrily. Cat was starting to feel her own lack of strength. She should have eaten when Sean had brought her food. She needed about three days of sleep.

"I'm sorry," Cat said. "I didn't bring you any clothes. I didn't know you were . . . Maybe we could find you something inside. Lea's a lot shorter than you though."

Kekona looked in confusion down at her body. "Sorry if I make you uncomfortable."

On top of the box, Cat stuck the key into the lock and flopped open the hatch. Heat billowed out. She wrestled with the ladder, pulling it up off the floor then sticking one end into the hole and sliding it down to land right at Kekona's feet. It made a terrible noise and slipped from her grip, but Kekona didn't even flinch.

Kekona put one foot on the bottom rung, her hand on the ladder, and started to pull herself up. "Why did Michael want you? You're a Secondary, I presume?"

"Yes," Cat replied, thinking it might grant them some sort of solidarity. Thinking that she'd never had difficulty speaking to people, except when it came to this most unusual woman.

"Well, what are you?"

The ease and speed with which she climbed the ladder left Cat agape. Kekona crouched next to her, awaiting an answer.

Cat wondered if she should say. Lea was responsible for Kekona's capture, but Lea didn't represent the whole race. However, Kekona was a victim here and she deserved faith.

"I guess I'm Ofarian."

Kekona's pupils and irises were nearly indistinguishable they were so dark, and Cat could have sworn she saw a tiny flame flicker across them. But then it was gone and Kekona's direct, enigmatic gaze set on her again.

"You guess?"

Cat swallowed. "I only just learned I was. Days ago. I don't even know how to use my . . . magic."

A muscle in Kekona's jaw ticked. How could someone who'd spent God knows how long in a fireproof box look so healthy and strong and focused?

"Where are we?" Kekona asked. "Where did they bring me?"

"You're in Colorado. White Clover Creek."

"Colorado? Shit." Her eyes shifted back and forth in thought. "Is there a car here? Anything to get us away?"

Cat started to pull up the cumbersome ladder, her muscles screaming that they'd had enough. Kekona leaned down and yanked up the ladder with one arm. She slid it back down over the side of the box.

"No, sorry," Cat said, thinking of Jase and how he'd said he was going to return Michael's rental car. She hadn't seen any other vehicles on site. She frowned at the garage door. How had Jase gotten back? Now that she thought about it, she hadn't heard the telltale sounds of a car prior to his reappearance out front.

"The Ofarians told us to sit tight," Cat said as she started to climb back down.

Kekona didn't bother with the ladder. She jumped off the box and absorbed the concrete landing with her muscular legs, straightening immediately. She tossed back her long hair with a shadowy smile.

"Come on. Let's get you inside. Find you some clothes." Cat had to skirt around Kekona to move toward the door into the house. Kekona didn't move aside, just followed Cat with her eyes.

"No, Cat the Ofarian. I'm not going inside."

A bolt of flame shot straight across Cat's path. With a scream she stumbled backward. Whirled around. Kekona was sitting into one hip, a thin trail of smoke leaking out from between her lips.

"And neither are you. You're going to sit right here with me," Kekona said with a terrible smile, "and wait for your people."

**That crash Xavier had heard while inside the house had been** the leftover Christmas tree, toppling from the dry fountain and knocking off one of the stone angels. There was no wind.

Jase stood next to the splintered angel. Alone. No rental car or taxi in sight. His skin was pasty, his lips tinged blue. He was trying to hide his shivering.

Xavier jogged down the front steps, the Colorado nighttime cold hitting his damp, bloodied shirt and making it feel like he wore a sheet of ice. "How the hell did you get back so fast?"

Jase didn't respond, but his eyes flicked to the snow-speckled night sky.

"The car?" Xavier prompted, not caring if Jase was a Popsicle. "Everything go okay?"

"Taken care of." Jase shoved his hands into his hair. Gone was the indifferent air elemental who'd so casually thrown Xavier around the basement room with little more than a thought. He was anxious now, *invested* in events. And, if Xavier wasn't mistaken, on the verge of tears. "Tell me; I'm dying here. What happened inside?"

"Lea's ours. So is Sean."

Jase's knees buckled. He caught himself, straightened. "Are you serious? You got them?"

"Yeah. The two Ofarians are unconscious in the basement. Sean gave a half-assed attempt to kill them but it looks like they'll live."

But Jase wasn't listening. He was staring somewhere beyond Xavier, a dazed look completely transforming his face. The rigid set to his torso and shoulders shattered, and when he exhaled, it seemed like he'd been holding his breath for years. Maybe he had been. "You get Lea's phone? That's her lifeline, man. If she presses any one of those numbers, I'm screwed. The Ofarians, too."

Xavier remembered hearing a clatter as he'd chased Lea through the hall. The phone had fallen off the desk. It should still be there. "I know where it is. We'll get it. It'll be taken care of."

"Where?"

Xavier told him and Jase dashed into the house before he even finished. Xavier followed. Jase found Lea and Sean first, prone and helpless on the couch. He stood over the Ofarian woman with fists balled. She glared up at him.

"Strange," Jase murmured to her, "but I feel like I should be thanking you. For all you did for her, how you saved her." Then his voice changed, darkening. His mouth twisted. "But

I'm not yours to order around anymore, so it looks like she and I both win."

Lea's eyes narrowed. A million questions perched on Xavier's tongue, but he was too entranced by the scene, too mesmerized by the massive, complicated web Lea had woven.

Jase swiveled away, heading for the hallway. He scooped up the phone where Xavier had told him it was. As his arm fell back, Xavier knew what was about to happen.

"Wait!" Xavier dove for Jase. "We might need that—"

But the phone was already exploding into tiny pieces against the wall. Jase picked them up, dumped them in the sink and turned on the water, then flicked on the garbage disposal. The jangling screech and grind of metal and plastic made Lea flinch.

"You might need it," Jase shot over his shoulder, "but I don't. I'm sure she's got a fail-safe somewhere. That one's for you. This one was for me. And the others." Then he headed for the front door.

"Jase." Xavier went after him. "There's still a lot of loose ends. We've called the Ofarian leaders and they're sending a team our way for cleanup. We just need to sit tight—"

"Fuck *that*." Jase threw open the front door and the wind rushed inside. He lifted his face to the snow for a brief moment, then bounded down the front steps.

Xavier stood in the doorway, knowing he had no say over what Jase did or did not do.

The air elemental just stood there in the driveway, then lifted his arms and turned around to face Xavier. He was smiling. "Well, goddamn. I'm free."

He was, and it showed. The Jase Xavier had been introduced to was not the same man who stood before him now.

"So long, Xavier." Another tip of the invisible cowboy hat. Jase turned. Sprinted down the driveway.

Where the hell did he think he was going in the middle of the night, no car, trapped high up in the mountains, dressed in nothing but—

A great gust of wind barreled down and lifted Jase clean off his feet.

He threw his arms out, head tossed back. Spinning, spinning like a corkscrew, he rose into the night sky. Breathless, frozen by more than just the weather, Xavier watched him fly—higher and higher, the snow eddying around his diminishing body. Jase soared over the road and disappeared into the blackness above the evergreens.

Even though the air elemental was no longer visible, Xavier heard Jase laugh. Joyous, relieved, anticipatory laughter. The sound drifted over the mountainside, mingling with the snowflakes. And then Jase was gone.

Xavier was standing there, staring into the sky, when a scream ripped through the night.

Cat's scream. From inside the garage.

Xavier whipped around and charged toward it. He grabbed the garage door handle, found a little strength left in his shoulders and legs, and pulled with everything he had. It didn't budge. Not a centimeter.

"Cat!" he roared. "I'm coming!"

He sprinted for the front door and ran back through the house. As he careened through the great room, Lea was laughing behind her gag. He burst into the garage.

Cat cowered in the far corner. A naked woman, dark in both hair and skin, stood in front of her, flames licking up one arm. As Xavier watched, the woman drew a deep breath, opened her mouth and blew another coating of flame over her opposite arm.

Xavier lunged for her, blinded by the need to get Cat away. The fire elemental tossed a fireball at his feet. He skidded backward, heat searing his face.

"That's far enough," she said.

"Don't you fucking dare hurt her."

At least he had known Michael's intentions. He'd wanted Cat alive. This . . . this *thing*, he knew nothing about.

His eyes watered, his lungs burned. Through the haze, he saw Cat coughing, her eyes red and tearing.

"I'm so sorry," Cat said.

He knew she was. She'd just come out here to help someone she'd thought was trapped like her.

The lingering smoke swirled in carefully controlled spirals, racing inward toward the fire elemental. The place between her ribs collapsed into an unnatural concave shape. She sucked in her cheeks and drew in the coils of smoke between her lips.

When the smoke was gone, the fire elemental smacked her lips like she'd just drank ambrosia.

She turned a wicked grin toward Xavier. "And who would you be?"

"Let Cat go."

"No."

"She took down Michael. She just came in here to free you."

"And now she's my barter," the fire elemental said. "My ticket out of this alive."

"Your life is not in danger. You're free. You can walk away."

She put a hand on her hip, and Xavier was suddenly acutely aware of her nakedness. "In the middle of a snowstorm. On a mountaintop. With no car or clothes. Oh, and here's the kicker, the *Ofarians* are coming." She came forward, fire still dancing over one arm. "It's very clear what's going on here."

Maybe to her. Xavier didn't back away. Let her come. "What do you *think* is going on?"

"You must not be Ofarian," she said. "Otherwise you'd be a little smarter, a little more egotistical."

Fire, apparently, had no love for water.

"This Ofarian, however," she nodded at Cat, "has the humble and almighty act down pat. Bravo, by the way. You'll fit right in."

"Kekona, I told you," Cat said, "I don't know them at all."

Xavier had lost his patience about five seconds ago, and he growled, *"What do you think is going on?"*

Kekona moved to the side, giving Xavier a straight line of sight to Cat. It was a sickening tease.

Kekona said, "I came to the mainland to advance the next Senatus meeting, set up security. Which means the Ofarians had a pretty good idea where I was. They're not part of the Senatus but they know when and where the meetings take place. Two Ofarians, one of them Lea, got past my guards, and snatched me in my sleep. The male Ofarian used his water magic. Caged me here. Lea told me I was a present for Michael, but now he's conveniently gone. Next thing I know, Cat tells me Griffin Aames and Gwen Carroway are headed here? To set me free?" She laughed, shaking her head. "No way. Nuh-uh. There's only one reason the two of them are coming. And that's to pick up what their little kidnapper Lea gathered for them.

They'll dangle me in front of the Senatus and bribe their way into the leadership."

Xavier remembered Gwen mentioning something like that. About some big misunderstanding that had led to bad relations between the Ofarians and the Senatus. Gwen had also said that she'd wanted to find the missing Secondaries with the hope it would buy them some brownie points with the Senatus. Kidnapping and bribery were hardly the Ofarian style, especially given Gwen's bleak history. They wouldn't anonymously steal Secondaries, "rescue" them, then try to wedge their way into power. Would they?

"You're wrong," Xavier said.

Kekona moved closer to Cat. "Then this should be a no-brainer. If they don't want me, they shouldn't have any problem letting me go. But I still need some reassurance. I'm going to keep Freckle Princess close to me until they get here. I'm sure they'll want one of their own back, so we'll make an exchange: her for my freedom."

There were so many things wrong with this situation, not the least of which being: what on earth had Lea been playing with, taking this creature?

"A fair exchange," he told Kekona, knowing that Griffin would want nothing to do with this woman.

*Hurry, Gwen.*

Flame rolled over Kekona'a eyes. Actual petals of fire. "Then I guess all we have left to do is wait."

Xavier saw a lawn chair and went over to it. Sat down. If he kept calm, maybe Kekona would be, too. He found Cat's eyes and stared into them. Kekona's nakedness faded into the distance, became white noise. All he wanted was to focus on Cat. Most of her fear had worn away and now she just looked pissed off and cold.

*This will be over soon, sweetheart. Soon.*

# THIRTY

**Cat fell asleep sometime in the small hours of the morning.**
Xavier went back into the house and brought her a blanket,
which Kekona took from him and draped over her. The chill
in the garage kept him awake. There was no way in hell he was
going to sleep until the Ofarians got there. And neither was
Kekona.

To get out from under Kekona's silent scrutiny—because
she refused to answer anything he asked—he made the rounds
in the house. Lea had fallen asleep on the couch, and Sean had
transitioned from fight-induced unconsciousness into sleep. He
checked their restraints and went upstairs to Michael.

The bedroom stank of old blood and sweat and damp carpet. The top of the bloodied rug had started to crust over.
Michael's eyes had straightened out, and they eerily followed
Xavier as he went toward the bed. Xavier stood over him for a
moment. Michael's mouth opened but the only sound that came
out was a low, garbled mumble. When Xavier untied him from
the bed there was no resistance in his body. However, when
Xavier tossed him over his shoulder, Michael's arms shifted
all on their own. If his sight was coming back, it was possible
mobility couldn't be too far behind. The question was: how
much?

Xavier lay Michael on the floor between Sean and Lea. Sean
awoke, saw Michael, gave a good struggle and tried to *split*.
But two tied-up and gagged Seans weren't any better than one.

When Xavier went into the basement, Robert and Shelby
were conscious and talking. Their plastic restraints still tightly
clamped their wrists and ankles, which meant that Sean had

succeeded in dosing them with enough *nelicoda* to destroy their water magic. Otherwise they'd have gone liquid and flowed right out of there. The twinge of sadness Xavier felt over that took him completely by surprise.

He told them everything that had happened, and instead of looking overjoyed at being freed, they exchanged shameful, worried glances. Whatever Lea had been holding over their heads was about to come out. In front of Griffin and Gwen, no less. They were glad to be free of Lea, though, and offered to stand guard over their former captors.

Xavier gestured to Shelby's neck. "I'm sorry about that."

"I'm sorry, too," she replied.

Exhausted, Xavier went back to his lawn chair in the garage.

Cat woke up when the sun rose and a line of light appeared under the garage door. Xavier leaned forward on his chair. "Hey," he said, his voice sounding too loud in the garage. When Cat gave him a weak smile, he asked Kekona, "Can I get her something to drink and eat?"

Kekona relented, but refused all food for herself. As Cat sipped water and ate a hard-boiled egg, Xavier crouched as close to her as Kekona would allow.

"It's not going to end like this," Xavier told Cat. "Gwen isn't going to let anything happen to you. Neither will I."

Cat stared right into him, and even with the deep smudges below her eyes, her gaze still had the power to level him. "I know you won't. Just as I won't let anything happen to you."

He couldn't help it. He smiled.

Kekona made a sound of disgust. "Love is so stupid."

*Love.* A warmth settled into his body, spreading out and chasing away the chill.

Cat turned to the other woman. "You say that because I bet it's never happened to you."

Kekona was sitting against the garage door and she rolled her head on the metal, staring someplace far away. "It has. That's why I think it's stupid."

Several times during the night, vehicles had chugged up the road, their lower gears kicking in with a whine as they negotiated the curve up the mountain. None had stopped. Until just then, when one vehicle, then another, turned off the road and sped toward the house.

Kekona kicked off that weird coat of melancholy, hoisted Cat to her feet, and ushered her to the back of the garage. Xavier jumped up and slapped a silver button on the wall. The white garage door rolled up, admitting a gust of arctic air and a swirl of snow. The door rose and rose, revealing a boxy, blue van and a small, white SUV careening up the curved driveway. Xavier rushed outside, lifting a hand. The SUV flashed its lights in acknowledgement.

He never thought he'd be so relieved to be surrounded by Ofarians again.

The van braked hard, sliding on the fresh, six-inch layer of snow. The doors flew open, and Ofarian soldiers poured out. It had been five years but Xavier remembered the way they moved, the way they took over an area like water gushing into a canyon after spring thaw. Like they were in charge. Two soldiers broke off and went for the front door. Three others circled around back.

The SUV came to a stop. Gwen Carroway stepped from the front passenger seat wearing the same all-black uniform as her soldiers, minus the weapons. Her blond hair was pulled into a tight ponytail. She looked the same—still gorgeous, still highly focused—maybe even more so, on both accounts. Her long legs ate up the ground between them, and he found himself moving toward her, too.

"Xavier." She looked like she wanted to embrace him, but made no move to do so. There was a sadness to her eyes, and the set of her mouth reminded him of that day he'd taken her through the Plant and showed her the hell of his birth and life.

"Gwen," he said, drawing a breath. "It's good to see you."

And it was. Great stars above, it was. She smiled, and the wistfulness of it pulled something tight in his chest.

Reed hopped out from behind the wheel and jogged around the front of the SUV. He didn't wear the Ofarian black, but jeans and a thick jacket, a skullcap pulled over his shaved head. And just like five years ago, he kept Gwen within several feet of him while his stern blue eyes swept over the scene.

Reed stuck out his hand and Xavier took it. It had taken a long time to acclimate to this, the Primary custom of shaking hands. Reed gripped hard, as Xavier had expected, and looked straight into his eyes with a firm nod. Reed let go and stood back with his big arms crossed over his chest. "Can I help inside the house?"

"If I remember correctly," Xavier said, "you were pretty good with restraints. Mind checking on the people we have by the fireplace?"

With a clap to Xavier's shoulder and a touch to Gwen's waist, Reed hopped up the front steps into the house. He always did know when to leave Secondary business to Secondaries.

"Where's Cat?" Gwen asked, and then her voice choked. "And Delia?"

"Cat is"—he turned and looked toward the back of the garage—"there. Not the naked one."

Gwen followed where his gaze led, and sucked in a breath. "Who the hell is that?"

"A fire elemental," he said. "You said there were other Secondaries taken? Well, she's one of them."

Gwen pushed past him and hurried into the garage.

"That's far enough," Kekona said, and blew a little ball of fire into her palm as a warning.

"Whoa." So Gwen had never seen this sort of thing either. "Cat, I'm Gwen. Are you okay?"

"I'm not hurt," Cat said, starting to come forward.

"Ah, Gwen Carroway," Kekona said with a bland smile, curling her fingers over Cat's shoulder and yanking her back.

If Gwen was surprised, she didn't show it. Used to being recognized, he supposed. "I am. And you are?"

Kekona's smile curled wickedly. "As if you don't know."

"I don't. And there's no reason for you to be holding one of my own."

A car door opened behind them. Xavier glanced over his shoulder to see Griffin Aames, leader of the Ofarian race, sliding from the backseat of the SUV, phone to his ear and one hand harshly cutting the air. "Yeah, it's a mess. Keep two teams on standby. We're in the middle of fucking nowhere. Get as close to White Clover Creek as you can."

While Reed looked pretty much the same, Griffin looked older. More lines on his face, a harder glaze to his dark eyes. He had thick, straight eyebrows that made him look perpetually serious. He'd once been a soldier, an obedient do-gooder to the extreme, but his posture seemed even stiffer now. Carrying the weight and fate of an entire race had worn on him.

He stalked up to Xavier and Gwen, the phone still at his ear. When he looked up, into the garage, he did a double take. The hand holding the phone dropped from his ear and his mouth fell open. But he wasn't looking at Xavier or Gwen. He was looking at Kekona.

"*Holy shit*," he murmured. Griffin pushed the phone back to his mouth, but his voice had lost its stern authority. "Sorry. Get it done. Check back in thirty." Then he shoved the phone into his pants' pocket.

He went right past Xavier, right past Gwen, to stand just feet from Kekona. Closer than she'd ever allowed Xavier to be.

"Well, well, well." Kekona tossed her long hair, revealing one breast and the curving dents of her defined stomach muscles. "If it isn't the high and mighty himself."

A muscle ticked in Griffin's clenched jaw. "Keko."

*Keko?*

The Ofarian leader and the naked fire elemental stared so hard at one another, Xavier didn't think he could break the line with a sword.

"Griffin," Gwen said, half whispering. "You *know* her?"

He swallowed and nodded once. "Kekona Kalani. General of the Chimeran forces."

"Wait." Gwen gripped Griffin's arm. "Did she have anything to do with—"

"Gwen." Reed poked his head into the garage, and his eyes were filled with regret. He opened wide the house door that led into the great room, revealing the bound hostages. "Is this your sister?"

Gwen let out a strangled cry then checked herself. She lifted her chin in that way Xavier remembered, drew a deep breath, and went to Reed. The door closed behind them.

If Griffin and Kekona noticed that Gwen had left, they gave no indication. They had yet to break eye contact. Xavier circled around them and held out his hand to Cat, who looked at it longingly.

"Don't even think about it." Kekona's voice crackled with flame, and the palm cradling the fire shot out to prevent Cat from going anywhere. Then she turned to face Griffin. "This plan of yours isn't going to work."

Griffin raised his hands, weapon free. "I have no idea what you're talking about."

Xavier believed him.

"We don't kneel before bullies. We've survived centuries without Ofarians in the Senatus. This shit, kidnapping me then holding me hostage to bribe your way in, is going to blow up in your face. You've already screwed up big-time. You actually think this is going to make them change their minds? You're a bigger egomaniac than I thought."

Griffin's eyes widened in surprise, then narrowed in anger. "What the—"

The door to the house opened again. Reed stomped into the garage, carrying a laptop. "Griffin, you need to see this."

"That's the computer Lea worked on," Xavier said.

Griffin finally snapped his focus away from Kekona. "Who's Lea?"

"Lea is Delia," Reed said. "Gwen didn't want to believe it all the way here, but"—he threw a pained look at the house—"apparently it's true." Then he flipped the laptop around to show the screen.

Griffin leaned over it and shoved a hand into his short black hair. "Shit. *Fuck.*"

Xavier peered over Griffin's shoulder. "What is it?"

Griffin's finger swept around the display, and his hand shook. "She's in the Ofarian communication system. The goddamn *mainframe.*"

"That's not all." Reed toggled between screens. "Late last night she sent an e-mail." The e-mail popped up.

To: Senatus Premier
From: The Office of Griffin Aames

*We want in.*

Attachment: photos

Reed clicked on the attachments. A very clear succession of images showed Kekona being subdued using water magic, then being hauled unconscious into the fireproof cage . . . by Lea and Robert.

From inside the house trailed a low, throaty laugh. Lea's laugh.

Gwen raced back into the garage, white as snow, her eyes and nose red from crying. "What's happened? What did she do?" But she could barely get that much out, and she was sobbing again.

"How did this *happen*?" Griffin yelled.

"I think she's got someone inside your office," Xavier told Griffin. "Or at least someone pretty high up. She locked me up with a neutralizer cuff, the kind from the Plant. She got them sent here on short notice, because she didn't even know I existed until a couple days ago. And she had *nelicoda*."

Griffin turned away, hands on hips, staring at the ground.

*"What did she do?"* Gwen demanded.

Reed snapped the laptop shut and tucked it under his arm. Xavier could tell he wanted to pull Gwen to him, but didn't. Gwen was positively *vibrating*.

Griffin turned back around and raised his eyes to Gwen's. "Delia's starting a war."

Now Gwen reached for Reed. She clung to his side as his big arm came around her shoulders.

"There's other crap on here." Reed lifted the computer. "Videos of Secondaries. Proof positive of their powers."

Griffin made a terrible sound in the back of his throat. "Find out where else those videos might have been saved, who might have seen them."

"Try Raymond Ebrecht," Xavier said, remembering Michael's cryptic reference to the other man.

Hands on his hips, Griffin stared at Lea through the door. *"Why* would she do this?" he asked, more to himself.

In a very small voice, Gwen said, "Because she's not my sister anymore."

Kekona started to clap, little bursts of firecracker flame sprouting from her hands with every strike. "Very nice. Fine acting, all around."

Griffin glared at Kekona, but he looked more hurt than angry. "I had nothing to do with this."

Kekona jabbed a finger toward the house. "That bitch is

Gwen's *sister*. And she didn't work alone. The fact that you're here, that you and Gwen came for me and you didn't send your henchmen, that I have no way out of this place except going with you, tells me a whole hell of a lot."

Kekona hauled Cat backward, one muscled arm around Cat's neck. Cat scrabbled in Kekona's grip but the Chimeran was much stronger, and it took all of Xavier's power to keep still.

"Let me go home," Kekona demanded, "without incident, without any more excuses, without any bargaining with the Senatus, and you can have your water virgin."

Griffin advanced another step toward Kekona. "You'll let her go anyway. This isn't about her."

Kekona raised an eyebrow. "Is it about us then?" Then she licked her lower lip. Long and slow.

As Gwen might say, *Holy stars in hell.*

"There is no us," Griffin growled. "Remember? That wasn't exactly my choice."

A glimmer of emotion swept across Kekona's face. She tried to swipe it away and just barely succeeded. "It wasn't mine either."

A prolonged silence followed. Then Reed pitched his voice low. "Griffin, bud. This is looking really bad for you."

"Look," Griffin began, and inched even closer to Kekona. Xavier watched him desperately trying to look only at Kekona's face, but he knew the signs of anger mixed with arousal all too well—the labored breathing, the constant shifting of his stance, the flush on his neck—and Griffin was having a hell of a time keeping his under control.

The Ofarian leader ripped off his coat and held it out to Kekona. She just looked at it.

"Go on," he said. "Take it."

She laughed, deep and sensual. "Why? It's nothing you haven't seen before."

Gwen gasped.

Griffin ground his teeth together and Xavier knew that reaction, too. Griffin may have been all over Kekona at one point, and whatever had happened may have been long over, but that didn't mean he liked anyone else looking at what he still wanted for himself.

"Put it on," Griffin ordered. "Let Cat go to Xavier. And go

back and tell your people I had nothing to do with this. The Ofarians did not take you. Just one lone, messed-up woman who went rogue from us years ago. There is no hostage situation here."

"Really?" There went that eyebrow again. Kekona still didn't take the coat. "You don't 'want in'?"

"I—" Griffin cut himself off, lowered his eyes to the floor. When he raised his head he wore the look of a confirmed, dedicated leader. "We want a seat in the Senatus, yes."

Kekona looked disgusted and satisfied at the same time. "Well, there you go."

She snatched for Griffin's coat, but he didn't let go. He gave his own jerk, making her stumble. He pulled her another foot closer. She hated *that*. And Xavier was starting to feel shameful and awkward, standing here witnessing this exchange that so clearly had *SEX* written all over it.

"Just do it, Keko," Griffin begged, barely loud enough for Xavier to hear. "Please."

She snarled, pulled the coat from his grip and swung it around her shoulders. It was big enough to cover her ass, but just barely. After she zipped it up, only her fingertips jutted out of the sleeves.

Kekona turned her face just slightly into the collar of his coat. Inhaled. Griffin went bone still.

"I'll deliver your message," she said. "Just don't expect them to believe it."

Griffin exhaled, as did Xavier. He stretched that hand for Cat again.

"All right," said Griffin. "Good."

Kekona grabbed Cat and walked her backward toward the driveway. Toward the cars. "I'll take your wheels, Griffin, if you don't mind."

"No fucking way." Xavier charged forward. "Cat stays."

"Xavier . . ." Griffin warned.

Xavier rounded on him. "She's not leaving with Cat."

Kekona left the garage and stepped into the snow, the white flakes instantly melting under her feet, under her fire. A wave of heat shimmered around her body. She looked at Xavier with a tilted head, studying him for a moment, then shoved Cat toward him. "Here. Take her."

Cat fell into Xavier and he caught her, wrapping her up in his arms. Probably held her a bit too tightly, but then, the grip she had on his neck wasn't exactly comfortable either. He didn't care. He kissed her hair, her face, her lips.

"I think I'm done with this, being someone's plaything," Cat whispered against his mouth, and her words tasted almost as sweet as her lips. "Unless that someone's you."

He clung to her then, feeling her firmness and warmth, vowing to never let her go again.

"Oh, Griffin!"

Xavier looked up. Kekona had made it to the SUV and now stood on the running board, her head sticking up over the roof. Cat turned in his arms and he tucked her head under his chin.

Griffin slowly emerged from the garage. *"What?"*

"I totally lied. You screwed the wrong woman. Your people started something here, and mine are going to finish it. We're coming after you, and when we're done, the Ofarians'll no longer exist. See ya."

Griffin screamed something in Ofarian, a raw, anguished sound. He sprinted for the white SUV.

Kekona drew a deep breath and blew a straight, raging shot of flame from her mouth. It struck the blue van, turned its body yellow-white-gold with intense heat. The interior ignited and melted. And then the flame must have reached the gas tank, because the whole thing exploded.

Xavier whirled Cat in his arms, throwing his back to the explosion and pushing her into the garage. Heat scorched his legs and shoulders and spine.

Outside, the SUV's engine whined, the tires spinning on the ice. Xavier swiveled back around to see Kekona peeling down the driveway. Gone.

Griffin and Gwen ran for the burning van and started chanting in Ofarian, their voices rising as one. They knelt just outside the flames' reach and ran their fingers through the snow. They pulled the flakes to their bodies with invisible force, in a white fury. When the snow touched their hands, it instantly melted, and they flung the new stream of water outward like a hose, spraying it over the burning van, extinguishing the fire before it could lick the house.

Cat gasped in Xavier's arms. He understood. This was no tiny stream of liquid coiling innocently around her arm. This was her first witness of the full extent of her people's magic. She looked equal parts fearful and fascinated.

The van fire died out, leaving behind a charred, smoking husk, and Griffin and Gwen came back into the garage, faces grim. Reed slapped the button to close the rolling door. Gwen immediately went to Reed, and Xavier was amazed to see how the Primary had taken the whole magic show in stride. How things had changed over the years.

Griffin walked right up to Kekona's fireproof cage, put his hands on it. "Was she kept in here?"

"Yes," Cat said, pulling gently from Xavier's arms. "I don't know for how long. I let her out."

Palms still on the cage, Griffin bent his head and shook it slowly. He stayed that way for a long while, everyone in the garage watching him, wondering what the hell had exactly happened between him and Kekona Kalani.

Then the Ofarian leader pushed off the box. When he whipped around, there was absolutely zero emotion on his face. "We need some serious cleanup and cover-up work here. Call in the standby teams."

"I'm on it." Gwen pulled a phone from her pocket and punched a number. She moved away to speak in low tones, one finger in her opposite ear.

Griffin threw open the door to the house and stomped into the great room. Xavier followed, finally starting to feel the cold, the way his blood-stiffened shirt abraded his icy skin. Griffin came to a halt just inside, taking in the three tied-up Secondaries, and Robert and Shelby, who were talking to Ofarian soldiers in the kitchen. The faint thump of footsteps trickled down from other parts of the house.

"*Great stars*," Griffin whispered, going to stand over Lea. "Delia . . ."

That's right, Xavier thought. If Griffin and Gwen had known each other since they were teenagers, he would have known Lea, too.

Griffin turned to Xavier and Cat while gesturing to Michael and Sean. "And these two?"

Cat was about to open her mouth when, surprisingly, Reed

came forward. He nudged his chin at Michael. "That's Tracker. Remember the guy I told you about?"

No shit. Xavier recalled that name. Five years ago, Nora, the Tedran leader, had hired Reed to kidnap Gwen in order to force her to destroy the Plant and end the slavery. To keep Reed on a tight leash, Nora had threatened to reveal Reed's identity to Tracker, the client whose contract Reed had skipped out on.

Looked like they'd just been reunited. Funny—and awful? And amazing?—how the world worked out.

Gwen came back inside. "Backup's on its way. ETA two hours. One team to scrub this place clean, another to get us the hell out of here."

The Ofarians would leave. Was Xavier just supposed to go back to his life? The house he'd bought with Gwen's money, the kitchen he'd outfitted so well to deal with all his . . . issues? Shed? How could he look at any of that the same way ever again?

Was Cat included in that "us"? Now that she'd met her people, would she leave with them? Leave him? She was standing just two feet away and already it felt like two miles.

Griffin started to pace, and Xavier couldn't help but notice how Robert and Shelby watched him with respectful fear.

Gwen said, "We need to find the Chimerans. Appeal to them directly. Grovel, if we have to. Kekona just declared war on false pretenses. We have to try for peace before the shit hits the fan. E-mails aren't going to do it. Phone calls aren't going to do it."

Griffin stopped pacing and every eye turned to him. The sarcastic edge to his voice sliced through the air. "Sure. Yeah. Find them for me and I'll take care of it personally."

"I thought," Reed said, glancing between Gwen and Griffin, "their stronghold has never been located."

"It hasn't," Griffin snapped.

Gwen took a deep breath and Xavier knew she was preparing to say something big. "But there may be someone who can help us find it."

"Who?" Griffin demanded.

Gwen, strangely, looked to Cat. "Heath Colfax. Cat's father."

# THIRTY-ONE

**"You know my father?"**

They were sitting in the formal front living room, Cat and Xavier on a striped loveseat, Gwen and Reed on the longer couch opposite, Griffin pacing again under the arch to the foyer. Cat tightly gripped Xavier's hand, and he let her.

Gwen shifted to the very edge of the couch. The big, bald man named Reed sat close enough to her to say she was his, but far enough away to declare him not the possessive type. He sighed deep into the cushions, unzipped his coat, and stretched his thick arms across the back of the couch.

"I don't know him," Gwen said carefully. Xavier had been right; there was a magnetism to her. A confidence. "I know *of* him."

"Yeah, but you found him?" Her birth father. Just thinking that was strange. And stirring.

"I did." Gwen glanced at Xavier. "I used the information about where you grew up, Cat, your birthday and such. The former Ofarian Board kept a lot of information covered, tried to keep certain situations under wraps. They wanted to twist what the general Ofarian population knew about their own people. They wanted to ensure there were no uprisings, no dustups. And if there was any sort of behavioral problem or a lesson to be learned"—her eyes flicked toward the great room where her own sister was restrained—"then they trotted out the rule book and made a public spectacle of someone to keep us all in line."

Gently, reassuringly, Xavier placed a hand on the small of Cat's back and just held it there.

"So I dug into the hidden records," Gwen went on, "from around the time of your birth. There was this account of a couple who were deeply in love, Heath and Jessica, but who the Board didn't match in marriage. The family lines weren't compatible or some director owed another one a favor, or other such bullshit. Anyway, the couple was devastated to say the least. Jessica was already pregnant, you see, and even though she hadn't told Heath about the pregnancy, she couldn't bear the thought of raising the baby with another man. Jessica told the Board she wanted to travel before marrying—which wasn't that uncommon of an occurrence—and ran off before she started showing. She had the baby in some other part of the country. When she came back to San Francisco, no one was the wiser."

"How'd she get away with that, if the Board kept such tabs on their people?" Cat asked.

"There was a note attached to the back of the file, filling in pieces of information years after all this had happened. The Board searched, but the kid was never found. They thought you had been born in Alabama."

Xavier began to rub little circles on Cat's back. "So she had me in Indiana and returned to San Francisco. Did she marry the man the Board wanted her to?"

Gwen nodded tightly. "Yes. That's what you did back then. And if you didn't . . ." Another glance at the great room. "Things are different now, thank the stars."

One of Reed's hands left the back of the couch and stroked down Gwen's ponytail.

Cat was almost afraid to ask. "Is Jessica still alive?"

"Yes. We haven't contacted her about you. I thought that should be left up to you."

Cat exhaled. Her birth mother. Alive. "Okay. Thank you. And my . . . father?"

"Years after Jessica married the other guy, Heath was still distraught, became a completely different person—withdrawn, depressed, alcoholic—by all accounts. He refused all other marriage matches and instead applied for work in the Plant."

The circles on Cat's back stopped. She reached around and pulled Xavier's hand to her lap.

Gwen looked pointedly at their entwined fingers, her eyes soft. "He's told you?"

Cat squeezed Xavier's hand. "Yes."

"I don't think you knew, Xavier, that many Ofarians who applied for work in the Plant—not doctors or scientists or those who we thought were creating *Mendacia*—were oftentimes people who felt they had nowhere else to go. You had to give up your connection to the greater Ofarian world when you went to work there, and Heath wanted that more than anything."

Oh, God, this wasn't happening. Her own father . . . part of the machine that had made Xavier. "Where is he now?"

"Still at the Plant. It's a prison."

Inside her hand, Xavier's fingers went slack. Then he pulled them away entirely. She turned to him and he was looking down at her with a face like granite. It was one thing for her to be Ofarian, another for her birth father to have been somehow involved in his imprisonment.

He ripped his gaze from Cat and looked to Gwen. "Why do you think this Heath guy would know anything about the . . . what did you call them? The Chimerans?"

All that terror, all those nightmares Xavier had bled out to Cat that night in Shed—he was pushing them aside. For her. She didn't know if she wanted to take him in her arms and thank him, or send him from the room. He didn't have to be here for this. He didn't have to know this.

But he chose to stay.

Gwen drew a breath and stood. "Because after Jessica came back, married the other man, and then finally told Heath about the child they'd made but could not have, Heath went AWOL. Completely off the radar. He reemerged years later and the Board had to consider his punishment for desertion. He bargained for mercy by trading information."

"The Chimerans," Griffin said from beneath the arch.

Gwen nodded. "Heath claimed that while he was away, he'd discovered another Secondary race. Said that he found the stronghold of the fire elementals, but refused to say where it was or to give the Board more information. I think, because the Board didn't allow him to love whom he wanted, he liked withholding information from them, and they couldn't touch him because they wanted what was in his head. The Board sealed the scant bit of intel in a classified folder called 'Others.'" She turned to her leader. "Heath's story started the hunt for the other Secondaries, Griffin, but they never found the Senatus until you came along."

Griffin pressed his lips together. Perhaps he didn't claim that as such a great achievement, given all that had happened. "No travel records?" he asked. "Plane or train tickets? Anything?"

"Nope," Gwen said. "Which means he drove . . . or traveled by water."

By the grave look Gwen and Griffin exchanged, Cat realized they weren't talking about a boat ride.

"I'm thinking," Gwen said, "that maybe he might finally be willing to talk for the chance to meet his long-lost daughter."

"He's not going free." Griffin put his hands on his hips. "No exceptions. We make one, we have to make others. The lines are too blurry."

Gwen held up a placating hand. "I *know*, Griffin."

"Yes." Cat jumped to her feet. "Yes, I want to meet him. And if it can help you guys, who helped me, then that's all the better." Beside her, Xavier rose, too. But much, much slower.

"Thank you. I'll make the call with the offer," Gwen said, turning away.

They waited for interminably long minutes, at least a thousand of them, as Gwen moved into the game room and spoke into her phone in a voice too low to overhear. Cat hovered in the doorway, wondering if by meeting her father she'd actually be able to prevent a war.

When Gwen came back in, all eyes snapped to her. No one moved. She gave Cat a small smile. "He cried, Cat, when I told him we'd found you. And he agreed to the exchange. Meeting you for the Chimerans' last known whereabouts."

Cat clasped her hands together. The room went blurry beyond the sheen of her tears. She tried to dab them away but they kept coming. And she kept smiling.

"Done." Griffin removed his phone from a pocket in his vest, clicked a single button. "David, hey. Need a change in travel plans. Yeah, we're headed to the Plant instead."

The Plant.

Cat turned to Xavier. He lowered his eyes to the carpet, but not before she saw his beautiful face twist with anguish. Asking him days ago to go to Chicago with her was one thing.

Asking him to go back to the Plant was entirely another, and she would never do it.

**Two hours later, Xavier stood on the front steps of the house** with Reed and Griffin. He watched Cat talk with Gwen next to one of the newly arrived trucks that would bear the prisoners and the handful of Ofarians to the local airport, where private transport would take them to Nevada. A flatbed was loading up the vehicle Kekona had burned to a crisp.

Swarms of Ofarians covered the house and grounds, turning everything that had happened here invisible. They were really good at that.

Xavier had exchanged his blood-soaked shirt for a clean extra one of Reed's. Cat now wore an Ofarian uniform. They'd discovered her suitcase and personal belongings—taken by Lea from her hotel room after she'd "checked out"—but she'd chosen to wear the offered black.

She was leaving, going back to the place of his birth.

"I'll be here when you get back," he'd told her, but he was keenly aware that neither of them had any idea when that would be. If at all.

She'd never belonged here in Colorado. The only place he belonged was with her, but he couldn't go where she was headed.

He would return to the sanctuary he'd constructed here over the past three years. The sanctuary he was now loath to return to. Couldn't go forward, couldn't go back. Stuck in limbo and hating himself. All that "healing" Cat had given him? Down the shitter.

The front door opened behind Xavier, and a soldier ushered Michael out. He was walking now—like a man who'd done a whole bottle of whiskey with a beer bong, but walking. Still no speech, but plenty of coherent looks and a messy flapping of the lips. He was covered in blood. He ignored Xavier as the guard helped him down the steps, but as he passed Cat, he stared at her good and long. Cat faced him without fear, and Xavier's heart swelled with pride.

The soldier stuffed Michael into the truck holding Sean and Lea.

"I want to learn about him," Griffin said, almost to himself. "And the kid. What's his name again? Sean?"

Reed had pulled the skullcap over his head again and watched the scene with arms crossed. "Are you taking them to the Plant?"

When Griffin nodded, Xavier shuddered. "Experiments, Griffin?"

The Ofarian leader moved to stand right in front of Xavier. "Those days are over. Just discussions, I promise you. You told me what Michael and Sean can do. I haven't heard of anything like it. I may be wrong, but I don't even think the Senatus knows. Maybe if we find out something new, we can present it to the Senatus and be granted a seat—"

"You mean the Senatus that's about to declare war on you?" Reed scoffed.

"You mean you'll *use* them?" Xavier added, disbelieving.

"Fuck." Griffin's troubled eyes swept over the line of vehicles surrounding the fountain and landed squarely on Lea, who was barely visible through the tinted truck windows. "When did this become such a mess?"

Xavier had an answer to that. When Nora had hired Reed to kidnap Gwen five years ago, that's when the Secondary world had shifted.

"I won't use them," Griffin said. "Who knows what the hell's going to happen to Michael, what sort of state he'll end up in, but Sean is alert and young. Maybe he'll be willing to partner with us, if he's no longer under Michael's thumb."

"Sean used to be in a federal hospital," Reed added, "under government surveillance. They knew about his powers, or at least, they thought they knew. If Adine's willing, maybe she can patch in, try to gain access to his old files. Maybe Sean's looking for a little bit of extra protection. Keep that in mind."

Ofarian orchestration, Ofarian manipulation. Xavier looked to the snow-filled sky.

"So what about Michael?" Griffin asked. "He can't just disappear. That's when Primaries start asking questions. He lived in their world, not ours."

Xavier took a deep breath and told them how Jase had returned Michael's rental car. "But that's not enough," he added, and he couldn't believe what he was about to say. "The Primaries need to think he's dead."

Griffin's thick eyebrows drew together. "Go on."

Xavier looked to Cat. He'd do this for her—to protect her and the bond she'd just formed with the Ofarians. "Michael's a high-profile guy. You're right; he can't just disappear. He needs to die. In the Primary world, at least."

"Wait." Reed pushed past Griffin and came right up to Xavier. "You're talking about what you did with Gwen five years ago. How you made that dead homeless guy look like her."

Xavier shivered with the memory, but nodded.

Griffin's expression brightened. "Shit. Yes. We completely fell for it."

Xavier held up a hand. "But I didn't use my own power." He really, *really* couldn't believe he was doing this. His next words came out barbed, resisting their exit. "It worked because I made that man swallow *Mendacia*. I can make a tennis racket look like Michael's dead body, but the second anyone touches it the illusion will die. I need *Mendacia*."

Which would be impossible, considering Xavier had used every last drop of *Mendacia* to disguise the ship carrying the freed Tedrans as it rose out of Lake Tahoe and soared out of Earth's atmosphere. He still remembered how terrible and glorious that had felt. All that power, underneath his skin. All that power, made from Tedran lives.

"I have a bottle. At my house." Griffin's olive skin paled. He slanted his gaze toward the sun gleaming behind the mountains. "I've kept it all this time to remind me what we once were. What we're trying to be."

*Trying* to be. If that wasn't telling.

"I'm not killing anyone," Xavier told him, "but if you can get it to me, I'll help you out."

Griffin immediately spun away, muttering into his phone.

A hollowness ate away at Xavier, but he would do this, because Cat's safety depended on it. How strange, given that just two weeks ago he had been so intent on wedging himself into the Primary world. Now, once again, he was trying to sweep it away.

The wind picked up, making him think of Jase.

"Gwen will take care of her," Reed said at his shoulder, with a meaningful look toward Cat.

He exhaled, the pain in his chest worth the weight of a mountain or two. "I know. There's so much I don't know, but I know that."

"All right." Griffin came back to them. "The bottle will meet us at the Plant."

All strength left Xavier's body. "No. I can't—"

"Xavier, if we wait for it to get here we lose time with Heath Colfax. We need Cat to get what's in his head and we need it *now*. My people can drive the *Mendacia* to Nevada faster than they can get it to Colorado by plane. Who knows where Kekona is now, who she's contacted. We're relying on hours here, not days."

The wind swept Xavier's hair across his face and he swiped at it, wishing, for once, that he had the nerve to go as bald as Reed. Cat hadn't asked him to go to the Plant with her, and he hadn't offered. Now he had no other choice. *Face it like a man. A healed man.*

"All right," he said.

Griffin had the grace to look humbled. "Thank you, Xavier. I feel like I say that to you every time we're together." He clapped a hand on Xavier's shoulder and Xavier winced. The adrenaline had vanished hours ago. Now rushed in the pain from all the fights and the debilitating exhaustion.

Griffin frowned, then waved over an Ofarian soldier. "My EMT will look at you. Don't say no." Then he lifted his phone to his mouth again and barked into it. "I want evidence Michael Ebrecht is leaving Colorado on a private plane tonight. False departure records. Aircraft registration. Everything. And I want a plane we can set on autopilot to drive into the ground outside of Reno . . ."

Xavier didn't hear the rest. He was already walking toward Cat. Gwen saw him approach, gave Cat's arm a squeeze, and fell back toward Reed.

Xavier stood in front of her, his beautiful, brave Cat. "I'm going to the Plant."

Her chin quivered, but she clamped her jaw shut and the emotion transferred to her eyes, making them all clear and lovely. Like water. Never in a million years would she have asked him to go back there. He knew that. But some tiny part of her was glad they'd be together. And maybe he felt the same.

"Xavier," Griffin called out. "Everything's all set."

Xavier acknowledged the Ofarian leader with a lift of the chin.

Cat blinked up at him. "Set for what?"

He inhaled deeply. "I'm going to Nevada in order to fake Michael's death with glamour."

She touched her lips. "Oh, God. You'd do that?"

"I don't have a choice. They need to make sure Michael's not a threat while all this stuff with Kekona goes down . . ." He reached out, slid his arms around her waist. "And I'm going for you, too."

She smiled, but it was broken. "Don't say that. I don't want to be the one responsible for sending you back there."

"You're not sending me." He pulled her even closer. "I can stay here in Colorado and watch you fly away. I can be a prick and demand that I'll only help Griffin on my terms. But the thing is, this place, this town, won't ever be the same to me without you. It's my fucking hang-ups that screwed everything up between us—"

"No, that's not true."

"But really, what am I going to do? Go back to my job, my house, and sink back into that hole that I'd tricked myself into believing was contentment? I'm going back to Nevada because that's where Griffin needs me. It's where—and I can't believe I'm saying this—innocent Ofarians need me. I'm going back to Nevada because if I want to move on with my life, I should be able to leave my past in the past, right?"

Now her hands slid around his back, making his whole body come alive. He touched his forehead to hers, breathing her in. "And I'm going back with you. If you want a hand to hold when you meet your father, I'll give you one."

"Yes," she whispered. "I want that."

At this point, he'd do anything she asked. Anything.

# THIRTY-TWO

Cat got her first and last look at *Mendacia* when an Ofarian named David met them in the middle of the Nevada barrenness. When he passed the small vial to Griffin, she could see the worn-out places on the silver label where the leader's fingers fit so well. She could picture him sitting alone in his office or home or wherever, holding the bottle and staring into everything that had gone wrong for his people.

For *their* people, she corrected herself.

Without emotion, Xavier snatched the bottle from Griffin and the cage holding two rats from David. Xavier held one rat in his palm, popped the vial's cork with a thumb, and poured the thick liquid down the rat's throat.

Cat gasped. *Mendacia* was the exact color of Xavier's eyes.

She stood with David—who said he'd been good friends with Gwen since junior high and Griffin since high school—and watched, fascinated, as Xavier manipulated his magic.

He fed the other rat, then wove an illusionary spell on both animals, making one into a pilot—whose identity the half-Tedran tech master Adine Jones had created in less than an hour solely to serve his death—and the other into Michael Ebrecht. Xavier had gotten it eerily right. Cat went up and touched the new Michael, his skin real but chillingly not real. An Ofarian stuffed Michael's wallet into the faux-Michael's pocket and they sent the small plane up in the air on some sort of sophisticated remote and autopilot.

Cat and Xavier, Griffin and David, were speeding down the highway, deeper into the cold Nevada scrub, when David, sitting next to her, played with buttons on a handheld computer.

She swiveled in her seat to watch the tiny plane fall from the sky and crash in a great fireball in the middle of nowhere.

She thought of Helen and how, despite Michael's many, many shortcomings, his "favorite former stepmom" would be devastated.

The whole ride to the Plant, Xavier sat next to her with his head bowed. He didn't fidget; he didn't wield that invisible knife. He just sat there, breathing, eyes on his knees. When the giant, gray building, with no outside markings and nothing else around for miles, appeared in the distance, she knew it had to be the Plant.

She reached for Xavier. He'd said he'd hold her hand, but she wanted to take his first.

The moment Griffin and David guided them into the Plant, Xavier's head lifted. He was going in with his chin raised and eyes opened, and Cat felt a surge of love for him. He didn't have to go inside. He'd done what he came to Nevada to do. He could have waited in the car out in the parking lot. But he didn't.

Gwen and Reed should have arrived hours earlier with Lea. Griffin had refused to allow Lea time with her father until they knew everything she knew. Gwen had volunteered to interrogate her sister regarding her actions and the probable Ofarian mole, an assignment that garnered Gwen a whole heck of a lot of respect from Cat, given that the only two surviving members of Gwen's family were imprisoned here.

Michael and Sean would be given quarters and taken care of in the Plant until their situation was evaluated. The two Ofarians who had also been Lea's victims were to be taken away for questioning and medical checks by the head Ofarian doctor, who was also David's wife.

Now Cat and the three men—two Ofarian, one Tedran—walked slowly through the quiet, dimly lit corridors of the Plant. When they passed through a narrow hallway lined with doors that had been bricked over, the newer rectangles a lighter shade, Xavier shut down. He squeezed her hand so hard she lost feeling, but there was no expression on his wan face. Griffin awkwardly cleared his throat.

It was a world without windows, a life without light. And somewhere in here was Cat's father. Gwen had said anyone and everyone directly involved with the Plant—anyone who'd knowingly perpetuated the horror without trying to stop it— had been imprisoned here. Cat wasn't sure if that seemed fair, especially given Colfax's circumstances for seeking employment here in the first place.

They entered a cell block, a wide corridor whose cinder block walls had been painted a light blue. The place was carpeted, and each cell had a bed and a couch. Books. Not cushy by any means, but comfortable.

Xavier stopped, tugged his hand from Cat's, and slowly turned around to face Griffin. "I see you redecorated."

Griffin shifted under Xavier's harsh stare and said carefully, "There was a lengthy debate over how to modify the Plant to accommodate the new Ofarian prisoners. Some felt the place should be left exactly as it was so the Ofarians would get the exact same treatment as the Tedran slaves. Others wanted to essentially make it a hotel."

"So you made the executive decision to spruce the place up?" Xavier bit out. "Make it a little cheerier for your own?"

Griffin's jaw ticked. "Big decisions are done by vote now. I'm a moderator and, in some cases, a tiebreaker. Not a dictator."

"Aha. So the Ofarian people at large didn't want to see their own criminals sitting in a gray cell with the constant buzz of neutralizer lights picking at their brains and destroying their sanity."

Griffin drew a deep breath through his nose. "There are basic rights that all people deserve—Primary and Secondary. We recognized the grave mistakes we'd made for many generations and wanted to send a message that we are changing. Evolving. It was a very, very difficult choice to make, Xavier. Do not walk in here and assume these criminals have it easy by any definition. They've all been given enough *nelicoda* to fry their water magic, the very thing that makes them Ofarian. They are incarcerated. They are being punished. They will be in here the rest of their lives. And you are free."

The two men stared at each other. Xavier had four inches on Griffin, but Griffin looked every bit the born leader.

Griffin's phone rang. He answered it without breaking eye contact with Xavier. He grunted into it, shut it, then turned to

Cat. "David will take you to meet Heath in the conference room. I'll meet you there in a few minutes. Gwen needs me." He jogged off, leaving Cat to wonder and worry about how things were going between Gwen and Lea.

With a tight smile, David gestured her and Xavier out of the cell block and toward a *T* intersection. David was blond, too, but in a muddier fashion than Xavier. There was a casual air to his personality and posture, but he wore that same intense focus that all Ofarians seemed to have. Like they were forever trying to shift the weight of their worries around on their shoulders. That worry never went away; they just had to figure out how to bear it. She wondered if she'd ever get to be like that, and the prospect frightened her.

The panic returned without warning. That awful feeling of being engulfed by the flow of something she couldn't stop or manage.

When they came to the *T* intersection, Xavier stopped walking. He stared off to the left, where the carpeted hallway curved around in a gentle arc and disappeared into complete darkness.

David slid his hands into his pockets and nudged his chin in the direction of Xavier's glassy-eyed stare. "It's storage now. Nobody wanted anything to do with the Circle. And did you see? We bricked over the old draining rooms."

Xavier swiveled around, ignoring David to find Cat's eyes. "Let's go," he barked. "We're not here for me."

David brought them to a part of the Plant devoted to offices, the space utilitarian and plain, but clean. He opened a door between two fake ficus trees, flipped on the light inside, and gestured them into a conference room. A round table occupied the center of the room, with six cushioned rolling chairs positioned around it. Another door stood on the opposite end of the room. David pointed to it.

"They'll bring him in through there. I'll wait for Griffin out in the hall."

David stepped out, leaving the door open a crack. She and Xavier turned to each other.

"Are you—" she began.

A blaze of passion rolled over his gunmetal eyes and he was on her in an instant, pressing her back against the wall, his mouth hot and wet over hers. She gave in to him, because he was Xavier and he ignited something fierce in her. She was the match, forever waiting for him to strike her into flame. And, like a match, that flame happened instantly and with a brilliant, intense burst of color and heat.

His kiss was hungry and hard, as only he was capable of. The crush of his body against hers, the strong length of his thigh pushed between her legs . . . it had been ages since they'd touched like this. The improperness of the situation and location and timing just barely registered. It was there, faintly poking at the back of her mind, but she skillfully ignored it. Ever since the morning after they'd first had sex, when she'd twirled the water, she'd felt Xavier slipping away. Now he was here, against her, kissing her like he wanted to regain every inch lost.

"I want you out of these clothes." He was against her mouth, in her brain, in her bloodstream.

*Yes.* She wanted that, too. Just the two of them and their skin. And he'd loom over her, chest to chest, and slide into her. He'd . . . Wait.

She was wearing a black Ofarian uniform. When she'd emerged from the bathroom at the house in Colorado wearing it, Xavier had turned away, but not before she saw how much the clothing bothered him. Did he want to sleep with her again? Or did he just want her, literally, out of Ofarian clothing? Was this an angry kiss? One of those he didn't *want* to want?

And hadn't he once told her that just the walk from his cell to the Circle had automatically switched on his libido? He'd been conditioned to want sex just by being here. What exactly was he reacting to? Her, or something entirely out of her control?

Xavier reached around her neck and pulled her hair away from her skin. *There.* He found that spot just below her ear that made her knees crumple. She whimpered, tilted her head more to give him better access.

"I miss that sound." He swirled his tongue, the words seeping into her. "I've missed *you*, Cat."

The best possible thing he could say.

She clutched at the waistband of his jeans. He'd accepted a shirt from Reed and a coat from David, but had refused to put on anything Ofarian black. At her touch, his stomach muscles clenched and she traced the hard ridges with her fingertips. Just below, his erection nudged hard against her belly and it was all she could do not to reach for it right there.

"I've missed you, too," she said, and he groaned.

Suddenly Xavier stopped. His lips left her skin and he turned his head away from her. "Go away, you bastard," he snarled, even as he ground himself between her legs. "You don't belong here anymore."

"What?" Cat managed to whisper. She could barely stand, barely think.

A strange man's voice rumbled through the conference room. It sounded like a wild animal had clawed out the man's voice box and he'd tucked it back in, tatters and all.

"And where exactly do I belong then, 267X?"

Cat froze. Xavier froze.

He pushed off but kept her caged within his arms. He squeezed his eyes shut and his breath hissed in and out of his nose. "Cat," he whispered. "Tell me you don't see him. Please tell me you don't see him."

But Cat did. Across the table, she saw the paunchy Ofarian prisoner dressed in a gray jumpsuit, half his face melted from fire, and eyes she recognized as her own.

Heath Colfax, her father.

Heath Colfax, the Burned Man.

**Xavier spun away from her and flew out of the conference room** so fast that by the time Cat dragged herself out from under the shock and ran after him, he'd already reached the end of the hall.

"Xavier!"

He didn't turn around.

From the opposite direction, Griffin called her name. She half turned toward the Ofarian leader, now stalking toward her. "Not now," she told him, so afraid to lose track of Xavier.

"Yes. Now."

Griffin's severe tone cemented her boots to the floor. He jogged up, his thick eyebrows drawn tightly together. "Keko has made it back to her people. She's rallied them against us. The Chimeran chief has called the Senatus together for immediate war council. I need the fire elementals' location. I need it *now*."

She whirled around, but Xavier had disappeared from sight.

"Shit!" The curse came out surprisingly easy. "Shit! Fuck!" She wrapped her arms around her head, spun in a circle.

She couldn't let him just run off like that, not after all that he'd told her that night in Shed.

"Just wait," Cat told Griffin, then sped off down the corridor after Xavier.

The place was a maze. On the way in she'd paid more attention to him than to the pattern of lefts and rights. She called his name again and again. No answer, just the sharp, jangling echo of the cinder block walls throwing her own voice right back at her.

She sprinted down one hall that dead-ended in a large room divided by floor to ceiling windows. Reminded her of a hospital nursery. Only this place was empty and spooky and filled with ghosts. Spinning around, she backtracked and came face-to-face with the curved corridor leading into the Circle. She remembered now. They'd turned right coming through that door there, so that meant she had to go left to get out.

And there, at the *T* intersection, yawned the entrance to the first cell block they'd walked through. That meant it was close to the Plant exit, which was where Xavier was undoubtedly headed.

She burst through the double doors and let them swing wide behind her. He'd almost reached the end. When the squeak of the door hinges filled the block, he stopped. Turned around. His face burned red, his silver eyes swirling and tormented. His lips pulled back from his teeth, like she was about to attack him.

These past weeks together? All the progress he'd made? Gone. The connection they'd tenuously formed and then cemented that night in Shed? Severed. To him, she was his enemy again, and now he had the blood connection to prove it.

She stopped but he slowly started to move backward, toe-heel, toe-heel, toward the exit. She held up her hands. "We've gotten through this once. We can do it again."

He jabbed a finger deeper into the Plant, his face twisted with unspeakable pain. "Before it was just in my head. A hallucination, a fucking nightmare. But that man is real. He's *real*. And he's your *father*." He opened his arms, so long, so full of strength. "Ask me how I'm supposed to get over that. After all I told you that he did to me, and everything that I didn't."

Those words sliced and stung and bled like one of those fancy knives he kept in his kitchen.

"I am not him. And I'm just as shocked and horrified as you."

"I need to get out of here."

"Cat." Griffin again, coming through the double doors and sounding a little out of breath.

"I have to talk to Heath Colfax," she told Xavier. "He has information we need."

*We.*

Xavier winced and turned his face away.

"I am Ofarian," she said. "There's no changing that."

At length, he finally nodded, but it didn't mean, "I accept you." It meant, "I understand what you just said . . . and I don't like it."

"Can you just wait here for a bit? Until I'm done?" She was pleading with him now, her hands even pressed together in prayer. "Please. Don't go anywhere yet. Not until you and I have talked more."

Though he raised his eyes to her, his face was still pointed away and down, his hair grazing his cheek.

"Please." She whispered now. "Just wait."

There were other things she probably should have said. One thing in particular. But she hadn't even fully worked it out in her mind, so how could she voice it? Her entire life had been thick and cloudy as a river bottom, and then suddenly Xavier came along and everything he'd told her about her heritage had washed her away in a flood. Her body and emotions and life had spun so furiously she had no idea which way was up, which way lay the sun and the air.

One problem at a time. What she and Xavier had created couldn't disappear overnight. She would be there for him, always, but the Ofarians needed her help *right now*. She couldn't let an entire race—her race—be a victim of war if she had the means to stop it.

Griffin said her name again, his impatience widening the cracks between her and her Tedran.

"It's just talking, Xavier," she said. "I can help innocents. You of all people should understand that."

He didn't move—not forward, not backward—and she allowed herself to be fueled by it.

She'd done all she could at this point. Telling him she loved him wouldn't change a thing, because it wasn't *her* he feared. It was what ran through her veins.

It was the man who'd given her life. The same man who'd stolen Xavier's away.

"I can't go back in there," he said, his voice the lowest she'd ever heard it. "I won't go any farther than this spot."

"All right. Good." Small victory, and she ran with it. "I'll go talk to Colfax, then come back for you."

She left the cell block with Griffin.

"What the hell's going on?" he asked as they hurried back through the halls.

Maybe it would have been easier for her to say if Griffin was a hard-nosed, stoic leader who barked orders and wasn't so good at sounding like he cared. Except that she was pretty sure he did care. He cared greatly for his people, and she was one of them now.

"Heath Colfax . . . my father . . . was Xavier's guard in here. Xavier didn't tell me everything, but what I know, it was bad."

"*Shit*," Griffin swore under his breath. "Does Colfax remember?"

They reached the door to the conference room again. Her hand shook as she touched it, and all that rattled around in her brain was the awful way Colfax had slurred Xavier's prisoner number.

"He remembers," she murmured.

She opened the door and stepped back inside.

# THIRTY-THREE

**That morning in the coffee shop, Cat had told Xavier: *I feel like*** *I've been treading water my whole life. Just sort of lost . . . out there. To me? Finding out about my parents would be sort of like a raft floating along. I could grab on, rest a bit, get to safety. But I always thought that knowing them would be a new beginning, not an end.*

She'd gotten both: an end to any hope of family, and the beginning of a whole new chapter filled with deceit and hate.

Heath and Jessica had been in love, had created Cat out of that love, but weren't allowed to keep her. She expected to see evidence of that on Heath Colfax's face as she looked at him from across the conference table. She expected to see some measure of love or yearning, that burst of emotion that came with bittersweetness. Maybe a smile. Maybe a flash of regret.

There wasn't any of that. And yet Gwen had said he'd cried when she told him Cat had been found.

Colfax rested his forearms on the table, his wrist shackles jingling. His frown was made even more considerable by the smeared half of his mouth. He watched her, but it was only with disappointment.

She was here for a purpose. A very specific purpose. She had to remember that.

Behind her, the door clicked shut. Griffin stood just inside, his back against the door.

"They said your name is Cat." Colfax's voice was choppy and rough, like he was speaking around a bag filled with jagged marbles.

"It is." Though she didn't really want to, she pulled out a chair and sat.

"That wasn't what Jessica was going to name you."

She wasn't going to cry. She wasn't.

"She wanted Josephine or Jennifer . . . something that started with *J*. She told me that . . . after." A little bit of emotion crept into the light brown eyes that were the exact same shape and shade as hers, then he shook it away with a jerk of his chin. He kept running his good fingers over the pattern of scars on his bad hand.

He cocked his head, giving her more of the good side. "You don't really look like her, but I can tell you're hers. It's the freckles, maybe. You look more like me. Or how I used to look. When I knew Jess."

Griffin shifted. *Get on with it*, the rustle of his pants seemed to say.

Heath Colfax was her father, but she couldn't call him Dad. Not after how he'd treated Xavier and hundreds of other Tedrans. Not after the way his memory had haunted Xavier for so long, and how that memory had destroyed what little life he'd been given. She wanted to tell Colfax a million things, none of which had to do with the fire elementals or her mother, but she didn't even want to look at him, let alone talk to him.

Xavier had given himself to Lea and Michael—had put himself in chains again for her. The least she could do was face this horrid man. Feeling brave, she, too, leaned on the table. "What happened to you?"

He grinned, and while it wasn't malicious, it certainly wasn't pretty. He turned his burned side to her. "You mean this?"

She nodded, her throat tightening.

"Fire elemental," he said.

She straightened in her chair. Griffin went still.

"That's what you wanted to hear, right?"

"Was that not how it happened?" she asked.

"No, that's how it happened." He coughed and it was a gruesome sound. "I was coming off a massive, two-day bender. Still drunk. Nothing but Jessica and what's-his-name, the lawyer they ordered her to marry, on my mind. I literally stumbled into their territory. Didn't even recognize the shift in signatures until I was surrounded." He shrugged and the movement of his shoulder below his melted ear was stunted. "I could've gotten out of there easily. They didn't know me from Adam, to borrow a Primary phrase. But I wasn't thinking and I opened my big mouth. Told them exactly who I was. Who I thought they were."

"What did you say?" Griffin asked, a little impatiently.

Colfax shot a steel glare at Griffin. "How the fuck should I know? Was half in the bag and ready to slit my own throat because of your boss."

Griffin pushed off the door. "You mean the boss who's imprisoned in here with you?"

Cat threw out her arms, one to each man. Griffin settled back against the door. Cat laced her fingers on the table and pushed herself into Colfax's line of sight.

"You told Gwen Carroway," she said, "that you'd tell us what you remembered about the fire elementals' location if I came here and met you. I'm here."

He just stared. And stared. One of his eyes looked slightly foggy, like maybe the fire had stolen half his sight, too. "Did he come back here for you?"

Cat looked over her shoulder in confusion. "Who? Griffin?"

"No. 267X."

Cat's stomach tumbled. A sudden and terrifying hate made the blood surge in her veins. "He has a name and it's Xavier."

"Did 267X come back to the Plant for you?" Heath snarled, bending over the table. "Or did he come back because he was forced to? Because something was held over his head?"

She didn't say anything, because the answer to those last two questions was *yes*.

"They're a weak race, Cat. They depend on us to tell them what to do. You don't want someone like that. You don't want a *Tedran*."

"Xavier has absolutely nothing to do with the reason I'm in this room with you." *You son of a bitch.* She struggled to not explode, to not set off Colfax in the process. "Leave him out of it."

Colfax drove a fist into the table and she jumped. "He has *everything* to do with you and me. He's a filthy whoreslave.

And he was touching you. Had his hands all over you. Dirty, fucking Tedran. And you let him! My daughter, my blood, with one of *them*."

*Now* Colfax was crying. No, not really crying. His sobs had nothing to do with love and everything to do with hate and rage.

"Do you know what he's done?" he said, trying to catch his breath. "Do you even understand what he *is*?"

She began to shake. A barely contained fury exploded in her heart and made her skin vibrate. How much could she say? How much was worth it? If he got upset enough, would he withhold the information about the Chimerans, just to spite her? Heath Colfax would always be locked up in the Plant, where his words couldn't hurt Xavier or her, but the Ofarians still needed protection. They needed what was in his head.

She gritted her teeth and replied, "Of course I understand what he is."

How her mind would have been poisoned, if she would have been raised by this man.

"You don't want him." Spit flecked his lips.

"Yes. I do."

"I've known him since he was fourteen. He's nothing. He'll turn you into nothing."

"You didn't *know* him at all!"

"I know enough. He's empty. He's ruined. He'll soil you."

She jumped up, turning. Griffin's eyes widened with panic, his hands pressing in a "sit down" gesture. "The Chimerans," he mouthed.

She only half turned back to Colfax, finding she couldn't look straight at him anymore. "Where are the fire elementals?"

He leaned back in his chair, shackled wrists falling to his lap. "You have to do something for me first."

"What? I'm here. I met you. And let me say, it hasn't been the experience I was hoping for."

He ignored that. "Here's what I want you to do." Colfax raised those familiar eyes up to Griffin. "I want two radios. One here in this room, the other I want taken to 267X."

The sudden heaviness in her limbs tried to drag her to the ground. "What? Why?"

Colfax fixed that stare back on her. "Because you're going to cut him loose. And I want to hear you do it."

She opened her mouth but no sound came out. Not a refusal, not a scream, not even a gasp. It was impossible to believe she'd heard those words correctly.

"You're going to tell him," Colfax went on, kneading at his throat like too much talking had hurt him, "that you choose your people over him. Whatever it is you think is between you two is held together by wishes and spider silk. Invisible, thin, made of nothing but an idea. Nothing that delicate is ever meant to be permanent."

*Fuck you*, was what she wanted to say. Was *dying* to shout in his face. This wasn't about him and Jessica. She wanted to fly across the table and tear into that disgusting webbed skin.

She shook her head. "I won't do it."

He looked pointedly at Griffin. "Then you don't get the location."

Griffin surged forward. For a moment she thought he'd strike Colfax, but he pulled up. "Goddamn you. Xavier has nothing to do with this."

Colfax looked up at Griffin, incredulous. "She's my blood. She's an *Ofarian*. And you let this happen?"

Griffin held his ground. "The marriage rules you despised, the very rules that took Jessica and Cat from you in the first place, you'd have had me uphold? Cat's a grown woman and can do what she wants. Who the hell do you think you are?"

Colfax didn't blink. "I'm the guy with what you need most."

Cat stared at the table, considering everything her father demanded and all the possible repercussions.

Even if she did as Colfax wanted, Xavier wouldn't believe her. He *couldn't* believe her.

Except . . . what if he did? What if he left here thinking she was telling him the truth? It would destroy him. And she hadn't told him she loved him because she thought it wouldn't have mattered. That the timing hadn't been right.

She was a horrible, selfish person.

She didn't want to reject Xavier, but she had to give her people a chance to plead their case to the Chimerans, to stop violence and death before it happened. He *shouldn't* believe what Colfax wanted her to tell him, but because Xavier had always feared she'd eventually choose her people over him, he would.

He would.

And because he wanted to be far, far away from her people and this place, he would leave.

"Cat," Griffin said next to her. "It's your call."

But she knew Griffin didn't really believe that—or want her to take the time to find another way.

She felt completely disconnected from everything. A puppet. A breathing husk of a person. "Okay." The single word sounded like it came from far above and beyond her body.

Beside her, Griffin exhaled, but with it came a little groan of sorrow. She would never let anyone say the Ofarian leader was heartless, or that he didn't struggle with making tough decisions.

"It's the only thing to do," Colfax said, his voice softening like all of a sudden he was this sympathetic, warmhearted father. "You'll learn I was right, and then you'll come back and—"

"Enough," Griffin snapped. "I'll take Xavier the radio."

*Yes.* Cat perked up.

Griffin had heard everything that had gone on in this room. He knew how she truly felt about Xavier—suspected, at least, but it wasn't exactly a secret. He'd give Xavier the radio, tell him that everything that was about to come out of Cat's mouth was crap, and Cat would tell Xavier whatever the heck Colfax wanted. She and Xavier would disconnect, Colfax would give them the Chimerans' location. *Voila.*

"Nuh-uh." Colfax waved a finger. "You'll call for another guard. You'll tell the guard, within my hearing, to bring 267X the radio. After Cat's done, if the stars-cursed Tedran hasn't left on his own, I want his ass thrown out of here. For good. And if I hear anything from the two of you that might tip your hand, my lips are sealed. Also for good."

Cat had thought she'd hated Michael, but what she felt toward her own father at that moment made Michael's machinations seem like a minor annoyance, a fly in the ear.

Griffin caught her gaze and held it. He knelt before her. "We have to. There are no other options and no time."

She just stared. The cheery yellow wall paint had chipped away in a spot, showing the dismal Plant gray underneath. Just a show, that's all this was, inside and out.

"You'll get him back," Griffin whispered.

She had no response to that. Wishes and spider silk. Her bastard father had spoken the truth. Maybe, if that's all that had tied them together, it was never meant to last in the first place. That had been their thought from the very beginning, hadn't it? Maybe they'd been wrong to fight it.

She nodded at Griffin. He stood and spun for the door in the same movement. Opening it, he gestured to someone outside. "David." He waggled an invisible phone. "Need two two-ways."

David had them on his person and handed both radios to Griffin, who only took one. David raised an eyebrow.

Griffin cleared his throat. "Take the other to Xavier. He should be in Cell Block One. When we're done talking to him, escort him out."

David blinked. "Out of the Plant?"

"Yes. Let me know when it's done."

"Yes, sir."

Cat silently pleaded with the stars—those tiny, sparkling things she'd once only thought of as pretty—that David had been clued in by Griffin's behavior and would give Xavier some sort of warning.

But then, what sort of allegiance did David owe Xavier? None at all.

She sat on her shaking hands. Her elbows vibrated against her sides. After many long, heavy minutes, the radio in Griffin's hand crackled. Xavier's voice filled the silent conference room. "Griffin?"

Griffin turned the radio in his hand and held it out to her.

She took it, clicked the button on the side and closed her eyes. Feeling Xavier over the line, his presence that large in her consciousness. "It's me."

"Cat. What's going on?"

*Something awful.* "You have to leave."

"Leave. Leave the Plant?" There was unspeakable strain in his voice.

*Don't leave me.* "And me."

*"What?"* The radio exploded in static.

*I need you.* "You can't be here anymore. And I'm staying."

"You just told me to fucking stay. That you were coming back."

"I know what I said." *And I meant every word.*

A deep, long silence. "Is *he* making you do this? Did he force you to choose between me and the Ofarians?"

*Yes! Yes, he is! It's not what I want at all.* "No."

"Bullshit. That's bullshit, Cat."

*It is. Don't believe a word of it.*

It was too hard. She opened her eyes. She didn't want to look at Colfax, but her gaze traveled to him anyway. *Your people*, he mouthed.

"The Ofarians . . ." she began, but her voice was shaking so much Colfax gave her a furious look and Griffin tensed at her side. One slip—one moment in which Colfax became unhappy—and all the Ofarians were lost. Griffin had said she'd get Xavier back. She had to hold on to that. She pressed the talk button, cleared her throat, and started again. The button was slick with her sweat. The less she said, the better.

"The Ofarians are my people." *But I found my home with you.*

"You're letting me go. For them. For *him*."

*No. Never.* "Yes."

She remembered the late night in Shed, how he'd described her people like he might describe cannibals or child molesters. How, in his eyes, she'd ceased to be just Cat and had become another Ofarian.

Then she'd touched him, whispered to him. He'd put himself inside her, filling her in more ways than one. In those moments, he'd forgotten her label and she'd just been Cat.

She had to believe that would happen again.

Except right now, she was forced to say the opposite. "This should be easy for you, Xavier. You hate what I am. You don't want me to be Ofarian. We could be together for a hundred years and you'd never be able to get over it. It would always be there, in the back of your mind, what I can do. What my people did to you."

Oh, God. That was the ultimate truth. And it hurt more to say than the lies.

He roared, the radio falling to the floor with a crash. Then there was a string of horrendous sounds—*bang bang bang bang bang*—and Cat knew he was punching or kicking the bars of one of the cells. Every blow made her jolt. Every blow sent tears to her eyes.

The radio rustled. He'd picked it up again. She could hear the angry hiss of his breath, in and out, in and out. He didn't say anything for a long time. Then . . . "If this isn't love, then I don't know what is. I won't ever know."

*It's love. It's love. It's love.* "It's not love."

The pause that followed weighed three tons and lasted an eternity. "Well, if you're not willing to fight for us," he said, "then neither am I."

There was another crash, a high-pitched screech, then silence, and she knew he'd thrown the radio against the wall.

She could barely see Colfax through her sheen of tears. All sound went muffled, tuning to some bland frequency. She could no longer feel the chill of the windowless room or the hard planes of the plastic chair under her thighs. The whole world had been drowned and she didn't care if she'd ever surface.

Griffin lunged for the door.

"Uh-uh!" Colfax's voice cut through the buzz in her ears. "Don't move until your man comes back with word that 267X is gone. You leave, my mouth stays shut. Same goes for you, Cat."

They might have sat there, locked up with the most hideous man on the planet, for an hour or a minute. Time meant nothing. When the hesitant knock finally came at the door, Cat didn't even move. Griffin opened it.

"It's done, sir," David said. "He's gone. Took him out myself and locked the door behind him. Security said he headed straight across the parking lot and then disappeared."

*Glamour*, thought Cat.

"Thank you."

"What the hell was that all about?" David asked.

Griffin stalked to the table and braced his hands on it, leaning toward Colfax. "You heard the man. It's done. Now give us the Chimerans."

In the doorway, David gasped.

Cat heard none of the rest. Heath Colfax talked but his rocky voice bounced off her. He talked forever, it felt like. Vaguely she was aware of David carting in a tablet computer, his hands flying furiously across the touch screen. Griffin was asking questions of Colfax and scribbling something on a notepad simultaneously. Other Ofarians drifted in and out of the conference room. They were always in a hurry.

Cat sat in the same place, staring at the same chip of yellow-revealing-gray.

Someone touched her shoulder. Spoke her name.

She blinked, looked up. "Griffin." Her stomach growled. "Are you done?"

Colfax's seat was empty, the chair askew. She was glad she hadn't seen him get up and leave.

"Yeah. We're done. I'm getting ready to head out."

"Right now? Right away? What time is it?"

"Well, as soon as we get everything together. I want to meet with Reed still." He ran a hand over his head. Though he kept his dark hair short, enough feathered between his fingers. "No time to lose."

"Are you going after Kekona?"

He pulled on a vest over his black Ofarian shirt, started to buckle it. "No. I'm going to find the Chimerans. I'm going to try to talk with their chief. Make him hear my side. Again." He shook his head. "Straighten this out before it explodes."

"How many are going with you?"

He frowned. "Just me. If I take any more it could be construed as an act of aggression."

She watched him test the zippers on his vest, then start in on the side buckles. "What happened between you two?"

He paused mid-yank, then gave the strap an extra hard tug. "Too much. Not enough. Take your pick."

Smart man, to know she wasn't talking about the Chimerans as a whole. He finished encasing himself in gadgetry and took Cat's upper arms in a gentle grip. "I promise you, I'll make what you did worth it."

Had she sacrificed? Or was her relationship with Xavier doomed to begin with and she'd just put it out of its misery before it got too ill and just lay there gasping for breath?

"Does it matter? He believed me. He left." And she couldn't help but feel a little pissed off she'd been placed in this position, by the Ofarian leader no less.

He ducked his head, looking at her from under eyelashes that cover models would die for, and moved his hands to her shoulders. "So go after him."

She blinked, at first not understanding. It seemed so simple, to take the loss because she'd convinced herself that it was what Xavier truly wanted deep down—this separation. Except that he'd fought for her—chased after her—*after* he'd learned what she was.

She reached up, gripped Griffin's forearms. He gave a single, firm nod.

She nodded in return, pushed his hands from her shoulders. She shoved past him, burst out of the conference room, and sprinted back down the corridor. This time she remembered the way, the old nursery wing and the hall to the Circle passing by in a blur. She ran and ran. The cell block opened up and she raced through it. There was nothing outside the building, nothing but a weed-filled concrete parking lot and frozen Nevada ground. He couldn't have gotten far.

There. At last. The exit.

A shock of bitterly cold air slammed into her as she charged outside. Wind fought her as she ran for the parking lot. She reached the asphalt and swiveled in a circle, scanning the area. To the west, soft hills covered in snow. To the east, the giant, gray box of the Plant. To the south, flat nothingness. To the north, far in the distance, a stretch of highway and the zip of an occasional car trailing white exhaust.

No sign of a tall, beautiful man carrying rejection and anger and sorrow in a heavy load on his back.

"Xavier!" Her bones rattled inside her skin, her throat aching from the scream. *"Xavier!"*

No answer. He could be cloaked in invisibility glamour, standing there, watching her. But then he'd know that she'd come back for him, that she was here to apologize, to tell him the truth. He wouldn't just stand there. Would he?

She jogged along the perimeter of the parking lot, casting out the net of signature awareness Gwen had taught her to use while they'd been waiting for the cleanup crew back in White

Clover Creek. Sensing signatures had nothing to do with sound, and the sharp gusts of wind couldn't whip it away like a plastic bag or a swirl of leaves, so if he was anywhere close by, she would feel him.

She must have spent an hour outside, but what he'd said over the radio was true. He wasn't fighting for her. He was gone.

# THIRTY-FOUR

**The Nevada wind snapped at Cat's clothing, making sure she** knew she was surrounded by emptiness. As she turned back to the Plant, a black Jeep pulled around from the back and sat, idling. Griffin's ride to wherever he was going to find the Chimerans. By himself. To "try" to convince the Chimerans to stand down. To "try" to make up with the woman he called Keko. To "try" to persuade the entire Senatus that his race shouldn't be judged and punished for Lea's actions . . . or his.

"Try" just wasn't good enough for Cat. She didn't just destroy the only good thing in her life for a "Gee, I sure do hope this will work because I got nothing else."

She refused to lose Xavier for nothing. And damn if she knew what she was going to do about it, but she was through with having forces act upon her and her having to dodge and react. She stalked across the parking lot. The cold wind punctured her thin shirt and pants, and slid across the fine sheen of nervous, furious sweat covering her whole body. The guards at the main door buzzed her through.

"Where's Griffin right now?" she demanded.

"Uh, he's in prep to—"

"I know that. Where is he?"

After a long look, the guard punched a few keys and stared at monitors she couldn't see. "Front offices. Just down this hall, past the potted plants."

The front offices made a rectangle around a central station with a low counter manned by more black-clad Ofarians. Movement everywhere: talking, typing, pointing, planning. A din of conversation and orders and arguments. As she passed one desk, the computer screen showed a scene that made her shudder.

War preparation. In a big warehouse somewhere. Rows upon rows of weapons being loaded into nondescript vehicles. A few hundred Ofarians rushing about.

All in case Griffin should fail. Or, in their minds, *when* Griffin failed.

A few hundred Ofarians against how many? And where exactly would this stupid war take place? Where could the Secondaries possibly fight one another without bringing down any sort of attention from the Primaries? Weren't the Secondaries all about secrecy? Absolutely none of this made sense.

Across the central station she caught sight of Griffin. He was with Reed in a side office, hunched over a table, his finger sweeping over a giant touch-screen computer. It was a map, a big blob of green and red sitting in a field of blue. Reed nodded shallowly then replied, slapping the back of one hand into the palm of the other. Two men of action, radiating tension. Thinking about mechanics but not about emotion.

Gwen and David stood just outside the office, and as Cat approached she heard them talking about Gwen's dad and the sister she called Delia, but whom Cat would never think of as anyone but Lea. They'd found the mole, who'd been feeding Lea information and *nelicoda*, and who'd overnighted to her the Tedran neutralizer. He was an elected member of Griffin's cabinet who'd shared Lea's ideas about using the Senatus to tame the Ofarians. Gwen had learned he'd been in contact with Lea for years, after she'd secretly contacted him with her plans. Soldiers had been sent to apprehend him in San Francisco.

Gwen looked wan and upset, completely different from the focused woman who'd put her arm around Cat so easily in White Clover Creek. But as she looked up and saw Cat, the desolation on her face vanished.

Cat hadn't mastered that ability to mask emotions. She was fairly certain that she looked every bit as drained and heart-broken as she felt. She stood there, completely immersed in the scene but still separate from it. Her mind was filled with this familiar, muted hum, a constant reminder that she was surrounded by people exactly like her . . . but not. Because blood was supposed to create this impenetrable connection, and Gwen had done everything in her power to strengthen that connection, but she still felt like she stood outside of it.

And she was okay with that.

The realization came to her so sharply she gasped. She recalled all those agonizing days spent wondering what it was inside her that consistently pressed water to the forefront of her mind. All that frustration. She remembered how her awe over the spiral around her arm had so quickly shifted to panic.

What exactly did it mean, to belong? Was it blood or magic or water that bound her to her people? And did she *need* to be bound? Or had that frustration arisen from something else entirely?

She covered her face with her hands, closed her eyes, and searched inside herself. That agitation—that constant churning of the unknown making her distracted and ill and lonesome since she was twelve—had disappeared. It didn't exist anymore because she now knew what she was. She *knew*. That knowledge had been the key. Not the magic, not the whole of the Ofarian race standing at her back.

She went to Gwen. "Can I talk to you? You and Griffin?"

Inside the office, Griffin glanced up at the sound of his name. His eyes pulled down at the corners, making him look tired. Unsure. "You okay?" he asked as she stepped into the office, Gwen at her heels.

"You can't go to the Chimerans," Cat said, laying it all out.

Griffin sighed deeply and started to tap a pen on the table. "It's not a choice I have."

"No, I mean *you* can't go."

The pen stopped. "What do you mean?"

Cat took a deep breath. *Here we go.* "It's not going to matter what you say to them. From what I witnessed, just the sound of your name raises Kekona's defenses. And she's in some position of power. Am I right?"

Griffin's jaw made a stiff circle and he nodded. "But it's not just about . . . her. Keko and I, three years ago . . . we were a secret. The fact that you all know about it now is . . ." He waved a hand. "That doesn't matter anymore. I fucked things up with the Chimerans and the Senatus in other ways. I thought I was offering them help; instead I gave offense because I didn't know their customs. I mistakenly thought they should conform to ours, when it was the other way around. They think us even more arrogant, even more power hungry than before the Board came down. Everything I tried to do backfired."

"Okay," Cat said. "So if that's the case, if you show up to the Chimerans, they'll immediately turn their backs. You can't reason with that side of a person. Not unless you can get them to turn around. To listen."

Reed started to rub his bottom lip with his thumb, regarding her under his lashes. He nodded almost imperceptibly.

Griffin's hands slid to his hips. "There's one thing I haven't done yet, and that's beg. I tried arguing. I tried reasoning. I tried ignoring. I'm the one who screwed it all up. I should be the one to prostrate myself and grovel for mercy. What else would you suggest I do, Cat? Send in a random Ofarian to say, 'Hey, our self-important prick of a leader couldn't make it, but he's sorry for the serious cultural faux pas three years ago. And, by the way, he never kidnapped Keko Kalani.' Yeah, I don't think that would go over so well."

"So don't send a random Ofarian," she said.

He rubbed at his face. "You've just been introduced to this world, so I know that you can't possibly understand the silly politics, just as I didn't three years ago, but let me be clear that the Chimerans—and the vast majority of the Senatus, by the way—won't listen to *any* Ofarian."

"Then don't send an Ofarian."

Griffin let out a huff of exasperation and opened his mouth to refute her again.

"Send me," she added.

"What?" Gwen said at her side.

Reed was eyeing Cat like he suspected where she was going with this, but Griffin's patience had snapped and now he glared hard at her.

"I have news for you," Griffin said. "You're Ofarian. If you want to see what Chimeran backs look like, go right ahead."

She raised her chin. She felt every beat of her heart like a punch against her ribs. But she knew she was doing the right thing. "What if I wasn't?"

"Wasn't what?" Griffin said.

She licked dry lips. "What if I wasn't Ofarian?"

"Holy shit," Reed whispered.

Gwen gasped. Silence hung heavy in the small office, the only sound the clicking of the computer as it dove into sleep mode.

"Go on," Griffin finally said, his voice dark and firm.

Cat blew out a breath between tight lips. "Kekona knows me. She also knows that I'm brand new—a 'water virgin,' she called me. What if I walked up to her and her leader—the chief, you said?—and declared that I left the Ofarians? What if I had no water magic?" She turned to Gwen. "What's that chemical that erases it?"

"*Nelicoda*," Gwen said. She was clutching her throat with one hand, the skin underneath red and blotchy.

"Yes, that's it. Shoot me up with it, take away what . . . Heath Colfax's blood gave me, what makes me part of you. Make me neutral. If they see I'm not technically on your side, but that I believe in peace, do you think they'll turn their backs on *that*?"

Gwen touched Cat's elbow. "But you haven't even learned what it's about yet. Are you sure you want to do that?"

Cat gave her a sad smile. "Then I won't know what I'm missing. And honestly? What you've shown me already—the little bit of magic you had Xavier teach me, the Ofarian greetings, that cool thing you and Griffin did with the snow to put out that fire—I don't know . . . I don't think it's really ever been about *magic* for me. I mean, I understand now why my mind has been so fogged for half my life. The moment Xavier told me what I was, it became clearer. It was like just *knowing* about my origins solved so much.

"And then I met you, Gwen, and you, Griffin, and I see how you're fighting to make things good and right for so many people. How you're trying so hard to create this huge family. How you're . . . one. It's what I've always wanted to be a part of, and maybe for a short time, I was. And I think that it could be enough." She gave a small, confident nod. "Yeah, it's enough."

When no one said anything, just stared at her, she kept going. "If I can save lives, if I can stop something terrible before it starts, I want to do that. I have a better chance than you, Griffin. Admit it."

"Would this work?" Reed asked, breaking the long silence that followed her speech. "Sending in Cat?"

Griffin and Gwen exchanged a look. Griffin told Cat, "You do have a better chance than I."

"That's all I'm asking for," Cat said.

Reed gave a little cough. Gwen's expression shifted, her eyebrows drawing together. She pulled Cat so they faced each other. "You need to know," Gwen said, "that the absence of powers has a stigma attached to it. *Nelicoda* has been used as punishment since before we immigrated here. Most Ofarians consider using it worse than death. If you took it voluntarily, even to do something as noble as what you are trying to do, some still might not see it in a good light . . ."

Cat was already shaking her head. "Doesn't matter. The opinions of people I don't know won't bother me. What matters are the people in this room, and the lives I can hopefully save."

For a brief moment, she thought about painting. How just a short week ago, she'd wanted the favorable opinions of everyone she'd met, and those she hadn't, even while knowing that was impossible. Would she ever be able to paint again? Maybe. Maybe not. But she wasn't what was important here, and she couldn't think about her brushes and canvases right now.

"Cat, that's so brave of you. Let me give you something else to think about. And please know I'm not trying to make you change your mind, it's just that a *nelicoda* overdose is permanent." Gwen pressed her lips together. "What about your birth mother, Jessica? What if she's one of those who will judge you for what you've given up?"

The Burned Man's appearance had shot down all Cat's high-flying notions of a joyful family reunion and sent them careening to the ground in a ball of flame.

"If my mother decides she wants to know me," she said, "to really, truly know me, she won't care if I can touch water or not. I'll still be her blood. And if she's like Heath and wants to judge me, then I won't want to know her anyway."

The truth hurt like spicy food—pain on her tongue, satisfaction deep in her belly, a sick little twinge shortly afterward.

Griffin came around the table, slowly shaking his head.

There was so much emotion in his eyes: regret and gratitude, loss and fear. His voice was terribly low. "You'd do this for me, for *us*, after what I just made you do?"

"You didn't make me do anything. I could have refused. You probably don't want to hear that, but I could have walked away from all of you, grabbed Xavier by the hand and just disappeared." She drew herself up. "But I see where the greater importance lies. It hurts, yeah; I won't lie about that. So I want to make it worth it. I *have* to make it worth it. I won't throw away Xavier only to watch this fail. I can't live with that, and I certainly wouldn't be able to live with myself."

She looked to Gwen. "Xavier told me what he did, how he stayed behind on the Earth he hated in order to hide the escape of his people. How he sacrificed his own happily-ever-after to protect the fates of two races. I understand why he did that. And this is worth it. Please, let me make it worth it."

Gwen took Cat's hands. "You would *still* be one of us, to me and to many others."

Griffin nodded vehemently. "Granted full access to all of our Rites, given our protection. Absolutely." His eyes turned glassy. If she wasn't successful, there would be no more Rites—whatever those were—and no protection to give.

"Thank you," she said. But this wasn't about loyalty or fealty. It was humanity. And in Cat's eyes, there was no difference between Primary and Secondary.

At length, Griffin asked softly, "Are you thinking that if you're not Ofarian, you can get him back?"

Griffin didn't have to say who *him* was.

She met his sympathetic eyes and knew what he was thinking: maybe, if he weren't Ofarian, he could get his Keko back, too.

For her, it was a big enough reason to take *nelicoda*. "I can only hope so."

**Cat had a window seat. Commercial air. Griffin had said it would** negate the whole purpose if Cat showed up on the Chimerans' doorstep having come by Ofarian transport. Private plane was out. So was any Ofarian guard. She was on her own.

And on her way to Hawaii.

Twenty-five years ago, that's where Heath Colfax had

stumbled upon the Chimerans. His only love, Jessica, had finally returned home to San Francisco and married someone neither of them knew. Shortly thereafter, she'd told Colfax about their daughter she'd birthed and then abandoned. Colfax had thrown himself from the Golden Gate Bridge. The Primary press had eaten up the story about the unidentified man who'd tried to commit suicide but whose body had never been found. The Ofarians knew better. He'd disappeared into the water, and even they hadn't known if they'd ever see him again.

Colfax had swum all the way to Hawaii.

No, *swimming* wasn't a good word for it. The way Gwen described it, Ofarians just . . . became one with the water. They could slide through it faster than humans could swim or some boats could race. They moved like lightning, easier than oil, encased in something they loved and something that loved them back.

Not that Cat would ever know.

For the millionth time, she spread her fingers over her knees and stared down at them. They wielded no magic. Not anymore.

Gwen had offered to give her the *nelicoda* shots, but Griffin had insisted on doing it himself. When Cat and Griffin had been alone with three syringes, she'd asked why he wanted to do it.

"I want to be part of this," he'd answered. "I want to feel your sacrifice."

Losing her magic didn't feel like a sacrifice. Not compared to losing someone else.

One dose of *nelicoda* only temporarily took away the powers. But three needlefuls stole the magic and hid it away in a place where it could never be touched again. By the time the third needle punctured the skin on her arm, Cat hadn't even winced. The *nelicoda* had felt cold, sluicing through her veins, but otherwise there'd been no pain. Maybe a slight tingling just beneath her skin, a little lightheadedness, then . . . nothing.

And there was still nothing. She kept waiting for the regret to blindside her, but it never did. The memories of her days before she'd stepped foot in White Clover Creek burned incredibly strong. She remembered what it had been like, to stand every day with her toes in the turquoise water of the Florida

Keys and be on the verge of tears, not knowing why her body reacted so strongly to the ocean. And lakes and rivers and ponds. It hadn't been a good feeling.

Only when she painted had she found some measure of peace, but even that had never given her answers.

Now she had them.

She remembered her great exhale when Xavier had revealed her heritage. The relief in finally *knowing*. All those days of frustration. The persistent, annoying niggling at the back of her brain . . . gone.

She remembered that one moment when she'd spoken those unknown Ofarian words and the water had wrapped around her arm. For a second or two, it had been heaven. Pure heaven. She'd felt the ancient language in her heart and soul, and the element of water had been hers.

She'd owned it.

She'd once read that the reason addicts became addicts was because they were forever chasing the feel of that very first high. It would never come back, of course, but they chased it anyway. She imagined that many Ofarians—many other Secondaries, too—might spend their entire lives trying to get back that feeling of using magic for the first time.

But Cat would always have it. That first feeling was her *only* feeling, and even though it had quickly descended into panic, those first few seconds had been wondrous. That memory would never be diluted, never fade.

She realized, soaring at thirty thousand feet, that just that tiny taste of power would be enough to sustain her for the rest of her life, but the wound Xavier's exit had caused would never heal.

God. Xavier.

Before takeoff, at the airport in Reno, she'd called his house in White Clover Creek. No answer and, of course, no voice mail.

She pressed her forehead to the chilly airplane window and stared down at the never-ending expanse of blue. So beautiful. No more confusion in her mind, no more mystery.

*Hello, old friend. I know your name now. I know who you belong to and who belongs to you, and the reality is far lovelier than I ever thought.*

Just then, a million new paintings came to her. Canvases full of knowledge and confidence. Solemnity. Love. Power. Colors she'd never before used. The fingers that had been curled around her knees for several hours now itched to hold a brush, and she almost cried in relief.

Out of anything, that had been her biggest fear in taking the *nelicoda*: that it would take her art along with her magic. Painting had started as an outlet, but when she'd been given the chance to make a career out of it, she knew instantly that that was where she wanted to take her life. Her art would be different now, yes, but she was also a different person.

The plane touched down on Oahu, and then she transferred to a smaller plane over to the Big Island.

At the tiny Kona airport, the giant, unmarked plane parked on the far end of the tarmac gave her a very bad feeling. It was big enough to cart a sizable force of Chimerans to wherever they planned on attacking the Ofarians. But it was empty and unmoving, which meant she still had time.

She rented a Jeep that looked like it had been plucked straight from an off-roading commercial and headed south on Route 11. She didn't need the GPS; she was going off Colfax's recollections, and they had been surprisingly distinct.

She drove through trapezoids of green coffee fields covering the rolling land all the way from the inland mountains to the wild shore. She blazed by Punaluu Black Sand Beach, where Colfax had said he'd met a local who'd offered to bring him inland to see a part of Hawaii most tourists did not. And Colfax, perpetually drunk and despondent and having nothing better to do, had gone.

They'd ended up in a small town along the western edge of Volcanoes National Park, where Colfax had gotten wasted at the only local bar several nights in a row. He'd slept outside, in the cool mountain air. One night, after passing out in the bushes and then awakening with little memory of where he was, he'd set off wandering, trying to find his way back into town. Instead he found a road that wasn't anything more than two parallel gouges in the dirt. A road, he'd thought, always went somewhere, right? So he'd stumbled along it, thinking he'd be back in the familiar bar before noon. He hadn't found the town he knew, but instead a really small enclave of tightly packed buildings. The last bit of civilization, he recalled, before the land gave way to Volcanoes National Park.

Cat found the two-lane road off Route 11 easily enough, and made it to the town Colfax had described, even spotted the building in which he'd done all his drinking—now a beauty salon. She went inside the salon and asked about a rough, hidden road that skirted the edge of the park, maybe one that led to a little village higher up? The lone hairdresser eyed Cat's rugged vehicle outside and assumed she was a hiker. She directed Cat around the cafe, where she found the first tire tracks.

Then the hairdresser gave her a funny look. "If you go up there, get whatever water and food you need here. And don't be freaked out by the locals."

Though there were no Secondaries around, Cat's skin tingled. "Why?"

The hairdresser shrugged. "They're just weird. They come down here every now and then to get supplies and food and stuff, but the way they keep to themselves is, well, like I said, weird. No one knows how many of them there are."

Cat nodded, thanked her, and left. Throwing the car into four-wheel drive, she headed around the cafe and found the start of the narrow tracks, draped with foliage. Her eyes felt sandy and her body weary. Local time said it was early morning; her mind told her it was late afternoon. Nerves bounced around in her stomach.

Driving up to Colfax's party town had been a bumpy, swerving haul from the main route, but the tire ruts rising up to Chimeran territory were downright treacherous. Rocky and curving, the drive made her teeth rattle in her gums. She lost her way a few times and had to backtrack to find the fading path. Hours dragged on.

Then . . . *there*. The land flattened out a bit. The trees thinned. A slanted pasture with a few grazing horses lined one side of a dirt road. Three buildings, each no bigger than a small house, sat on the other side. One claimed to be a school, which might have been true if the year was 1890. Another had no signage, but the third was a little convenience store. No homes. No people.

*This* was the mighty Chimeran stronghold? Home of the people who threatened to wipe the Ofarians from Earth?

Cat crookedly parked the Jeep in front of the convenience store door. She sat, staring at the door for a moment, then realized she had no moments to spare. She went inside. Dusty, peeling floors. Three lonely rows of goods, most looking out of date. A cooler along the back wall that didn't look plugged in. An ancient cash register that was clearly just for show.

A girl in her late teens wearing a tank top and jeans stood behind the counter, reading *InStyle* magazine. She had a shade of dusky skin and shiny black hair like Kekona—native Hawaiian mixed with all sorts of other handsome and strong bloodlines.

And her Secondary signature was making Cat's head spin. *Nelicoda* hadn't taken away that ability.

"Can I help you?" said the girl all casual, like this place was used to customers and she was the Best Salesgirl Ever.

"Yes." Cat went right up to the counter. "You can help me find Kekona Kalani." The Chimeran shopgirl blinked and made a startled, feeble attempt to deny knowledge, but Cat held up a hand. "That's really not necessary. I know she's somewhere around here. I know she's Chimeran. I'd like to speak with her. And your chief."

The shopgirl slowly spread her hands across the counter, leaned over it, and Cat could see the outlines of pretty much every muscle in her chest and arms. "And you would be?"

"Cat Heddig. Kekona knows me."

The girl's eyes briefly shifted to a spot over and above Cat's shoulder. A camera, no doubt. Sure enough, not three seconds later, as the two women stood staring at each other, a radio buzzed and crackled. The Chimeran slid her hand below the counter and pulled out a clunky hunk of metal. She put it to her ear and listened. Still watching Cat, she returned it to its place below the counter.

"They'll be here soon. Sit over there." The Chimeran pointed to a single chair in the far back corner, near the Doritos and Fruit Roll-Ups—things with a scary long shelf life.

Cat nodded and did as she was told. They'd get no physical fight from her; that's not why she'd come.

The Chimeran moved to the front door and started to take deep, deep breaths, the curve of her waist sucking in, her lungs expanding. Preparing her weapons, so to speak.

Thirty minutes later, a battered four-wheel drive vehicle careened into the dusty lot next to Cat's rented Jeep. Kekona hopped out of the driver's seat, wearing clothes, thank God, but not much: an orange tank top and a tiny pair of white shorts that made her legs look impossibly strong and sleekly dark. She was still barefoot, though, and looked perfectly warm even though Cat had huddled further into her zip-up sweatshirt in the cool mountain climate.

An enormous Chimeran male burst out of the passenger side of the vehicle and pushed past Kekona to storm inside. Same dark hair and skin as the others. Shirtless, worn jeans slung low on his hips, his feet also bare, he surged across the store. He stomped down the yellowing-postcard-and-expired-battery aisle, right for Cat. By the time she'd risen to her feet, he was right in front of her. No, he was over her, nearly pushing her backward over the chair.

"What are you doing here?" His incredible baritone voice shook the walls. "Talk."

"Are you the chief?" She prayed her voice wouldn't reveal her nerves.

His eyes narrowed, a spurt of flame crossing their darkness. "No."

Cat peered around the big Chimeran's shoulder, which was wrapped in a flame tattoo. Subtle.

"Kekona . . ." she began.

The Chimeran woman stood just behind the man to whom she had a striking resemblance. She coolly regarded Cat with her legs apart, muscular arms across her chest. "How'd you find us?"

Absolutely no sense in beating around the bush. Minutes meant everything in this game. "Have you heard the story about the Ofarian man who found this place twenty-five years ago and came out burned to within an inch of his life?"

Kekona nodded once. "Of course. It was a warning to stay away that has served us well. Looks like we might need another one. Oh, wait—"

"A warning?" Of course. That made sense then, why they

hadn't just killed him all those years ago. A walking, barely breathing, hideous-looking *Keep Out* sign. "Well," Cat said, "he's my father."

A sound like a blazing, crackling fire emanated from the Chimeran male's body. "You're *Ofarian*?"

"Easy, Bane. Let me handle this. I know her." Kekona reached out, took the big man's arm and pushed him aside. Bane backed off toward the counter, where Shopgirl stood. When he was out of earshot, Kekona lowered her voice and asked Cat, "Did *he* send you?"

"No," Cat replied, knowing she meant Griffin. "I offered to come. And I'm here alone. Please. I'd really like to speak with your chief."

But Kekona had *no* stamped all over her, so Cat raised her voice enough for Bane and Shopgirl to hear. "War doesn't mean death just on one side. I doubt you really want to risk your people's lives, when there's a chance they could be saved, too."

"You have news?" Bane asked, inching forward.

"It's why I've come to speak to your chief." When Kekona didn't move or answer, Cat unzipped her sweatshirt to show she had no weapons, then opened her empty hands. "They're just words."

Kekona smiled, but it wasn't backed by the bravado Cat'd seen in that garage in White Clover Creek. In fact, there was a little bit of fear. "The chief wants to see you. Otherwise I would have had Akela over there send you back to them like Daddy. You'll ride with us, but I should warn you, you're a day too late."

Cat raised an eyebrow. "Then why do you look so worried?"

Kekona opened her mouth to show a flame sparking in the back of her throat, then swiveled around and punched out of the store.

# THIRTY-FIVE

**The Chimerans' vehicle picked and dug its way higher up the** mountain and then slowly pitched back downward. When it stopped abruptly, Kekona told Cat, "You can take off the blindfold."

Cat ripped the yellow bandanna off her eyes at the same moment Kekona and Bane opened their car doors. The sights and sounds assaulted her, filled her with dread.

Kekona had parked on the edge of a vast, oblong meadow. Around it rose the steep slopes of mountains, covered in all possible shades of green, closing them in. Shutting out the world. On those slopes clung rows and rows of small, tightly set houses and buildings, similar to how White Clover Creek had been built overlooking the main square, only far less affluent. Here no roads ran between the homes. There weren't even cars, just footpaths. The air, though cool, reeked of sulphur and smoke, as though just over that ridge to the north sat the volcano that constantly spewed lava.

And on the flat of that great meadow, an army prepared for an offensive attack.

A whole field of warriors, five hundred at least, all as strong and lethal-looking as Kekona and Bane, moved and worked and shouted back and forth to one another. Some loaded up run-down buses from another era, piling in huge duffel bags. Families—numbering another five hundred, at least—lined the far end of the meadow. Women and men and children of all ages, watching, waiting for their time to say good-bye. Shoulders back, no tears.

The mobilization struck fear in Cat's heart and made her

breath lodge in her throat. It wasn't just a threat anymore. This was real. It was happening.

To the west, a small pocket of male and female Chimeran warriors sparred. Half-naked, barefooted, their bronzed skin slick with sweat, they fought each other under the unrelenting sun. The grunts and roars of practiced battle soared over everything else, and Cat could hear death within the sounds. They fought with their hands—a combination of slugging it out and a nasty form of martial arts—and with fire.

Streams of orange and white and yellow shot from fighters' lips, and their opponents dodged them gracefully. Others spit balls of flame into their hands and hurled them from powerful arms. It was almost balletic. It was a show, Cat realized, to display their might in front of the entire race. It was all choreographed, a ritual before battle.

Water would put out those fires. Water would always triumph over fire, unless there was simply too much fire to overcome. And if there were other races involved in the offensive. If Cat didn't succeed here, Griffin would have to surrender in order to prevent an annihilation. But Griffin wasn't the surrendering type.

"This way. The chief's waiting for you." Kekona nodded toward a tilting brick house painted white that hugged the edge of the meadow. It was larger than all the others, but still average by mainland U.S. standards.

Bane gave Cat's shoulder a sharp shove, as if that's all the contact with her he could stomach. As Kekona marched through the ranks, Chimerans everywhere stopped and turned and bowed, murmurs of "General," trailing after her.

The whole of the Chimeran army started to follow Kekona, waves of huge, fire-wielding warriors swarming across the meadow to gather around the house. Even the sky seemed darker now, the clouds trailing, the sulphur odor intensifying, as though their anger had coalesced into ash and smoke and drifted upward. The Chimerans had no "bloodhound" powers like the Ofarians, but they knew Cat was different, that she didn't belong here. All strangers were a threat.

A shallow stone veranda with crumbling posts circled the white house. Kekona disappeared through the front door, leaving Bane to loom at Cat's back. She had no choice but to go inside, and stepped into the colder shadows as the murmur of the gathering Chimerans continued to rise. The house felt larger on the inside, its rooms spotted with white wicker furniture that had seen better days, and rippling white curtains hanging at the small, arched windows.

Bane pointed to a set of narrow steps curving up from the front room. "Upstairs."

Kekona stomped up ahead of them. The close quarters and the creaking wood under Cat's feet made her even more tense. Behind her, Bane's shoulders brushed the walls. At the top, she pushed aside a curtain and stepped out onto a balcony overlooking the meadow. An ocean of dusky-skinned Chimerans spanned below . . . and they all looked up at her.

No, they looked to Kekona, who gave a mighty shout, then ran right for the balcony edge. Without slowing, without fear, she hopped up onto the railing. No hands, no overcompensation for bad balance, just pure muscle and raw, physical power. With a feral growl, she thrust one fist into the air. A short phrase in a language Cat didn't recognize burst from Kekona's mouth and echoed across the valley.

As one, nearly a thousand Chimerans roared their reply.

The entire population—children, too—dropped to a crouch, shouted something fierce and emotional in unison. They stamped one foot, then the other. Shouted something more, their faces twisting in determination. They shook their heads, chanting. Stomped again. They slapped one elbow, a thigh. The chanting rose and rose, and it was beautiful and petrifying and moving. All together, the Chimerans straightened, brought one fist across their chests, then the other, and bowed.

Cat couldn't disguise her full-body shiver.

Kekona screamed something else in Chimeran, then jumped down from the railing, twisting to land facing Cat and Bane. She walked up to Cat wearing a satisfied smile.

"Keko. Enough."

The new voice was low and gritty. Cat turned to the corner of the balcony from where it had come. A man, who could have been fifty or sixty or seventy, rose from a rickety wood chair. He, too, wore no shirt. No longer as trim and strong as the younger men on the field below, his power came through in his carriage and the calm confidence of his attention. His hair was still black as ink, dusted with only a few silver strands at his temple. He went to the balcony and raised a hand. The Chimerans lifted a thousand hands in response. Some blew tiny flames to dance on their fingertips. When the chief lowered his hand, his people sent up a joyous new cheer, and then started to disperse.

The man placed his hands on the balcony railing and did not face Cat. "Why have you come?"

"Chief," Cat said, bowing her head in the way Griffin had coached her. "I've come to explain Kekona's capture. What she thought happened, did not. The basis for your whole offensive is incorrect."

Now he turned, and the weight of his look made her feel heavy and small. "And who are you, to come to us like this? An *Ofarian*, begging for mercy for your people?" There it was: the loathing, the disgust.

"No, Chief. I'm not Ofarian."

Kekona stomped forward. "Yes, you are, you lying—"

"I'm not." Cat bit out. "I left them. I gave up my water magic. By choice. Griffin is my leader no more than you are."

Bane and Kekona didn't move a muscle. Cat held her breath. The chief ambled toward her. "So why are *you* here?"

Cat searched for the words Griffin had given her, but decided nothing would sound as true as her own.

"I'm new to this life, to this"—she waved a hand at the warriors and the unseen volcano and the hidden little town—"world. Two weeks ago I'd never even heard the word *Secondary*. I thought I was an emotionally messed-up orphan, nothing more. I'm here now because this is a stupid misunderstanding and both sides are being hotheaded. Sorry if no one's ever put it in such blunt terms before, but I'm no politician. I'm no leader. Look, whatever Griffin did all those years ago to upset the Senatus is tearing him apart. He wants to fix his mistake, and he's tried every way he knows how, but his wheels are spinning in place."

"You just met him," Kekona sneered. "You can't know all that."

Cat evenly met her fiery eyes. "And sometimes that's all you need, to really know a person."

Suddenly the memory of Xavier sprung up, twisting her

heart in a vise, making the emptiness there achy and palpable. Her words must have meant something to Kekona, too, because the Chimeran looked away first.

"And you," Cat rounded on the chief, "want to believe what you've always believed about the Ofarians. They're a different people than what they once were, how you knew them before Gwen Carroway took down the old empire. I didn't have to have been born into their society to know. I can see the pain on the surviving members' faces, the frustration in their voices. They are *trying*."

Kekona's head snapped up. "Their leader kidnapped me."

Cat shook her head and told Lea's story. How the banished and neutered Ofarian woman had been trying to eradicate Ofarians by enflaming the Chimerans and, ultimately, the Senatus. "I know this because she told me herself after she captured me, too. Griffin had nothing to do with it, and Lea is sitting in his jail right now. You were there, Kekona. You saw him come, heard us talking. You saw Lea be taken into their custody."

Kekona and the chief looked at one another so long Cat wondered if the Chimerans possessed some sort of telepathy. Bane stood off to the side, glowering.

"I didn't see or hear anything to convince me," said Kekona.

The chief opened his hands. "You expect us to just take your word for this?"

"No. I expect you to listen to someone who was actually there, in Michael's house, when Kekona was brought in."

Other than the widening of Kekona's eyes, the Chimeran general didn't move.

Cat reached into her bag and pulled out a little video device. "This is for you. Press *play*."

The chief looked skeptical. "What's on it?"

"Just press *play*."

He did, Kekona and Bane crowding their leader on both sides. Even though Cat couldn't see the screen, she could hear Sean Ebrecht's voice rise up. She hadn't been there when he'd offered the information. She hadn't been there when he'd recorded this, as he'd cried over Michael and threw a chair across the room when talking about Lea. He told Lea's story: how she was a lone wolf, and had been working with Michael for years.

The Chimeran leader looked up.

"All I'm asking, Chief," Cat said, "is for you to stand down. For now. There is no need for loss of life on either side. Not over this. Call the Senatus together. Allow Griffin Aames to speak his piece and listen. He will listen, too, to whatever lectures you want to give. I promise you."

The chief pursed his lips and shifted his focus to Kekona. "General?"

Fire flared across Kekona's pupils. When the fire died, there was so much pain and humiliation and sorrow in that stare. Kekona finally looked away, and Cat was sure that she'd succeeded.

"General," the chief pressed.

"Don't be fooled by that, Uncle," Kekona said. "Sean's their prisoner. He's a kid who's used to being told what to do."

"No—" Cat began, horrified.

But Kekona ignored her and leaped once more for the balcony rail. She assumed a wide stance on the narrow slat of wood, like the warriors on the ground had done earlier, and screamed something in Chimeran, the cords in her throat jutting out.

Everyone on the field paused in whatever they were doing and turned their faces up to the house again. Then, in a flurry, they rushed toward the waiting buses. Deploying.

Cat saw it all—the fighting, the scorched skin, the blood, the needless deaths. When it ended, all that Gwen and Griffin— and especially Xavier—had accomplished and sacrificed for, would be washed away. Gone, because of people being obtuse. Gone, because Griffin had once given unintentional offense to Secondary leaders.

Gone, because that offense had driven a massive wedge between Kekona and Griffin's secret relationship.

Dear God . . . could all this be happening over a reason even stupider than a cultural misunderstanding?

Kekona hopped down, not looking at Cat as she made for the stairs. Bane fell in behind his general.

"Kekona," she called, desperate. "I have no idea what happened between you and Griffin, but please don't make this war some sort of ex-lover's vengeance."

At the top of the stairs, Kekona froze.

*"What?"* The chief's roared surprise almost knocked Cat over.

*"Sis."* Bane gripped Kekona's arm and spun her around. "You didn't."

Kekona's shoulders dropped, along with her dark eyes. She wouldn't look at either her brother or her uncle.

Well, now, how about that? Cat had just let her namesake out of the bag.

She'd assumed that the Chimerans had known. She'd assumed that part of Griffin's ostracizing had been due to Kekona's revelation to her people of their affair.

The chief loomed over his niece. Sixty-plus years or not, he was, without a doubt, the most fear-inducing man in that valley. "Is this true? Are you involved with him?" Kekona lifted regretful, lovesick, forlorn eyes, and he amended the question. *"Were* you involved with him?"

The general said nothing.

Sparks danced across the chief's eyes. "You and I will talk," he told Kekona, pointing toward the great field, "after you call them off."

# THIRTY-SIX

One week later.

**The Turnkorner Film Festival had ended. The movie stars had** fled, the tourists trailing in their wake. The sidewalks of White Clover Creek sat empty. Wind whipped fresh powder from the rooftops and swirled it around the town that finally got to pull a blanket over its head and sleep after a two-week party. A few cars were parked along Waterleaf now, but most townies were likely at home, thrown over the couch in an exhausted heap. Mr. Traeger, however, was brushing snow from the front steps of the Tea Shoppe.

It was like Turnkorner had never happened and Xavier had gone back in time to the period when he'd lived anonymously and shrouded in demons. Only, in a vicious turn of events, he was allowed to keep the awful memories he'd made in the future.

Xavier had thought she'd be here.

The week-long trek from Nevada back to White Clover Creek had started with a despair so deep he contemplated chipping a hole in the frozen ground, burying himself, and just huddling there until spring. But a funny thing happened when he started moving eastward. He thought about everything Cat had said to him in the Plant—had been *forced* to say to him, he was sure—and decided that digging a hole couldn't possibly bring him any lower. The only way to go was up, and he actually allowed himself to hope.

By the time he'd hitchhiked his way across two states—using glamour to disguise himself as pregnant or disabled women, and to steal food, because he had no money or ID to speak of—he'd convinced himself that there had definitely been something wrong when Cat had shoved him away, and the problem hadn't been him. When he got back to Colorado, he told himself, she would be waiting for him.

But she wasn't.

There was no reservation for her at the Margaret. Or any other hotel or motel within the town limits.

There were no new tracks in the unshoveled snow leading up to his house.

In a daze, he got his key from under the thyme pot in the greenhouse and went inside his cold, silent home. He stared at the red plastic phone on the wall and released a howl of frustration. Why couldn't he have forced himself to join modern society and signed up for something as basic as caller ID? Maybe she'd tried to call and he hadn't answered. Maybe she was waiting for him to call her.

He snatched the receiver from the cradle and stabbed out Cat's cell phone number. Disconnected.

He sank onto one of the chairs around the kitchen table.

Disconnected. That pretty much said it all. It hadn't rung and rung, like she'd left it on too long and it had run out of juice. Disconnected meant *I don't want to be found*. Disconnected meant *The people I've joined don't want me to be found either*.

He could call Gwen or Griffin, but he didn't want to hear it from their lips, too, that Cat had made her choice and left him. For the Ofarians.

All that shit he'd convinced himself of on the way home was just that: shit. He'd been right, what he'd said to her over that radio. Maybe they had made her say those things to him, but in the end, she hadn't been willing to fight for them.

He could have walked up to the Drift and tried to talk to Helen again, but after the way he'd approached her last time, and then the violent way he'd left, he seriously doubted she'd tell him anything about Cat. Could he really blame her?

Cat was gone and he was back in White Clover Creek. A big circle, that was life. And his life? A set of overlapping circles laced with razor wire.

He stumbled into the bathroom and showered until the hot

water heater couldn't spit out anything more, then somehow made his way into his bedroom, kept in shadow by the drawn curtains. He deliberately didn't look at the bed. He wouldn't sleep there again. He didn't look at the clothes he pulled out and put on. Didn't care.

Then he locked up his house, and walked into town.

Pam would probably be at Shed, even though it was early on a Sunday. He paused at the back delivery door, hand on the knob. If it turned, he'd go in. If it didn't, he'd go back the way he came and not look back.

It turned.

Pam was in the kitchen, trailing her fingers over the dangling pots and pans, notebook in hand and pen stuck behind her ear.

"Hey," he said.

She turned and he was reminded of Kekona's blazing eyes, the streams of fire that had erupted from her throat. And as frightening as Kekona had been, she had nothing on Pam.

"What the *fuck* are you doing back here?"

Being thrown from the Primary world, into the Secondary, and back again, gave him terrible mental whiplash.

Pam snatched the pen from behind her ear and whipped it across the kitchen. "How *dare* you. I mean, really. Leaving me a message, a goddamn voice mail, that you were taking off before the end of Turnkorner? Turnkorner, for chrissakes! Only the biggest two weeks of the year for us." She threw up a hand in disgust and turned away like she'd just eaten McDonald's. "You actually make me a little sick. Get out of here."

He just shoved his hands in his pockets. "I'm sorry, Pam."

She sighed, turned back around. "Is that why you came back? To apologize?"

"Yes." He realized, above all, that that was true. Pam had helped him so much. She'd created him, essentially. She'd given him the dream of a career, a bigger life, and had unknowingly granted him a sliver of happiness. To disappoint her, to fail her . . . "I'm sorry," he said again.

"Tell me you at least got her."

He put a hand to his chest, where it hurt the most. "No."

She calmed down a bit, setting the notebook on his old station. Her lips tightened. "Aw, man. That sucks."

He stepped farther into the kitchen, ran a hand over the burner knobs. "She hasn't, um, been back here, has she?"

"No." Pam looked at him funny. "What's going on with you?"

Never had he ever been tempted to tell any Primary anything about his former life, until now.

He traced his fingers over the cold, black metal burners. He'd learned the most in Shed. He'd discovered quite a large part of himself here. Pam had seen promise in him back in San Francisco, and she'd brought him here. She'd planted him and watered him, and he'd grown so much.

"I'm leaving," he told her.

"Ah, fuck." She'd picked up the pen and it clattered to the tile again. "Knew that was coming."

He cracked a smile. "Just last week you were wondering when I was going to head out."

"Yeah, but I didn't think you'd actually do it." She sighed dramatically. "Where are you going?"

He knew she meant which kitchen. He shrugged. "Don't know."

That was the truth. He had no idea where he was going, where his steps would take him once he left White Clover Creek. Wandering sounded like the best idea, although "best" was a relative term.

So rarely did he see Pam genuinely surprised. Her face whitened, her eyes going wide. "Xavier. Are you okay?"

He touched the same pots she had earlier, sending them clanking. "I will be."

She ran a hand through her short hair. "Jesus, X. Quitting your job over some girl—"

"It's more than that." He swept a gaze over the quiet dining room, lingering on booth six and seeing, against his will, Cat's gorgeous body draped over it. Open and waiting. For him. "Remember those ghosts you mentioned?"

"Yeah. I do."

"Well, I've got some that need fighting."

She didn't look at all surprised by that. Just nodded. They stood there in companionable silence for several minutes.

"If you need a reference," she said, "you've got mine.

Despite what you did to me last week. You're very talented. I'd hate to see you throw it away."

So would he. But he just wasn't sure where or when he'd want to cook again.


Three weeks later.

If Cat could have transported herself to Colorado with a snap of the fingers the moment the Chimeran chief had called off the attack, she would have. Instead, it had taken three long weeks to get back to White Clover Creek.

The Chimerans had insisted she remain in Hawaii until the situation had been smoothed out. Threat of imminent attack had calmed, but had not been killed. At least the two sides were talking. Both Ofarians and Chimerans had agreed that keeping Griffin and Kekona apart was a wise choice. Griffin had kept his leadership, but Kekona had been relieved of her command.

After the Chimerans had stood down and unpacked their transports, Griffin had asked Cat back to San Francisco to rehash everything that had happened in Hawaii for the Ofarian cabinet.

Then the Senatus Premier had called. He'd offered Griffin a stilted apology and allowed Griffin to make a heartfelt one of his own. When the Premier extended Griffin an invitation to a sit-down with the Senatus, Griffin had exhaled on a powerful sob. He'd pushed away from the table and left, disappearing for half a day. When he'd returned, the lines on his face had smoothed. He moved with a renewed grace.

Then he'd corralled Cat in private.

"How is Keko?"

It hadn't been a question meant to gloat or belittle. The intense emotion on Griffin's face screamed of his affection for the Chimeran woman. Cat had been forced to swallow her own tears, because she knew what it meant to be separated against your will.

"I think she's full of regret," she'd told him. "I think she's sad."

"Where is she?"

Cat had to shrug and answer honestly. "I don't know. The chief gave her position to Bane, her brother."

Griffin had nodded, then dismissed her. Then she'd literally run to catch a cab to SFO. The first available flight to Denver cost an arm and a leg, but she didn't care.

In Hawaii, and then in San Francisco, she'd called Xavier's house every chance she got, even though she hadn't expected an answer. It wasn't like he was going to install voice mail now. Not when he surely never wanted to speak to her again. And if he *had* tried to call her using the only number he had for her, he wouldn't have gotten through because Lea had taken her cell phone all those weeks ago.

She'd been hoping that Xavier would've called Gwen, but at the same time she knew that hope was foolish. Made of wishes and spider silk.

That didn't mean she was going to give up. Not like Griffin and Kekona, who'd surrendered to outside forces way too easily three years ago.

Now, back in White Clover Creek, she picked her way up Waterleaf from the square. The town was emptier now, in more ways than one.

Given that she was barely standing due to exhaustion, and her San Francisco jacket was wildly inappropriate for the winter that was still raging strong in the Rockies, she should have walked right over to the Margaret, maybe inhaled a burger or two, had a good, long sleep, and then bought some ridiculously overpriced but more suitable clothing in the gift shop.

She didn't do any of that. She went right to Shed. It was nearing the end of lunch hours and Turnkorner was over. She didn't expect Xavier to be there; that wasn't why she went there. Pam was in the kitchen, behind the glass in the spot where Xavier used to work. Cat went up to the glass and caught the chef's eye. Pam did a double take then nodded in acknowledgement. Cat took a seat at the bar and waited an hour for Pam to come out.

"He's gone," Pam said without preamble, and Cat almost melted into the white leather bar stool cushion. It was what she'd expected to hear; it didn't hurt any less.

"When . . ." Her voice died and she cleared her throat. "Do you know when he'll be back?"

Pam pressed her lips together. "No, I mean like he's gone. For good. Packed up. Gone."

All oxygen left the world. Just . . . vanished. All those atoms swooped up into the sky, leaving Cat to choke. The sympathy on Pam's face was killing her.

"You'd think he would've learned," Pam added, "but he doesn't have a cell phone as far as I know. Didn't give me any other phone number either. I don't know where he went. I'm sorry."

She was so grateful that Pam didn't ask what happened, but by the look on her face, Cat knew that Xavier had, at one time in the past three weeks, returned to White Clover Creek heartbroken or angry. He'd stayed just long enough to tell Pam goodbye. A solitary guy like Xavier wouldn't have left word where he was going.

And that broke Cat's heart a little more, because that morning in her hotel room, when he'd held her while she first talked to Gwen, he'd been on the verge of breaking away from that solitary existence. He'd actually agreed to go to Chicago with her.

She left Shed and walked to the top of Waterleaf.

It felt strange—almost like an out-of-body experience—for Cat to be back in the Drift, surrounded by the paintings that had started this all. Helen greeted her with a tight hug, telling her all about Michael's death in between sobs. Cat had done some superior acting with her customers back at the hotel bar in the Keys, but nothing rivaled what she did for Helen that afternoon, pretending to just now learn about Michael's plane crash. And it ripped her apart with guilt.

"There was a memorial," Helen said, wiping her nose and pulling Cat over to sit on the chairs in front of her desk. "But the whole thing was very odd. Some horrible information came out after his death."

"What kind of . . . information?"

Even though they were the only two in the small office, Helen leaned closer. "He'd been keeping his father alive, in an irreversible coma on life support, in his house, when everyone had thought he'd died two years ago."

Cat's blood iced over.

"There must have been someone living there with Raymond,

taking care of him, because they found evidence of a nurse. But this person was gone by the time his house was opened. Raymond's machines had been disconnected. He was dead, too." Helen shuddered, looking so confused and sad. Then the curator waved her arms as if dissipating smoke. "I haven't cried in over a week. I'm so sorry. I've been so worried about you. I haven't been able to reach you anywhere."

All Cat could do was apologize and hold Helen's hand.

Helen searched Cat's face. "Is everything okay at home? Did you lose everything?" When Cat just stared, Helen prompted with a frown, "In the fire. The reason you went back."

"The fire." So that was the excuse Lea had given for Cat's unexpected disappearance. "Yeah," Cat answered truthfully. "I did lose everything."

Helen teared up again. "Maybe you can start over, with what you've made here. You've sold through. Every painting on display here, spoken for."

Cat couldn't breathe. "Every painting?"

"Every one. And Jim Porter, remember him? He wants your next show to be in L.A. He can represent you better than I can from here in the boonies. How do you like that?"

On the surface, Cat liked it a lot, but her state of mind wasn't letting her feel anything but deep sorrow and need.

"Helen," Cat asked, after they'd discussed Jim and L.A. a bit more, "you haven't seen Xavier around town, have you?"

Then Helen described Xavier's frantic behavior the day he'd realized Cat had gone missing, and Cat had to lower her head so Helen wouldn't see the true depth of her emotions. He'd sacrificed his job and his safety for her. And then she'd destroyed him.

She left the Drift and went right for those cursed stairs leading up to Xavier's neighborhood. Freezing, she stood on the sidewalk outside of his dark house. No *For Sale* sign. Maybe he hadn't completely abandoned this place. The walkway up to the front stoop hadn't been shoveled, but there was fresh snow settled into one set of old footprints going around back to the greenhouse, then the side door. Size thirteens.

She made new footprints. If he came back, he'd know she'd been there.

She went up to the front door and knocked. Hoping. Wishing

for a miracle. Telling herself it was the cold that was making her eyes water.

She pulled out the note she'd written on her SFO-DEN airplane boarding pass. She stuffed it between the screen door and the chipped wood with the tilted triangular window.

It said: *I am going to fight for you.*

# THIRTY-SEVEN

Six months later.

**Cat was back on an island.**

Dragging her small suitcase out of the airport doors, a hot blast of air greeted her. Enveloped her. She'd missed the tropical climate, living in San Francisco these past six months. The water magic was gone, but that didn't mean she'd abandoned her love for salty breezes and the lap of the warm ocean. It was different now, yes, but the connection to water was still there. Instead of buzzing just underneath her skin, the peace of water embraced her, seeped into her heart. Made her happy.

And her art had evolved to show that.

On the busy airport sidewalk, Cat wove her suitcase through the maze of bags and trolleys. Taxis and hotel shuttles wedged themselves into spaces along the curb, and at the front of the line idled a white Mercedes. A man with silver-blond hair, a straw hat, and an almost unnatural tan stood near the trunk, holding a sign scrawled with her name.

"That's me," she said to him, smiling.

The driver reached for her rolling bag. "Welcome to the Virgin Islands."

Though the car's air was on, Cat rolled down the window, feeling like a dog with its ears flapping in the wind. The colors here were so bright, the air so clean. Inspiration tugged at her.

Maybe after her show opened next year at Jim's L.A. gallery, she'd search for a permanent studio site someplace hot and tropical.

The Mercedes pulled into the drive of a nearly complete

boutique resort done in pale blue stucco. The main construction was done, but the landscaping was pretty much just piles of dirt and two-by-fours.

The driver told her, "Mr. Brighton asked me to tell you he'll meet you in the lobby after you've had time to freshen up. He apologizes in advance for any construction noise."

Mr. Antoine Brighton, general manager for the newest Wave Resort in St. Croix, could have tossed her a sleeping bag and told her to curl up on the beach, and she wouldn't have cared. Instead, the room she was given for the next two nights was a light, airy suite with a curving balcony that overlooked the central courtyard—currently dotted with orange construction cones surrounding what would eventually become a pool and waterfall—and the never-ending expanse of the turquoise Caribbean Sea. As far as resorts went, this place was going to be intimate but exotic. Pricey.

And Brighton wanted her artwork everywhere.

After rinsing off and changing into a light dress and heeled sandals, she grabbed her portfolio, made her way to the lobby and rang for Mr. Brighton. When he appeared, he looked exactly like he'd sounded on the phone: somewhere in his fifties, pasty British skin, on the shorter side, friendly but clearly "in charge." He wore khaki pants and a pale green button-down shirt with the sleeves rolled up. With a firm handshake, he said, "So glad you could make it, Ms. Heddig."

"Please. Call me Cat."

"And I'm Antoine. I'm excited to see what you have for me. Come, let me show you where we'd like to showcase your work."

He took her on a tour of the resort, pointing out the high, wide space behind the front desk, the taller, narrower spots between the windows in the lobby bar, and the rounded walls near the elevators. When they were done, they grabbed lemonades from the workers' break room and sat down in Antoine's office, an interior room that felt horribly closed in after what she'd just wandered through.

She opened her portfolio of works that were still available for sale and talked through her ideas for what could possibly go where. And because she'd learned well from Jim and Helen, she made suggestions for additional places Antoine hadn't mentioned. She must have talked for twenty minutes straight, all her ideas just spilling out. Antoine listened, nodding, a twinkle in his eye. And she knew she had him. She sat back, satisfied.

"What about your new series?" Antoine asked. "What Jim's seen, he says it transcends your earlier works."

Cat gave him a gracious smile. "That's very kind of him. I'm afraid the new pieces aren't ready yet. And I'm not sure they'd be appropriate for this setting."

The truth was, she didn't know if the new series would ever be ready for public viewing. She'd painted them for herself, and approached them as though they'd never hang anywhere but where she eventually decided to set down roots. But the buzz about her work had been building steadily since White Clover Creek and many of her current buyers kept asking about what she was working on now.

Three months ago, Helen had visited San Francisco and Cat had revealed to her a few of the new pieces.

"They're so . . . peaceful," Helen had said, pushing her glasses onto her nose. "To have something from your early collections, and then one of these . . . to see how you've grown . . . well, I think you can expect collectors to become greedy."

Cat had turned away at that, her first inkling that these would become private pieces.

"What are you calling them?" Helen had asked.

Cat had gazed at the seven-foot-tall tumble of green-white ice captured in paint and tried to ignore the tightening in her chest. The waterfall looked exactly as it had that day on the frozen lake. "The *X Series*," she'd whispered.

At the Wave Resort in St. Croix, Antoine Brighton chose which archived Cat Heddig pieces he wanted for his walls—including the places she'd sneakily suggested—jotted down their names, and said he'd contact Jim the following morning to arrange the sale and transfer.

"So you and Jim know each other well?" she asked.

Antoine chuckled and twisted his wedding ring. "Yes, we go way back. Met at Oxford, what, at least thirty years ago now?"

"How fortuitous," she said in a terrible British accent that made Antoine smile. "I'm very excited about this, about being displayed here. I'm so thrilled Jim recommended me."

Antoine blinked. "Oh, he didn't."

"Sorry, was it Helen Wolfe then?"

"No, sorry, I don't know who that is. Two or three months back I was arguing with my department heads about decor. It wasn't going where I felt it should go and . . . anyway, I got an e-mail the next day from a new employee, saying he'd overheard us talking. He suggested taking a look at your work. He included a link to your website—which is brilliant, by the way—and I learned you were being represented by my old mate's gallery in L.A. I rang Jim and here you are."

"And here I am," Cat murmured. She paged through every man she'd met at the Drift and through Jim, and tried to recall if any had resort connections. She came up blank.

Antoine checked his watch. "You know, I believe he's here right now. Would you like to say hello? Perhaps you know him."

Antoine beckoned her through the lobby and around to the opposite side of the resort from her room. What would soon become the spa was straight ahead, but Antoine turned right. Parting a plastic curtain hanging from the ceiling, he guided her into the restaurant. Semicircular, with a domed ceiling and central bar, it boasted incomparable views of the ocean from the wall of windows and outdoor patio. Huge crates of furniture and carefully stacked tables sat atop the plastic-covered carpet.

"Hmm," said Antoine, peering around the empty space. "He should be here. Let me go see if I can find him."

Antoine wandered toward the gleaming white-tiled and stainless steel kitchen, and Cat let her eyes follow, choosing to ignore the furious flutter of butterflies in her belly. Then she caught sight of the wood hostess stand shoved up against the far wall. A single word, silver and curling, was embossed on the front.

*Caterina.*

She reached out for something—anything—to steady herself in a tilting world. Her fingers snagged a crate labeled "chairs" and she clung to it, leaning into it. Letting it hold her up. Breathing. Eyes closed. Not moving.

Hope boiled inside her but she refused to let it rise to the surface, to believe in it. It had done nothing for her, all these months alone in San Francisco. Hope had started so strong, and then had died rather spectacularly. Not even the Ofarians' unfailing inclusion had healed her. Not even meeting her mother, who had been lovely and supportive. No, hope had not served her well. She'd waited for Xavier—and waited, and waited—and he hadn't come to her.

And then he was there. Behind her. Saying her name.

*"Cat."*

The sound of his voice surged over the persistent crash of the waves outside and the pounding of her blood in her ears.

She turned. There he stood, tall as she remembered, beautiful as a statue, his heart in his eyes.

"Oh, God. Xavier."

He'd cut some of his hair off, but it was still long and shaggy. Still surfer hot. And now he had the sunburn to go with it.

"Did you do this?" She could barely get the words out. "Did you bring me here?"

The restaurant door opened and she glanced over to see Antoine slipping out, grinning. When she turned back to Xavier, he'd lowered his chin but kept those incredible gun-metal eyes on her.

"Is this *your* restaurant?"

"No. It's the resort's. But the menu is mine." He looked to the hostess stand. "And the name."

"I saw." Her knees were as shaky as water. "How—"

"Pam. She hooked me up. She knows someone who knows someone who heard about this place opening up." He shook his head. "She's been an incredible mentor to me."

But that meant . . . "You went back to White Clover Creek?"

"Yes, right after I left Nevada. When I thought you'd be there. And again, when I needed to sell the house a month or two later."

She gasped. "I *was* there! I went back the second I could, looking for you. But I couldn't get there for several weeks and by then everything was so messed up. I called and called."

The molten silver of his eyes started to swirl and darken. She'd missed that so much. So very, very much.

"Please believe me," she said. "I was there. I went back for you."

One corner of his mouth twitched. Was that a smile? "I believe you. Pam told me you came to see her. And then there was this." He stuffed a hand into his back pocket and pulled out the boarding pass note she'd left in his front door. Heavily creased and faded, he held it out, and there was blinding intensity in his expression.

"You kept this?"

He nodded, reached into his pocket again and pulled out an equally creased note on Griffin's own letterhead. It read: *Everything Cat said to you in the Plant to make you leave was untrue. Please forgive me. Please forgive us. Please forgive her.*

She made a fist, confused and a little angry. "So why didn't you try to contact me? Or Griffin or Gwen, even? I know I've been moved around, but Gwen's still in the same place. Xavier, I've been going out of my mind, thinking you thought I'd shoved you away on purpose."

He smiled and it might have been the most beautiful thing she'd seen in months. He exhaled deeply. "Come with me." He backed toward the door leading out to the patio. "I want to show you something."

She followed him, dazed, into the brilliant sunshine. He turned his face to the cloudless sky for a moment, then looked over his shoulder at her, the smile still there. Her heart gave a little flip, but her mind was racing after him, wondering what was going on. Still trying to believe this whole thing was real, that he was close to her again. That he was *smiling*.

He crossed the patio, his shoes making prints in the sand that had blown onto the bricks. When he hit the beach he just kept going, walking slowly over the sand and down to the water.

She followed, saying, "Xavier, I'm so confused. Why—"

"Let me talk." He turned to her then, right at the edge of the water, where the highest waves slid up the wet, packed sand. His words were a caress, his eyes like hot steel. "Please."

And she shut her mouth, because she realized that she'd never seen him so at peace. Gone was the tension from his shoulders, the hard set of his mouth, the drifting focus of his eyes due to discomfort. He'd never spoken with such confidence. He'd never smiled like that, unbidden. He'd never turned his face into the sun. She was entranced.

"You sent me away," he said, "and I was angry for a long time. But I don't blame you for doing what you did at the Plant. I figured out you were forced to do it, I just didn't know why.

It was hard. So, so hard." He shook his head, the warm breeze tangling in his hair that was now a whiter shade of blond.

"I'm so sorry. You have no idea how sorry."

"You did what you had to. I was selfish, thinking that you and I were the most important things in that building that day. But I kept thinking, after some of the rage wore off, that maybe it had been easy for you to set me aside, because of the way I treated you."

It took her a moment to process those words. "The way *you* treated *me*?"

This whole scene was beginning to feel unbearably surreal, like maybe she'd fallen asleep in her hotel room and was dreaming every moment of this.

"Did you know that the first thing that drew me to you, that really made me want to get close to you, was your smile? Your laugh?" He looked off toward the horizon and shoved his hands into his pockets. "And then I figured out what you were, and I took away that joy. I didn't mean to, but I did. Not with my revelation, but with my reaction. You didn't think I accepted you—and I didn't—and you lost your spark."

He looked back at her, and his eyes burned with an emotion she hadn't seen since the morning after they'd first slept together. No, it was stronger than that. Ten times stronger.

"I want your spark back," he said. "I want *you* back."

Her fingers pressed to her lips. She tried to speak, choked up, tried again. Xavier looked almost deliriously happy to see that.

"Why did you wait so long?" she demanded, her hands dropping. "If you found my note, if you knew all along I was in San Francisco with Griffin, why didn't you come to me sooner?"

"When I first got back to White Clover Creek and you weren't there, I left and didn't look back. I traveled everywhere, all over the country. For two months I just wandered. Then finally one day I called Pam on a whim and she told me you'd come back to White Clover Creek looking for me. She told me how upset you were. And oh, Cat"—he put a hand to his chest, and his palms must have been sweating because when he pulled it away, the faint imprint of his big hand remained over his heart—"it sucks to say, but that made me believe that everything between us would be all right."

Frustration started to get the better of her. "But *why*? Why wait so long? Do you have any idea how unhappy I've been without you? How horrible it's been for me imagining you out there, hating me? Thinking I wouldn't ever be able to tell you the truth about that day in the Plant?"

"Yes, I have a very good idea. Because I bet it's about as unhappy as I've been without you. But I couldn't go to you yet. Not without doing this." He started to back toward the water and lifted his voice. "Not without finding a piece of something I could share with you. Not without getting over my own shit. Otherwise we'd just find ourselves back where we were before. I know you've been living in San Francisco, so I know you're neck deep in the Ofarian world. I could have gone there to tell you I accept you, but I'd said that to you before and it didn't work out. I wanted to prove it to you." He stretched out his long arms. "This whole place is surrounded by water and I want to see you in it. I want you to be here. I want you to be here, with me."

She just stood there, dumbfounded, as a strong wave rushed the beach and splashed over her shoes. Xavier kicked off his own shoes, peeled off his wet socks, and went right for the water. He waded into the ocean, the water blackening his jeans and making them suck to his strong thighs. He stopped, turned around. Looked her so deeply in the eyes she could swear he was touching her.

"What are you doing?" she called.

He trailed his hands through the impossibly blue water, then raised his arms and let streams trickle from his fingertips. "I'm showing you me. Standing in the one thing that has scared the shit out of me for so long. I'm showing you me, surrounded by what makes you *you*."

*Holy crap.*

"Xavier, I'm not—"

"I'm telling you," his voice rang clear and strong, "that I don't care what you are, whose blood you have. I'm telling you, Caterina, standing here soaked to the skin, that I don't love you despite you being Ofarian. I love you because of it."

The very first moment she'd ever touched water—the intimate connection that defied words, the ever-expanding high, the joy, the love—was *nothing* compared to how Xavier made her feel just then.

And then she was splashing into the water toward him. Running over soggy sand and kicking into the warm ocean. She slammed into him and he caught her, wrapping those long, strong arms around her. He kissed her, and a new universe exploded on her tongue, with Xavier the sun, the center. Her arms folded around his neck and suddenly her feet were no longer touching sand. He lifted her, buoyant in the water, and they kissed and kissed and kissed.

When he finally released her, letting her slide back down his body, they were both shivering in the hot Caribbean air.

"Do you really love me?" she whispered against his mouth.

One hand slid around her hip, his fingers teasing that crease between butt and thigh. He smiled against the skin of her neck, then turned his face to kiss her softly once more. "I started that day on the ice, once I got a taste of what we could be. I never stopped."

By the confident way his hands were smoothing over her back, making dirty promises to her skin and igniting a desire she'd thought dead months ago, he didn't seem to be looking for a response. He wasn't that man anymore—the man who'd been drifting unsure and unattached through the world—and it floored her.

So she told him how she felt, just to surprise him. To feel his reaction. "I love you, too."

He didn't disappoint. His body sagged against hers. For a brief moment she felt his whole weight, physical and emotional, and it didn't scare her. Not one teensy bit. She'd take care of him, just as she knew he'd take care of her.

"No one's ever said that to me," he whispered.

"And now you can't claim that anymore."

He took her face in his hands and slid his mouth over hers again, his tongue wet and delicious. She kissed him until she couldn't breathe. Her dress was drenched, her shoes ruined, and she couldn't have cared less.

"There's something I should probably tell you," she

murmured against his lips. He just nuzzled her. "I'm no longer Ofarian."

With a splash he pushed her away, holding her at arm's length, searching her face. "What? How?"

"*Nelicoda*. Enough to kill the magic."

"When?"

"The day I sent you away."

"Oh, Cat . . ." His grip on her shoulders tightened. "Why?"

She took fistfuls of his wet shirt, pulled him to her again. "For many reasons. Just one of them you. Another being my father. But I'm okay with it. I'm more than okay, actually."

Because Xavier had declared his love to her while standing in the ocean, still thinking she was his enemy.

He pushed a wet lock of her hair over her shoulder. "What the hell happened?"

"It's such a long story. Bitter lovers, hot lava, half-naked warriors tossing around fire, Hawaii—"

"Holy shit. Tell me everything. No, wait." His eyes dropped to her chest. In the water, her dress had pretty much gone transparent, and his hand slid over one breast. "Tell me everything naked. Where's your room?"

He carried her from the sea and they left trails of dripping water all through the resort. He had her halfway naked before she got her room unlocked—her shoes off, her thong pulled down and over her feet. Inside her suite, he pushed her up against the wall and covered her from the back. His hands moved hot and slow over her body, stripping the straps of her wet dress down her arms. She could feel all of him behind her, through his wet clothes. One hand curled around her front, teasing her nipple, then dipping lower to find the place inside her as wet as the ocean.

"God, I love you." Her voice was as shaky and unstable as her legs.

He kept touching her, making her rise and rise while he made low sounds of approval.

"I want to be in you," he said. "But not like this."

He pulled away and turned her around so they faced one another. As he kissed her, he backed her toward the bed. He peeled off his wet shirt and went to work on his soaked jeans.

From one pocket, he pulled out a condom and dangled it between his fingers with a grin. She marveled at the body she'd never forgotten, at his height and lean build, at the skin that now had sun lines she wanted to trace with her fingers and mouth.

He loomed over her, every part of him hard except for his eyes. With a gentle nudge, he pressed her body into the comforter and then followed her up, settling between her legs but not entering. He stared down at her, the ends of his hair tickling her face.

"I love you," he whispered. "And I want to do it like this. Looking into your face."

She smiled, lifted one leg around his hips. "You can do anything you want to me, anytime."

Then he entered her and she was lost.

An hour or so later they lay in a tangle of damp sheets on the floor between the bed and balcony door. She didn't remember falling from the bed, but whatever. Tremors still pulsed through her body and her mind was floating somewhere over the ocean, somewhere between Earth and heaven.

Xavier was still kissing her, everywhere but on the mouth.

"Was Antoine lying when he said you'd e-mailed him about me?"

He grinned. "No."

"You mean you've actually turned on a computer?"

"Yes. Just don't time my typing speed."

"If you say you have a cell phone I might have to name you an impostor."

His mouth covered her bellybutton. "I don't."

She pushed at his shoulder, not wanting him to move away, but not wanting him to get in trouble either. "Don't you have menus to plan or cooking to do or something?"

"I thought you knew." He drew a wet line with his tongue between her hip bones. With a wicked, wicked look up at her from under his lashes, his eyes glowed pewter. "I've never tasted anything as good as you."

**Jen Haverhurst swerved onto the gravel shoulder of Route 6** and braked the rental car with a jolt. On the other side of a sturdy fence, Loughlin's highland cattle swung their giant horns and hairy heads toward her. Those beasts had always made her uneasy. Beyond their field, across a cracked, weed-filled parking lot, rose the vacant Hemmertex headquarters. And directly ahead, tucked into the bend in the road, still sat the produce stand.

That's where Leith had parked his dad's boat of a Cadillac convertible that summer night ten years ago. The moon had been a sliver, each star its own atmosphere. And Leith had given her her first orgasm not from her own hand.

Jen turned up the weak air conditioner and whipped out her phone, pressing the single button to connect her to her office. She needed a dose of her real world. Fast.

Her assistant picked up. "Gretchen, it's me."

"You made it up there okay?"

"Yeah. I'm here."

And here she was. Back in Gleann, New Hampshire, after all this time.

"What'd I miss today?" Jen stuck the Bluetooth earpiece in place and pulled back onto Route 6, following its curve down the hill and into town.

Gretchen started talking, but Jen drifted off, her mind following the roads she'd gotten to know so well by spending every summer here growing up. She still knew the way to the Thistle, the Tudor-style B&B once owned by Aunt Bev. She parked in front of it, but couldn't yet bring herself to get out and physically step foot in the town that had given her her only happy childhood memories.

Down the block, past the park, the Stone Pub remained, its faded sign still swinging out over the sidewalk. That's where Leith had first brushed against her during their shift. That's when they'd gone from being old friends to sneaky, desperate, teenaged lovers.

Gretchen let out a singsong whistle. "Yoo-hoo. Jen."

Jen shook her head. "Sorry. What was that?"

"I asked if I should switch the setup for the Umberto Rollins cocktail party. The table pattern doesn't quite work, I don't think."

Jen snapped back into focus. "No, no. Don't change a thing. Everything is all taken care of. This is the same party they throw every year for their employees, and I had to make do with a drastically reduced budget. All you have to do is see it through."

"All right. If you say so." But Jen could hear the reluctance in her assistant's voice.

"Gretchen, I'm serious. They're very particular and traditional. They trust me, they trust the company. Just follow my directions for Umberto Rollins and then we'll tackle the Fashion Week event when I'm back in the office in three weeks."

"I thought it was four."

"Nah." She peered out the side window, at the ivy creeping up the side of the B&B she'd once considered home. "This should be a piece of cake. In and out."

"The bosses were okay with you taking leave now?"

Jen pressed her lips together and forced confidence into her voice. "The bosses are okay with it."

They had to be. She'd worked her ass off for them for six years, almost single-handedly tripled their client list, and snagged a prestigious fashion house account. She deserved this partnership. She *needed* this partnership.

And when she got back to New York after this leave was over, the promotion would be waiting for her. She could finally kill the heel-biting fear of mediocrity that had chased her all the way from Iowa.

"I still can't believe you're leaving Umberto Rollins to watch guys in skirts throw heavy shit around."

Neither could Jen, but she'd make it work. She always did.

"They're called the Highland Games, and Gleann needs them." Gleann needed *Jen*. Someone moved behind the B&B's upstairs curtain. "Listen," Jen told Gretchen. "I gotta go, but call me if you need me. For anything. I'll check in from time to time."

"You're on leave."

"Oh, honey. In this business, you're never really on leave. Nor do I ever want to be."

She disconnected and stared out at the empty streets of Gleann. They hadn't replaced the sign welcoming people to the downtown. GLEANN, A WEE BIT OF SCOTLAND IN AMERICA. HOME TO HEMMERTEX CORPORATION.

The whole place was quiet and still. She reached into the passenger seat and lugged her giant purse across the center console. It hit the car horn hard, sending a loud and nasal blast echoing up and down the curving streets. In New York, a single horn meant nothing. Here it was a day's excitement.

So much for a quiet arrival.

The front door to the Thistle flew open and Aimee bounded out, her light-brown hair streaming behind her. Jen hoisted her bag higher up her shoulder and went around the car, heading for the taller and older sister she hadn't seen in three years.

Jen's foot struck something, and she toppled forward, all balance and grace gone.

Aimee caught Jen and hauled her to her feet. "Whoa. You okay there?"

Jen righted herself and frowned at the slab of cracked concrete poking up from the sidewalk. "That wasn't there before."

Aimee gave a little laugh, but there was familiar strain behind it.

Jen eyed the tree in the bed and breakfast's tiny, fenced front yard. "That thing's enormous now."

Aimee winced. "Did you expect the place to stay the same? Waiting for you to show up again after ten years?"

Maybe not to that extreme, but the distance between northern New Hampshire and New York City had stopped time in her mind.

Unexpectedly, Aimee pulled her into the tightest hug they'd ever exchanged. Or maybe that was just distance and time again, pulling them together instead of pushing them apart as it had been doing for so long.

"I'm so glad you're here," Aimee said into her hair, in that serious, pleading way Jen remembered well. "Thank you. Thank you for helping us."

Jen awkwardly patted her back and pulled away. "I said I'd *try*. Even I can't guarantee how it'll all turn out."

Aimee nodded. "I know." But there was hurt and worry behind her green eyes, the same shade as Jen's.

If Jen didn't succeed here, if she couldn't fix the local Highland Games and keep the Scottish Society from moving it across state, Aimee could lose the B&B. The town could lose a lot more.

Jen glanced at the Thistle, which upon closer inspection looked a little threadbare and weedy. "Where's Ainsly?"

Aimee rolled her eyes as she smiled. "At a friend's. Who's a boy. I don't know how I feel about that."

"She's what? Ten?"

"Oh, God. Nine. Please don't make her older than she already is."

Her twenty-nine-year-old sister had a nine-year-old daughter. There went time again, churning up dust as it zoomed past.

"Come on." Aimee took her arm with a small smile. "I'll show you your room."

It was same room Jen had slept in all those summers ago, from age eight to eighteen. The same room, different everything else. Frilly and soft and pale—not at all what she'd have chosen for herself. She dropped her bags outside the connected bathroom and went back downstairs to where she could hear Aimee clanking around in the kitchen.

"What are you doing?" she asked, stepping into the kitchen that hadn't changed *at all*, shiny red refrigerator and everything.

"Cooking."

"But I'm your only guest."

"You're still a guest, right?"

A guest. Right. A guest in the house that had once been the only place she'd considered home. Maybe she deserved that, since she'd been out of the country during Aunt Bev's funeral. Bev had left the place to Aimee, after all.

Jen pushed a smile onto her face. "The next meal is lunch. Your sign says 'breakfast.'"

"Please, Jen. Let me do this."

Jen got it. She'd spent her life taking care of her older, crazier sister, and now Aimee had something to prove.

"Okay," Jen said, levering herself up onto the familiar wood barstool at the kitchen island. "I, uh, saw that sign out on Route 6."

Aimee slid a cutting board on the counter. One dark eyebrow twitched. "Which one was that?"

"You know."

"Ohhhhhh. That one." Aimee craned her neck to peek at the clock. "Wow, only twenty minutes."

"For what?"

"For you to ask about him."

Jen supposed it had to have taken coming back here to finally ask about Leith, considering neither of the sisters had mentioned his name in ten years. "They put up that huge sign? Just for him?"

Aimee took out a roast from the refrigerator and started to carve thin slices from it. It looked like she actually knew what she was doing. "It was a big deal then, a local winning the Games so many years in a row. And after that football season and that state track championship and all . . . It's a small town. He's a bit of a celebrity. He doesn't compete anymore, but they still love him like he won the Olympics or something."

"I'd say. That sign was like a shrine. An effigy shy of a temple."

Aimee gave her a weird smile and started to assemble sandwiches.

Jen gazed out the window, to the backyard that sloped down to the creek. Old images of Leith struck her hard in the heart, and she felt more than a little dirty picturing his eighteen-year-old body, big even back then, moving on top of her in the back of that Cadillac. How cliché to have lost it to each other in the backseat of a car.

How wonderful to have lost it in the cloud of teenage obsession.

Aimee went to the pantry. "You should ask him to compete again."

Jen felt like she'd tripped over something again, and she hadn't moved an inch. "Wait. What?"

"You know. Get him to come out of retirement or something. I bet the town would love it."

"You mean he's still here?"

Aimee tipped down a bag of pretzels from the top shelf. "Sure. He owns a landscape business, though word is he's hurting, like everyone else."

But he was still here. Oh, God, Leith was still in Gleann. Jen didn't feel guilty for leaving him ten years ago—it was what her life had demanded of her—but the possibility of seeing him again . . . "Why didn't you tell me?"

Aimee shot her a hard look. "Because everyday news about Gleann hasn't interested you in ten years. Until you learned it was dying."

Jen swallowed, dropped her head in the face of the truth.

She'd chosen to keep her memories as just that: particles of the past drifting around in her mind. They weren't allowed to affect her life in New York. She couldn't afford to move backward.

Leith had once kissed her under the giant maple tree out back, up against its trunk that curved over the creek. How could something she hadn't thought about in so long still feel so fresh? "Has he ever, um, said anything? To you? About me?"

"How old are you again?" Aimee shoved a plated sandwich in front of her. "No, he hasn't. When we run into each other, it's smiles and small talk. You remember how he was, like nothing could ever faze him."

A little piece of her heart crumbled off and knocked around inside her chest. She'd managed to faze him, the night before she'd left Gleann for good and he'd begged her to stay. Told her he loved her. But what was she supposed to do? Sacrifice college and career and risk suffering the drunken, aimless, bitter lifestyle of her parents?

"So he doesn't know I'm here?"

Aimee shook her head. "No one does except the mayor and me. What if you'd said no, Jen? We didn't want to get everyone's hopes up and then be denied. I've had enough disappointment."

*I*, not *we*. Jen knew Aimee wasn't talking about today as

much as her and Ainsly's visit to New York three years ago. The same week the fashion house had called and Jen had had to drop everything to secure the prestigious new client.

Aimee took a bite of sandwich and talked with her mouth full. "When's your appointment with the mayor?"

Jen flicked on her phone to check the time. "About ten minutes."

Which, if she remembered correctly, gave her about six minutes to eat, since it took four minutes to walk to city hall. They ate in silence, and then Jen fixed her hair and makeup, grabbed her purse, and headed for the front door.

A hard wave of memory slammed into her. This moment felt like all those other summers, leaving for job after job after job, her college fund bank account growing with every hour worked. It was as though ten years hadn't passed at all. Even the feel of the front door's oblong brass knob brought back memories. She'd drown in them if she wasn't careful, and she'd only been in Gleann less than an hour.

She opened the front door, the scent of thyme and rosemary wafting in. The herb garden, surrounding little metal breakfast tables, was new.

"Jen."

She turned around to find Aimee standing in the hallway, at the foot of the narrow, creaking staircase leading up to the guest rooms, her eyes filled with emotion. Jen's eyes swept over the foyer. "Anything for this place," she said. "Anything for you."

"I want you to know that I feel bad asking, for taking you away."

"Don't. It's no biggie. Came at the perfect time."

She hadn't told Aimee about the impending partnership. Or the risk she'd taken coming here now.

Aimee wrung her hands. "I'm older. I should have been taking care of you, instead of the other way around. And here you are again."

"And here I am." With a final smile, as reassuring as she could make it, Jen left and headed downtown.

Gleann legend said that its founders had used Celtic magic to transport a chunk of old Scotland into this out-of-the-way valley, from its stone-facade shops crowding the narrow sidewalks, to the meandering path of its streets. Gleann reality was that little plaques hung from every building and fixture, describing how the immigrants had constructed their new home.

Jen had always found it magical, truth to the legend or not. Now, however, the place was practically deserted. The ice cream shop where she'd scooped out orders one summer had long since closed, but she could see that at its last use, it had been a scrapbooking store. The Picture This sign still hung over the door.

A faded poster was taped inside the window, one corner curling back. GLEANN'S GREAT HIGHLAND GAMES! DON'T MISS IT! Looking around town, it was the *only* mention of the Games anywhere, and the thing was supposed to happen in three weeks. If this was the kind of hills she'd have to scale, she was in deep shit. But then, that's what she was good at: climbing her way out and putting on the best events any amount of money could buy.

She looked closer at the poster.

Leith. His brown hair longer than the last time she saw him, wet and clinging to his jaw. His rugged face contorted in exertion. Hammer clutched in his great fists, arms extended out, his body even bigger and more muscular than she remembered. And he wore a kilt.

Good God, a kilt.

She'd seen him wear his family's tartan before, in high school when the whole town had turned out for the Games. But a kilt on a boy was a much different thing than a kilt on a *man*. In the photo, the wind had kicked up the hem of the kilt, displaying the hard lines of his thigh muscles, set in a wide stance. Black knee socks showed off bowling balls for calves.

None of the men in New York were *that* kind of gorgeous.

The shrine out on Route 6 had said he'd last won the heavy athletics competition five years ago. What did Leith look like now? Looking at the poster and seeing how much he'd improved from age eighteen to twenty-three, the curve for hotness progression over time indicated he should be approaching godhood right about now, at twenty-eight.

Her phone blared a warning and at first she didn't recognize the sound of the alarm. She was never late. Ever. *Crap.* She hurried down the street to the small brick house that served as Town Hall.

**Jen rang the doorbell to the locked Town Hall front door. When** the door finally opened, a silver-haired woman in jeans and a Syracuse sweatshirt frowned down at her. It was an expression Jen remembered with painful clarity.

"Hi, Mrs. McCurdy. It's good to see you."

Mrs. McCurdy, former manager at the ice cream shop and a steady dog-walking client of Jen's, stepped back and opened the door wider. "Here. Let me show you the mess you've inherited."

Jen took a deep breath. "Ah, great. Thank you, Mrs. McCurdy."

"It's Mayor Sue now," the other woman threw over her shoulder as she headed toward the back of the hall.

"You . . . you want me to call you that?"

"Everyone else does."

Mayor Sue turned in to what must have been a bedroom at one time, but was now a tiny, corner conference room with a giant box fan whipping warm air around. A laptop sat on the table. Mayor Sue hooked her wiry hair behind each ear and flipped the laptop around.

Jen bent over and squinted at the spreadsheet. At the tiny number in the bottom right rectangle. "That's what's left? Where'd DeeDee run off to again?"

"France, we're told." Mayor Sue snorted, and Jen wasn't sure if the disgust came from the fact that the long-time organizer of the Highland Games had run off with a sizable chunk of the town's money, or that she'd run away to a place that wasn't Scotland with a man who didn't have a drop of Scottish blood in him.

Neither did Jen, which might have accounted for some of Mrs. McCurdy's disdain over the years.

The amount left in the Games's account wouldn't even have covered Jen's fee back in the city, but she wasn't here for the money. A part of her got way too excited at the challenge. She wouldn't be sitting on her ass the next few weeks, that was for sure. Her goal? Put on the best Highland Games Gleann had ever thrown, and convince the state's Scottish Society to keep the event here next year and beyond. With the departure of

Hemmertex—and its employees and monied executives—the Games were all Gleann had left.

It was, quite simply, a matter of pride.

"Think you can do it?" Mayor Sue crossed her arms under her generous boobs.

Jen pulled her dark hair back into a ponytail and took a seat. "I think so. Yes."

Mayor Sue frowned again before leaving, as though she'd had hundreds of other event planners lining up around the block to take this gig for free, and Jen had to prove herself.

She *would* prove herself. To Aimee, who'd been so clearly disappointed in Jen's absence the past decade. To Aunt Bev, whose love and encouragement had brought her to Gleann in the first place. To Leith, who'd been so hurt and angry when she'd gone.

And to her parents, who probably wouldn't give a shit but whose negativity and laziness had driven her out of the house in the first place.

Jen spent the next hour flipping through old files, memorizing spreadsheets and totals, and rearranging numbers in her head. There were very few resources, even less money, and practically no organization or innovation. She needed to take inventory. She needed to contact vendors, renegotiate terms. Check up with the competitors and judges and—

Her phone rang. Aimee.

"Hel—"

Screeching and sobbing filled her ear.

"Calm down, Aim, I can't hear a thing you're saying."

"Oh, my God, the whole place, Jen!" There was splashing and squishing in the background. "The toilet or the bathtub or something up in your room. Something must have burst. Water everywhere. Totally flooded." A sob, a sniffle. "It's dripping through the floorboards, into the guest rooms downstairs. Oh, my God! I don't know what to do!"

Jen's first instinct was to run. To swim like hell far, far away from this mess, grab onto the first floating thing she could find and paddle in the opposite direction. Why on earth had she ever thought this would be an easy three weeks? Especially if Aimee was involved? Why the hell was her sister calling *her* now? Ah, of course. Because she was here, and when Jen was here, Jen took care of things.

All her clothes and things were in that room, sitting right outside the bathroom. Probably floating down the hall by now. *Shit.*

She ground fingers into her temple. "Maybe you should, I don't know, turn off the water at the source and then call a plumber?"

"What? No." More crying, more splashing.

"Why the hell not?"

"Because I can't call *him.*" It came out like *hiiiiiiiim*, in a child's voice, and Jen finally got it. Aimee had probably slept with whoever *hiiiiiiiim* was and they hadn't moved past the After-Sex Awkwardness.

Lovely.

Jen Haverhurst to the rescue. "Just hold on, Aim. Be there in a second. Can you at least find the water shutoff?"

"Okay. Yes. I think so."

Jen hung up and sighed. She pushed back from the table and poked her head out of the conference room door. "Mayor Sue? Know of any places in town I can rent? Like, today?"

# LOVE
## ROMANCE NOVELS?

For news on all your favorite romance authors, sneak peeks into the newest releases, book giveaways, and much more—

**"Like" Love Always on Facebook!**

 **LoveAlwaysBooks**

M1063G0212

# Can't get enough paranormal romance?

Looking for a place to get the latest information and connect with fellow fans?

## "Like" Project Paranormal on Facebook!

- Participate in author chats
- Enter book giveaways
- Learn about the latest releases
- Get book recommendations and more!

**facebook.com/ProjectParanormalBooks**